The Geographer's Library

Jon Fasman was born in Chicago in 1975. He worked as a
journalist in New York, Oxford, Moscow and London and
now lives in Brooklyn. *The Geographer's Library* is his first book,
and has been translated into eleven languages.

The Geographer's Library

JON FASMAN

PENGUIN BOOKS

PENGUIN BOOKS

Published by the Penguin Group
Penguin Books Ltd, 80 Strand, London WC2R 0RL, England
Penguin Group (USA) Inc., 375 Hudson Street, New York, New York 10014, USA
Penguin Group (Canada), 90 Eglinton Avenue East, Suite 700, Toronto, Ontario, Canada M4P 2Y3
(a division of Pearson Penguin Canada Inc.)
Penguin Ireland, 25 St Stephen's Green, Dublin 2, Ireland (a division of Penguin Books Ltd)
Penguin Group (Australia), 250 Camberwell Road, Camberwell, Victoria 3124, Australia
(a division of Pearson Australia Group Pty Ltd)
Penguin Books India Pvt Ltd, 11 Community Centre,
Panchsheel Park, New Delhi – 110 017, India
Penguin Group (NZ), cnr Airborne and Rosedale Roads, Albany,
Auckland 1310, New Zealand (a division of Pearson New Zealand Ltd)
Penguin Books (South Africa) (Pty) Ltd, 24 Sturdee Avenue,
Rosebank, Johannesburg 2196, South Africa

Penguin Books Ltd, Registered Offices: 80 Strand, London WC2R 0RL, England

www.penguin.com

First published in the USA by The Penguin Press,
a member of Penguin Group (USA) Inc. 2005
First published in Great Britain by Hamish Hamilton 2005
Published in Penguin Books 2006

5

FT Pbk

This is a work of fiction. Names, characters, places and incidents
either are the product of the author's imagination or are used fictitiously,
and any resemblance to actual persons, living or dead, business establishments,
events, or locales is entirely coincidental.

Set in 11.75/14 pt Monotype Garamond
Typeset by Rowland Phototypesetting Ltd, Bury St Edmunds, Suffolk
Printed in England by Clays Ltd, St Ives plc

ISBN-13: 978-0-141-01984-0
ISBN-10: 0-141-01984-0

For Alissa

I find myself always torn between two beliefs: the belief that life should be better than it is and the belief that when it appears better it really is worse.

— GRAHAM GREENE, *Journey Without Maps*

LIST OF OBJECTS

꘍

The Alembic	20
The Castle	58
Ferahid's Golden Ney	104
Ferahid's Silver Ney	143
The Ethiopian	164
Xinjiang's Ivory (Earth)	192
The Crying Queen	229
The Sheng (Air)	264
Rainbow Dust and Peacock's Tail	307
The Kaghan's Cages (Fire)	332
The White Mediko	372
Al-Idrisi's Kamal (Water)	408
The Yellow Sun	448
The Red Mediko	484
The Sun and Its Shadow	515
The Suitcase	541

Dear H:

   *I thought you would be dead by now. Certainly I never expected
to hear from you again. And maybe I haven't: the handwriting
looks familiar, but forgery would probably be among the mildest of
your new friends' skills. But I'll give you the benefit of the doubt.
Unwarranted assumption seems a fitting way to pay you tribute.*

   *Enclosed you'll find what you asked for: 'A full and objective
account of our time together.' You told me it wasn't for you
alone, but even if it were, I doubt I could've written it differently:
you couldn't have been 'you' here, even if I had wanted you to be.
And however much I wanted to keep silent and ignore your request,
I found I couldn't. Anyway, I wasn't doing much else. I've been
holed up here for longer than I knew you, and however shaken
I remain (and will, at least for a little while longer), your face is
already growing indistinct, and for that I'm grateful.*

   *I worry about you, though. I wish you a longer and happier life
than I fear you'll have.*

   Paul

True it is, without falsehood,
certain and most true.

For a journalist at a weekly paper, especially one as small as the *Carrier,* The Day the Paper Comes Out is a day of rest. I usually strolled into the office around eleven, caught up on correspondence, read all of the magazine articles I hadn't been able to read during the week, made some long-distance personal calls, pretended to start thinking about next week's pieces, and left at five sharp. If I was feeling virtuous, I'd file some of my week's notes and clear a landing strip on my desk, but usually I saved that for when I was on deadline and needed mindless industry to clear my head. Not that a deadline really mattered all that much: Lincoln, Connecticut, like many small towns, specialized in news with a long shelf life. Anyway, nobody was going to lose a job if an article detailing the controversy over the high-school's mascot – the Fighting Sioux: culturally insensitive,

3

respectfully traditional, or traditionally respectful? — didn't make it. First of all, the debate would recur next year, probably in the fall, right about the time ambitious seniors wanted to polish their agit-cred for college. Second, we had an endless supply of ads, announcements, notices, and just plain filler we could recycle or resize if the cub reporter couldn't quite ride without training wheels.

And the times when I couldn't were getting more and more infrequent. I had been working at the *Lincoln Carrier* for almost a year and a half, ever since graduating from Wickenden University. I had friends who had slid seemingly without thought from college to med school or law school, or to fancy consulting jobs or some sort of literary underling work in New York, as though those things were just what you did. I had no such prospects, nor did I much want to go back to New York, where I grew up. Actually, I had a vague plan to attend graduate school and eventually settle down to live the cloistered, quiet life of a history professor in some picturesque little college town (steeple, main street called Main Street, movie theater with a marquee), someplace where I could get all of my aging out of the way in my early thirties and live without crises or surprises, changing only incrementally for the rest of my allotted threescore and ten.

I hadn't really thought of becoming a journalist, mostly because I didn't really understand how one did it. I had turned out a few music and book reviews for my college paper, mainly for the free books and

CDs; I would read or listen to something, write a couple hundred words about it, and a week later I'd see my name above some prose that bore a passing resemblance to what I had written. A racket, not a career.

After graduation I had just stayed on in the same apartment I lived in during the year: I had no reason to be anywhere else. A month into that stagnant summer, I declined my father's offer/mandate to work as a paralegal at his friend's law firm in Indianapolis, where my father had moved after my parents finally split. He made me feel so guilty about not having a job that I went, for the first and only time, to Wickenden's Career Promotion Center. There I filled out questionnaire after questionnaire, and I talked to chipper recent grads with sweater sets and pearl necklaces, loafers and the beginnings of beer guts. I looked through job ads that made no sense. My favorites were from the consulting firms: 'You will learn to implement strategic management protocol decisions,' et cetera. I worried that I would turn into some sort of cyborg after three weeks at one of these places; I would return home for my first Thanksgiving and communicate via streams of ticker tape issuing from my mouth.

After a couple of hours of Career Promoting, I felt certain that I would live a long, lonely, useless life and die alone and unmissed (did I mention that I never bothered filling out any grad-school applications?). It's self-indulgent, I know, but this is what happens to the overachieving but essentially useless children of parents who raised their children to do well on tests but failed to equip them with the poison-tipped spurs of true ambition.

Art Rolen called Career Promotion as I was getting ready to trudge home and maintain a full schedule of feeling sorry for myself. I remember watching the face of my Career Finder become radiant, just beatific, as she nodded with increasing excitement and finally said into the phone, 'Sir, I think I have someone for you sitting right across from me. He's not from the college paper, but his Gibson-Montaneau scores indicate that he might be a *rilly, rilly* good fit for you.'

She winked twitchily at me and handed me the phone with one hand while making a 1983-vintage thumbs-up sign with the other. I said hello, and this drawly growl in the earpiece said, 'Well, I hear those Gibbon-Martindale numbers of yours are really adding up. But here's what I want to know: What do they mean? And can you write?'

I tucked the phone into my chest and turned away from my Career Finder's blinding enthusiasm. 'Well, I don't really know what they mean, to tell you the truth. They seem to put some stock in them here, I guess. And technically I'm not from the college paper: I wrote for them every so often. I guess I can write well enough. Where is it you're calling from?'

'Lincoln, Connecticut. About two hours west of Wickenden. I run a small weekly paper here, about

6

sixteen pages. What I need is another full-time, little-bit-of-everything kind of person. Right now it's just me and a columnist, and we got an ad lady. The other full-timer we had just left, got a job in Storrs. Greener pastures, I guess. Anyway, you'd do a little reporting, little writing, little editing, little paper shuffling, some office work.' I heard the muffled *hoosh* of a cigarette being smoked. 'Some phone answering, but no more than anyone else. Nothing fancy. No Woodstein stuff. Maybe a way to see if you want to do something like this or not.'

I shrugged, then remembered that shrugs don't translate over the phone. 'Sounds interesting. Sure. You want me to send you my résumé?'

'Yeah, do that. But do me a favor: send it by mail. My new fax machine's having some trouble making it from the box to the desk, and I'd rather see a hard copy than something on the computer screen. You do that?'

'Sure, no problem. Should I come out and see you? Do you want to interview me or anything like that?'

'I thought that's what we were doing. For now just send your stuff up here. My name's Art Rolen, by the way; send it to my attention. Résumé and a few writing samples. We'll go from there. Sound okay?'

It sounded fine, and sixteen months later, here I was in Lincoln, hauling myself out of bed at the crack of ten on a chilly Tuesday morning. I had stayed at the printing press until all the papers rolled off at 3:00

A.M. Art liked one of us to stay at the printers' until the job was done, and technically the duty was supposed to rotate among the four of us on staff, but as I was the youngest and the only one who wasn't married, it fell to me more often than not. I didn't mind, really: the drive back from New Haven at that hour was always fast and peaceful, and I liked the smell of the air late at night. Strange to think of what was happening back in sleepy Lincoln during that particular drive. I suppose I won't ever know, exactly.

I lived in the commercial part of town, called Lincoln Station, where in the 1920s, when this was a real farming village instead of an Escape from New York, trains brought grain and feed in and took butter, milk, and cheese out. Cute little stores with actual green patches of lawn behind actual white picket fences now filled the area of the old train depot. The paper's offices were in the town's residential section, which was called Lincoln Common because (my Brooklyn eyes couldn't believe it when I first moved here) at its center was an expanse of lawn in front of an old white wooden church with a steeple: the Village Common. Of course, the number of people who observed that distinction decreased yearly, as Lincoln natives died, or sold the houses their grandparents had built to lawyers and magazine editors from the city. The newcomers gutted and colonnaded the houses, then showed up three weekends a year to barrel through town in their SUVs. Manton's General Store now stocked chèvre, five kinds of olives, and took the *New York Times,* the *Wall Street Journal,* and *Crain's.* Of course, I was a newcomer myself, but I had a rickety little compact, no life elsewhere, and – rarest of all honors – I was a Friend of Townies (the Rolens). Anyway, I'm temperamentally inclined to talk about the Good (or at least Better) Old Days; I feel nostalgic for every era that preceded my birth.

As I walked into the newsroom – a kind and self-conscious exaggeration for what was essentially an insulated garden shed with four desks and four computers – that afternoon at one, Art was at his desk smoking and reading the *Times:* glance, puff, turn the page; puff, glance, puff, turn the page, puff. 'There he is,' he said, not even looking up when I shut the door behind me. 'Bright and early.' Now he looked pointedly at me over the tops of his reading glasses.

The room smelled like cigarettes and perfume; Art was responsible for the first, but the last belonged to Nancy Llewelyn, who sold our ads and ensured, as best she could, that we didn't go broke. Like Art, she was a lifelong townie, and according to Mrs Rolen, she had nurtured a low-level, harmless crush on Art since the seventh grade. I sniffed ostentatiously, and Art laughed.

'She stopped by earlier to pick up some reading, she said, for her vacation. You imagine that? Taking work from the *Carrier* with her? Dedication.' He puffed, closed the front section, and reached for the sports. 'Got a call from the Panda a little earlier.'

'Who's the Panda?'

He laced his hands behind his head and looked out the long window toward Lake Massapaug, cigarette in the corner of his mouth. I loved the way Art smoked, with a quiet, straightforward satisfaction instead of either the furtive guilt so common among older smokers or the forced, noisy, almost defensive pleasure of teenage and Californian smokers. He smoked because he smoked, not to prove a point and not shamefully, but because it somehow completed him.

His thick white eyebrows, deep-set dark eyes, long jaw, and white beard gave his face a perpetually mournful cast; he looked like a cross between an older Humphrey Bogart and Leo Tolstoy near the end of his life. Art was a lifelong foreign correspondent (Vietnam, Cambodia, Paris, Beirut, Jerusalem, desk editing in New York) and, like most longtime reporters, a cynic, and, like most cynical reporters, a big-hearted sentimentalist of the worst, best sort.

He dropped the remains of his cigarette into the remains of his cup of coffee, pulled a business card from his shirt pocket, and slid it across the desk to me. 'The Panda. Says for you to call him. I told him your name, so he knows who you are.'

I turned the card over. VIVEPANANDA SUNATHI-PALA. WESTON COUNTY CORONER. NEW WESTON HOSPITAL, NEW WESTON, CONNECTICUT. About forty-five minutes away, the closest town of any size. I tilted my head questioningly to the side, and Art half nodded in response. 'That's the Panda. Sri Lankan, his name is. And he is. Old friend of mine: chess partner, drinking partner, bridge partner. His daughter and mine went to school together. I guess he's lived up in New Weston about thirty years now. Right about the time I started tromping all over the world, he settled down here.' He stretched and yawned, as though thinking about how old his daughter was made him tired.

'Any advance warning what he's calling about?' I asked.

He pulled his notebook toward him. 'J-A-A-N. Guess that's pronounced "Yan," right? Right. Jaan – this name's a little tricky – P-U-H-A-P-A-E-V. Got umlauts over the *u* and the second *a*. Pronounce that one however you like. Lived right here in Lincoln. Never met him, never even heard of him. Died last night. That's about all I know.'

But that wasn't all *I* knew: Pühapäev was a professor in Wickenden's history department. I didn't remember what he taught. He always seemed more like a piece of department furniture – old, drab, tattered, inoffensively present – than an actual living, breathing professor. I told Art that I knew him, or at least had heard of him. He nodded and ran his hands along his beard. 'You want to write his obit for us? See what there is to say?'

'Sure.'

'What else you got this week?' I reached for my notebook, and he waved it away. 'No, no, forget that. Just make me feel guilty about overworking you. That was a joke, by the way. Listen, I don't really know why someone called the coroner. Seems unusual. Might be something to say. Might be something juicy, something interesting; might just be a regular old obit. Which, for our paper, I guess, qualifies as something interesting. But you want to see what you can do with it, right?'

'Of course.'

He pointed to the phone, and I called the New Weston coroner's office.

'Pathology. Chief medical examiner speaking. How may I assist you?' The voice was clipped and direct, with a military cadence and a lilting accent.

'I'm trying to reach Mr Panda.'

'*Dr* Sunathipala, if you please. You are right now speaking to him. Who is this, please?'

'Sir, my name is Paul Tomm, T-O-M-M, and I'm calling from the *Lincoln Carrier*. Art Rolen told me to call you.'

He laughed. 'Art, yes. Is he fine? Is he well?'

'He's both fine and well.'

'Yes, yes. You are calling, I presume, about this dead man here, Mr . . .' I heard papers shuffling. 'Mr Pühapäev, yes?'

'Yes, I am. I just wanted —'

'Nothing yet to tell you, I'm afraid. I arrived early to attend to other matters and cannot yet say one thing or another about Mr Pühapäev. One moment, and I will walk with this telephone into the examining room itself.' I heard a door open and shut, then footsteps. 'Yes, here he is. The entire room to himself. Very recently arrived, I see, and I am looking at him right now, and he looks recently dead. Old man, the features and the body. Old man.' I heard a scraping sound that I didn't want to think too hard about. 'Smoker. Beard and mustache yellow around the mouth. Very general signs of wearing and tearing. This could be consistent with . . . well, with almost anything, I am afraid to say. Consistent at the very least with having lived for enough years to be a yellow-bearded whitebeard.'

I heard a slamming sound, and his voice seemed to gather itself, turn its attention back toward the phone. 'Yes, Mr Tomm. Nothing to say or report just now, except the smoking. Very nasty habit, smoking. Nasty but pleasant. Your friend Art knows this well. In the end, though, smoke or don't smoke, whiskey or no whiskey. "Golden lads and girls all must, / As chimney-sweepers, come to dust." You know that one, maybe, or is it only dancing on the television and spy novels for you?'

I shut my eyes. I knew those lines. I *knew* I knew those lines. 'Shakespeare.'

'Yes, of course, big big bravo, Shakespeare. But *which* from Shakespeare?'

'Late, probably.' I guessed blindly. I had a one-in-six chance. '*Cymbeline?*'

'Yes, excellent, most impressive and good. I could naturally hear the guessing in your voice, but remember, too, your Martin Luther: "Sin boldly." Better guessing loud than quiet. Well then, Mr Tomm the Shakespeare scholar, I would very much love to discuss poetry with an educated reporter all day over this telephone, but the dead await me. My very own captive audience. Maybe you will call again this afternoon, or perhaps tomorrow morning. I hope very much that I will have peeled him open by then. Good-bye and Godspeed to you.'

'Nothing to say, really,' I told Art.

'In all the years I've known the Panda, he's never had nothing to say,' Art laughed. 'You going to call him back?'

'This afternoon or tomorrow. He said he'd have something by then.'

'So what are you doing now?'

'Now? I guess . . . well, where's he live? Where *did* he live, I guess?'

'That's the spirit. Here's his address.' Art slid a sheet of paper across to me. 'You know, just something to think about: you might want to tootle out to Wickenden. What's it, noon already? Maybe go this afternoon, you feel like driving fast. Maybe tomorrow. Just to see if any of your old running buddies have anything to say about him. Long as we got the time – and we got the time – why not do right by the guy?'

*

I had never seen Pühapäev's house because, in all the time I had lived in Lincoln, I had never noticed his street. Drooping willow branches and fat oak trees concealed the turnoff; even now, when the leaves were sparse and falling, I nearly mistook it for a driveway. The street itself was almost too narrow for a single car, though it swelled slightly as it dead-ended unceremoniously at a patch of scraggly trees and dirt. Across from each other and closest to the turnoff from the main road, two identical flagstone houses with gray-blue shutters and wraparound porches stood like sentries in silent communication with each other. On a different street or a different day, the effect would have been precious; here it was unsettling, particularly as smoke rose from both chimneys but I could see lights in neither house.

The next home back on the left was a large, rambling, yellowish clapboard house that looked as though it had been airlifted in from Rockport or Gloucester, right down to the widow's walk on top. Across from it was number 4, Pühapäev's house: squat and brown, with peeling white trim and sagging gutters. A forlorn-looking maple tree stood in the center of a yard of patchy grass, mud, and twigs. On the small front porch, a swing that still bore a few scabs of pink paint had come off its chain on one side, and it slumped on the porch like a fat old man too tired to move.

I pulled in behind a Lincoln police car – *the* Lincoln police car, actually. As I walked toward the house, I glanced across the street and saw a hand draw the shade back from an upstairs window. I knocked at the open front door of Pühapäev's house, then called out and stepped over the threshold.

'Jesus Christ,' said an exasperated voice. 'This isn't a museum; this is somebody's house.'

'Is it also a crime scene?' I asked, stepping back outside and craning my neck in.

'That your business? You a tourist or looking to be a homeowner?' A pudgy policeman packed into his uniform like a sausage stepped into view, holding his cap under one arm and a clipboard in the other. He had a goofy little sleeping-caterpillar mustache parked on his upper lip, and several strands of reddish hair whirled strategically around an otherwise bald head. I had seen him before but never met him: my father always advised keeping well away from small-town cops, and as a result I had never even gotten a parking ticket in Lincoln. I usually saw him with a partner, a slender guy who always seemed about to disappear from sheer vagueness. If Art had ever told me his name, I had forgotten it. 'Who are you?' he asked.

'I'm from the *Carrier*. Name's Paul.' I extended my hand, and he shook it silently, without changing his expression or his stance, as though he had neither control over nor interest in what his hand shook.

'Bert,' he replied flatly.

'Anything interesting here?'

'Just checking for signs of a robbery. So far nothing but a lot of junk.' He looked back over his shoulder, and I leaned in to see a large room barely managing to keep the forces of entropy at bay. In one corner was a dusty grand piano on which sat stacks of books and papers. Across the room was a low table strewn with overflowing ashtrays, plates smeared with ketchup (I hoped it was ketchup) and scattered with old bones, and crusty bowls with spoons sticking out. A mottled sofa completed the picture. Domesticity gone haywire, home for the perpetually solitary. The house had a musty smell: a mixture of cigarettes, grease, mildew, dust, and old man. 'Don't know how we'd know if anyone took anything.'

'Can you tell me where you found him?'

Bert sighed and rolled his eyes, as if I had just asked him to wash the windows, then pointed to the couch. 'Over there. Lying down, sort of sprawled out. Looked peaceful, though. My money's on heart attack. Still, got the call from the state, middle of the night, someone hadn't heard from him or something. Gotta check everything. Anyway, we're getting ready to leave, though. Right, Al?'

His forgettable and funereal-looking partner – Al, I supposed – trudged down the stairs. 'Guess so,' Al said in a voice so uninflected and quiet that it seemed resigned to its ineffectuality even before the words left his mouth. 'You're ready, we can go.'

'Yeah, let's beat it. Nothing here for the papers,

right?' Bert looked darkly at me, then at his partner, who was standing with his back to us, facing a huge clock against the far wall.

'Nothing yet,' said Al. 'No way of knowing if anything's missing, 'cause I guess he lived alone, but nothing looks broken. He lived messy, but there's no law against that. But come take a look at this.' He was probably talking to Bert, but I took it as an invitation all the same.

Al nodded toward the old grandfather clock. It had two golden pendulums swinging down from the mahogany body, and its face was decorated with interlocking geometric patterns. The hands were stuck at 10:25, and the bottoms of the pendulums were dusty: it hadn't moved in a while. 'Bert, you remember Grandpa Per had a clock like this? Old windup thing in the bedroom?'

'I don't know,' said Bert curtly.

I sauntered as slowly as I could across the front hall toward the doorway, past an overflowing bookcase in the middle of which was a glass-fronted display cabinet. It was closed and empty. Inside, there were fifteen wooden tripod stands: three each on five shelves. It wasn't clear whether Pühapäev had kept anything on top of them. I decided not to draw the policemen's attention to the cabinet, though I'm still not sure why. Stubbornness, maybe. Why do you kick a stone across the sidewalk instead of letting it alone? Something about that cabinet, though – a display cabinet with nothing on display, the only

bit of empty space in the whole cluttered house –
stuck in my mind.

'C'mon, Al, I'm hungry,' said Bert, jangling his
thick key ring and walking toward the door. 'Let's
get some eggs at Vinchy's and talk this through. I'm
buying.' He put his hand in the small of my back
and pushed me, gently but firmly, out of the house.
'We hear anything, we'll let you know. Right, Al?
Meantime, you head out first, and we'll lock up
behind you.'

THE ALEMBIC

✂︎

Is not our universe itself little more than an alembic on the shelf of the Creator? By practicing this our science of transformation in our modest little vessels, are not we then doing God's work in miniature? To say so aloud would surely be to allow ourselves to be mistaken for blasphemers, when in fact we are the most adept and dedicated followers of God, and this our mission most holy, and our experiments nothing other than prayers most divine, howsoever unsanctioned by any church save our own.

— SANOPLUS OF ALEXANDRIA,
On Natural Practices

Early in the spring of 1154, when frost no longer edged the wild sage and the palace gardeners could remove the cloth coverings from the royal lemon, orange, and olive trees, King Roger II of Sicily summoned his geographer to the court at Palermo. The geographer was the renowned cartographer, herbalist, medic, composer, oudist, illustrator, and philosopher Yussef Hadras ibn Azzam Abd Salih Jafar Khalid Idris, known to history as al-Idrisi, wandering librarian of Baghdad. His early life and origins remain a mystery: some chroniclers claim he was born to a wealthy merchant family in Tunis; others, that he spent his adolescence as a beggar in Aleppo, cursed with a piercing voice and the dubious gift of inaccurate foresight; still others, less believably, that he was the son of Solomon ben Avram, sightless rabbi of Merv.

Al-Idrisi first gained fame as a scribe, later illustrator, later vizier to Haroun Ali Haroun in the city of Yazd, whose labyrinthine streets permit a cooling circulation of air even in the midday desert sun. From Yazd he traveled to Baghdad at the caliph's request, and there he created the thirty-six libraries of Baghdad, whose fame spread throughout the civilized world, reaching even as far as Christendom. Scholars, imams, musicians, men of science, men of God, and men of divine science from Córdoba to Bukhara to Mikkouni arrived, manuscripts in hand: they were permitted to copy one of the libraries' holdings in exchange for the one they carried. In that manner al-Idrisi cultivated libraries whose holdings exceeded even those in Alexandria, before the tragedy, of which we need not speak, struck that unhappy city.

An unscrupulous adviser to the Baghdadi caliph, jealous of al-Idrisi's fame and of his master's high regard for 'a bastard scribe,' circulated unsavory rumors pertaining to the librarian's religious faith and personal proclivities, especially as they related to the caliph's favorite nephew. Al-Idrisi fled and found the licentious city of Beirut filled with spies and dangers, and so sailed west to Sicily, whose learned king knew of al-Idrisi's treatise on the epidermal and enteric benefits of chewing, but never swallowing, certain wild thistle flowers.

There al-Idrisi found employment as the royal geographer and as a herbalist: he kept a large and varied garden, as well as several orchards, in whose groves the king and queen frequently strolled when the Sicilian heat became unbearable. King Roger called upon al-Idrisi frequently, for cartographical projects of increasing scope and ambition. His first map depicted every stitch, thread, and embellishment on the queen's royal robes; his second showed the location of every plant, herb, fruit, root, tree, and grove in his garden.

He completed a series of hypothetical maps for the king's enjoyment – the Lion Room at Ounanga, an underwater chess museum at Atlantis, the secret rock gardens of an initiate gnostic sect of Khazars in the Khamantor Mountains – which remained available to the public until a myopic and rather graceless librarian, in a torrid affair with one of the junior proctors and hasty to make her afternoon assignation, misfiled the collection at the Bodleian in 1972; the maps have not been seen since.

He drew from memory street maps of Yazd, Esfahan, Ahvaz, Dimashq, Beirut, and Jerusalem. His map of Palermo hangs still in the office of the city's mayor, and Roger gave al-Idrisi's maps of Malta and Minorca to Theobald the Pious and Carlos the Fabulous, respectively.

The king summoned al-Idrisi on this March morning in 1154 with an affirmative answer to his geographer's request. Al-Idrisi would be given leave, expenses, a ship, and a staff to embark on the greatest cartographical undertaking of his life, and certainly the greatest in Sicilian history: to draw a map of the known world. He would begin, of course, with Europe, and he would begin in the north; letters to King Sweyn III of Denmark requesting favor and safe conduct had already been dispatched. Not without a degree of sadness, Roger granted him freedom to leave at will; al-Idrisi commended into his liege's keeping his gardens, orchards, and his home, requesting only that he always keep the library – the curiosities as well as the books – together. To the queen, al-Idrisi gave his jewels, 'precious gifts from a life of wandering that I had hoped would pass to my wives and daughters. I see now that I will have none, and if you should take them in remembrance of me, perhaps you will do me the honor of passing them to your daughters and so, together with the comfort and presence of God, lessen the dolor and quiet the regrets of a lonely old man.'

Late that summer al-Idrisi paid his visit to the Danish king Sweyn, who was curious to meet a foreigner from the south, permanently tanned by the desert sun. The cartographer's stay was not a long one; he wrote to Roger that 'moving northward, a man naturally passes from civilization into barbarism; indeed, one might reasonably question whether civilization is possible in the northern climes. Where a man's energies must principally be expended on defending himself from the cold in winter, infernal mosquitoes and disease in summer, and infidel raiders at all times, how can he expect to develop those arts of the soul and intellect – I speak here of music, learning, conversation, cuisine – that, by the grace of God, prevail at your noble court, which I so dearly miss?'

He wrote that he would depart the Danish court as quickly as possible, 'for, if I would speak truly here (and pray God that this message falls into no hands but your own), the men are given only to drunkenness, brawlings, contests of brute strength, and an artless chanting which they mistakenly call singing. By God's provident design, a young bishop named Meinhard is at the court now. He will sail east after the days begin to wane and cool, and, for the sake of your name and the justly earned fame of your most royal court, has agreed to grant me passage in his convoy to Lübeck, and from there into the undiscovered regions which some call Livonia, some Karelia, some Lettgallia, and some Astlanda. I have heard that among Astlanda's towns there is also Qlwri. This is a small town like a large castle; if it is God's will, I shall arrive there before the first snow falls.'

Astlanda was al-Idrisi's translation of Estonia, and Qlwri one of the many names of the city we today call Tallinn. Meinhard and his company sailed no farther than the Christian outpost of Riga; al-Idrisi continued his cartographic travels along the Baltic coast until a storm brought his ship aground on the island of Hiiumaa. He wrote that during that winter 'we were shamed to see all manner of misery and unhappiness. Men ate horseflesh, tree bark, dogs, dead grasses and mosses, and, on occasion, each other. Fathers and mothers set their children in boats, hoping that they would reach a safer land elsewhere; we found scores of these babies frozen stiff upon the island shore. It falls beyond my power to convey the depravity which hunger and cold can bring.' What is most extraordinary about this note is not its tone – Adam of Bremen and the Novgorod Chronicles report similarly miserable events – but its existence: it reached Roger's court in April 1155. How did al-Idrisi, who had never ventured farther north than Sicily, survive a winter that, according to the Chronicles, killed one in three Novgorodians?

The following spring, Canute V, king of the Danes, received a letter from Bishop Meinhard. The cleric mentioned that, traveling from King Sweyn's court to Riga, he had, 'for the purposes of increasing the Holy Church's stock of souls and for the greater glory of our Lord Jesus Christ, passed some time in conversation with a dark Sorcerer also traveling to the cold and untamed regions, a pleasant-spoken heathen with all manner of knowledge meet and unmeet of the natural world and things unseen. He carries constantly about his person a satchel, inside of which he boasts is that which can save a man forever, or dash one all to pieces.'

Item 1: An alembic is the top part of an apparatus used for distilling. This one is made of sturdy green glass, 36 centimeters tall, 18 centimeters around at the widest point of its base. The top part of the vessel is narrow and fluted, and turns sharply to the right; alembics are set over a still to collect and carry vapors to another vessel. The vessel's inside bears a

crust of gray material that seems to be a mixture of lead, iron, and antimony, as well as some organic matter, including canine and human bones. Scorch marks are visible on the outside bottom, extending 5 centimeters up. No discernible odor.

Date of manufacture: Unknown. Estimates range from 100 B.C. to A.D. 300.

Manufacturer: Unknown. Considering its age, the workmanship is exceptionally fine; the apparently simple design belies the thought, care, labor, and skill that produced such a vessel.

Place of origin: Hellenistic Egypt. 'Alembic' comes from the Arabic *ul-anbiq*, which comes from the Greek *ambix*, meaning 'cup' or 'beaker.'

Last known owner: Woldemar Löwendahl, Danish-Estonian governor-general of Tallinn. The alembic was unearthed during the construction of Kassari Chapel on Kassari Island in April 1723, and brought to Löwendahl's office that June. The governor-general placed it on the top shelf of an unfilled bookcase in the back corner of his office and never noticed when it went missing two years, six months, and seventeen days later.

Estimated value: Unknown. Such antiquities rarely sell on the open market. If they are discovered on an archaeological dig, they will usually pass to the sponsoring body's museum. If they are discovered accidentally or by a private citizen, discretion begets higher prices. In 1997 the Dutch enthusiast and licorice magnate Joop van Eeghen paid $70,000 for a distilling spoon that supposedly belonged to Roger Bacon. In 1999 an Arab gentleman rumored to be acting as an agent for the Iraqi government paid $790,000 to an Italian baron-in-exile who had come into possession of an original manuscript of Aub'l-Qasim Muhammad ibn Ahmad al-Iraqi's *Book of Knowledge Acquired Concerning the Cultivation of Gold*. The morning after the purchase, he was found in his hotel room without the book, his head, and three fingers from his left hand.

*That which is above is like to that
which is below, and that which is below is
like to that which is above, to accomplish
the miracles of one thing.*

By the time I got back to the office, Art had already gone home, and it was getting dark. If I started for Wickenden now, I'd find a locked and empty history department when I got there. The day was over. I would have typed up my notes if I had taken any. Instead I turned off the office lights, locked the door, and drove back to my empty apartment by the train tracks. Dinner was two beers and a sandwich eaten staring out the window. When I first moved here, I liked these small-town quiet nights: I sort of narrated them to myself. But there's a fine and time-sensitive line between monastically romantic and boring. I had been treading it for a while and was finally slipping over to the Dark – or at least the Dull – Side. I was asleep by ten.

*

When I got to the office the next morning, Austell McFarquahar had arrived. I should have expected as much: it was ten-thirty, and Austell bounded through the door every working day, without fail, at ten. In all the time I worked at the *Carrier*, he was never sick. He took the same vacations every year: Nova Scotia to fish and sail at the end of July, and Christmas holidays with his wife's family in England. He went home for lunch and what he called 'perusal time' from eleven-thirty to two, and then he left for the evening between six-thirty and seven. When he walked through the door in the mornings, Art would say to whoever else was around, 'Austell McFarquahar – set your watch by that guy.' In response Austell would hold an imaginary watch in his left hand and wind it with his right, grin with boyish self-satisfaction, and say, 'Like clockwork.'

Austell used his 'perusal time' to gather material for his nature column, which was his only duty at the paper. He had changed the title of his column so frequently – 'Housatonic Tomfoolery,' 'Arboralia,' 'Oddments and Woodments,' 'Willow Winds' – that Art had finally eliminated the title bar altogether, which sent Austell into a funk that lasted nearly five full minutes. He always refused payment for his column, and several times Art had hinted to me that the *Carrier* owed its existence to Austell's largesse.

He and Art had been grade-school and high-school classmates. After graduation Art had gotten a copy job at the *Hartford Courant* and came back to

Lincoln only in semiretirement. Austell, meanwhile, had attended but never graduated from Yale and eventually moved home to become a full-time putterer and town legend. His family had lived in Lincoln (Lincoln *Common,* he always stressed, though he admitted shamefully that some cousins had lived in Lincoln Station before moving to San Francisco) for over two hundred years, and he spoke constantly of the history of Lincoln he was compiling. The more he talked about the project, the longer it became: a history of a town comprising every event in the town's existence fully researched and retold in precisely the same amount of time the initial event lasted. I stopped asking him about the project after sitting through an eyelid-fluttering, multiple-hour explanation of the rationale behind an 1892 Lincoln ordinance banning the consumption but not the sale of horehound drops. Art joked that he always carried a couple of smoke bombs in his pockets so he could create a diversion when Austell had him alone in the office.

We were about halfway into the season that Art called 'The Trials of St Austell,' by which he really meant the trials of everyone around Austell. From Thanksgiving until he left for England, Austell worked himself into a babbling frenzy of excitement about his upcoming trip. His goal for each visit was to re-create as precisely as possible the experience of the previous year. Twelve months smoothed aberrations into traditions; if one year the pub where they always went to dinner on December 27 was closed, then the following year the new pub became a part of the family itinerary and the old one was erased. His excitement, which began as pompously boyish – 'Nothing like an English Christmas, you know, though that part of the country hasn't seen snow in yonks, of course. All the same, Mum (that's what I call Laura's mother) lays out a posh spread every year . . .' – dissolved after several days into a jumble of references to mince pies, Christmas crackers, and roast goose on the sideboard. Whether this was due to Austell's increasing inhabitance in his own Dylanesque reverie or his gradual passing into background noise for the rest of us remains an open question.

He resembled a human pinwheel: tall and thin, with a perpetually surprised expression, a loping, reeling gait, and a shock of clumpily wild red hair. This particular morning he sat in front of a long window; when I walked in the office door, his hair jumped to attention in the cross breeze, and he turned his long scarecrow face with its large, round tortoiseshell glasses toward me. 'Ahoy there, young scribe! Invigorating morning, isn't it, absolutely invigorating. The trout running, hunting season's on, there are chanterelles for whoever can find them in the woods. Just explain to me exactly why anyone would ever wish to live anywhere other than western Connecticut.' I actually was about to throw caution to the wind and answer when he turned away from me to open the window, take a deep, chest-puffing breath of freezing-cold air, and slam the window shut. That habit of his grew more trying over the course of the winter. 'You're not from New England, right?'

Answering Austell's questions was like walking between huge, teetering stacks of books: the slightest misstep and he'd bury you beneath cascading mounds of words. I settled for direct, to the point, especially since he'd asked me this question at least a dozen times before. 'No, I grew up in Brooklyn.'

'Brooklyn, eh? Big Apple and the Dodgers and all that. Why there?'

'My father worked in Manhattan and my mother grew up in Brooklyn. Different part, though.'

'Ah, work. Of course. I suppose there isn't all that much work out here. Naturally, your people must come out here every chance they get, what-what? Escape the smog and so forth.'

'Well, my dad moved back to Indianapolis, where he comes from. He's never visited. My mother still lives in New York, though. She comes up every once in a while.'

'Grand. That's wonderful. So you're not completely bereft, right? I'm glad to hear that.' He leaned back in his chair and started to pick his teeth with a ballpoint-pen cap while blithely rooting around in his ear with the pen itself.

'You know,' he said, removing the pen and examining it, 'I think perhaps this week I'd like to write about the differences in cap structure between the deadly and less deadly *Amanita* mushrooms. Our Fearless Leader says I've done something like that in the past, but do you know that I checked, and as it happens I had written about the various kinds of logs that the two types of *Amanita* can be found on? Or near. Or at least . . . Anyway, my point is that there is no difference in cap structure, and if you're going to go mushroom hunting, you've got to have either a trusty field book to hand or someone who knows what he's doing. I thought, you know, how many people can really be bothered to buy an entire field book about mushrooms, so I ought to just explain the differences myself. Might save a lot of amateur mushroomers a spot of unsightly stomach trouble, or worse. What do you think of that?'

'Sounds like a great idea, Austell,' I said as cheerily as I could while edging away from his desk. 'Is Art in his office?' I peered around the corner, but his door was closed.

'Should be, should be. Fearless Leader? Fearless Leader! Minion here to see you!' He laughed, and Art's door opened. Art had a set of headphones draped around his neck and held a Walkman in his left hand. He smiled thinly and waved thank you to Austell, then ushered me into his office.

He shut the door and held up his Walkman. 'Anti-Austell defense mechanism. I love the guy, you know, but he's in one of his chatty moods. And we're one target short with Nancy gone for the next couple weeks. Just have to wait it out. Little too early in the morning for him, too. He still talking about the deadly whatever-the-hell-it's-called?'

I nodded, and Art smiled, shook his head, and took a pack of cigarettes from his shirt pocket. 'Least I know that if I'm doing this' – he held a match in one hand and a cigarette in the other – 'he won't come in here. Guess that means maybe the benefits to my mental health outweigh the lung damage.'

I didn't say anything, but apparently he didn't want me to either, because immediately afterward he asked about Pühapäev's house. I told him about the two cops snooping around the house and chasing me out. 'The Olafsson cousins. Can you believe that? Name for small-town cops – right out of central casting. Only one way they're dependable – report a crime in progress, and the Olafsson cousins will be there thirty minutes too late. At least. That and end of the month they'll write you up for speeding down on Elias Road whether you're speeding or not. Never met 'em before?'

'Seen them a few times, but we never met,' I answered. 'Never knew they were called Olafsson. How long have they been cops here?'

'Were here when I moved back, five years ago about. When I was a kid here, their grandfather was the town constable, then their father, and when the town grew, he hired his brother as deputy. Now there they are. Rumor is their grandfather, who came with the first wave of Swedish farmers in the twenties, couldn't work a field, so he convinced the mayor to hire him as sheriff. You might want to ask Austell about this; he'll tell you. Of course, you might want to avoid asking him about this, since he'll start with their ancestral Swedish village.' His eyes glazed over for a moment as he thought about the story as told by Austell – New England biblical, generations begetting generations, all good people of the soil.

'So Allen,' he continued, '– that's the thin one – inherited the job from his father, who was the constable, not the deputy. He was fine, as far as his job went. Small-town cop, town like this – what do you need to do, really? Treasury's running low, park your car at the bottom of Station Hill and start handing out tickets. Get some cats out of trees. Or is that the fire department? I think it's the fire department. Anyway, the deputy's son, Bert – that's the fat one – was a cop in Hartford for maybe five, ten years. Then suddenly he's back in town. Allen hires him as *his* deputy, but look at the personalities: Bert just runs the poor guy. Story is Bert failed his sergeant's exam over and over, and had a lousy record – drinking, beating, all kinds of nasty stuff – so he headed back here. Clean slate, I guess. Problem is, to make the slate really clean, he'd need to change his personality, which he hasn't done. Still drinks, still lazy, still rude. Wouldn't be surprised if he convinced Allen to head over to the dead guy's house so he could pinch something.'

'So why not do a story about that?' I asked.

'Town corruption, police misconduct: isn't this what journalists are supposed to salivate over?'

Art made a noise midway between a sigh and a grunt and straightened up in his chair. 'Yes. Yes, it certainly is. But this paper, for better or worse, isn't the place for it. Hartford is. Waterbury, maybe. Even New Haven. But this is a community paper. Weddings and football games. Carnivals. New store opens, old store closes. Besides, most of our readers come up from the big city to get away from that kind of corrupt-cop stuff.' He drummed his fingers on the desk, looking pained and a little embarrassed by the conversation. 'Running that story will also ensure that *you* get every sort of moving and parking violation under the sun, plus a few they'll make up. Problem is, though, my friends in Hartford won't want to do it, because who really gives a shit about Lincoln? You want to do investigative stuff?' He looked across the desk at me inscrutably – I couldn't tell whether he wanted me to say yes or no. I nodded. Why not: it wasn't like I was doing anything else for the next sixty years.

'You want to do investigative stuff, I'll find you a job somewhere bigger. Hartford, Stamford. New Haven, maybe. Might even be able to find something for you at the *Record,* in Boston, but that's pushing it. You decide you want to do it, let me know. You know, you've been here sixteen months, and it's been great having you here. But you can't stay here forever. Either you'll turn into Austell or one day you'll climb up the steeple with an AK and start picking our readers off, one by one. Can't have that. Go see the world, make some noise. You could do it, you know.' He stubbed out his smoke. 'Here endeth the first lesson.'

He checked his watch. 'Meanwhile, you got anything to do today? Anyone to call about this dead professor of yours? Got to be something, someone, somewhere, who knew him, right?'

I nodded. 'Well, why don't I drive out to Wickenden and see if anyone in the history department knows anything else about him.'

'Commendable lot of work. You don't mind? What else are you working on here?'

'I don't mind. I'm sort of curious about the guy anyway. I was going to work on that piece about Verrill's garden store moving indoors and building a fruit-and-honey section. That can wait, though.'

'What do you mean, wait?' asked Art, eyes popping in mock anger. 'That's not a Lincoln evergreen; that's breaking news here. Seriously, though: you go out wandering around on this, we got enough to fill a paper this week?'

'Should have, I think. I'll have Verrill's for you. Then there's that zoning piece held over from last week, and the Christmas list. Also, don't forget the photos from last year's Christmas we can put in. Plenty of excitement. Anyway, I'll be back here this afternoon.'

He slapped his desk with the palm of his hand.

'Great. Go forth and prosper, my son. May the road rise to meet you and all that.'

The drive from Lincoln to Wickenden usually took a bit less than two hours, traffic permitting. I drove this route a lot when I first took the job and was spending every weekend with Mia. Mia Park was two years behind me at Wickenden and light-years ahead of me in poise, sharpness, and tenacity. We had the sort of uneasy, leaves-over-bear-traps romance that jitters along when neither person wants to be the first to relax. We had met just before my graduation and, with a little effort on my part and a good deal on hers, had continued dating until the end of the following fall semester (we were still on academic time: a dangerous sign). We split amicably, predictably, and remained in ever-dwindling contact. After she graduated, I figured that I would probably not hear from her again, though I suspected I would at some point read about her. I was curious to see how she was doing, but I figured it wasn't worth the awkwardness this time, particularly as I was due back in Lincoln this afternoon. I'd have probably thought differently if there were any chance of a nostalgia fuck, but weekday-afternoon sex is one of those things you give up when you get a day job. (And sex, I had been discovering to my increasing dismay, is one of those things you give up when you move to a tiny town in New England where you're younger than the average citizen's children.)

I headed east through the old industrial cities of Connecticut that had turned bleak, broke, and half scrapped. By the time I joined the interstate, I could have reached Wickenden with my eyes shut; I had driven up and back from New York seventy or eighty times. I knew the distances and vistas as well as I knew the inside of my house: the way the pavement gets rougher as soon as you cross into Rhode Island; the forest on either side of the highway that seems somehow out of place in the Ocean State; the anonymous 1970s-vintage concrete office blocks, truckyards, and bus stations in Staunton and East-wick. As you approach Wickenden, fifty years drop away. Pastel-colored three-story clapboard houses with balconies on every level crowd the highways, teetering unsteadily above it. Then comes the red-brick industrial section, once abandoned and now gussied up with art galleries and cafés where $5.50 gets you a geographically precise cup of coffee in a wide ceramic mug handmade by a friend of the café's owner; and a downtown stuffed to bursting with rickety old buildings, steel-and-glass new ones that shine obnoxiously like a made-it-big uncle at a family reunion; quirky streets that started in a parking lot and dead-ended at the side of a building: America's grandmother's attic. I loved it, everything about it, with a possessiveness one reserves for indefensible (or semidefensible) loves: anyone could move to New York or San Francisco or Los Angeles, shed his past and join the nativist chorus, but this place offered little except its strangeness and ramshackle charm, and it ruined those it charmed for anyplace else.

I pulled off the interstate on Firwell Street, just down the hill from the university. Wickenden's buildings sprawled over a few square miles on a hill overlooking the city's east side: it was isolated enough, geographically and culturally, so that unadventurous students never had to venture into the big, bad (in fact, midsize and friendly) city below, and close enough so that when older students started to get cabin fever, they had somewhere to escape. I drove up the hill past the courthouse and the town's University Club, and when the buildings became institutional instead of professional, I pulled in around the corner from the history department.

When I got out of the car, a skinny, tattered man in a huge blue parka talking to an unspecified number of imaginary friends sauntered down the street toward me. He waved a finger in the air and brought it down in my direction like an orchestra conductor. 'Say, brother. Say, man, them ponies are a motherfucker. Gotdamn bitches spit a grown man out.'

I suppose I was staring, because as he reached me, he looked me up and down and asked, 'Anybody the fuck talkin' to you? Shee-it,' he spit, removing a greasy MENDES BROS. GARAGE SERVICE cap and scratching his bald head.

'You best get in that jive-ass shitheap you call a car

and get on back to St Lou.' He started walking past me, then stopped, turned around, and held his arms out, palms up, shaking his head. 'And tell Miss Ethel she don't need to worry about nothing no more. I be right there behind her, little man.'

I was still puzzling over possible meanings as I walked up the department steps. It felt like a couple of years and another lifetime ago that I'd shuffled around this place as a decent but unmotivated student, one who wrote good essays out of habit and considered graduate school as a means of avoidance, but really could never make himself care quite enough about colonial American sock darning or gun barrels in czarist Russia. It wasn't a lack of curiosity as much as it was a lack of *committed* curiosity: I'd love to know about, say, hardtack production in Vermont or how the innovations of Catherine the Great's chief gunsmith prefigured the Kalashnikov, but I didn't really want to do much with the knowledge other than consider it, turn it around in my mind, imagine it into three dimensions. I certainly didn't want to spend decades poring through archives and nitpicking over secondary sources in order to dispute it.

Still, I liked the department. I liked the way it felt, the way the stairs sagged in the middle, the pervasive smell of books, pipe tobacco, old coffee, dust. I liked the hum of conversation, too: the arcane topics and quiet voices. When I was twelve years old, I went on a Sunday-school trip to a monastery near Oneonta;

42

this department had a similar feel of cloistered seriousness. The monastery, however, offered far more comfortable digs – fires, soft couches, well-insulated rooms, a warm kitchen – than the history department, which was stuffed into a nineteenth-century Queen Anne house that hadn't seen a fresh coat of paint in decades and whose walls, in the howling midwinter (and even now, in early December), were the merest formality.

At the main desk, one secretary was talking to another about either her disobedient husband, son, or dog – '. . . and he goes *right there* on the floor, so I told him, I said, "Angelo, you're gonna clean that up, and you're not going out tonight until you do," so he says . . .' – when I knocked on the open door.

'Help you?' she asked.

'I hope so. My name's Paul, and I'm a reporter for the *Lincoln Carrier* in Lincoln, Connecticut. I was wondering if the department had a sort of biography, or any sort of biographical information, for Professor Pühapäev.'

She craned her neck and looked over at the mail-boxes. 'Pühapäev hasn't been in yet today. Couple of days, actually, it looks like. You can ask him when he gets here, or you can leave a message and I'll put it in his box.'

I looked around me, a little panicky. How could nobody in the department know? But then it was clear: he lived alone and two hours away, probably had few close friends here, and kept irregular hours.

The perfect person to go missing or drift away. The perfect person to realize our most knee-buckling fear, the one that saves uncountable marriages and holds families together with the unconquerable mixture of love and terror: the perfect person to die alone, unmissed and unnoticed.

'I'm sorry to tell you this, but Professor Pühapäev died the night before last. He lived in my town. I'm just looking for some information about him so I can write an obituary.'

She blanched and looked down. The other secretaries stopped typing. It was like a western when the stranger walks into the bar and everything stops. The secretary crossed herself. 'Died? How? What happened?'

'I don't know yet, actually. He lived alone, and they only just found him. I'm just up here looking for some background stuff about him, something so I can write an obit. Do you by any chance know how old he was?'

'Pretty old, I think. I don't know, though. He was here when I got here, but I've only been here for a few years.'

I put on my 'harmless idiot' face, which was probably in any case not too different from my normal expression. 'Do you maybe have any papers or forms that could give me some idea of where he was from, when he was born, or anything like that?'

She sighed and cracked her gum sympathetically. 'I don't know. . . .' She trailed off. 'Feels kind of strange to just, like, give it to you before the family or anyone gets here. You know?' I nodded, again as harmlessly as I could. I figured it wasn't worth arguing with her quite yet. 'You could go talk to Professor Crowley.' She leaned back in her chair for another mailbox check. 'He's been in today. I think he's even here now, but I'm not sure. Check his office. I think he and Professor Pühapäev were friends. Anyway, their offices are – were – next to each other. Third floor, turn right, all the way back.' She nodded and smiled thinly. 'Tell his family we're so sorry and we're praying with them.'

'I certainly will. I'm sure they'll be glad to hear that.' It seemed the best thing to say.

I knocked on the last door of the third floor's right-side hallway, and a harrumphing 'Yes?' barked back.

I opened the door and poked my head into the office. A whey-colored face glared up at me. 'Office hours are tomorrow, one to three P.M. Come back then or make an appointment.'

'Sir, I'm not a student, I'm a journalist, and –'

At this the man bounded up from his desk like a friendly dog and walked over to me. 'Ham Crowley. Good to meet you. Sorry about that gruff welcome, but I thought you were a student. What can I do for you?'

His eagerness caught me off guard. I had, in fact, taken one class from him (Power and the Press Under Khrushchev and Kennedy), but it was a large class and I never spoke to him directly. He had a reputation as a disinterested discussion leader, a bullying adviser, an erratic reader, and a drunk. He had published a book in the late 1980s that, through assiduous self-promotion and selective reading, laid claim to 'predicting' the fall of the Soviet Union. During the early 1990s, he enjoyed fourteen of his fifteen minutes – dinners with senators, Sunday-morning talking-head panels, articles in *Foreign Affairs* and op-ed pieces in the *New York Times* and the *Wall Street Journal* – and had spent the rest of the decade scrounging for the last one. I expected he would throw me out as soon as I told him why I had come.

'Well, sir, I'm writing an obituary of Jaan Pühapäev, who died yesterday. The receptionist told me you might be able to tell me a bit about him.'

He puffed his cheeks out bullfrog style, waddled back to his desk, and plopped flubbily down in his chair. 'Well, shit. I'm sorry to hear that. I thought you were here about my book. Thus far published to utter fucking resounding silence.' He waved me into a chair across from him and handed me a book from a stack of about twenty. *And Where the Bear?* by Hamilton S. Crowley. The front cover showed a brown bear teetering on a globe, with a hammer and sickle on one side and an American flag on the other.

'Hideous, isn't it?' he asked hemorrhoidally. 'Some jackass art designer at my cut-rate publisher thought it was cute. I hate it when they fag up my covers. And I didn't pick the title either. Two-bit fucking assholes.'

I wondered if Crowley had met the pony man in the street; I imagined them cementing their brother-hood with unbroken streams of profanity. 'What was your title?'

'*Market Reforms and Managed Resource Extractions in Post-Soviet Russia.* Sucks, doesn't it?' He pulled his lips into a grimace, revealing a mouthful of the worst teeth in New England: a dental postearthquake shantytown. 'So, what about Johnny?' he said, pulling his defeated face into something almost resembling interest.

'I'm sorry. Who?'

'Pühapäev. Jaan. When he first got here, I called him Johnny. I think he thought it was funny, but with him you could never tell.'

'What do you mean?'

'He wasn't really one to emote. Very Soviet, and very Estonian. You know, they have a proverb, the Estonians: "May your face be like ice." Jaan's was. Almost totally un-fucking-readable.'

'Was he teaching this semester?'

'Probably. Taught the same two courses every year, for God knows how many years.' Crowley picked up a course catalog and leafed through it. 'First semester: Baltic History, 1200–1600. Second semester: Baltic History, 1601–1991. I think he wrote the lectures on the flight over here in 1991 and hasn't changed them at all. I hear he sometimes had students, but not many. Don't know if he ever directed a thesis, and I think he only published occasionally, in these obscure Baltic journals.'

'Did he do departmental work? That seems like an awfully light load.'

'Well, he was an awfully strange guy.' Crowley put his hands on his desk and nodded once, firmly, at me: so there. 'I used to tell my students to take his courses, but I stopped recommending him a couple of years ago. No point, really. You know, this one girl told me a funny story about him. Said one day a student asked him a question he wasn't prepared to answer, and he just grabbed the lectern with both hands and looked up for a long time. Then he bolted. Just left in the middle of a lecture. He showed up at the student's door at two A.M., still dressed in professorial tweed, to answer the question.'

'What was the question?'

'Well, I sure don't know. Is that really the point?' The charm of talking to a member of the press was clearly starting to wear off. Crowley untucked his shirt and scratched his armpit for a while. I took this as a sign of my journalistic unimportance to him.

'Do you know where or when he was born?'

'His name's Estonian, and I'm pretty sure he is, too. I can't speak the language myself – totally incomprehensible Finno-Ugric mess, fourteen cases, unpronounceable vowels, and so on. But I know he spoke Estonian, Latvian, Lithuanian, Russian, German, and even occasionally some English. And the other question: when? Not sure. He arrived on a wave of euphoria; everybody wanted to hire former Soviet scholars. Standards lowered, know what I mean? Not to say Johnny was unqualified, but I don't think anybody needed to know much about him except that he was an Estonian university professor, not a Party member, and kind of an odd duck.'

'Does the department have his CV?'

'Maybe. Doubt he'd want you looking at it, though. Good old bred-in-the-bone Soviet paranoia. You can try downstairs.'

'I did that. They sent me up here. Can you please just tell me something, anything about him so I have something to write?'

He looked at me sourly and shuffled some papers on his desk. 'Look, Mr . . .'

'Tomm.'

'Mr Tomm?'

'Yep. T-O-M-M, Tomm.'

'What the hell kind of name is that?'

'Long story. You don't want to hear it.'

'You're right. Mr Tomm, Johnny and I were collegial, friendly, but that's it. We weren't best buddies. When he first came to this country, my wife and I had him over for barbecues a few times – rah, rah, July Fourth, wave the flag and all that horseshit. I went out drinking with him occasionally, but not in a few years. That's all. Now, if you'll excuse me, I have to get back to whatever crap I was doing before you showed up.'

I stood up and, as I was leaving, asked where they went drinking.

'You know, it's funny, but I still remember. It was this roadside dive called the Lone Wolf, a little ways past Westerly, just over the border on the way back to his town. Think it was in a place called Clougham. God knows what possessed me to drive out there. He only drank there, and he only drank this hideous homemade brandy. A few of those and they'll peel you off the floor. This one time, my wife . . .' He waved his hand and grinned briefly, before his face slumped back into defeated doughiness. 'Story for another time. Anyway, Lone Wolf: that's where we went. Good luck with the digging, Mr Tomm. Shut the door on your way out, if you wouldn't mind.'

I silently wished Crowley all the good reviews, fawning midlevel politicians, and C-SPAN interviews he could handle and prepared to head back to Lincoln, no more enlightened than when I'd left.

At the second-story landing, a familiar cultured voice spoke in a familiar inimitable accent from behind me. 'Do you know that I once had a student who looked remarkably like you? My student, however, was a well-mannered, almost timid young man, one who would never neglect his duty in courtesy to pay at least a brief visit to an old friend, were he in that friend's vicinity.'

Professor Jadid stood in his doorway, papers in one hand, glen plaid blazer draped over his arm, with his eyebrows raised in greeting and his characteristic half smile under his push-broom mustache and half-moon glasses. He was the first professor I'd ever met – my randomly assigned adviser from whom I had taken one course freshman year – but I had consulted with him at the beginning of every semester, and in my mind's eye, his image appeared first whenever I heard the word 'professor.'

I extended my hand – first checking to see that my shirt was tucked in (it was) and that I wasn't wearing sneakers (I was), and he shook it warmly. 'I don't remember the last time an ink-stained wretch progressed this far up the stairs. Usually my colleagues meet their admirers in the lobby, before allowing one august publication or another to pick up the check for an extended bibulous lunch. What brings you here today?'

'Hello, Professor.' I nearly reached over to hug him, but I think he would have considered that a breach of decorum. 'I was wondering whether you were around.'

'Around? And where should I go? Lovely to see you. So what does bring you here today?'

'Work. Reporting, believe it or not. Professor Pühapäev died the night before last. He lived in Lincoln, and I'm trying to find just the most basic biographical information so I can write the obit. No luck so far.'

His face fell as he exhaled and looked down, scuffing a shoe against the doorjamb. 'I'm very sorry to hear that. Very sorry indeed. I supposed he . . .

Well. Well, well.' He composed himself and straightened up.

'Do you know much about him? Where he was born, when, that sort of thing?'

'Oh, not terribly much. I know that his name was Estonian, and I know that he occasionally translated articles for me from all three Baltic languages. Do I know, beyond doubt, that he was born there? No. By the way, his name – Jaan Pühapäev – means "John Sunday" in Estonian. Very unusual, and probably completely fictitious. I had always assumed he had a Jewish name and background and had changed it during Soviet times, to avoid, or at least minimize, religious persecution. That assumption of mine, however, is precisely that: an assumption, without factual grounding. I know that he was quite a good linguist and that in this department he was considered an expert in his field, perhaps because there are so few Baltic historians outside of Germany, Russia, and the Baltics themselves. I know that he was also a remarkably poor teacher.' Professor Jadid paused, again tapping the toe of his shoe in thought. Both of his shoes were particularly worn at the toes. I had never noticed this habit before, but this might have been the first time we had spoken standing up.

'I also feel that I shall miss him terribly, not because we were particularly close but because he carried himself with an air of mystery and perpetual gloom, and I always found that a sovereign antidote – and please, Mr Tomm, do not take this as a generational slur – an antidote against the Frisbee-tossing cheerfulness so prevalent here.

'I can see in so many of my students an absolute certainty that nothing bad will ever happen to them. Wars, plagues, detentions, beatings – all things to sign petitions about on their way from the post office to the gym. As a fellow immigrant, I can tell you that it takes more effort than you might think to preserve a manner such as Jaan's: generally either we become more American than the Americans or we develop a hard shell of contempt for everything about our new home. Jaan was invariably himself, and that is praise of a high order.'

I glanced down at my watch. The professor, sensitive and tactful as ever, glanced at his and pulled the door shut behind him. 'Wednesday afternoons this semester, I find myself teaching a Hansa seminar, and I fear I shall be late. Are you rushing away quickly, or might I be able to convince you to stroll around your old stomping grounds for ninety minutes and then join me for an afternoon drink at Fitzgerald's?'

The invitation alone was worth the trip – I felt as though I had just passed a test of some sort – even if I had to leave. We began walking down to the lobby together. 'I'm sorry, but I need to get back to my office this afternoon. A two-hour drive.'

He pressed his lips together, shut his eyes, shrugged, and tilted his head to one side, then the other: a Groucho Marx pantomime of resignation.

'Ah, well. An old man is a ridiculous thing. If you plan to return at all, I should very much like to buy you a glass of beer. And if you have no plans to return, I'll sweeten the invitation to include lunch, and so give you an excuse. I always enjoy hearing news of the outside world.'

'I'd love to. Maybe later this week, after I finish this obit? Any day that doesn't inconvenience you, really.'

'Why don't you come up on Saturday? Neither of us will be working then, I hope. I'll reserve a booth at the Blue Point with a window facing west, and we can conclude our lunch as civilized people do in the winter: by drinking brandy and watching the sun set.'

I agreed immediately, and he extended his hand again. 'Until Saturday, then. And do keep me informed about Jaan. I shall be quite curious to hear what you learn, as well as how you will learn it.' We stepped outside and into a gust of Wickenden wind: I had forgotten that the east side of the city generated its own gales. He clamped one hand on his papers, gave a short roll-of-the-fingers wave with the other, and walked off – head down, long strides, quick pace – toward the class buildings. After a few steps, he turned around and walked back toward me.

'You know, Mr Tomm, I dislike telling tales out of school, but Jaan was a singularly strange man. Obsessively private, rather paranoid. I wish to tell you something about him you might not otherwise find out, but you must promise me something.'

'Of course.'

'Fine. First you must promise not to use this information in a salacious manner. If it helps you write a fuller obituary, fine, but you must promise that you won't simply drop it in for the sake of a little spice. Do you give me your word on this?'

'I do.'

'Good. Jaan's relationship with the local authorities was at times rather more fractious than a tenured history professor's should have been. I believe he was arrested, though I do not think he spent any time in prison.'

'Really? What for?'

As I opened my notebook, a grimace flashed across Jadid's face, as though impropriety was too painful for him to consider. 'Well, as I said, he was a private and paranoid man, and he also had rather a violent temper. Apparently he used to carry a small handgun on his person at all times.' He gave an embarrassed little mirthless chuckle.

My eyebrows raised: an armed professor?

Jadid continued: 'We discovered this surprising fact when he fired his gun out his office window at a stray cat on the eaves across the courtyard. I believe he saw a shadow move and mistook it for a prowler.'

'Do you remember when this happened?'

'Oh, a few years ago I should think. While you were still a student, most likely.'

'Really? I don't remember hearing anything about it.'

'As well you should not have. The department and the university went to considerable trouble to keep this matter quiet.'

'Why?'

'Why?' he mocked gently. 'A gun-toting professor at a university of this caliber, in this state? There would have been a scandal.'

'Why wasn't he fired?'

'He was tenured. We would have had to give a reason, and hold an official hearing, and we wished not to do that. We told him that under no circumstances was he to arrive armed at this department again. He agreed reluctantly, though, needless to say, he would hardly have been frisked as he came through the front door.'

'And did this happen again?'

'I'm not certain, to tell you the truth. I never heard of it again, but then few members of the department knew about the first incident. No reason, really, for everyone to know everything. But if you are curious to get all the details correct, you might want to phone my nephew Joseph, who serves on the Wickenden police force.'

'You have a cop for a nephew?' I asked incredulously.

He laughed. 'Yes, of course. My favorite nephew, in fact, my favorite among seven others, and two nieces as well. Do you simply assume all Jadid males are handed sport jackets with elbow patches as they emerge from the womb? No, I'm the only one, and . . . Anyway, I really am going to be late. We can discuss families over lunch. But please do get in contact with Joseph if you're curious. He's not to everyone's taste, you know, but he's quite intelligent, and if you mention that I suggested you call, he should be able and willing to assist you.'

'Thank you. Just out of curiosity, do you know whether Professor Pühapäev had anything to be paranoid about?'

'One of the enduring legacies of the Soviet Union, Mr Tomm, is mistrust, of everybody and everything. Of course, paranoia as psychosis does not negate the possibility of actual, tangible reasons to be paranoid. In Jaan's case I wouldn't hazard a guess either way. He was a dark one. At any rate, I look forward to discussing him this weekend.'

THE CASTLE

❧

When we say of the castle that it is where the transformation takes place, this is not a limiting but an expanding statement: it refers to the vessel itself, the outer vessel in which the first one is sealed, the laboratory, the laboratory's building, the building's city, the city's county, and so forth. An experienced and introspective metaphorist could point the telescope inward rather than outward, referring to himself as the ultimate vessel of transformation, for turning sights and sounds into thoughts and so forth. We were best to leave this approach to ladies and novelists.

— CLARKE CHUMBLEY, *Too Little, Too Late:*
The Tragic Peregrinations of a Victorian Alchemist

If the most accurate judge of time is a clock, the most sensitive is surely a thief. Omar Iblis was the best and, in A.D. 1154, the year where this telling begins, the least-heralded thief in Sicily. He cultivated his anonymity carefully, wearing forgettable clothes, keeping his hair and beard trimmed neither stylishly nor unfashionably, walking neither too near nor too far from others, neither too quickly nor too slowly, and never drawing attention to the thing he most wanted. He taught himself to pay more attention to the edges than the center of his vision. At night he trained his memory: behind his house he would gather up one handful of stones and one of dried beans, extend his arms straight out from his body, drop the beans and stones, stare at them for a short while, prepare dinner, and, after eating, draw the pattern into which the objects had fallen. Before going to sleep, he trained his body, spending hours moving nothing but a single muscle in the center of his hand, controlling his heartbeat, timing his breathing to coincide with the upswell in the locusts' song.

He had graduated from stealing fruit from orchards at night to stealing animals from their pens to stealing merchants' trinkets to stealing merchants' profits. He eventually became an accomplished house robber, because he could always tell – by the cut of their clothes, the look of anticipation on their faces, the amount of luggage they carried – when the occupants were departing for a long journey. Only then would he enter the house, examine its contents at leisure, and take what he wanted, and only provided he could do so without causing spectacle or commotion. He never robbed churches, synagogues, or mosques, nor would he steal from priests, rabbis, or imams; though he did not attend prayer services himself, he liked to avoid unduly inciting God or His representatives on earth. King Roger II tended to protect all servants of God with equal vigilance, and his sentries exacted retribution in gruesome and varied ways.

Early one afternoon Omar passed a young novice, freshly tonsured and still awkward in his cowl, and asked him what day it was. 'Today is the feast day of St Theodore of Sykeon,' the boy answered, holding out an iron-ringed arm as evidence.

'I see. And tell me, if you know, what house is that on the hill, surrounded by such fine gardens?'

'Our abbot covets that house. But the occupant was a singularly strange fellow who worshipped at no house of God and built odd-smelling fires at all hours of the night. Some say he was a witch, but he always enjoyed the king's protection. His name is something I could not tell you.'

'You speak of him in the past. Is he dead?'

'No, put to sea yesterday. The abbot says His Holiness King Roger will make the house into a second palace, far from the bustle of Palermo. But even so, it would take his guards until tomorrow at least to reach this place. The house stands abandoned until then, with entry barred by order of His Holiness King Roger.'

'Is that so? Indeed. Well, thank you for your cheer and conversation, friend.'

'Go in God's grace, friend.' Turning around, the monk tripped on his cowl, rolled over twice, righted himself, and continued quickly downhill.

Omar weighed his options: On the one hand, an abandoned house, rich in appearance, owned first by Roger's friend and now by Roger himself, no doubt well appointed. On the other, it was only rumored to be abandoned, and if he was caught in the house of a royal friend (or worse, of the king himself), it would mean, at the very least, death. He finally decided that there could be no harm in looking, and if he was found on the grounds, he would identify himself as an itinerant field laborer searching for work in the orchards and gardens. No harm at all.

He stayed to the side of the path, under the trees but not too far under, walking purposefully but not too quickly, casually but not too jauntily. He circled the house and approached through the groves of orange, lemon, and almond trees, stopping to shove a few oranges into one of the pockets that he had sewn onto the inside of his tunic. He stooped beneath the window and listened. A wasp landed on his lip and crawled across his face to his ear. A second wasp landed on his nose, then a third on his left eyelid, a fourth on his right. His thighs and knees trembled as he crouched, perfectly still, and the wasps' antennae made him want to sneeze. The wasps, each as big as a man's pinky, moved like an advancing army, crawling to a fixed point and pausing, as if waiting for instruction. Then, in the same order that they came, they flew away, and Omar crept around to the front of the house, slipped in the front door, and shut it behind him.

The hallway floor was marble; a white line down the center divided the front room into two identical parts: a black-and-white chessboard pattern on either side of the floor, staircases ascending in either corner of the room and converging into a single ladder, two doors on either side, and between the doors a shelf, on which stood two identical blue glass vases, each holding a white rose in the early stages of decay. Omar had never set foot in such a grand house. Crossing the line to the left, he opened the door closest to him: it opened onto a stucco wall. The door farther from him on the same side also opened onto a wall, this time painted with some sort of red beast with a long forked tail, rows of sharp teeth, and fire coming from its mouth. He crossed the room and opened the door farthest from the entry on the right side. A darkened hallway began at this door but curved sharply almost immediately. Omar walked onto the path but left the door open behind him. Like any Sicilian thief, he always carried a pocketful of dried chickpeas with him to use as trailmarkers or a makeshift meal, and he dropped them along the path behind him. The path twisted and turned, but Omar had followed it for less than a minute when he came to another door. He opened it, and it led back into the entryway: the only door he had not yet tried. Confused, frustrated, his hopes of a rich take slipping from him, he climbed the staircase that turned into a ladder; when the ladder stopped at a trapdoor, he shoved it open and climbed through.

He emerged in a long, low, dark stone room, with three ovens leading to three chimneys, as in a bakery. Along one wall were more books than he had ever seen in one place, even more than his grandfather Maulvi Azzam had. Along the other wall were shelves holding vessels of various sizes, colors, and shapes. Omar was walking along the shelves, hefting first a broad stone bowl, then a tall copper beaker, when he heard the door creak open downstairs. Peering through the trapdoor, he saw two men, both wearing short and long swords, with the royal crest on their shields. He moved away from the door quickly and silently and searched the room for something, anything valuable he could take with him. Now he thought not of riches but of escape – he was bargaining silently with the God he never visited, promising to lead a quiet, pious, sheep-tending life, if only if only if only – and of a single trinket he could show his friends and children, and say that he took this from under the king's nose.

A burlap sack lay shapelessly in a corner. When Omar bent to pick it up, he noticed a small wooden chest wedged into the alcove behind one of the ovens. He lifted and shook it: it made a rattling sound; it was locked, not too heavy. He considered putting the chest into the sack, but it fit awkwardly and would have been cumbersome to carry at a fast clip. Instead he grabbed a heavy stone vessel and brought it down as hard as he could on the lock, which split with less noise than he feared. He emptied the contents into the sack, distributing them evenly so he could tie it securely around his waist, and again peered through the trapdoor. He saw two guards, one sitting on either staircase, so still he couldn't tell if they were asleep. They both sat on the third step, and both held their heads in their hands in the same position, as if assimilated somehow into the room's living mimicry. He considered waiting in the room upstairs, but he had no food other than the path-marking chickpeas, the day was waning, and he knew that if the guards were occupying the house in the king's name, sooner or later they would have to patrol upstairs.

He eased open the trapdoor gently and descended the ladder as quietly as possible. When the ladder divided into two staircases, he paused – the guards had not heard him – and, grabbing the bottom rung, swung himself as far forward as possible and let go, landing in the middle of the room still on his feet. The guards jumped up at the same time, but Omar ran out the door ahead of them and started down the path, running now as fast as he could away from the house. 'You've been seen!' one of the guards called out behind him. 'You've been seen by the king's men, thief, and will be broken for it!'

*

That night he slept in a thicket and awoke to discover that what in his dream was the mouth of an amber-skinned girl was in fact the warm, wet nose of a curious hedgehog. Keeping his pace quick and not stopping to eat, he reached Palermo by dusk. He knew the back alleys and rooftops better than any man alive, and he made his way unseen to a rude, squat hovel by the water's edge, where the scent of seawater and rotting fish mingled with fish roasted over rosemary branches and apple tobacco wafting from the window. He had barely poked his head through the front door when a booming voice asked him to state his business, his name, and whether he wished to be drowned, impaled, set alight, or flayed.

'Frighten those who live in comfort, Uncle. I have been scared enough these past two days.'

Laughter loud enough to rustle topsails answered him. 'My quick-handed Omar! Come in, sit; sit, come in. Will you eat and keep an old man company?'

Omar walked through the door and saw his uncle Faisal in the candlelight and gloaming. Faisal's size seemed to increase with the city's. He was massive and imposing rather than corpulent; his chestnut skin, a certain awkwardness of posture, and a reluctance to move unless absolutely necessary gave him a petrified appearance. A scar in the shape of the Arabic letter faa' ran from just above his right eyebrow almost to the dome of his bald head, and a beard the size of an eagle's nest ran from his nose to his belly. His eyes were milky, indistinct.

Omar had learned his trade from Faisal, before the older man had been caught in the home of a lesser duke's factor and had a red-hot sword put to his eyes. Now Faisal merely directed most of Palermo's crime from this shack by the docks; though Omar saw nobody else in or near the house, he knew that his uncle kept himself at least as well guarded as the king. The large man made an incongruously girlish trilling motion with his fingertips, and a tall, lean, armed man appeared with a plate of dates, almonds, bread, and cheese and set it before Omar, not looking at him. Omar ate ravenously, noisily, without even offering any to his uncle, who kept his voided sockets fixed, as if sighted, on his nephew.

'Why don't you tell me what has happened, boy?'

'I have been seen. I have been seen by the king's guards, stealing from the house of the king's friend, and I must leave this island immediately. Where I go, what I do, how I go is of no importance, but if they find me . . .' He whimpered at the thought of what might happen to him.

'No decree will ever be as effective as physical pain,' his uncle said thoughtfully. 'What were you taking, and where were you seen?'

'I have taken nothing much, nothing of con-sequence,' Omar began, his voice rising. His uncle moved a hand up and down: calm. 'I took these trinkets,' he said, loosening the sack, 'from a house on a hill, some two days' quick walk from here.'

His uncle reached into the bag, examining with his hands. He pulled out oddity after oddity – a gold flute, a painted coin, a knotted rope attached to a copper board – and returned each to the bag. He closed the bag and handed it back to his nephew, then sighed. 'Did this house have orchards and gardens?'

'Yes, both.'

'Was one side of the entryway the same as the other? Did you take these from an upstairs room?'

'Yes, Uncle, but how could you –'

His uncle pounded a massive, piglet-size fist on the table. 'Fool! Imbecile! Curse of my blood! If you could return these things . . . But you can't. No matter.' He sighed again and ran a hand over his bald head, tracing the scar with one finger. 'My brother your father is dead. My wives are barren, and they hate me. I do not know my own children. You are my only living family. I will put you on a ship and give you safe conduct from here. Either reform yourself or go be foolish someplace else, but I will not hear of your death here.'

Omar put his head in his hands. 'How will I go? And whose house was I in?'

Faisal clapped his hands twice, and the same lean man entered. They whispered to each other, and the man withdrew. 'As for how: you will go with a Genoese merchant who sails for Sudak at first light. Do you know where Sudak is?'

Omar shook his head.

'Ignoramus. I study every new map, and I cannot even see them. The world is expanding, nephew, perhaps it is even expanding enough to hide a careless idiot like you. As for your other question, you have stolen from al-Idrisi, the king's geographer and many other things besides. That you escaped his house without being run through by the guards I would expect; that you escaped without something infinitely more horrible happening to you . . . well, we will see whether you have or haven't. The Genoese owes me favors for the introduction I provided him to Assaf Qidri and his daughters. But he is not an honest man, and I expect you will have to part with some of your treasure, too.'

A rhythmic, low whistling came from just outside the window. With great difficulty Faisal stood, placed a hand on his heart, and bowed. 'Go now. Follow Asif to the ship silently, and do not ever look back at this house. Go and be well. God will do as He will. May I never hear of you again.'

On the ship Omar worked at whatever the merchant Silvio asked – cooking, scrubbing galleys, sail rigging – and after a month they sighted land. The merchant called Omar to his cabin. 'That is Sudak in the distance. Your new home. Do you wish to work or steal there?'

'Work. I worry that my instincts for thievery have left me.'

'Good. I expected no less intelligent an answer, even if it is not a true one. Now, I have taken this sack from your cabin. This is what got you in trouble in Sicily, is it not?' Omar nodded. 'Yes. I will relieve you of this burden.' Omar began to protest, and Silvio moved his hand to his sword. 'I am not entirely heartless, though. You may choose one item from among these – I see fourteen in the sack – as a memento of your former life.' He held the sack open toward Omar, who reached in without looking, and what he withdrew he quickly shoved into his tunic pocket.

'Good. A proper respect for chance, or fate, or God's will, or luck, or whatever it is you wish to call it. Now, when you get ashore, leave this ship at once. You are an able-bodied young man and will find work easily along the docks. Venture inland only when you tire of life: the Golden Horde and the Polovtsy fight for control of this island, and when one of them becomes strong enough to eliminate the other, then we Genoese, too, will have to leave. You will be doing yourself a service, though, if you remain among us civilized people for as long as you are able. Now gather your remaining things and go ashore with the rest of the crew. If you ever trouble me again – if you ever claim knowledge of me or even hint that we have spoken – I will bone and flay you like a pigeon.'

Omar walked quickly to the bow. When the ship reached shore, he fairly jumped off. A man transformed, with nothing to his name except a carved rock of questionable value in his pocket, he breathed free and deeply for the first time since leaving Sicily, and he toddled with his bandy sea legs in the dying light up the wooden walk.

Despite his initial misgivings and concerns, Omar found Sudak a congenial city: not as advanced or as cosmopolitan as Palermo, but, like most seaports, teeming with intrigue, mongrels, and all the pleasures a man's purse could buy. He lived through several summers in Sudak, never reverting to thievery. His ability to converse in Arabic, Latin, and vulgar Sicilian made him unusually valuable as a negotiator, a job that not only fed and clothed him but allowed him to save enough for a bride price and a small piece of land in the mountains. When he retired from Sudak, he swore never again to look on the sea; he planted grapevines and orange trees on his land and earned some local fame as a vintner.

Rumor spread that his distillations bestowed on the drinker unusual longevity, for Omar outlived not only his wife but all seven of his children, dying at what some called an unnatural age: on his deathbed he told his eldest grandson, then an abbot of advancing years and stern reputation, that he had been in Sudak for more than a century. On the day of his death, in the silent hour between cricket song and birdsong, he used his last strength to pull himself from his bed to a secluded and barren spot between his home and vines. There he dug a small pit and, with all rites and rituals, buried the one item that came with him from Sicily, wrapping it in virgin white cotton, as if he were at last burying his younger self. When his valet came to rouse him at daybreak for prayers, he found his master cold and white, with dirt lodged beneath his long fingernails.

As for the Genoese captain, Silvio Freschi, he became known not only as the bravest and most intrepid sailor from a land of brave and intrepid sailors but also as the wealthiest trader in a country of wealthy traders. He established Genoese trading settlements at Qingdao, Kwangju, and Fukuoka. He supposedly took a wife in Axum, where he spent long months in conversation with the guardian monk of the Ark of the Covenant. On the rare occasions he came to Genoa, it was always a cause for celebration and wonder, for he returned with his hold full of spices, nuts, fruits, seeds, fabrics, musical instruments, and books. He always sailed with the same crew, and when one of them died or deserted or remained in a pleasant city, that man was never replaced; Silvio said that he would retire when he was left with a skeleton crew.

When that time came, he put ashore in Genoa with his twelve remaining crew members, and together they sank their ship, using a black powder they had obtained in Qingdao in exchange for a crate of crushed rose petals from Masqat. Silvio invited the men to his house for one final supper together, where he gave each of them a thirteenth part of his wealth. Then, in a gesture that became common practice in Genoa at the end of a career at sea, he ceremonially burned an empty sack, signifying the end of his trading and traveling days. The sack he burned was sloppily woven from Sicilian hemp; the crew remembered the jumpy little thief who had carried it aboard, wrapped around his waist.

Item 2: A castle carved from an elephant's tusk, 40 centimeters tall, 20 centimeters across, 20 centimeters back to front. Hollow inside, and completely blackened, as if it had sat for long periods of time over a fire. Scorch marks also visible rising from the outside castle windows, as they would be from a razed castle on land. Vermilion and aquamarine decorative designs around the castle's base, turrets, and minarets. Design taken from the hashish dream of Ali Rasul Ali (A.D. 1034–1134), architect and chess

player of Lahore. Ali carved a complete chess set, all of elephant tusk and all of pieces much larger than usual. Toward the end of his life, he became myopic, though his love of chess never diminished, and played with the larger pieces to ease his eyestrain and maintain his strength.

An alchemist's work takes place within the castle, which describes what a castle is, or can be, not at all: one could say that an alchemist's work takes place within a green pea, if one could find a sufficiently large and hollow pea. The castle ought to physically contain all of the equipment and effluvia relating to the alchemical process, and therefore they vary widely in size (this one is among the smallest; the Domesday Book mentions 'ye fortresse nr to Greate Brizes, blackened ronde the tops of the turrets, all encompassed with foul vapours and excrescences, though none professe to live there, nor indeed do they know who does).' Nor need they invariably be castles in design. The ultimate and final castle is, of course, the world.

Date of manufacture: Late eleventh century A.D.

Manufacturer: Ali Rasul Ali.

Place of origin: Lahore.

Last known owner: Yussef Hadras ibn Azzam Abd Salih Jafar Khalid Idris. Stolen from his library in

1154 by Omar Iblis, born a Sicilian thief, died a Feodosian vintner. Omar kept the castle on his person until he became gravely ill at an unnaturally advanced age, when he buried it in a secluded spot between his grapevines and his grand house. It remained undisturbed there until 1943, when a series of explosions blamed on Crimean Tatar separatists unearthed it. The bombs were, in fact, planted by KGB agent Yuri Starpov to provide a pretext for the deportation and eventual liquidation of the Crimean Tatar populaton, at Stalin's behest. A Lithuanian Soviet army major found the castle in a tangle of vine roots and blood and brought it back to Svencionis, where it remained in the back of a kitchen cabinet, behind stacks of cheap china plates and chipped glass cups, perhaps even forgotten, until a burglary in 1974.

Estimated value: Based on sales of antique chess pieces and sales of pre-Moghul craft, between $24,000 and $70,000. Other pieces from this chess set exist but are scattered throughout the world. The corresponding white rook sits in the back of an antique shop in Pecs, where the ignorant owner's requested price is 400 forints; the two black rooks – painted with a mixture of goat's blood, soil, and burned cardamom husks – sold at auction in Pondicherry for $65,000 each. The Irish child-grandmaster Sean Lallan of Roscommon, now advanced in age and fortune, due to shrewd investments in Donegal's collective wool industry, owns both white knights and one black bishop and has let it be known that he would trade twenty acres of land for the other black bishop. A forged version of the white queen sold for $54,000 at a Toronto auction to a philandering orthodontist.

*And as all things were by the contemplation
of one, so all things arose from this one thing
by a single act of adaption.*

Professor Jadid bounded away, and I started to
regret not taking him up on his offer of a drink.
Maybe I should have been more concerned with
getting back home, but I was intrigued: guns and
conspiracies – even academic conspiracies like this
one – made a welcome change from the usual stories
about school-board meetings and zoning disputes.
As I looked at the clear and lapidary blue sky
and inhaled the city's distinctive autumn scent –
smoke and sea tang, with an occasional whiff of dock
brackishness – ninety aimless minutes here seemed
appealing.

The thought of catching up with the professor
appealed even more. He was courtly, classically educated, dignified, and European in a pre-1914 sense,
and as such had won more than his share of campus

enemies who considered him a dinosaur. One reason I liked him so much was how little that affected him: I had seen students refuse to walk through doors he held open, but I had never seen him fail to hold open a door. We had fallen out of contact mostly because of my laziness – I forgot to respond to a letter, never thought of picking up the telephone, and here it was almost a year since I had heard from him.

I don't know if I missed him personally as much as I missed the feeling of a benevolent approver, something that had disappeared once I graduated and found myself on my own, making decisions that actually mattered. And I missed the city, too, its cozy strangeness and, compared to Lincoln, its liveliness. As I looked up and down Roderick Street – the main student drag – hundreds of site-specific stories popped into my head, and the stories' ghosts became clearer to me than the people wandering around. After two minutes of this, my enthusiasm for staying here poured out of me as if I had been stabbed. Wherever I would go, I would be trailed by so much past, so little present, and no future. I decided to get in my car and drive back to my real life.

A bit more than an hour into Connecticut, I noticed the sign for the Clougham turnoff up ahead and remembered the bar that Crowley mentioned. It wasn't even 2:00 P.M.; if I stopped for a single beer, I could still make it back to the office with time to spare before close of business. Besides, maybe Pühapäev had drinking buddies. Maybe he was the type who confided in his bartender. Maybe I was the type who rationalized shamelessly to justify a beer during working hours.

Clougham was one of those innumerable little one-road towns in western Connecticut, one of an ever-dwindling number that had not yet become an extension of New York's Upper East Side. It had a two-pump gas station, a white clapboard general store (instead of a Ye Olde General Store), and next to it a combination post office and package store. When I first arrived in Lincoln, I had spent my weekends exploring the surrounding area, which is how I had discovered Clougham. In the past few months, though, I had stopped exploring and started freelancing for a couple of midsize Connecticut papers and for a magazine or two (mostly regional, historical, and garden-related). Art had tossed me a few assignments that some editors had thrown to him, saying I needed the clips more than he did. He also told me that if I ever found another working journalist who handed well-paid freelance assignments to a colleague just for the hell of it, he'd buy me my own magazine.

In front of the package store, I turned to gawk out my window at two couples, probably, God help me, a little younger than me, drinking beer in the beds of adjoining pickup trucks, one with fire detailing and the other with ocean. One of the guys stood up as I slowed down and tossed a beer can toward my car. I thought it was an empty until it hit the driver's-side door hard enough for me to swerve a bit, and as I slowed down to check the damage in my mirror, the guy who threw the can grabbed a tire iron from the bed of his truck and started striding toward my car. There was a dent in my door, but no comparable weapon in my car, so I just kept driving, my white-knuckled hands shaking and gripping my steering wheel. I heard them laughing loudly, even through my closed windows, and in the rearview I saw him slap his friend five.

A few streets down from the package store, around a sharp bend in the road, was a squat two-story maroon house with Christmas lights wrapped around the drainpipes and twinkling in the broad daylight. There was a parking lot where the front yard should have been, and at the entrance to the yard, a small wooden signpost was driven into the grass: THE LONE WOLF.

I pulled into the parking lot, between a navy blue Crown Vic and a rusty Datsun. Except for the neon Schlitz sign in the window and the parking lot in place of a yard, it looked like every other house along this street. Behind it, just visible around the side, was a backyard with a large grill next to some Dumpsters and a sad-looking, broken swing set behind them: Norman Rockwell seen from the bottom of a bottle, a view that could kick you sweetly in the chest like a poem.

I entered the bar through what should have been the house's front door, and for a moment I really did think I had walked into someone's residence: the bar and all the walls were covered in that flimsy, fake-wood paneling common to basements and rec rooms; no two chairs or tables matched, and they all looked like Salvation Army castoffs. A black-and-white television set quietly played soap operas in the corner. A thick-necked bartender with jet-black hair and a Pancho Villa mustache glanced up at me from behind the bar when I came in. Three other guys, all sort of grim and sleepy-looking, glanced up at me, too. They were sitting singly; when they looked up, it didn't seem as though any conversations had stopped. The bar felt rough and purgatorial. I like local color as much as the next outsider, but still I tended to steer clear of bars like this. As I walked in, my hands – still shaking a bit from the beer-can incident – began to sweat.

'Help you?' the barman asked. I couldn't place his accent, but it wasn't American.

I shut the door behind me and nodded. 'You open?'

'Maybe. You member?'

Did he mean 'Are you a member?' or 'Do you remember?' I guessed the first one. 'A member of what?'

'This private club. Social club, not bar. Need to be member to drink here. You got membership card?'

'No, I'm afraid I don't. Could you maybe make an exception and sell me a beer? I won't tell anybody.'

He plonked his forearms on the bar and leaned

forward. 'No exception, my friend. Must be member. But you could maybe make temporary member for this afternoon only.'

'Sure. How can I do that?'

'Invitation only,' he declared, grinning, as if the entire conversation had been leading to this point. 'Sorry.'

A skinny guy wearing a peacoat and silver granny glasses piped up from the end of the bar nearest me. 'C'mon, Eddie. Give the kid a beer. I'll invite him. Chris' sake.' He waved me over to an empty seat. 'Siddown here. This is the only bar for three towns around, and the only decent one left in this whole part of the state. Siddown already, why don't you?' He had a reedy voice and a local accent, the New England chowder thinned out a bit this far inland, all slippery endings and round vowels.

The bartender shrugged, feigning indifference, though he seemed upset not to have been able to kick somebody out. I've never understood why some proprietors derive so much pleasure from denying service. 'So okay, so sit. He invite you, so sit. What kind of beer you drink?'

'Bud?'

'Don't have.'

'Rolling Rock?'

'Also don't have.'

'What *do* you have?'

'Busch, Schlitz, Genesee, Heineken.'

'I'll have a Genesee, then.'

'Might be out. I check.' He poked his head into a refrigerator below the bar. 'No. Yes, we have. You want can or bottle?'

'A bottle, please.'

'Only have cans.'

'Okay, I'll have a can. I don't need a glass.'

He slid the can across the bar to me and handed me a streaked and grimy glass with a spent match in the bottom.

A man with a white beard at the end of the bar caught the bartender's eye and gave him the curt chin raise of someone used to being obeyed. He looked like some kind of mountain animal made temporarily human. The bartender poured a shot of viscous, clear liquid from an unmarked glass bottle and walked away only after the older man had nodded his approval of the drink.

The skinny guy – my host – turned to face me, and the light caught his glasses so I couldn't see his eyes behind them; it looked like two iridescent quarters were suspended in front of his face. 'Nate's body?' he asked.

'I'm sorry?'

'You here for Nate's body?'

'What? Who's Nate?'

He laughed. 'Guess not. Nate's Body Shop and Repair. It's a garage right behind this place. Does good work, pretty good prices. A lot of times, people waiting for their cars, Nate tells them to come wait here while he works.'

'I thought you had to be a member.'

He drained the rest of his beer and pointed at the bartender. 'This guy never turns down a buck. Might give you a hard time at first, but he'll always let you sit down. Right, Ed?'

The bartender grumbled and made a weird clicking sound with his tongue against his front teeth, most of which were gold. He poured the skinny guy another beer (Schlitz, can). 'So,' the coin-eyed guy said, 'why's a handsome young man like yourself wasting a nice Wednesday afternoon with a bunch of drunks in Clougham?' At that, a fat guy sprawled on the sofa raised his glass — 'Hey, he's talkin' about us!' — and everybody laughed just enough to take the discomfort off the self-identification.

'A friend of mine drinks here. He recommended it to me if I was ever out this way. Don't really have to be anywhere for another couple hours, so I figured I'd stop and check the place out.'

The bartender stopping polishing glasses and looked up at me. 'Your friend maybe told you about the membership, then. Who you know comes drinking at place like this?'

'An old professor of mine,' I lied. They already thought I looked suspect; I might as well add to the suspicion by admitting that I went to college. 'Name's Jaan.'

'Hey, I know him,' said the heavy guy on the couch. He turned to face me, and I saw that he was wearing a cap that read CHARLIE REED'S FEED &

SEED. 'Old guy, kinda sloppy, big beard. Yeah, he's here a few times a week. Doesn't say much.'

The bartender went back to his glasses, polishing and polishing, not so much as looking up at me. Given the state of my glass, he was making a surprising show of his fastidiousness.

'Kind of talks funny? Black glasses? Always wears that same churchy tie?' asked the guy sitting next to me. Feed & Seed nodded. 'Yeah, I know him, too. Real quiet type. Never even knew he's a professor. We got some real class here, eh?' Feed & Seed laughed; the bartender kept at his glasses. 'So what's he got to say for himself?'

'Well, nothing, actually. I'm sorry to tell you this, but he died,' I said. The bartender barely glanced up, and the white-bearded man behind him looked at me with stern and unblinking hawk eyes. The skinny guy turned around to face me. 'He died a couple nights ago. I'm a reporter for the newspaper in Lincoln, where he lived, and I'm trying to get some basic information so I can write his obituary. I stopped by his office and his home, and I heard that he drank here, so I thought maybe one of you knows something about him that you could tell me. Really, just basic stuff,' I said, shaking my head and putting my palms up in preemptive surrender: the No Threat position.

'Ah, shit,' said the skinny guy. 'That's a damn shame. He was real quiet, though. Don't know too much about him. Hey, Eddie, pour us a drink for Jaan, how about?'

84

Eddie shrugged again and arranged five shot glasses on the bar, filling them from the unmarked bottle, heading one to each of us, keeping one for himself, and whistling sharp and short for Feed & Seed to come get his.

I raised the glass to my nose, but the odor beat the liquid by about six inches. I reared back. 'What is this stuff? It smells like paint thinner.'

Eddie laughed. 'Always I thought so, too. Never drink it until now, but Jaan, he make it at home – make it from fruits, you know, also from roots, sugar, leave it sit, then drink – then bring it here. A sort of brandy.'

'He made his own booze but brought it to the bar? Did he buy it from you?'

'Yes, you know, we have arrangement: I buy the bottles, then he buy it from me, one glass, two glass, three glass, so on, so at the end everything even.'

A strange arrangement, but there was a distinctly strange feeling to this place, something ramshackle, intimate, and improvised. It felt both temporary and timeless; if I left and came back tomorrow, the Lone Wolf might be gone, but if I came back in thirty years, I wouldn't be surprised to find these same people in the same positions doing the same things. I looked dubiously at the glass, and Eddie grinned, opened his eyes wide, and nodded. Two of his top front teeth were gold. I inhaled, exhaled, and bolted the brandy in one shot. I felt it searing a hole in my throat and leaving a flame trail down my gullet.

I nearly fell off my stool. Eddie laughed; so did the three other guys. The skinny guy pushed his glass back to Eddie. 'No disrespect, Albie, you know, but I don't drink this stuff. No hard stuff until sundown, what I say. That's my line in the sand. Only beer until sundown.' The bartender shrugged again and poured the brandy back in the bottle.

'Did you just call the bartender Albie?' I asked, leaning close so the bartender wouldn't hear.

'Yeah, that's his name, that's what we call him.'

'I thought you called him Eddie.'

'Yeah. Albanian Eddie. That's what everybody calls him. Sometimes Eddie, sometimes Albie, some-times, if we're feeling formal, the Albanian. All the same, though.'

The skinny guy's voice had been beerily increasing during our discussion, so by now the bartender was standing in front of us, hand extended to me, his gold-fronted grin more menacing than a scowl would have been. I shook his hand. 'Eddie. My place here. You want maybe to mention in your newspaper, I tell you some advice: don't. This quiet place. My place,' he said, squeezing my hand harder, his grin becoming wider. 'We don't like trouble. People who ask too many questions, where I come from, we have name for them: corpses.' I tried to pull my hand away, and he grabbed my wrist with the other hand, still grin-ning, leaning even closer so I could smell his garlic breath, sweat, and dishwater hands. 'We drink toast to Jaan. Sorry he died, but always people die. We drink toast, then you leave. You don't come back.'

The skinny guy had shrunk down in his seat. Eddie gave me my hand back. It looked like raw chicken skin. I rubbed it, and the color drained back in slowly. Still grinning, he turned around and put the bottle back on the shelf. The skinny guy threw an arm around my shoulders and said confidentially, 'The Albanian, sometimes he's a little hotheaded. C'mon, lemme walk you to your car.'

To me 'a little hotheaded' means you pound a bookcase when you stub your toe or scream at the TV when some indistinguishable Jets quarterback tosses a dying quail in the fourth quarter. It means you snap at someone when you shouldn't. Trying to rip my hand off while comparing me to a corpse seemed far worse than 'a little hotheaded.' Still, I wasn't about to argue with the one person in the bar who seemed to care whether I got out with all my bones intact.

'Listen, Jaan was just a drinker, you know,' said the skinny guy as we walked across the parking lot. 'This is just a drinker's bar, not really a social place. All of us come here because we like to drink and get left alone. So nobody really talked about where he's from, or what his kids were doing, or what his daddy beat him with, or any of that crap, because nobody here cared. We sit down, hurt ourselves, and leave. Eddie keeps the place quiet and cheap, and he don't want anything else.'

'So you and Jaan never really talked?'

He sighed, spit on the ground. 'Sure, we chatted, said how ya doin', but that's about it. I don't know the first thing about him, and he don't know the first thing about me. I been here long as this place has been open, and so's he.'

'When did this place open?' He breathed in like he was about to restart his lecture, so I reassured him. 'I won't write it. I'm just curious. When did the Lone Wolf open?'

He put on a black watch cap from his inside pocket. Something about him – the lost expression, the agelessness, the aquiline dissoluteness – made him look like a figure from New England's past, a bookish crewman on the *Pequod*. 'Well, let's see. I remember when I first come here, my kid still lived at home, but just barely. He's in the army now, lives in Germany. Says he's about to make captain, I guess. But I haven't seen him in . . .' His voice trailed off, and he looked down. Suddenly, like an otter popping up from underwater, he refocused on me. 'That would mean 1991, I think this place opened. Yeah, gotta be early '91, 'cause I remember watching Scott Norwood miss that field goal in this bar, while Eddie and I were laying the floor tiles. He'd never seen a football game before. Yup, 1991 early.' With that, he nodded, hit the roof of my car, waved good-bye, and went back into the bar. Eddie opened the door for him, and as he walked in, Eddie clapped him on the back of the neck, a gesture somewhere between affectionate and threatening. To me he flashed his death's-head grin, gave me a thumbs-up, then drew his extended thumb across his throat.

Against my better judgment – and probably against the law, too – I drove back to Lincoln without waiting for the brandy and beer to fade. Something about Clougham unsettled me: it was as though the town itself didn't want me there and had animated its citizens to make sure I left quickly. All except that skinny guy from the bar, whose name I didn't know and to whom I may well have owed my intact body.

When I reached the office, I found Austell and Art in the same positions: one staring out the window, the other seated behind his desk with his door mostly closed and his headphones on. Only the light had changed; the soft afternoon sun made Austell look more boyish and made Art, his long bearded form bathed in poured gold, seem a Byzantine icon made flesh.

Closing the door, I gave Austell a quick wave and walked straight to Art's office before the columnist could waylay me; he still followed me, perching just outside Art's door. Art shut his music off. 'Well, kid, what's the story?'

'None. I'm exactly where I left off. Nobody knows where or when he was born, although his name was Estonian. One of his colleagues thinks his name was an alias but doesn't know his real name.'

'Did he speak Estonian?'

'He did.'

Art blew a line of smoke into a sunbeam, where it slowed down, as if reflecting, and dissolved. 'Estonia, huh? Tallinn. Went there in '89, then again in '93. One of those professionally cute little European towns. Postcard hawkers at every corner, this piddly cobblestone Old Town tarted up with restaurants and souvenir shops. Professional cuteness,' he repeated, shuddering theatrically. 'Sorry. So what you're telling me is you spent all day in Wickenden and you're right where you started this morning.'

'Not exactly. Both the professors I talked to said he drank at this bar in Clougham, the Lone Wolf' – I paused to see whether Art knew the bar, but he raised his eyebrows and shook his head – 'so I stopped there to see if maybe his bartender or one of his drinking buddies knew something about him.'

'And?'

'They didn't. It was a strange place, though. I didn't like the feel of it.'

Austell piped up from behind me. 'Well, Clougham, yes, I'm not surprised. They've always been a bit odd over there. You see, during the War of 1812, and then again during the Russo-Japanese War –'

'Hey, Austell,' Art interrupted, 'what do you say I claim that drink you owe me tonight? Let me just listen to what this kid has to say, and I'll be right there, okay?'

Austell's face lit up. 'The Fearless Leader, drinking sherry in front of *my* fireplace? Well, this certainly is an occasion. Let me call Laura and tell her.' And like a friendly dog chasing a thrown stick, he bounded out of Art's office.

Art shook his head, exasperatedly but affectionately, and motioned for me to continue.

'Something about the place didn't feel right. This bartender, Albanian Eddie –'

'Albanian *Eddie*?' Art laughed. 'What did you do, get caught in a Damon Runyon story? Besides, who ever heard of an Albanian named Eddie?' He lit another cigarette. 'So what happened?'

'Eddie just didn't want to talk. He made it clear he didn't want to see me again.'

'You okay?'

'Fine, fine. I don't know if I'd like to go back there alone, but I want to know why that guy was so hostile. The thing is, it seemed like he knew that Pühapäev had died, you know? When I said it, he didn't even look up, just kept polishing the glasses, and this one other guy – this skinny drinking buddy of Pühapäev's – said that he'd been coming for about a decade.'

'And?'

'And? Same guy, same bar, same bartender, more than ten years, and he doesn't even look up when I say the guy's dead? I mean, it's not like it gets a lot of traffic, right, this small-town bar? I don't know. Just didn't feel right to me.'

'Yeah, maybe. Maybe he's just strange.'

'Maybe. But he seemed unusually hostile, you

know? More protective than strange. Hell, he told me he'd kill me if I mentioned his bar.'

'Well, that's one way to drum up business, I guess. Look, you think something's there, then find out if something's there,' Art said. 'Really, go to it, and let me know if I can help. From the other side of the desk, I'm just telling you it might be nothing, is all.'

'Fair enough. Oh, one other thing, too: my old professor told me Pühapäev had some legal troubles.'

'What kind? Like tax problems?'

'Well, no. Like he carried a pistol around with him and winged a cat out his window late one night.'

'He shot a cat?' Art cackled. 'A gun-toting history professor? This just gets stranger and stranger. You confirm it with the Wickenden police?'

'No, not yet. I was going to call them this afternoon. My professor's nephew, he's a cop there.'

Art ran his hand over his head. 'See, this is why we got to get you to a real newspaper. I can tell you're getting restless, and you're getting curious, and those are the two best things a reporter can be. Listen, why don't we think on it tonight? Tomorrow we'll decide whether you want to keep poking around or whether you'll go back to the usual stuff.'

I nodded, and he got into his coat. 'Hey, one other thing I forgot to mention,' I said, 'the fat cop –'

'Bert.'

'Bert, right. Bert said that they got a call about Pühapäev's death in the middle of the night. Someone else reported it. Any idea who?'

He stopped, one arm in and one arm out of his coat. 'Good question. You know, I have absolutely no idea.' He took his coat off. 'Give me just a sec, I'll call the Panda.'

He put the phone on speaker, dialed, and waited until that deep, clipped voice picked up. 'Panda. You have a waiting room full of clients or you got a second for me?'

'The world, my friend, is my waiting room full of clients. For you I anytime have several hundred seconds.'

'I'm sitting here with Paul Tomm, ace reporter.'

'Shakespeare scholar Mr Tomm. Is he quite fine today?'

'He isn't complaining. How are you?'

'No complaining from me either here. What can I do for you gentlemen this afternoon?'

Art motioned for me to stay quiet. 'Panda, we'd like to know who reported Jaan Pühapäev's death.'

'You know this is information and a matter for police only. You know I should not tell you anything and refer you instead to official authorities.'

Art sighed and winced. 'Yeah, I know, but look, can you just tell me? I promise we won't print it, and your name won't appear anywhere. But we're having a hard time finding anything out here, and the ace reporter is getting restless.'

'Again, my friend, I will do for you things which I do for nobody else, if only because you are the only man this side of Brighton Beach who provides even the remotest of challenges to me at the chessboard.' We heard papers flipping over the phone. 'Ah, here it is. Telephone call at 3:23 A.M., number 860-555-7217. No name given. Anonymous. Very sorry.'

'Well, shit. Thank you anyway, old friend. I'll see you soon, right?'

'Not soon enough, I think. You and Donna must come have dinner with me and Ananya next time. We will play chess while the ladies drink and giggle and snooze on the settee. And before we sever our connection, about this ace reporter's story: I am keeping the body now until and unless someone makes a claim on it. For now I will say only that he possesses unusually smooth skin, you know? For a man so old in the face. And inside, too, from what I've seen: insides in surprisingly tip-top shape. There is something worth further investigating in this body. Something I cannot . . . No, nothing now. We will wait for the scalpel. Soon, soon. And I think you or the Shakespeare scholar will call me back in the morning, yes?'

'He will,' Art said. 'You will, kid, right?'

'Absolutely.' I nodded.

'You hear that? He said "Absolutely." That's four syllables of yes.'

'Four syllables of his life which he will never get back. Next time, Shakespeare scholar, simply say yes and save three for "I love you" to your young lady. Queen to Rook Four, Arthur. You gentlemen will call tomorrow.' With that, he hung up.

Art passed me the phone and sat back. I was lost. 'We'll call him tomorrow, I thought.'

'Not the Panda, kid. The number he gave us.'

So much for the ace reporter.

I punched in the number the Panda gave us, and the phone rang twelve times before I stopped counting and several more before someone picked up. At first all I could hear was a whooshing sound, like someone was holding the phone out an open car window. Then something or someone tapped on the mouthpiece, three times, then a pause, then three times again.

'Hello? Hello?' I called down the phone.

'Not this one. Not this one. Not this one. Not this one. Not this one . . .' A deep, expressionless voice droned on as I looked across at Art flicking a cigarette with his thumbnail. I held the phone away from my ear, and when I listened again, the words had changed to 'I'll find her. I'll find her. I'll find her.' I gently knocked on Art's desk to get his attention and handed it to him. He put the phone to his ear and looked at me strangely.

'What do you think?' I whispered.

''Round these parts we call this a dial tone,' he said, handing the phone back to me. Sure enough, a robust dial tone sounded in the earpiece. 'What happened, you get cut off or something?'

'No,' I said, bewildered. 'No, there was this guy on the other end, and he kept saying "Not this one" over and over again.'

'Uh-*huh*,' Art said skeptically. 'Tell you what, why don't you try the number again? And don't just hit redial.'

Art's evenness and his skeptical look had me almost doubting what I had heard. Still, I punched in the number again, and this time a man answered.

'Yeah.' Man's voice, sounded peeved.

'Yeah, uh, did you just answer the phone?' I asked.

'No, fucknut, I'm talking to you through a tin can. What do you think?'

'No, not now. I mean just before now. Who was talking here before?'

'When before? You mean just now?'

'Yeah.'

'Nobody. Before you, nobody. Scared the shit out of me when the phone rang. What the hell do you want anyway?'

'I'm calling from the *Lincoln Carrier*. I'd like to speak with someone there about Jaan Pühapäev.'

'Poo *who*? The fuck is it?' The voice stepped up from peeved to angry. It sounded like a man with a mustache. I heard a car horn, loud: the phone was outside.

'Someone there reported a death last night. I'm trying –'

'What do you mean *there*? Who are you calling for?' Flannel shirt, pickup truck, inland New England accent, big Jerry Remy fan.

'I don't know, that's what I'm saying. This telephone number showed up –'

96

'This is a pay phone, friend.'

'A pay phone?'

'You know, a phone you put a dime in, except now it's thirty-five cents 'cause they keep jewing the price up. This is a pay phone in front of Arliss's place.'

I got out my notebook as Art raised his eyebrows. 'Where is Arliss's place?' I asked the man.

'Trawbridge Road. Edge of Lincoln, not quite Stevens Bridge.'

'You mean that little general store just at the edge of Lincoln Common? I never knew it had a name.'

He puffed, sighed, and growled all at once. 'Well, it does, and that's it.'

'Hmm.' If I were a real reporter, I would have known what to ask; instead I just went 'Hmm.' Inside my head, too: 'Hmm.'

'So someone reported a death from here? Must have been the killer, right?'

I sat up straight, like someone had dropped ice cubes down my spine. 'Why do you say that?'

'Nothin' around here, chief. This little store gets locked up at eight P.M., and nothing but empty fields and ponds for a good ten miles in every direction. Town starts about half mile up, but why would you hike up here from there to use a phone? Only people use this phone is Arliss and people driving through somewhere. Back when, they used to say Trawbridge was the fastest way out of Hanoi.'

'Why? Where does it go?'

97

'Chunk of Route 87, goes pretty much due north from Bridgeport at the Long Island Sound. Goes through Massachusetts and Vermont, wild New England country, no one around. Ends outside Drummondville, on the St Lawrence River.'

I looked at the New England map on Art's wall. I didn't see any St Lawrence River. 'Where's the St Lawrence?'

'Where?' He snort-laughed. 'You don't do much fishing, do you? Good steelhead, good salmon in that river there. It's up in Canada. Geography lesson same time tomorrow if you need it, dicksuck.' I heard him and a woman laughing, and then the line went dead. I imagined him hanging up the phone angrily, but I guess all hang-ups sound the same.

'One of rural Connecticut's less charming residents,' I told Art. 'The telephone used to report Pühapäev's death is outside Arliss's place, on –'

'Arliss General Store. I know where it is. But why were you talking about the St Lawrence?'

'Apparently that's where Route 87 ends. Up in Canada, near someplace called Drummondville.'

Art scratched his beard and stared at the ceiling, quiet for a long time. 'Strange. Could be a mistake, you know. The Panda's handwriting. Misdialed number.' He looked over at me as I shifted defensively in my chair. 'Okay, before you try the number back again, you should call your professor's nephew, see if he'll tell you more about Mr Estonia with the six-shooter.'

I nodded, swiveled in my chair, and dialed. Someone picked up before the phone rang.

'Gomes speaking.'

'Ah, I'm not . . . I'm looking for the Wickenden Police Department.'

'Well, you found it,' he said. 'This is Detective Gomes. What can I do for you?'

'I'm trying to reach Joseph Jadid, please.'

'Just a moment, please.' Gomes clunked the phone on the desk. 'Line two, big man. Someone's asking for you,' he said in the background.

A deeper, sleepy-sounding voice clicked on. 'Cold Case, this is Detective Jadid.'

Behind him someone said, 'Go on with that "Cold Case" bullshit, man.'

'Yeah, this is Paul Tomm. I'm a reporter with the *Lincoln Carrier,* and –'

'I don't talk to the press. Hang on and I'll transfer you to our PR liaison.'

'No, wait, hang on. Your uncle told me to get in touch with you.'

'Yeah? Which uncle?'

'Anton.'

'He told a reporter to call me? How do you know him?'

'He used to be my professor. He gave me your number this morning.'

Jadid sighed, cleared his throat. 'Well, okay. But listen: you don't use my name anywhere in the story. You need to quote me, you make it anonymous. This

99

is a small enough town, and I've had some trouble with the papers recently.'

'No problem.'

'That's right, no problem. Now, what do you need?'

'I'm working on a piece about a guy named Pühapäev. Lived in Lincoln and worked in Wickenden. Actually, he worked with your uncle; he was a professor. Anyway, he just died, and I understand he'd been in trouble with the law in Wickenden before. I was just wondering what kind of trouble.'

'Let's see here.' I heard the sound of typing on a computer keyboard. 'Poo-hah . . . what's the rest?'

'P-A-E-V. Two dots over the *a*. First four letters P-U-H-A. Two dots over the *u*.'

'This is a police computer; we don't do umlauts. Here we go. You know, before I give you something I'm not supposed to give you, I just want to tell you that I wouldn't do this for anyone but Uncle Abe. He knows you well enough to give you my number, I'm going to assume you're okay, too. Don't fuck up all three of our reputations by printing something stupid, okay? You want to use any of this information here in your article directly, you run it past me first, you got it?'

'Of course.'

'Good. Here we go. Jaan Pühapäev. Connecticut resident, Connecticut driver's license. Two incidents, bunch of charges. We got two counts carrying a concealed weapon. We got two counts disturbing the peace. We got two counts misdemeanor mayhem for firing said weapon, and we got one count drunk and disorderly filed when they came to arrest him. On all counts of all charges, got away with fines and time served.'

'When was this?'

'This was . . . hang on a second. Fucking computer,' he snarled, banging either his desk or the offending machine. 'Here it is: Count one, January 12, 1995. Count two, August 24, 1998. Nothing after that. I guess that means the good professor died an officially reformed character.' He said this in a way that made it clear he thought the opposite.

'Yeah, maybe. Anyway, thanks very much. I appreciate the trouble.'

'No trouble for a friend of Uncle Abe's. Like I said, though, you call me if you want to use this. Wickenden police information appears in a Wickenden newspaper, people wonder how it got there.'

'I will. Just so you know, though, I'm not in Wickenden. I'm in Lincoln, Connecticut.'

'Lincoln, Connecticut,' he parroted. 'Where the fuck is that?'

'About two hours west of Wickenden. Near the New York and Massachusetts borders.'

'Oh, well, shit, if you're writing from there, use my name, my picture, my Social Security number, anything you want.' He chuckled and paused. 'I'm just kidding, you know.'

'I figured.'

'Good for you. Well, listen, have fun out in *Deliverance* country. Take care.'

Friends I grew up with in Brooklyn had the same attitude: Get past the city limits, you're in the sticks. Past the outer suburbs and you might as well be in the Third World. My asphalt-in-the-veins brother stood as a case in point. I repeated the highlights of the conversation to Art, who scratched his beard, reclined in his chair, and sought guidance in the ceiling.

'So here's what you're telling me: We've got a dead guy,' he said, extending his right thumb, 'but nobody knows how he died.' Index finger up. 'Nobody knows who reported the death.' Middle finger. 'Doesn't look like a robbery gone bad.' Ring finger. 'Local police don't care; state or federal police have no reason to get involved. Yet' – right hand open, palm up – 'he was a professor who barely taught and who carried a gun. No friends, no family, no nothing.'

'Yeah, that's pretty much the size of it. Don't forget that weird thing with the pay phone.'

'Right,' Art said slowly. 'Let's put that one on hold, relevance-wise. Okay, you got any other calls to make?' I shook my head. 'Good. It's about seven-thirty, and I'm due at Austell's for a drink. He serves me that acetone sherry again, Jesus Christ … Anyway, you show up here tomorrow morning ready to talk about this piece with a friend of mine. Okay?'

'Sure, who?'

'You'll see tomorrow. Don't look so skeptical: your face'll stick that way, and you'll never get a job except as a reporter.'

FERAHID'S GOLDEN NEY

~や~

Our gold is a perfect body, wanting nothing, mimicking God; our sulphur is an imperfect and active body, wanting its wife, acting the man. All earthly things begin from this marriage.

— HAMID SHORBAT IBN ALI IBN SALIM FERAHID,
On the Aims of Music and Sunlight

On the platform Yuri had taken a parting drink with every member of his family and two with his father, who maintained that his eyes teared from the vodka and the wind, though they stood against the station wall and beneath its eaves. While walking from the station to the train, his mother had assaulted him with angrily affectionate kisses. She tucked and retucked his shirt, tied and retied his scarf, drew his coat closer and closer around him, so by the time he reached the train, he had practically been mummified inside his clothes.

As soon as the train's chuffing settled into a regular rhythm, Yuri fell into a boozy and heavy-headed sleep. When he awoke, the familiar chaotic Moscow vista — squat brick factories either half built or half ruined, birch trees stationed haphazardly in front of massive apartment blocks, wires and streets radiating outward from the tracks into the city's heart — had given way to endless pine forests punctuated once in a rare while by villages consisting of little more than a few dirt roads and twelve to fifteen tiny dachas, aglow from the inside, nestled close together like gossiping smokers in a tavern.

Every time he glanced out the window, he thought, 'This is the farthest I've ever been from home,' and after reading or writing for a brief while, he would look again and think, 'No, now *this* is the farthest I've ever been from home.' Each time he checked the passing scenery, he felt a slight pang of nostalgia for the Yuri of forty minutes ago, who hadn't yet seen all that this Yuri had. He shed selves at irregular intervals, and by the time he changed trains four days later at Novosibirsk, he fancied himself a thoroughly more worldly man than the Yamoskvareche city boy who had left home almost a hundred hours earlier.

His journey lasted another three days. The almost mythically endless forests, so vast that Russian cities seem merely perfunctory, tentative dips into a vast and untamable wilderness, eventually yielded to mountains. And the mountains flattened and eroded into steppe: rags and swellings of white laid over a changeless, constant earth, the horizon so distant and visible it seemed an idea.

During a stop outside of Aktogay, Yuri saw a black scorpion scuttle onto the train before the *provodnitsa,* a formidable moose of a woman, shooed it onto the tracks with a broom. She told him that an Uzbek man had told her that scorpions bring good luck, so immediately she knew that they were no good, and she had ordered all the girls under her to stand watch at the doors with brooms, because they like to sneak their way onto the train. She said that if he should have the misfortune to get bitten by a scorpion, the only remedy was to soak a muslin cloth in vodka infused with St John's wort for three minutes and hold it to the wound for thirty-three minutes, so the herb could draw the poison from the body into the cloth. Then you must be very careful to burn the cloth well and scatter the ashes.

At this, the only conversation Yuri had for the entire voyage, he nodded obediently and said nothing. When he at last reached Leninabad and saw the corporal standing expectantly by the station's entrance, he felt suddenly apprehensive about returning to the world of human interaction.

'Engineer Kulin?' the corporal asked. Yuri nodded. 'May I see your documents, please? Internal passport and *propusk*.' The *propusk:* the all-important little sheet of paper whose official stamp and signature sanctified its information into unimpeachable truth. If the *propusk* said that the bearer was ten feet tall and covered in purple scales, and it bore an official stamp from the People's Deputy of Height Specification and Scale Certification, and the bearer appeared to be six feet tall and possessed of normal human skin, there was something wrong with the visual evidence: epistemologically, a *propusk* brooked neither contradiction nor appeal.

Yuri's *propusk* said that he was not a graduate student in linguistics but an engineer assigned to 'oversee the initial planning stages for the possible development of a proposed museum of Tajik Socialist Culture.' Clearly one of the selves Yuri had shed on the way to Leninabad had been that of an aspirant linguist, and instead this engineer stood in his place. Yuri handed the documents to the corporal as casually yet authoritatively as possible.

The corporal had a beefy farm boy's build, a ruddy and fair complexion, and a cloudy expression that defaulted to tentative joviality, as though he was always guarding against missing a joke. He and Kulin, also fair and in military dress, stood out among the lean, dark, sharp-featured men with long beards who surrounded them on the platform. The corporal seemed uneasy at making demands of an educated man, even one younger than himself; he returned Yuri's documents with a smart salute and led him to a waiting car, where he could return to his comfortable position of servility.

'You've been allocated private quarters at the officers' barracks in Leninabad,' the corporal told Yuri proudly. 'And my name is Kravchuk. I'll be your driver as long as you're here.'

The car, a rickety and mud-spattered Zhiguli, bumped and rolled along the half-paved road from the station to the outpost. By the time they arrived at the barracks – a drab, gray warren of buildings that seemed to suck color from everything around it and everyone in it – Yuri felt as though he'd been log-rolled for fifteen kilometers. At the officers' canteen, he ate a predictable dinner of meat cutlets (whose principal ingredient, of course, was day-old bread), oily cabbage salad, oily beet salad, oily carrot salad, and greasy potatoes, all topped with generous spoonfuls of slightly fetid sour cream and dill. The men around him either ate in boisterous groups or sat in furious, stony, self-contained silence.

'You must be our guest. The engineer.' Standing in front of Yuri was a man in late middle age, keen-eyed and trim, wearing an army uniform plastered with medals and ribbons. His hair was cut slightly longer than the standard military brush, and his posture was more relaxed than standard military bearing.

Yuri stood up. 'Engineer Kulin, sir. But if you don't mind my asking, I am in military dress. How did you know that I was a civilian and not a transfer?'

'Aha,' said the man, leaning close to Kulin's face and beckoning. He pointed at Kulin's plate. 'Your eating habits betray you. You have been cutting your meat with a fork and knife and carrying the food to your mouth with a fork. You also eat your salads with a fork. Your spoon lies undisturbed, right where the galley's assistant placed it. These men here, these enlisted men' – he gestured generally with his right hand and Kulin's eyes swept the room – 'most of them use the back of their fork to shovel as much food as possible into their spoons and then cram it into their mouths. Now, it is not impossible to have a recruit with decent table etiquette, but it is impossible that he should retain that etiquette after his military training. You yourself did service, did you?'

'Yes, sir, in the Tajik Republic.'

'And did your standards of decorum slip?' Kulin stayed quiet and involuntarily looked down. 'You see,' said the man, breaking into a tight smile, 'you would not have brought those manners home to your mother, would you?'

'No, sir.'

'Well. I came to welcome you, not taunt you. I am Colonel Voskresenyov. I live in my own barracks, not a hundred meters from where you're staying. Please call on me if you have any problems while you're here.'

'Thank you, sir, I will.'

'Do you play chess, Kulin?'

'No, sir, I don't.'

'Ah. Pity. Well, enjoy your meal. Good evening.'

*

In his room Yuri laid out his tools for the next day: paper, pencils, Tajik-Russian and Uzbek-Russian phrasebooks – he spoke both languages fluently but had been instructed to carry and make obvious references to both books – a photograph that he could not bear to look at and desperately hoped he would not have to use, and a padded velvet bag that fit into a hidden pocket in his suitcase. He reviewed the name and address of the man he was to meet, as well as the terms of the exchange. Trading two musical instruments for a human life seemed odd and cruel, but then, as he had been reminded, he was not a military man. If all went well, he would be on a train back to Moscow in two days, at his carrel in a week, and installed in a prominent position at the Ministry of Culture by the time he finished his junior thesis next June.

After a full breakfast of poached eggs, black bread, salted kasha, and tea, Kulin and Kravchuk climbed back in the car and headed north. 'So, Comrade Engineer . . .'

'Please, Kravchuk, if it's just us, call me Yuri. I'm not a military man.'

'But you did your service?'

'I did. In Dushanbe, in fact, though in three years there, I never did come up to the Ferghana region.'

'If you say so, Com — Yuri. Me, I'm just a *muzhik* from Kharkiv,' he said, puffing out his chest with a firm but self-deprecating giggle. 'Give me flat land

and black soil any day. So I hear you met the colonel yesterday.'

'Yes. Very polite.'

'Polite,' said Kravchuk incredulously. 'If you get on his right side. He's a strange one. But he's a Balt, you know, so a little . . .' He fluttered his open hand, palm down. A little unbalanced? A little crazy? A little homosexual?

Kulin cleared his throat. 'How long have you been here?'

'What is it now – September twenty-fifth, 1979? So that's eleven months, two weeks, and three days. If you're counting.' He laughed heartily and belched. 'Anyway, my friend works as a general's typist and says that they're going to be moving us into Afghanistan soon. An invitation by our socialist brethren, the general says.'

Kulin winced: riding around like an emperor here was one thing, but as part of his studies he had read accounts of the British army at Khyber Pass, and he worried that Afghanistan would be something else entirely.

'If you don't mind me asking, Yuri, why have you been sent here? I mean, why do we need a museum here of all places?'

'Corporal, I'll tell you, I didn't ask. My superior ordered me to report on this site. The local Party wants to document and display the cultural advances that the Soviet Revolution has brought to the Ferghana Valley. I shall evaluate the proposed site's 'suitability for the museum, and then I shall return home.'

'Moskovchik, right?' Kulin nodded. 'You can always tell!' Kravchuk exclaimed, slapping the steering wheel and grinning. 'Ah, well. I don't mean to pry. Let me see that address again. Here it is: we just cross this bridge, and it's that village up there on the right.'

The bridge spanning the Syr Dar'ya River marked the end of Leninabad, and, more to the point, the de facto end of the Soviet Union. Snow made the narrow, unpaved road between here and Tashkent, some three hours north, rough going between October and May, and bandits made it impassable for anything less than a battalion from May to September. The Pamir Mountains lay to the south; the Ferghana Valley, home to violent regionalist factions of countless types, was to the east, and beyond that was China. Leninabad's abrupt end: drab Soviet architecture hugged the river on one side; mountains poking through the snow like crumpled birds spanned the other bank, stretching and rising all the way to the Tien Shan Mountains in the distance. A photograph of this vista taken from upriver would look fake, as though a portrait of a city had been glued onto one of a valley.

Kravchuk pointed to nine cottages on the nearest hillside, clustered around a winding brown tributary of the Syr Dar'ya. 'Most of them still live like this, in these little villages . . .'

'*Kishlaks.*'

'What?'

Kulin opened his phrasebook to cover his mistake. '*Kishlaks,* it says here, is the Tajik word for "villages."'

Kravchuk nodded. 'Well, whatever you call them, they sure look nicer than Leninabad.' The road ended just below the village, and Kravchuk cut the motor. They got out of the car and began walking together, but Kulin asked Kravchuk to wait with the car. 'Just to be safe. You never know around here, leaving a car on its own like this.'

Kravchuk nodded, looking not unhappy with the decision. 'Shout if you need me, Engineer. I'll be right here.'

Kulin nodded, waved, and began trudging uphill. Three children came out of the first house he passed and began shouting 'Russian, Russian! Come see the foreigner!'; by the time he reached the village center, the shouting had stopped and he was surrounded by dark, silent, wide-eyed children. '*Assalom u aleykum,*' he began, when a raspy voice speaking Russian interrupted him.

'Why don't you speak your native language? We can. Some of us have the lashes, scars, and burns to prove it.' The voice had an ironic edge that stopped just short of threatening; it belonged to a tall man with a deeply lined face and piercing green eyes. He wore a multicolored, striped robe tied with a sash at the waist and stood absolutely still, neither warning Kulin away nor welcoming him.

'Thank you,' Yuri said awkwardly. He waited for the man to respond, but he just stood silent and watchful, not changing his expression. 'I wish to speak with Porat Badhmadullaev. I understand he lives in this village.'

'He does. Hajji Porat, he is called now. He made the journey with his son last year. Very difficult, very illegal. But if you are who I think you are, then you already know that.'

'I'm not KGB, if that's what you're asking. I'm an engineer, here to find a suitable location for a museum dedicated to Tajik culture. To your culture,' Kulin said, trying to smile but realizing as he did that it made him look weak and unsteady instead of warm and disarming. His interlocutor inclined his head forward, slightly cocked, a gesture whose meaning escaped Kulin. 'Could you take me to him, please?'

The man pointed to the village's last house, farthest up the hill, and turned away without a word. He clapped his hands twice, and the children dispersed. Kulin could sense eyes on him from inside the houses, but nobody came out to greet him, threaten him, or even stare at him. When he reached the last house, he paused before knocking at the wooden door.

A voice invited him in. He pushed the door open and saw a one-room hut, at the center of which was a small fire in a stone oven. Four men sat around the fire: they all had forked white beards without mustaches; they wore white turbans and robes; they had long faces, deep and watery eyes. They looked as though they had been sitting there for centuries, figures out of time, tried by fire, still watchers and guardians of secrets. 'Are you looking for Hajji Porat?' one of them asked in Tajik.

Kulin nodded, and three of them stood up and left, without saying a word or changing their expressions. The one who remained looked up at him gravely. 'I am Porat. Sit, please, and drink some tea.' The man poured weak tea from a battered aluminum pot into a grimy ceramic bowl and passed it to Yuri with both hands.

'You've been told who I am, why I came here?' Yuri asked.

'Of course. You wish to see about building a museum of Tajik culture. An unusual choice for a location, I would say, outside the city, on a hillside prone to avalanches and mudslides. An altogether unsuitable location.'

Kulin suddenly grew uncomfortable at having to explain the entire situation to Porat. The man who arranged to send him on this mission had told Yuri that Porat understood and accepted the exchange. Kulin was merely a courier, chosen for his intelligence, anonymity, ambition, and fluency in the region's languages. Kulin cleared his throat and was about to speak when Porat held up a long hand.

'You do not need to tell me. I know the real reason you are here. I was told you would be carrying Akbarkhan's photograph. May I see it, please?'

'Hajji Porat, I'm not sure that you –' Porat raised his cane and brought it down with both hands on Kulin's bowl of tea, shattering the pottery with the sound of a gunshot.

'I can imagine what he will look like. What you will have done to him. I am prepared. Let me see the picture.'

Kulin pulled the picture from between two pages in the Tajik phrasebook and handed it to Porat. It showed a young man in a hospital bed, a hand holding his head up. Ripples of black and sickening purple encircled his swollen-shut eyes. His nose was nearly flat, broken in uncountable places and ways. His split and puffy lips were opened slightly and revealed a bloody mouth of half-teeth. He looked like he had been soaked in wine and his head inflated. The bruises continued to his shoulders, where the photograph ended. Porat tried to stifle a sob, but it came out as a reedy exhale that collapsed his torso. Kulin didn't move.

'What has he been charged with?' Porat asked, sitting up and readjusting his turban.

'Hajji, I don't know. But I can promise you –'

'Promises from an agent of the Soviet government are worth less than the breath it takes to utter them. But tell me, what choice do I have?' Kulin said nothing. 'You see?'

Porat walked over to an ornate copper chest in the corner of the room. 'I am sure that you will be well paid for your troubles here. A young man like you can have cars, jobs, girls. Nice home for your mother. But whatever you receive will be less than the worth of what you carry back. And what you carry back I would give a thousand times over for Akbarkhan, my son, my only son.

'Akbarkhan is the last male descendant of the Samanid scientist and musician Ferahid. I can trace that line back for more than one thousand years, all through the fathers. Tell me, how far does your family line reach? Who are you?' Porat glared at him intently.

Kulin's father worked in a lathe factory; his mother was a secretary at a local Party office. His grandparents were farmers. His lineage ended there; he kept silent.

'I suppose it hardly matters,' Porat said, unlocking the copper chest and withdrawing a carefully wrapped parcel. 'It has taken me, and my father, and his father before that, and all our fathers, centuries to find these flutes. Now they are yours. Our family's greatest treasure in return for its continuance. A painful but, in the end, very easy choice.'

Kulin unwrapped the package and saw two little flutes, one gold and one silver. He turned them over and was going to check the inscription when Porat banged his cane against the oven. 'Put those away and listen; you are not a guest here. I expect that you will cable whomever you need to cable this evening, and that you can effect my son's release immediately. Curse you if you do not. I want him to come home.

Now go,' he said, turning his back on Kulin before he had even finished speaking.

Nobody confronted Kulin as he returned to Kravchuk and the car. Nobody even emerged from any of the houses, but from all of them came steady clicking sounds: the sound of disapprobation that his mother used to make when he'd done something wrong. Which, of course, he had. That he was only a minor participant consoled him little, if at all. He had wanted to come to the Ferghana for his entire life; now he had, and the first Tajiks he met hated him. Either the son was a criminal and Yuri was delivering a bribe to free him, or the son had been kidnapped in order to obtain these two strange flutes Yuri carried in his bag. He wondered what the flutes were that they meant so much to somebody powerful enough to free a jailed man and grant a rich future to an apolitical linguist. Wonder, in Kulin's experience, tended to cause more trouble than it was worth, so he willed the questions out of his mind.

When he reached the car, Kravchuk was sitting on the hood reading a book and drinking a beer. He drained the beer and threw the bottle as far as he could; it sank into the Syr Dar'ya with a satisfying *ploop*. 'Any problems?'

'None. What were you reading?'

Kravchuk held up the book, examining the spine. '*A History of Uzbekistan,* by the Soviet Committee on Caucasian and Central Asian Brotherhood.'

Kulin knew the book: a predictable, plodding, and

typically Soviet tale in which the fortunate lesser peoples of Central Asia were rescued from superstition and barbarism by the glories of Marxism-Leninism. 'Interesting?' asked Kulin disinterestedly.

'Very. I was just reading about the bug pit.'

Muzaffar Khan, an Uzbek ruler of the mid-nineteenth century, was famous for throwing his opponents into a deep hole, at the bottom of which were assorted rodents, scorpions, and worms. Every so often Muzaffar would have his royal beekeeper toss a hornet's nest into the pit. Soviet historians loved these stories; they spent less time on the Bukhara of Rudaki, Avicenna, and Firdausi (and, apparently, Ferahid: Kulin reminded himself to look the figure up when he got back to Lenin Hills). 'There really are much cleaner ways to take care of a dispute or do away with an opponent,' Kravchuk said, grinning.

Kulin nodded absently and got into the passenger seat, closing his eyes. He did not notice Kravchuk reaching beneath his seat and bringing up a gray metal object. If Kulin heard the click, he probably registered it as Kravchuk's adjusting his seat. When he felt something cold against the base of his jaw, he opened his eyes, and everything flashed white.

Item 3: A ney: an end-blown flute, cylindrical in shape, 28.3 centimeters long and 2.1 centimeters across, with six finger holes on one side and one for the thumb on the obverse. Just below the mouthpiece is a carving of a sun in the Persian style, and in Persian script an inscription reads 'Gold yet not our gold.' The flute is indeed made of gold, or rather of a hollow cylinder of gold filled with powdered sulfur and sealed shut at both ends and around the edges of the finger holes.

The sulfur buffers the ney's sounds; few musicians could produce anything more than a rasp or occasional hoot from it. Ferahid's use of sulfur in this flute became known, in fact, because so few skilled musicians could produce a sound from it, as reported by the Samanid historian Ghazi Jaffar Sharaf:

The exalted Ismail, having received from his musician Ferahid a most resplendent golden flute, attempted at great length and without success to play the instrument. In frustration he hurled the flute at his musician, whereupon it glanced off a castle pillar and released some yellowish powder. Some fell upon the fire and stank. Ferahid defended it as 'a secret and wondrous thing for all manner of transformation and sovereign medicines.' He then melted several of his own treasures to repair the flute and returned it to Ismail, the

summer flower of Bukhara, who was much pleased with
this display. Ferahid then summoned the oudist and the doura and
doira masters and played with much effort a tune of his own
composition, and the sound produced by Ismail's golden ney differed
from the sound of an ordinary one as the sweetest summer grape
from a clod of desert sand.

Like so many items in an alchemist's study, the ney
reminds rather than performs: it is a representation
of principles, and a tripartite metaphor:

1. Gold, of course, is a precious metal, and alchemists
   have (correctly or not) long been associated with the
   transmutation of worthless metals into valuable ones.
   As such, gold represents the end stage of the alchemical process, the ultimately changed and unchangeable
   substance.
2. The sun represents both gold and the transformative
   fire. It is the alchemical father, the active, hot, pene-
   trating force in the process.
3. Sulfur, with which Ferahid filled the ney, represents the
   same male principles as the sun. In Kabeljauw's theory
   of metals, sulfur 'is the root form of all metals, though
   it stink like the devil yet must we have some commerce
   with it, for by a brief knowledge of demonic principles
   we may triumph over the active doom – that is,
   temptation – and the passive doom of ignorance.'

Date of manufacture: A.D. 1000.

Manufacturer: Hamid Shorbat ibn Ali ibn Salim Ferahid. Ferahid was a musician and an astronomer in the Samanid court at Bukhara; he was also a tutor of Abu Ali ibn'Sina (Avicenna) and possessed the largest library in Bukhara. He spent his life in the composition of a single work, never finished and never found. His illustrious pupil reported that Ferahid 'has increased man's knowledge of God beyond what any man has done previously, but seeks no fame for his labor, for the thought of his discoveries' being used for purposes dark and contrary to divine wisdom haunts him greatly, so much that I fear for his health and sanity. He will in no case travel from his house, but I have seen the wonders of which he speaks and could attest their greatness to the world.'

When Ferahid died, Avicenna reported that his teacher 'went to the bosom of God this night just past under circumstances most grotesque and horrific. All trace of his mighty work has vanished, and indeed I fear that history will know him solely as an artisan.'

Place of origin: Although Ferahid served the Bukharan Samanid court, he lived and worked in Khojand, where this flute was likely made.

Last known owner: Porat Badhmadullaev, resident of the Tajik-Uzbek border town of Bilanjan, at the mouth of the Ferghana Valley and across the river from Leninabad (the once and future Khojand). Porat was the ninety-ninth male descendant of

Ferahid, and he completed the task begun by Ferahid's grandsons: he found and obtained his ancestor's neys.

During the declining years of the Samanid dynasty, in the early twelfth century, the flutes were sent as tribute to Baghdad, where al-Idrisi won them from the caliph in a game of skill. The geographer took them to his new post, as court geographer to the Sicilian king Roger II, but when he disappeared while completing a map of Europe in 1154, the existence of the flutes became rumor. One of Porat's fourteenth-century ancestors reported seeing them in Venice. Two centuries later another was hanged in Trivandrum for attempting to steal a golden flute from a wealthy landowner.

Porat never revealed how he obtained the flutes. Yuri Kulin, a promising young linguist specializing in Central Asian languages, was dispatched to Bilanjan, supposedly to record Porat's story for inclusion in a long-planned but never-built museum of Tajik culture. Bilanjan, like most of the Ferghana Valley, was at the time growing increasingly restive, gripped by late-twentieth-century Islamic religious fervor. According to the Soviet military's account – which is, of course, the official account – Porat's brothers shot Yuri Kulin, mutilated the body, and rolled it down the hill to the banks of the Syr Dar'ya. It landed at the feet of Kulin's military escort, Corporal Alexei Kravchuk, who reported the death – the earless, handless, and headless body – and Porat's brothers firing rifles triumphantly into the air from their village. Three hours later Bilanjan was bombed into rubble. Later that day Akbarkhan Badhmadullaev, in Lefortovo Prison under suspicion for terrorism, reportedly 'committed suicide by running repeatedly into the bars of his cell.' Three days later Corporal Kravchuk disappeared and has not been heard from since.

Estimated value: The gold alone would be worth several tens of thousands of dollars. Add to that its age and colorful history, and it could easily command seven figures.

What would you pay for Aladdin's lamp?

The father thereof is the Sun, the mother the Moon.

〜✺〜

The next morning, from the newsroom window, Lake Massapaug gleamed still and deep like an opal in the late-autumn sun. No boats or bathers or fishermen disturbed the surface. No phones rang in the office, and neither Art nor I was talking. It was a little after nine, so Austell hadn't arrived yet, and Nancy was on vacation. A calm breeze gently scalloped the lake's surface at the edges and scraped the nearly bare branches across the newsroom roof. We were sitting in Art's office, him with a cigarette and coffee and me with a newspaper. The morning hadn't yet begun to shape itself into a day.

I had spent the night before watching one of those dire midweek football shows on an all-sports public-access station. Around this time of the year, most Jets fans develop a case of heartburn that never really goes away. My brother, Victor, describes their strategy as 'suck, then hang on for dear life': after losing four games they should have won in September and October, they then win three games they should have lost in November and December, limp into the playoffs, and get mauled in the first round. Never fails.

Last year I drove home to watch them lose the wild-card game to Oakland with Vic; his wife, Anna; and Chris, my nephew. It was in the nasty stretch of my breakup with Mia, and I ended up drinking too much, bad-mouthing her to Vic and Anna, and passing out on the couch right before kickoff. Anna was one of those high-strung moms already plotting Chris's Harvard application; having a wayward uncle swear a blue streak and then nearly brain the kid with his falling, beer-swollen head didn't impress her. Oh, well. I was hoping for an invite to Art's for the playoffs this year – most of the time, he and his stable family were easier to take than my entropic and nervous one – but I would settle for an invite from my couch.

Footsteps, quick and deliberate, on the wooden stairway leading to our office door brought me and Art out of our reveries; we were both staring at the door as it flew open.

'You know, I make this lunch for you so you'll eat it during the day. You can't live on tobacco and caffeine anymore, not at your age and not with your heart.' Donna Rolen strode theatrically to her husband's desk and thrust a Tupperware container holding a sandwich and an apple out to him. He winced, also theatrically, and took it, lifting the lid and sniffing.

Donna huffed and turned to me. 'Hello, dear. Is he driving you too hard? Is that a ham sandwich? Are you eating your lunch already?'

I was, I'm ashamed to say, eating a ham sandwich at 9:00 A.M. 'No, yes, and no. The ham's breakfast – I have a Dutch mother. I didn't bring lunch today, though; I'm watching my girlish figure.'

She laughed loud enough to rattle shingles on the roof, much louder than the feeble joke demanded. 'You'll waste away! How can you think when you don't eat? You'll never get anything done!' She snatched the Tupperware container from her husband and put it in front of me. 'He'll never eat this! He's just humoring me. You take it. It's turkey. Do you eat turkey?' I nodded. 'Terrific. Don't let him bully you,' she said, pointing at her husband, wearing his Chastened Husband Face and slouching lower in his seat. 'If he starts giving you any guff, you know what to do, right?'

'Guff back? Use my secret antiguff ring?'

Donna looked at me like I had just sprouted a second head – I worried that I had offended her straitlaced New England sensibilities – and then she laughed even louder. 'You need to GET OUT OF HERE! Go find some other young people, go get into trouble! Really, Art loves having you here, doesn't he?' – she didn't even look to him for confirmation; still I saw the nod, followed by a less perceptible eye roll – 'but you should be staying out all night at your age. We'll survive just fine without you, you know.'

I did know, in fact; Art and Donna could survive pretty much anything. They had lived in more countries than most people ever visit, and their nagging wife/henpecked husband routine was just that – a comfortable, light comedy routine that concealed a deep and tested love. My own parents had not been in the same room with each other for more than ten years; these two had barely spent a night apart in four decades. Donna's family had lived in Lincoln for almost two hundred years, and as much as she joked about self-reliant Puritanism and the stoic frostiness of New Englanders, when I first moved here, she cooked me dinner every night for a month, and I had never left empty-handed from any sort of encounter with her, even if it meant she stole her husband's lunch and gave it to me.

'Did you tell him?' she asked Art. He shook his head.

'Should I be concerned?' I asked.

'Yeah, kid, you're fired. My only working reporter' – he rolled his eyes at me and talked to Donna – 'and he thinks I'm about to can him and let Austell turn the paper into *Carrier & Stream*. No, no reason to be concerned. Donna and I were talking about your obit last night, and –'

'I have never met this fellow,' Donna interrupted,

'and I think I know almost everyone in town by now. Well, everyone except the weekenders,' she said, pronouncing the last word the way most people would say 'cockroaches.' 'But I think I've heard of him.'

I reached for my notebook. 'How? Who from?'

'Our new music teacher.' Donna was the librarian at the Talcott Academy, the local prep school. 'She rents the first floor of Mary DeSouza's house over on Orchard Street. Did your guy live on Orchard?'

I looked at my notes and nodded.

'Then it must be him. She always talks about the strange old man who lives next to her, and how he doesn't have any friends and he's from a foreign country and he knows all this fascinating stuff and isn't it sad and so on and so forth. She cooks for him, and she plays checkers with him. Well, she used to cook for him and play with him, I guess.'

'What's her name?'

'Hannah Rowe. She just started this year, and already all the little boys have crushes on her.'

'Is she pretty?' I tried to make it a disaffected question, but my lack of recent romantic practice probably made it sound more eager than it should have.

'You see,' Donna said, breaking into a broad smile, 'he's human after all.' She laughed; I blushed. 'Hannah's perfectly nice-looking. Too tall, if you ask me, but there we are.' Donna paused and held her breath in a beat before continuing in a lower voice. 'You know, she isn't exactly a favorite among the staff. I've never had any problems with her, though.'

'Why? People dislike her?'

'Well, no, but, well . . . maybe I shouldn't say anything. A pretty young woman is bound to stir a little something in all those old fuddy-duddies.'

I nodded noncommittally. I had never known Donna to say anything remotely critical of anyone she knew, and it seemed to be making her uncomfortable. 'So you like her?' I asked.

'Oh, well, yes, of course, but you see I really don't know her terribly well. She's perfectly polite, and conscientious about chaperoning duties and so forth.' She paused and swallowed. 'I don't know that we'll invite her for supper or anything like that, right, dear? But she's cordial enough.'

'Fair enough. You think she'll talk to me?'

'Well, I should think so. I certainly hope so. With your charm I'm sure you'll have no problem.' She reached over and patted me on the knee.

'Not sure about that, but thanks. You don't know her home number by any chance, do you?'

'Her home number? Well. We do move quickly, don't we?' She winked. 'I don't know it myself, but I'm sure Information would have it. Better still, just call the school. She'll be there, I'm sure. And I should be getting back there, too; I told Joanie I'd only be gone for five minutes.' She checked her watch and glanced out the window: like most Lincoln natives, she always left the car running when she ran a short errand (I never got over my surprise at seeing people do that). 'Okay,' she boomed, turning to Art, 'you're going to eat today, aren't you? Paul's going to eat the lunch I made for you, and you can just run home and get something from the refrigerator.'

'You want to tell me what I should have? And might as well remind me, since you're here, not to stand in front of the refrigerator with the door open.' Art held his cheek with his hand in an exaggerated bored-schoolboy pose.

Donna shook her fist and kissed him on the forehead. 'He's lucky I love him, or I'd have to kill him. Don't work too hard, boys,' she said with a mock-coquettish wave as she shut the door and descended the outside stairs.

Once she left, I put Art's lunch on his desk, and he shoved it back toward me. 'You eat it. Really. I'll grab something from home.' I shrugged, took the container, and tried to remember the last time my own father had given me a homemade sandwich. I came up with never. He and I weren't all that close. I figured that Vic – college-to-law-school Vic, married-with-child Vic, home-owning, golf-playing, glad-handing Vic – stayed in close enough touch and good enough graces for both of us.

There was a certain defeated tone that crept into my father's voice whenever he asked me what I was up to. At Thanksgiving last year, he told me that 'a lot of very successful people had started out doing what you're doing.' That was when I'd said to Anna that it was looking like a three-bottle dinner. When he told me how sorry he was that I had 'screwed things up with that smart Oriental girl,' I upped my estimate to six. He had recently changed tactics, moving from hortatory belligerence to emitting an extended martyred sigh whenever I told him that I liked my work. I had been ducking the phone call I owed him because I was sure when we spoke he'd insist that I come out to Indianapolis to spend Christmas with him, his high-strung, bottle-blond new wife, and my meatheaded stepbrothers. I'd have preferred swallowing lye, but I'd have to make sure to buy the right brand of lye, or Dad would be mortified.

'You know, you're doing some real investigating for this piece,' Art said. 'Not the usual community stuff you do for me.'

I agreed noncommittally, not knowing where he was headed.

'Ought to place it somewhere bigger than the *Carrier.*'

'Like where?'

'Why I told you to come in early today,' he said, reaching for the phone.

'Who are we calling?'

'Leenie,' Art explained while dialing. 'Eileen Coughlin. She's the deputy editor at the big Boston paper, and she and I –' He broke off midsentence, listening. 'Lee-NIE,' he greeted the respondent, his voice rising on the second syllable as a small smile quivered, resolved, spread into a larger one.

'Yes, indeed it is. How's you? Wait there just one

minute – I'm going to put you on speakerphone.'

A throaty woman's voice with a thick Boston accent crackled from Art's phone. '. . . this fucking box and talk to you like a normal person.'

'Leenie, you remember at the Metzgers' the other night I was telling you about the kid reporting for me? Paul Tomm?'

'Yeah.'

'Well, he's in the office with me, and he's working on something that I think might suit you guys more than me.'

'Yeah? This kid comes with the Artie Rolen seal of approval, I'm all ears. Let's hear it.'

Art pointed at me and nodded: you're on. I told her the story as concisely as I could, playing up the darker parts (mysterious paranoid immigrant professor who carried and sometimes fired a handgun, no immediately apparent cause of death, unknown concerned citizen reporting the death from a pay phone, possible robbery, police record) and sidestepping the most banal conclusion (strange old man dies alone of natural causes).

'Well,' said Leenie after I finished, 'sounds like it could be something. Then again, sounds like it could be absolutely nothing. But it *is* interesting. Artie directing you or advising you?'

'Advising, sweetheart,' Art called into the box. 'Kid's dressing himself and uses the potty all on his own now, too.'

'Listen, Paul, do me a favor, would you?' she

asked, laughing. 'Pick up this phone so I don't have to listen to you shouting down a tin box. Thanks, that's better. Here's the score: Art speaks well of you, and I think well of him. He thinks that you think you're onto something, and you think you're onto something, and if you are, he's right that it's not for the *Carrier*. If it pans out, then give me a call again and we can talk about it. Meantime, whether it pans out or not, we occasionally run local-interest pieces from all over New England. You see something that's worth some ink, you give a shout here, too. Now, before I hang up, hand the phone back to Art, would you, please? Good luck, and keep in touch.'

I handed Art the telephone, and he said his good-byes, made courteous unfulfillable nonplan plans to see Leenie, and hung up. 'She say she'd make room for you?'

I nodded. 'If there's something there. She also said something about local-interest pieces from out here?'

'Yep. You should do those. Their current correspondent out this way's notoriously lazy and unreliable.'

'Who's that?'

'Me,' he said with a bashful grin. 'I do maybe one story every few months, but, really, you could do one a month, easy. Pay's decent, the stories aren't too tough, and it's a good clip and a great foot in the door if you want to go to Boston. And believe me, you do. Maybe she'd give you something that would let you skip a step, you know, so you wouldn't have to go from here to – I don't know – New Haven or Springfield or someplace like that. Meanwhile, you need to keep digging.' He lowered his head and pointed at the phone. 'You going to call the music teacher?'

The same way runners get sponsored by sneaker companies, reporters should get sponsored by phone manufacturers: nobody except telemarketers rides them like we do. I dialed the school number, and a pinched grammarian's voice answered the phone. 'Talcott Academy, this is Mrs Turley. How can I help you?'

'I'd like to speak to Hannah Rowe, please.'

'Miss Rowe is out sick today. Can I leave a message for her?'

'Actually, it's important that I speak with her. Do you have a number where I can reach her?'

'Whom am I speaking to, please?'

'This is her cousin Brett,' I said, to Art's silent giggles. 'I'm calling because I'm going to be coming through Lincoln tonight and wanted to stop in and say hello. The thing is, I left her number back in Philly, and I can't get through to my wife. Any chance you could connect me to her somehow?'

'Oh. Well, we don't usually . . . But I guess . . . oh, I guess you're family. Here it is: 555-0791. Tell her I hope she feels better.'

'Thanks so much, Mrs Turley. I sure will.'

*

I did not believe then in fate, destiny, predestination, or any of the other 'signs of divine action here on earth' that Hannah saw. Before meeting Hannah, I looked on such beliefs bemusedly, as the harmless imposition of narrative order on a fundamentally random world. Now I hold them in active contempt; they are dangerous if not delusional, and I know that people believe them out of vanity. I cannot hold her in contempt without thinking the same – less, even – of myself, who found her so enthralling for such a short time.

I also can't help thinking of that phone conversation as something extraordinary; I preserved it in a journal, which I began keeping that evening, but in fact her words remain clear, carved from ice and frozen, in my memory. I am telling this story not as a memorial but as a means of covering emotion in a blanket of words, and so defeating it. I will ruin her memory by preserving it. So:

On the third ring after dialing the number Mrs Turley gave me: 'Hello?'

'Is this Hannah Rowe?'

'Yes, it is.'

'My name is Paul Tomm, and I'm a reporter for the *Lincoln Carrier*.'

Her voice warmed; she had an audible smile that still catches me like a blow to the gut when I think about it. 'Oh, I love the *Carrier*. I know your name; you wrote that article about the reconstruction of the Old Mill.'

'That's right. You know how to flatter a reporter.'

'It's not flattery. Mr Relaford and I – he teaches visual arts – took our students to the mill after reading that article. They drew while I played for them in that huge stone room. It was like playing in a church. Such amazing acoustics. So thank you, Paul Tomm.' Hearing my name in her mouth, even then, made me uneasy and grateful. This is what happens when a healthy young man holes up in a small town with no female contact for months. But then I guess I always built romances in my head better than in the world.

'Thanks. Like I said, we're all egomaniacs over here. It makes us feel good to see our name in print. All we really want is recognition. So you made my week.' She laughed a tickled, pleased double-hiccup laugh.

'So the reason I'm calling is, I'm working on an article about Jaan Pühapäev. I understand he's your neighbor.'

'Yes.'

'Have you seen him recently?'

'Let's see. Not today, not yesterday, and I was chaperoning my church's youth-group trip Tuesday night. I usually stop in once on the weekend and once during the week, but I just haven't had the chance to visit yet.'

'So the last time you saw him would have been . . .?'

'Let's see. Last Thursday or Friday, I think. Are you writing an article about him? You should, you know. He's such a fascinating man.'

I paused. Not, I'm ashamed to admit, out of any respect for the dead, but because I didn't want to ruin our conversation by bringing up something sad. But then I thought about comforting her, holding her, this woman I had never seen, had spoken to for only a few minutes. 'I'm really sorry to tell you this, but he died. He died earlier this week.'

She didn't say anything. Then I heard her moan softly. 'I'm so sorry,' I told her, and meant it. 'Are you okay?'

She sniffed. 'Oh, I'm fine. I just hate to think of him dying alone. I'm sure he's in a better place, though.'

I didn't want to touch that last comment. 'Listen, is there any way I could maybe speak with you about him? I'm trying to write an article about him, and you seem to be the only person in Connecticut or Rhode Island who actually knew him.'

'An article? You mean an obituary?'

'Yeah.' Mostly. Maybe. I suppose so, technically.

She sighed. 'Sure. I'm officially sick, so I don't want to go out. Why don't you come by here this afternoon, and we'll have tea?'

'Sure. I heard you live near Jaan's.'

'I used to, I guess,' she said, with a mirthless exhale-chuckle. 'I'm sort of across the street and a bit down from his house. There's no number on the house, but it's brown with white shutters, three stories tall. I'm on the ground floor.'

'Okay. Thanks for doing this.'

She paused and started speaking twice before she finally pushed the words out. 'I loved him, you know. I loved him, and I want to see him remembered. Of course I'm doing this for him. Come by around four this afternoon, if you can.'

'I can. I'll see you at four.' We said good-bye and hung up.

Maybe it was because I hadn't slept with anyone – let alone flirted with anyone – since Mia. Maybe it was the thwarted academic in me that always saw promise in autumn. Maybe I was lonely. But I felt like I had just been shaken awake, and as I hung up, I noticed that my hand was trembling.

'Good. Four P.M. Now what are you going to do?' Art asked.

'Go home and get ready?'

He cackled and leaned back, cocking his elbows behind his head. 'Easy there. This isn't a date, right? You're still working on this story, aren't you?'

'Yes. Sorry. Now I guess I'm going to . . .'

'You're going to call the Panda and see if he had any news today.'

I dialed the coroner's office; the nasal, muffled female voice that answered wasn't the one I expected. 'New Kendal County Medical Office.'

'Dr Sarath . . . Schata . . .' I looked at the card and read slowly – 'Sunathipala, please.'

'Are you family?'

'I'm sorry – you mean, am I calling to claim a body? No.'

'No, were you related to Dr Sunathipala?'

'I'm not, and –'

'Who is this, please?'

'Paul Tomm. I'm a reporter. A friend of his,' I fibbed.

'Then I regret to tell you,' she said officially, 'that Dr Sunathipala died last night. He was struck by a car while he was walking home.'

'Dead? What is . . . ? But I just talked to him yesterday. I didn't . . .' Art was looking right at me, eyes wide, mouth slightly open, his hand frozen on its way to the pack of cigarettes in his shirt pocket. He shook his head but said nothing, his expression still registering shock, fear, disbelief.

'I know. We're all just shocked. He was such a dear man. We're holding a memorial service for him here at work. I don't know what the family's going to do yet.' Her voice grew tighter, as though she was trying to restrain sobs and only barely succeeding.

What could I say? I just wanted to get off the phone as quickly as possible. 'I'm really sorry.'

'Thanks.'

I thanked her again, hung up, and told Art. He held his right thumb and forefinger on the bridge of his nose for so long that I thought he might have fallen asleep. Like an ice sculpture under a hair dryer, he gradually stirred, sort of slumping onto his desk in a puddle. I stood up quietly and was going to put a hand on his shoulder when he sat upright.

'I'm just . . . You know, you work in enough war zones and you start to know more dead people than living ones,' said Art quietly. 'Never makes this any easier, though.'

He reached into his pocket and pulled out a sheet of paper gone soft and tattered with age. 'Bishop in Hebron gave me this about twenty, maybe twenty-five years ago. I was living in Beirut then, covering the civil war. Miserable time. I still remember . . .' He waved his hand and shook his head quickly, eyes shut, as though he was declining something. 'Another time. Anyway, this bishop had built a little lean-to on a hill. The settlers' movement was just gaining steam under Begin, and he wanted to protest this idea that God had promised land to people born this way and not that way. So he left his church and moved to this tiny shack, where he planned to stay for forty days and forty nights – he had water but no food – but after about three weeks, this doctor who had come from Brooklyn to cash in the chips God gave him shot the priest in the side, then took him to the settlement's hospital and operated on him – saved his life, actually. He didn't want to kill the priest; he just wanted him off the hill. So a few of us headed out there to interview the priest. I'll never forget this: he said anytime his faith was tested – which I imagine was pretty often – he turned not to the Gospels or Revelation or promises of heaven or anything like that, but to this one verse from Ecclesiastes' – and here Art read from the scrap of paper: "'Whatsoever thy hand findeth to do, do it with thy might; for there is no work, nor device, nor knowledge, nor wisdom, in the grave, whither thou goest.'" Art looked up at me. 'He said that it reminded him that faith came and went, even in priests – even we cannot believe all the time, he said – and that actions, not pure belief, matter more. I remember he looked up at me – a practicing Catholic can always tell a lapsed one – and said, "You came for a bullet, but you would not have come for mass." He was right.

'Now, what the hell that has to do with the Panda, I don't really know. But this scrap of paper – see, it's in Arabic on this side and translated into English for my benefit here – that he kept with him in the shack, I always read it when someone I know dies. And believe me, kid, that's going to be more often than you can imagine. Only if you're lucky, though, and it's not you.' He gave me a tired wink, stood up, and put on his lumpy green coat, patting down each pocket ritually. 'I'm going to go home and cry. Then I'll head out and see Ananya. See you back here in the morning.'

FERAHID'S SILVER NEY

❧❧❧

Hermes, Thoth, and Mercury: fleet of foot and wit, beloved despite inconstancy. The learned Galen named the female progenitor of my art after the Greek member of that triumvir. This metal itself is as predictable in its properties and character but not in its specific actions and any of these gods. In this way it resembles women, water, and music, which create, sustain, and flavor life.

— HAMID SHORBAT IBN ALI IBN SALIM FERAHID,
On the Aims of Music and Sunlight

Item 4: An end-blown flute, cylindrical in shape, 28.3 centimeters long and 2.1 centimeters across, with six finger holes on one side and one for the

thumb on the obverse. Just below the mouthpiece is a carving of a moon in the Persian style and an inscription in Farsi script that reads 'Silver yet not our silver.' The ney is made of a hollow cylinder of silver that has been filled with mercury and sealed at the ends and around the edges of the finger holes.

This instrument is the more famous of the pair; its Persian nickname translates as 'Sliding Facilitator of Madness.' 'Sliding' refers to the lack of fixed notes produced by this ney; as the mercury sloshes through the flute's body in response to the heat and pressure of the player's fingers, it redistributes the flute's weight and so changes the pitch and timbre of the sounds it makes.

Ghazi Jaffar Sharaf describes Ferahid giving the ney to Ismail: 'Ferahid presented Ismail, fruit of the noblest tree of the Samanids, with a second flute, composed of silver, with a moon and a learned inscription inscribed on the mouthpiece. "One may produce more notes with this flute than with any three others of variant sizes," he explained to his commander. "But it requires a fixity of spirit mirrored in a fixity of the player's fingers."

'So saying, he covered all of the holes and blew into the mouthpiece, and the sound indeed quavered and would not settle. Bowing, he presented the instrument to Ismail, who looked upon it with the beneficence and gentle good humor for which he is justly remembered. "Musician," he said, "will you grant me your only daughter if I can produce a single note of sustained clarity?" Without hesitation Ferahid agreed. "Musician," Ismail asked, "will you grant me your only daughter if I cannot produce a single note of sustained clarity, and I ask her of you?" Again the musician agreed without hesitation. "Musician," Ismail asked again, "have you an only daughter?" Ferahid replied that God had granted him but one son. Ismail, Garland of Bukhara, the head of all the world, placed the flute on the table nearest his throne and smiled.'

Like its twin, the silver ney represents three metaphors:

1. Silver, being slightly less precious than gold, symbolizes the near completion of the alchemical process; it represents the endeavor rather than the triumph.
2. If the sun is the father, the moon is the mother, and as such incarnates the cool, receptive, pure female principles of the process.
3. Mercury, often referred to as 'argent vive,' symbolizes transformation, or alchemy itself. Formless and quick, mercury is pure and untrustworthy possibility, and requires a hand made sure by knowledge rather than force to tame it.

The irony that Mercury himself was, among other things, god of commerce and wealth was not lost on most alchemists.

Date of manufacture: See 'Ferahid's Golden Ney.'

Manufacturer: See 'Ferahid's Golden Ney.'

Place of origin: See 'Ferahid's Golden Ney.'

Last known owner: See 'Ferahid's Golden Ney.'

Estimated value: See 'Ferahid's Golden Ney.'

The Wind carried it in its womb,
the Earth is the nurse thereof.

I left the office just after Art drove off: I didn't feel like discussing death with Austell. I took the purposefully devised 'aimless stroll' route Art had shown me when I first got there: out the back door, down the hill and into the woods, then along the stream until it crosses beneath the gas station that marks the beginning of Lincoln Common. Right as I reached the halfway point of the walk, it started raining: not a forgettable drizzle that I could pretend was just mist, and not a rainstorm that I could wait out under a tree. Steady, cold, late-autumn New England rain, the kind that chills and darkens the world from log to sky. I stopped by my apartment, which was just across from the gas station, changed clothes, put on a waterproof jacket, and grabbed an umbrella.

When I got back, the office was (blessedly) empty and there was an envelope addressed 'Paul' on my desk. I opened it to find a paper with the New Kendal County seal at the top and a yellow Post-it attached: 'PT – See attached if you're interested. If not, do the Panda a favor and see attached anyway. Pls put them on my desk when finished. Good luck with the music teacher. Remember: life is for the living. See you tomorrow. AR.'

Beneath the seal was the New Kendal police report of Vivepananda Sunathipala's death. The date and time next to the signature showed that it had been filed at 10:03 the previous night; the time stamp in the top right corner showed that it had been faxed to Art at 11:47 this morning. I wondered who he knew on the New Kendal police force. The report said that the Panda had been hit by a late-model car; either two- or four-door; painted black, gray, dark blue, or purple; with one or more occupants, either male or female. Five witnesses saw five different cars with five different drivers. Two paramedics saw one dead coroner in the street. All agreed that the car did not stop – barely even slowed – after running him down.

The second unexplained death that had crossed my path in the past few days: two more than in my previous twenty-three years total. I linked Pühapäev and the Panda for no reason other than circum-stance, and then I wondered whether there was, in fact, some connection between their deaths. It was certainly strange that the one man in Connecticut to get an intimate look at the dead man would himself be killed. But would anyone else see it as strange, or as just two random deaths that my work connected, however tenuously?

A Lieutenant Haynes Johnson had signed the report, and I called him to see whether he had anything else to add. When I told him I was calling from a newspaper, though, he transferred me to the public affairs officer, who said that 'information regarding an ongoing investigation, whether material or immaterial to said investigation, is not parceled out to the public until such time as the authorities can ascertain that having such information in the public domain would be beneficial to the end of apprehending the suspect or suspects.' A truly astronomical syllable-to-content ratio; I thanked him, hung up the phone, put the report on Art's desk with a note ('AR: Done as ordered – many thanks. Hope you, Donna, and the Panda's family are as well as can be. PT'), and headed out into the rain to interview the music teacher.

As I turned left onto Orchard Street, narrowly missing the branches that hung close on either side of the street, Allen Olafsson was heading the other way in the town's police car. He squinted at me through his and my rainy windshields, trying to make out who I was. When we were nearly bumper to bumper, he gave a little nod and half smile of recognition, then flashed his brights and rolled the blue-and-red at me soundlessly, pulling over to the side of the road and cranking his window down. I stopped next to him so that we were facing each other through our open windows.

'Second time we seen each other in this neighborhood,' he said flatly. 'What are you doing here?'

I thought about asking what business it was of his, but it's always a good idea to stay on the right side of small-town cops. 'I have an interview to do.'

'An interview? Who lives up here worth interviewing?'

'There's a teacher living in Mrs DeSouza's place.'

'Mary DeSouza, huh? Strange bird, that one. Interview got anything to do with our late friend?'

'Yeah, something for his obit,' I said. No reason to mention the coroner and his police record and the investigation for a Boston paper. Keep it simple. 'You find anything at the house?'

'Nah,' he said, taking his cap off and running a hand over his thinning straw-colored hair. 'Didn't even go in, really. Just driving by every so often, you know? Making sure nothing goes missing, no one comes back. Don't know how much good it's doing.' He smiled ruefully. 'Between us, Bert thinks I'm wasting my time. But it makes me feel better. Gets me out of the office.'

I nodded and didn't say anything, hoping he'd take my silence as an invitation to end the conversation. He did. 'Not going to keep you,' he said. 'But listen: you hear anything interesting about this guy, you let me know? I'll do the same, you know, so you'll have, like, a source.'

I wasn't sure if he was making fun of me, but I agreed. He extended a hand, and we shook on it. Then he drove off, the siren still flashing and rolling soundlessly atop his car.

The street dead-ended just a few car lengths ahead. On either side of me, smoke still rose from the two flagstone houses, and neither house had any lights on inside. Pühapäev's swing was still down for the count, and the rain had turned his front yard into a muddy, cratered moonscape. I parked in front of the three-story clapboard place (which was the only house on the street that gave any signs of habitation) and walked up to the front door. A white sticker just below the doorbell said DESOUZA, with an arrow pointing up at the bell, and ROWE, with an arrow pointing around the side of the house, so I followed the arrow, stepping over a puddle of rainwater. Walking to the side door, I slipped on something left in the path and sent it into the door with an embarrassingly loud *thwack*. It was a huge wrench. I picked it up as the door opened.

She was smaller than Mrs Rolen had led me to expect – an inch or two taller than me, but her thinness and long hair made her seem taller still – and she had light brown hair, gray eyes, and sharp, clear features. It was a face just on the perfect side of plain, one that grew deeper the more you looked at it. I always found it unreadable: changes of mood and thought swept across it like water and just as quickly sank beneath the surface. That, of course, came later, but even at this first meeting, she leveled me.

'Hannah Rowe?'

'Paul Tomm?' she repeated in the same tone. I wasn't sure whether she was teasing me or merely responding musically. She looked down at the wrench that I held in my hand and was now extending to her like a flower. She smiled broadly, and I blushed. 'I know the one about Greeks bearing gifts, but I've never gotten any advice on reporters bearing wrenches. You *are* Paul, aren't you?'

I nodded, and she invited me in, taking the wrench from my hand and tossing it carelessly back onto the path. 'You're a little early,' she said, waving me off as I began to apologize. 'Just an observation, no reason to be sorry. Would you like some tea?'

I said I would, and she invited me to sit down. She pointed to a pair of green armchairs in the corner of the room, on either side of a circular wooden table. I walked over to one of the chairs and, in taking my jacket off, upended the table. An odd assortment of junk – some pottery, a playing card, and a number of what looked like children's art projects – all fell to the floor with a crash. Hannah laughed; again I blushed. 'Paul Tomm, we're going to have to set you somewhere safe. I guess I should have put foam rubber on all the sharp corners.' My ears got hot and started ringing; I wanted to run out and redo the entire introduction. I stood next to the upended table – my dripping jacket in one hand and a reporter's notebook in the other – frozen, mortified.

'I was just kidding. A joke. No blushing necessary,' she said, taking my jacket and draping it over the radiator. 'Sit down and relax. No, don't try to straighten that up; just put the table back and leave everything else. Sit here,' she said, laying her hands on my shoulders and guiding me into the chair. Instinctively, I reached up to my shoulder and touched her hand – whether in thanks, acknowledgment, or apology I don't know – but she lifted her fingers and gave mine a polite squeeze as I sat down. 'Now. Stay there, and I'll put on some music and get the tea. What do you want to hear?'

'I don't really know that much about music. No strong preference. Whatever you'd like.'

She smiled and pressed a button on a stereo in the corner. The sound of a single cello – rich, mournful, plaintive, expressive – filled the room. The pattern of the notes fell just short of a melody; the register and deliberately irregular rhythm made it sound almost like human speech. I had never heard anything like it; it filled my brain; I hung on the completion of each phrase.

'What is this?' I called to her in the kitchen.

'Marais. It's a viola da gamba duo called Les Voix Humaines. Here arranged for a single cello. It's supposed to sound like a human voice. I think it sounds like a poem, or a prayer.' She set a tray with a teapot, two cups, a bowl of sugar cubes, and a plate of cookies on the newly clean table. 'See, you did good without intending to. Where would I have put the tea if you hadn't made a space for it?' She sat down next to me and gave one of her thawing smiles. I returned her look for longer than was merely polite, then took my notebook and two pens from my shirt pocket.

I always envied Art his ability to open a conversation with disarming small talk that led seamlessly into purposeful questions. He had told me repeatedly how important it is to make your interview subjects feel comfortable. Of course, Hannah was far more comfortable than I was; my stomach was doing the Pretty Girl Shimmy, and I was starting to sweat. I couldn't think of anything to say except what I had come to say. 'Can I ask you about Jaan?'

Her smile vanished immediately, leaving no traces of warmth on her aquiline face. She looked haunted; with the soft light on her pale skin and long hair, she seemed to have sprung from the pages of a nineteenth-century ghost story. 'I'm so sorry about that. That he died alone. I hope he knew where he was going.'

'Who *does*?'

'I do,' she said, turning to face me. She was so beautiful then, with the lamplight on her face and an expression that just bored into me, that I nearly sprang out of my chair and ran. Anyone who believes that beauty is alluring rather than terrifying is either ignorant or uncommonly brave. 'I *do*,' she said again softly.

'Do you think he did?'

She wrung her hands in her lap. 'I hope so. I really do hope so. He just . . . He was so old, you know? So old. I hope he had thought about it,' she said, more to herself, it seemed, than to me.

I cleared my throat. 'Do you know how old he was?'

She gazed at me directly, and the haunted look jumped off her face; her hair caught the light and set hard and fiery around her face, grave and deep as a carved stone angel's. 'Exactly? No. He talked about living in an independent Estonia, between the two wars. I guess that would make him about eighty. But please,' she said as she saw me taking notes, 'don't make me a reliable source for that. In fact, do you have to use my name in this article?'

I said no, I didn't; if she didn't want her name used, I certainly didn't intend to use it. I asked her how she knew him.

'I met him when I moved in, a couple of years ago. I knocked on his door to introduce myself, and he shouted at me to go away,' she said, chuckling, her face lit by the memory. 'So I started walking back down his steps. Then I guess he must have peeked out at me, because I heard the door unlock, and he goes, in this thick accent, "Why you do not tell me you are pretty girl?" Then he invited me in, we talked for a while, and that, as they say, was that.'

'Do you know where he was born, whether he had

family, what sort of work he did, anything like that?' I asked, playing dumb like Art had taught me. Better to get too many answers than too few.

She was looking down and pulling tiny balls of wool from the pilling afghan thrown over her chair. 'Well, he was Estonian. I guess I just told you that. He used to talk about Tallinn a lot, but also about the countryside and the islands. He had this book of photographs of one of the islands – Saaremaa, I think it was called – that he loved to show me. I think he had some family, but I don't know who, or where they lived. Last summer, though, he went back to Estonia for three weeks.' She walked over to her bookshelves and pulled down a garnet-colored bottle. 'He brought this back for me.' VANA TALLINN, the label said. I opened it and sniffed; it smelled like caramel and licorice and looked syrupy, like sherry that had been boiled for a while. Hannah poured a slug into my tea; it tasted sweet, and though it had no burn, I could feel the warmth down my chest as I swallowed.

'What about work? I know he was a professor, but . . .'

'I think he was sort of retired. I know he didn't teach that much. He didn't teach around here, I know that.'

'He taught at Wickenden College.'

'So you *have* done a little homework. Well done. He wrote a lot; he has notebooks full of his writings, but I don't think he had much of his writing published.

Every so often he'd pull some obscure magazine off the shelf and show me his name. It could have been the same magazine over and over, for all I know. No books, though, I don't think. You should go out to Wickenden and ask them, though, if you want to know about his work.'

'I already did. I graduated from there,' I said stupidly, boastfully. I really just wanted to tell her something about myself, lay it in front of her and see whether she picked it up.

'Did you? I wanted to go there. Didn't get in,' she said, knocking on the side of her head. 'Not enough brains.'

'Just tell me which admissions officer to shoot.'

She laughed. 'What do you think of this?' she asked, pointing to the speakers.

'I like it,' I said dopily, unable to come up with something smarter. It sounded like music. Pretty music. 'What instrument do you play?'

'Piano, a little violin, a little cello, nothing else,' she said, putting her head in her hands and shaking her head. 'It's my music-teacher badge of shame. I'm a fraud, I know.' She smiled ruefully.

'Not a fraud. An enthusiast.'

'Aren't you sweet?' In fact I almost answered her – *'Yes, yes, very!'* – when she asked whether I played anything.

'No. I really don't know anything about music. I have tin ears, wooden hands, and clubfeet.'

She laughed. 'And you also need a heart, a brain,

and some noive, right? I should give you a crash course.'

I looked up like a clumsy, overfriendly dog. 'Tell me when. I'd like that.'

She smiled, tilted her head to one side, and rested a long, slender hand on her forearm and nodded at my open notebook. 'Do you want to know anything else?'

'Can you tell me anything else?'

'Only that I loved him. I did love him,' she repeated, as if I had disputed her. She had said the same thing to me on the phone. And here I reached a romantic nadir and grew jealous of a dead Estonian.

'I shopped for him when he needed it, cooked him meals a couple of times a week. I talked to him. Actually, I just sat with him while he talked and smoked. That's all, really. Now I wish I had asked him more about himself, but . . . I'm sure wherever he is now, there's a fire, a stuffed chair, and endless amounts of books, tobacco, and pretty girls to listen to him.'

She shrugged and raised her eyebrows sadly. We stared at each other quietly, steadily, long enough so neither of us had any questions. The bookshelves, couch, and cello in the corner started to shimmer and darken; I could feel myself against my clothes, tingling, and could feel my pulse at the base of my jaw. She set her teacup down too close to the edge of the table, and it fell and shattered against the table leg. We both jumped and stood up. 'Well,' she gasped. 'I seem to have caught the dropsies from you.'

I looked at the porcelain shards among all the religious artifacts still scattered on the floor. 'What are all those anyway?' I asked.

'Oh, that's my God table,' she said, smiling, so I couldn't tell if she was serious. 'I believe in everything. Any religion. All religions.'

I nodded, unable to think of anything to say. 'Are you a believer?' she asked.

'No, I'm a mongrel.' I grinned.

She looked horrified. 'Don't call yourself that. It's okay, whatever you are, just as long as there's something, you know? I couldn't imagine anything worse than not believing in anything. What are you, really?'

'Lutheran, Catholic, Greek Orthodox, Jewish. A Dutch-Irish mother and a Greek-Jewish father. One grandparent in each church, and now they have twelve grandchildren in none.'

'Well, that's wonderful. Look at all the choices you have. Which one were you raised in?'

'It depended on where we were for which holiday, I guess. A long story,' I said, looking at my watch and gathering up my perpetually meager stock of courage. 'A long and occasionally interesting story, and one best told over dinner. What do you think?'

'The ace reporter's treating the struggling music teacher to dinner, right?'

'Wouldn't dream of anything else. The Longwood Inn?'

'You do have fancy tastes for a small-town scribbler. How about something a little farther away? I'd rather not worry about colleagues seeing us, and teachers'-lounge gossip, and so on. Have you been to the Trout?'

'No. Never even heard of it.'

'That's because it's in Pelton, about forty-five minutes north of here. Right on the river and almost in Massachusetts. Do you have a car?'

'I do. When should we go?'

'Tomorrow?' I nodded. 'Good,' she said. 'I haven't had Friday-night plans in weeks. I have some work I need to do at school, unfortunately, so if you could, why don't you pick me up around the back of Talcott, right where the hill begins sloping down from Common to Station? We'll go from there. Around seven?'

'Perfect,' I said as she opened the door. I put my hand out. She looked at it sympathetically, then looked up at me, said, 'You sweet man,' laid her hands on my shoulders, kissed me lightly just below my eye on my cheekbone, waved, and closed the door behind me.

As I walked around to the front of the house, out of the corner of my eye I saw something moving quickly on the porch. I turned to look, and a cat flew past my face, brushing me right on the spot where

Hannah had kissed me, and disappeared with a riffle into the bushes. I jumped backward, and I'm sure I must have yelped, or, at best, sworn at an embarrassing volume. The front door opened, and a skinny old woman wearing a shapeless quilted housecoat, a mismatched pair of slippers, and a lumpy blue blanket wrapped turban style around her head emerged. She jumped when she saw me. 'Oh. Gracious, I'm not presentable. My house is a bit drafty, you know,' she said, leaning forward and dropping her hand down at the wrist like she was telling a secret, 'and heat is so expensive. Why are you sneaking around the side of my house, young man?'

Taken aback, and trying hard not to laugh at her appearance, I said, 'I was visiting Hannah.'

'Oh, boyfriend, boyfriend, are we? I should have guessed you were. You know, I'm an old-fashioned woman, and I can't say I approve of the way you young people hop in and out of bed all the time.'

I wasn't sure whether to be offended or proud at her estimation of my prowess. 'Ma'am, I'm a reporter,' I stammered, 'and I was talking to her about your late neighbor. We remained seated – in separate chairs, of course – or standing at all times.'

'I'll bet you're sorry about that, aren't you?' She peered at me over the top of her glasses. It just made her look short. 'You don't look like you're from around here.'

'I'm not,' I said curtly, walking toward my car.

'Don't walk away from me when I'm talking to

you, young man. Did you say you were here to write about that old man who lived across the street?'

'Yes.'

'Well, I'm Mrs DeSouza, and you can quote me if you like.'

'Certainly. How did you know him?' I asked, my pen ostentatiously poised above my open note-book.

'I've lived in this house for seventy-two years. I should think that counts for something.' She wrapped her coat tighter around her thin frame and adjusted the blanket, which was beginning to wobble and pull her over with it. 'We never shared tea, if that's what you're asking. He never bothered introducing himself when he moved in,' she sniffed. 'Then, when I finally went to scold him for it, he wouldn't even invite me in. Can you imagine? Just opened the door one tiny crack and barely poked his head out.'

'So you got to know him after that?'

'After that? After the way he spoke to me? You must be joking. I wouldn't have given that filthy son of a sailor a match in a snowstorm.'

I couldn't help myself now; trying to stifle a laugh only made it come out harder. Mrs DeSouza straightened up to glare at me, but as she did, she upset the balance of the giant blue puffball on top of her head, and it slipped too far to one side, nearly toppling her. 'I don't use such language lightly, young man. Nobody takes etiquette seriously anymore. He should have come to me first.'

'Of course. I know. Well, if you don't have anything else . . .'

'*Have* anything else? What do you mean by that?'

'For my story. Anything else about Jaan.'

'The only person who, as you say, "had anything" from him was your little musical friend. I never saw him open the door to anyone else but her. I can imagine why,' she said, lowering her voice and leering salaciously.

'I'm sure nothing like that happened.'

'Oh, of course. An old man like that? Probably hasn't raised a mast since Harry Hopkins's time. I'm merely saying that Miss Rowe's charms are considerable. As are her wiles. An old man living alone would have been flattered, even if he would never even shake hands with anybody else.'

'Interesting. Thank you, Mrs DeSouza. This interview really has helped me.'

'Don't patronize me. And I don't want to see you sneaking in and out of this house at all hours of the night, do you understand me?'

'Of course.'

With that, she slammed the door and I got into my car. The cat peered skeptically at the porch from beneath the hedgerows.

THE ETHIOPIAN

After many a summer dies the swan, and after many an era dies the myth. My colleague Lönnrot believes that myths do not die so much as they are supplanted. But this seems to me not so much incorrect as based on a limiting and unimaginative view of matter. In full spring, leaves supplant blossoms, but it is equally true that in late autumn leaves that are 'are not' supplant the leaves that were. Within these brief emptinesses we would see wondrous things, if we but knew how to look.

— OLAV GRYNZSTEIN, *Menelik's Chamber*

November 19, 1979
Axum, People's Revolutionary State of Ethiopia

To: Comrade Colonel Virju Saarju, Army of the Union of Soviet Socialist Republics, Special Liaison to the Union of Researchers and Professors of Ethiopian Ethnography, Estonian Division

From: Captain Felix Armando Correa, Cuban People's Revolutionary Army

Comrade Colonel:

I send fraternal greetings in the name of the people's continuing revolution and the socialist struggle against menshevism, regression, bourgeoisism, counterrevolutionary thinking, formalism, and superstition. I send warm personal greetings also, to your wife, Natasha Georgovna, and your sons Grigoriy and Fyodor, and hope that this missive finds you and your esteemed family in no worse health than when we last saw each other in Santiago de Cuba.

Our units continue to fight bravely against the nationalist rebels, though we are at a distinct disadvantage in knowledge of the terrain. With barricades at strategic points of entry along roads and passes, our revolutionary forces control Ethiopia's major cities. Our writ, however, ends at nightfall and does not extend far beyond any city's perimeter. I hope that we are good enough friends that I need feel no shame at telling you of my relief at leaving Asmara.

My position here has been filled by Cesar Reyes, who, following what I assume were your instructions, has told my battalion that I have gone to scout ahead with a small forward regiment in the highlands. This has given rise to the most ridiculous stories of my bravery and commitment. As I departed, one of my sergeants, a crude and robust man named Juan Colón, surreptitiously placed in my hands a small mahogany cross that he said had belonged to his great-grandfather Ernesto.

With your permission assumed, I will now speak plainly, and leave the mouthing of phrases to our esteemed comrades with more strictly military temperaments. Perhaps you will do me the same courtesy and let me know, when next we meet, whether Juan Colón is also one of ours or whether he is simply one of the many men in both of our countries who might be sympathetic but is as yet ignorant of this particular mission. Whatever the case, I took his good wishes as a favorable omen, whether from you or from Someone Else, and traveled by military aircraft from Asmara to Axum without incident.

I have now been in Axum for some six weeks looking into this matter. I have a small villa in the Ethiopian style — mudbrick, low ceilings, small rooms, narrow tables — with one interpreter (a native of Axum named Gebredan), and one cook, housecleaner, and general errand runner. My accommodation suits me perfectly, though generally my reception has been anything but pleasant: the people here hate me. They hate Mengistu, they hate me, and they would hate you were you to set foot here.

Gebredan insists that wearing my uniform in public is risking my life unnecessarily; whenever a villager slaughters a goat or chicken, he shouts either 'Russian!' or 'Cuban!' as the knifepoint enters the beast. Despite events of this sort, with persistence, humility, goodwill, and faith, I was able to win my interpreter's trust. That has made my work here far easier, and far clearer. By this I mean that I have come to understand just how ambiguous an answer I am bound to give you.

Are you familiar with the German physicist Schrödinger and his theoretical cat? Like that cat, what we seek is in superposition; it both is and is not here.

Getting Gebredan to do something other than repeat socialist slogans to me took no small amount of money, debasement, rum, and cigars. He initially mistook the latter for a cured meat product, with results that compelled me to remain in my study for the better part of a day, but once that misunderstanding was eliminated, he grew quite loquacious. He is a religious man, a Christian, and once I had taught him the Nicene Creed in Spanish and he taught it to me in Amharic, we got on famously.

The Queen of Sheba, he explained to me, was Ethiopian (her supposed palace lies a short distance from the airstrip where I landed), and during a visit to Jerusalem, she became pregnant with the child of King Solomon. By him she bore a son, Menelik, who at the age of twelve traveled to Jerusalem and was received with all pomp and honor: his father and the courtiers recognized the boy. After Menelik had stayed for some years, Solomon's counselors grew jealous of the boy and compelled him to leave, which he did, taking the Ark from the Holiest of Holies in Jerusalem as he left.

He managed, somehow, to conceal his theft from his companions until they were, as Gebredan said, 'well beyond the reach of Solomon's long arm'; Menelik and his companions reasoned that such a daring, brazen, and poorly planned theft would never have succeeded had it not been God's will. So, with God's approval and grace, Menelik and his followers carried the Ark back to Axum, where they built a masterful temple to hide it in. My interpreter assures me that there it still remains.

But you knew this, of course, or else you would not have sent me here, with all the risk and subterfuge such a dispatch entails. You wish to know whether the legend is true. I tell you we shall never know; what I know is that this city exists to protect a single path in a single building that might lead to a single room where the Ark might rest. A combination of belief, terror, pride, and fear protects the Ark. This is not to denigrate the temple or those cowed by its legend: whether God himself has any powers beyond the instillation of such feelings remains an open question.

Only one man, the Guardian Monk, is permitted to see the Ark; on his deathbed he chooses his successor. Gebredan told me that the same man has been guardian for his life, and his father's, and his father's before that, a total of some seventy years. As the guardian is chosen from among the ranks of monks, not novices, his age must approach or exceed a century. When I wondered what a hundred-year-old man could do against a foe, or battalion of foes, armed and determined to seize the Ark, he laughed, and said that the Guardian Monk does not guard the Ark from strangers; rather, he guards strangers from the Ark. The chosen monk is not the strongest or the most battle-proven, but the subtlest, the cleverest, and the most persuasive: the monk best able to convince curious outsiders to forbear, for their own safety.

Should that fail, Gebredan told me, Axum has no shortage of men who would kill to protect the Ark. Nor does the church itself, where the Ark supposedly resides, lack traps, byways, labyrinths, mazes, and hidden alcoves that would either hinder an escape or conceal villagers who themselves would make the church an interloper's burial ground. About these traps he will say nothing, except that passing the simplest among them requires working knowledge of Hebrew, Aramaic, Amharic, and Tigrayan. The church itself is carved into the side of a mountain: there is only one entrance, and to reach it one must walk several kilometers along a narrow path with the mountain on one side and a sheer drop on the other.

I asked Gebredan two nights ago, again, to show me the inside of the church, but again he refused. Since then he has behaved strangely, refusing to stray far from the house, insisting that I engage a different man for 'outside work,' and remaining shut in his quarters for most of the day. I can only assume that he has said too much to me. *Whether he fears tradition or something altogether sharper remains unclear.*

My mission here, as far as I am concerned, is over. Either the Ark is in that church or it isn't, but the results for us are the same. Most of the villagers — all but one, in fact — have never seen the Ark, but they believe that it is there and behave as though it were there, which is enough to render the question moot. It might be possible, of course, to come into Axum with a heavily armed battalion and barrel your way into the church. Convincing the officially atheist Union of Soviet Socialist Republics to divert precious matériel from the front in order to obtain a religious artifact of questionable authenticity that might not even exist is a task that would probably outpace even your gifts of persuasion. Besides, I think it best, for reasons beyond the material needs of the fight against the Tigrayan People's Liberation Front, for reasons that a Soviet official would call 'regressive superstition' but that you and I know by a different name, to leave Axum in blessed peace. I feel I defile it by my presence, though I would like very much to return here under different circumstances.

I shall return to Asmara early next week, and from there hope to be back in Santiago by Our Lord's birthday (though I understand that your cultural attaché, that fat buffoon Gennady Shtarpin, insists on referring to Christmas as 'The Winter Celebration of the Workers' Seizure of the Means of Production and the Ever-Increasing Outputs of Collective Industry Under the Benevolent Iron Hand of Socialism').

Yours in comradeship and warm personal friendship,
Captain Felix Armando Correa de Todos los Santos

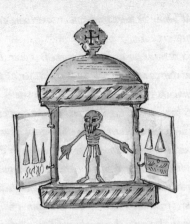

Item 5: A carved wooden triptych, with a main square panel measuring roughly 8 centimeters per side, concealed by two rectangular panels. A carving on the front of the two flaps depicts a wooden chest surmounted by two winged figures – cherubim – facing each other. Close examination of the carving shows traces of gold paint on the cherubim.

Opening the flaps reveals an icon depicting a slender, bareheaded, bearded man with dark brown skin standing in the extreme foreground, arms raised with hands outward and pointing, gesturing to the scenes depicted on either side of him (i.e., on the inside of each flap). On his left is a full-color representation of the same chest carved on the front, this time with two thin yellow cones, representing the celestial fire, emanating outward from either cherub. On his right the cones converge on three tall obelisks, as if the obelisks had somehow been raised by the fire. The steady gaze, large eyes, and tightly pursed lips give the foregrounded figure an air of worry and defiance.

Many European alchemists used the figure of a black man (or, by those who thought themselves worldly, an Ethiopian) to represent the initial stage of the alchemical process, wherein the substance to be transformed must first decay and blacken before it can be reborn. Alchemists in the Horn of Africa, however, who learned the trade from Arab scientists who guided trading convoys through the Red Sea, used self-depiction to represent not decay but the power and possibility of a substance freed from an inferior form: present liberty compared to past bondage, rather than present formlessness compared to future perfection.

Date of manufacture: The foregrounded man, with his disproportionately large and thin head and pursed lips, as well as the triptych's style (carved wood, with a single picture on the front spanning both flaps that presages the revealed scene inside the flaps), are characteristic of the Tereyu school of Ethiopian iconography, which would put the date of manufacture in the late eleventh or early twelfth century.

Manufacturer: The precise manufacturer is unknown but would have come from the ranks of Tereyu monks, renowed as artists from Gdansk to Constantinople and beyond, as well as for their strategic innovations in the battle against the Sons of Imam Ali Rashid, when for seven years and seven months they held the Fortress of the Shepherd's Dream against the invading Arabs.

Place of origin: Most likely between the present-day towns of Massawa and Zula, in Eritrea. The region between these two towns was quite active as a trading site from the eighth to the eighteenth centuries; virtually any item that left Ethiopia for Europe or Asia passed through this region.

Last known owner: The Center for African Ethnography and Culture, University of Havana, Cuba. This icon was in one of the four chests stuffed with 'Oriental curiosities' brought back to Santiago de Cuba by Felix Armando Correa, onetime captain in the Cuban army, later scholar of African Christianity. In 1980, after being discharged under questionable circumstances from the army, Correa devoted eight years to retracing the travels of the itinerant sixth-century monk Cosmas Indicopleustes. On his return in 1988, he retired to his family's tobacco farm, where he lived the remaining years of his life in fasting, study, and prayer.

Following a hurricane in August 1989, the museum had to be repainted and rewired; in order to complete the job quickly, a group of Russian-Uzbek electricians on a 'workers' retreat' were pressed into service. The icon was reported lost one day after the electricity was restored and two days after the electricians returned to Chirchik.

One year to the day after the Tereyu figure disappeared, Correa's grandson found him in the drying shed, his brains on the wall and a shotgun in his hands.

Estimated value: Optimists would estimate its value at roughly $70,000, realistic sellers at $55,000, and shrewd buyers at no less than $45,000. Tereyu icons, rare and old as they are, tend to fetch between $15,000 and $45,000, depending on condition, for a single stone panel, and $30,000 to $70,000 for a carved wooden diptych or triptych in good condition.

It is the father of all works of wonder
throughout the whole world.

❦

When I got to the office later than I should have on Friday morning, I found Austell there, fountain pen in hand and foolscap on his desk, books with etchings and photographs of mushrooms spread out on the floor in front of him. 'Ah, good morning, Paul. Or rather sad morning, eh?'

He gestured toward Art's dark office. 'He's gone to a wake for that doctor, the one whose name –'

'The Panda,' I interrupted.

'Yes, indeed. The Panda. Wonderful name. I never knew the man. Oh, well, I suppose I met him at one of Art and Donna's lovely bohemian evenings. Dark-skinned gentleman, wasn't he?'

I shrugged noncommittally – I'd never seen him.

'Yes, I thought so,' said Austell obliviously. 'Hmmm. Very nice chap, all the same. He died suddenly, I understand?'

'Hit-and-run. Car didn't even stop.'

Austell took his glasses off and peered at me as though seeing me for the first time. 'Really? Really? How awful. Well, that's just . . . Has anyone gone to the police?'

The way he leaned on the word 'police' emphasized its exoticism for him: violent men who wear cheap blazers and run through doors with guns raised. I wondered whether he had ever met a policeman (the Olafssons not included). 'Yeah, the police were called in just after the accident. No suspects yet; the witnesses couldn't agree on the type of car or who was driving.'

'You actually spoke to the police?'

'I did. Not that much came of it.'

'Pity. And how is the rest of your work coming?' he asked in an almost paternal tone.

'Fine, no complaints, thanks.'

'Ah, good. You know, I hear Verrill's is adding a vegetable section. Causing a lot of excitement around here, I can tell you. Any more visits to Clougham for you?'

'No, none on the horizon. Looks like everything's either local or in Wickenden.'

'Excellent to hear. As I advised you before, Clougham has always been a rather odd place. I wouldn't go there myself if I could avoid it.'

I nodded amicably and turned back toward my desk. For the rest of the morning, we worked in silence, broken occasionally by Austell's reading a sentence to himself and by my tapping on the computer keys, transcribing the previous day's conversation with Hannah. As I did, she kept jumping uninvited into my mind, and as I began counting first the hours and then converting into minutes the amount of time before I would pick her up, I found it increasingly difficult to work. Austell had taken to humming tunelessly while he worked; he sounded like a stoned hornet. By late morning I had gotten so antsy at the thought of an actual, real-live date with an actual, real-live woman that I couldn't sit still at all. I told Austell I was going to talk to the Verrills about their expansion. I left before he could ask me to bring something back for him.

By 6:40 the sun had set, the air had turned sharp and smoky, and I had paced a marathon in my apartment. I couldn't think of a productive way to fill that afternoon, so I resorted to the time-honored practice of throwing a tennis ball against a wall until my landlady pounded back. Then I watched the news. Small-town television news seemed purposefully arranged to refute the proposition that journalism chronicled a changing world; after I'd lived two months in Lincoln and its environs, the evening news for me became an exercise in combinatorialism: fire, councilman in trouble, high-school football team wins, weather; high-school football player in trouble, councilman proposes a new way to pay municipal taxes, fire, weather; snowstorm, high-school hockey news, judge fired for groping his secretary, fire, weather. Tonight the lead story was the opening of a fancy new grocery two towns over, which meant that weekenders no longer had to bring their quinoa, frisée, and coffee-chocolate-myrtleberry stout with them. When they showed the high-school basketball team advancing to state quarterfinals, I switched the television off. I put on a sport jacket for the first time since graduation (it seemed to have shrunk around the midsection from sitting in my closet untouched for so long), brushed my unbrushable hair into semiobedient clumps, and headed out the door, tossing my keys to myself, missing, and fishing them out of a puddle.

Talcott's long horseshoe driveway shone with its own private harvest moons, yellow lamps on either side, stretching from the entryway to the grand front, winding past the floodlit athletic fields and the dorms in a variety of styles – Olde New Englande Rusticke, ivy-covered redbrick, 1970s Hartford housing projects – to the plain glass-and-steel back doors. Hannah stood just inside, emerging when I waved and flashed my brights (why did I do that? I never do that; that's not one of my gestures – the evening was filled with silent recriminations issued against self by self). In the pooled warm light, with her green woolen cape, honey-colored hair, and long silver earrings, she looked timeless, enchanted, like some sort of liquid gazelle.

'You're very prompt,' she said, climbing into the car. 'I'm glad; I had just finished looking over some papers five minutes ago.'

'What on?'

'Oh, the usual. Music. I tried to have the older students do counterpoint. I played the first French Suite and then "When I'm Sixty-four," for that clarinet part in the last verse, you know?'

I didn't. 'Sure.'

'Judging from the essays, I'm not sure how well it took.' She looked in the rearview mirror and ran her fingers through her hair, pulling the strands apart. 'Oh, well. By the way, do you know where you're going?'

'No. No sense of direction. I get lost in parking lots.' She giggled – score one for the home team. 'Tell me.'

'Okay, you're going to turn on 87, which is up –' She suddenly got excited and put her hand on my arm. 'Oh, pull over, pull over here in front of St Stephen's.'

A large stone church loomed on our right; in front of it, two men in cassocks and parkas were pounding posters on stakes into the lawn. The men were opposites in nearly every way: one was fat, florid, jolly-looking, and white; the other was trim, neat, sober, and black. The black priest held the stake in place while the white one drove it into the ground, puffing with exertion. When I pulled over, they both stopped and looked up: priests in headlights. Seeing

Hannah, the fat white man carelessly dropped the hammer and stepped over to the car.

'Well, look who's here. Hello, Hannah. What a nice surprise. Where are you off to this evening? Luke, look who's here,' he called to the other priest. 'It's Miss Rowe.'

The second man walked over and gave a courteous smile and nod to Hannah, who returned the greeting in kind but spoke to the other one.

'We're on our way to dinner. This is my friend Paul,' she said. 'This is Reverend Hampden.' He took off his mitten and laid his flabby hand in mine like a dead carp, not even returning my grip, then hastily regloved his hand. 'And this is Reverend Makgabo.' He returned a firm handshake and even a 'Nice to meet you.' I couldn't place the accent.

'So where are you kids off to this fine, fine evening?' asked Hampden.

'The Trout.'

'Ah, lovely, lovely. Wonderful choice. Tell me, Paul, are you from our neck of the woods?'

'Not originally, but I live in Lincoln now.'

'Do you? Fantastic. What do you do? What church do you attend?'

'I'm not much of a churchgoer, but I work for the *Carrier.*'

'A reporter. I suppose that explains it,' he said, giving Hannah a showy mock wink. 'Members of the hardworking press can't be bothered to attend church much these days. No, even Art and Donna don't come on Christmas. Of course, Art's a Catholic, so maybe –' He broke off his sentence and held up his mittened hands as if I had rushed at him. 'No offense, none at all, if you're a Catholic, too, or anything else for that matter. But Hannah here, you know, is one of the few young people around who's active in our church. Isn't that right, Luke?' Makgabo nodded, but Hampden didn't even look back at him for confirmation. 'Matter of fact, she just chaperoned the youth group, didn't you?' Hannah nodded.

'You know,' said Hampden, raising a large hand to his head and shifting his gut beneath his coat and cassock, 'I wonder whether you couldn't step inside for just a second so we can talk about your chaperoning,' he said to Hannah. 'Paul, you're welcome to come inside. We'll just be a minute. Luke, could you finish with the announcements, please?' He turned to me and held his hands up again. 'It's these darn clumsy mitts I've got. No good for anything. Hannah?' As she stepped out of the car, he put an arm around her, and they walked toward the church. Hannah looked back at me, held a finger up, and mouthed, 'One minute.'

I turned off the car and stepped outside. 'Can I give you a hand with those?' I asked Makgabo. The posters advertised a bake sale and silent auction to raise money for the rectory.

'Yes, thank you. It takes two people, you know, to drive them in properly. And the ground is slippery after all of this rain. You must hold them steady, and

I will pound with the hammer. No, no. Hold the stem, not the top. I have no wish to make your fingers flat.'

'If you don't mind me asking, where are you from?'

'Uganda. I have come to the United States for a two-year exchange. A priest from New Haven, Reverend Jonas, has taken my place in Gulu for the same duration.'

'Why Lincoln and not New Haven?'

'To speak frankly, I am not entirely sure. I have just gone where I was assigned. I work in New Haven three nights each week, but more as a volunteer than a parish priest. There would seem to be more need of counsel there than here. Forgive me for saying so if it offends you.'

'Not at all. What do you do in New Haven?'

'I work at a canteen, a soup kitchen, as people seem to call it here, run by the church. Cooking, cleaning, listening.' He drove one stake firmly into the turf and grabbed another. 'And you are a reporter here? Do you like your work?' He looked at me steadily, with a warm and open expression.

'I guess I do.'

'Guessing is no good. You are an educated man, so you have the opportunity to select a profession that you may love, no guessing needed. Your friend Hannah seems fond of her work.' He paused and threw me a sly smile, his eyes twinkling mischievously. 'And you seem quite fond of her, too.

You looked at her all the way as she walked up to the church.' I blushed and said nothing, and Reverend Makgabo laughed. 'Ah, you see. I knew it. I have a wife myself, and I look at her in just the very same way. Because I am a priest, this doesn't mean I'm not human.' He had an infectious, full-throated laugh that I couldn't resist.

'Yeah, she's okay,' I admitted, which provoked even more laughter from Reverend Makgabo.

'Okay. Indeed. Yes, indeed she is that.' He looked at me again, in the same sidelong, half-smiling way. There was something lively, elfin, and winning about him. 'If you don't mind the observation, you would make an excellent hooker.'

'Excuse me?'

Twinkly eyes and more laughter. 'Yes, I know this word in American has a meaning perhaps . . . well, perhaps not altogether salubrious. I am talking about rugby, though. Do you play?'

'I never have.'

'Ah, well then, you must play with us. A group of about twenty of us plays on weekends, when we can. Aside from myself, nobody has ever played before. I put notices up in New Haven and Lincoln, and I corral my brethren in both places into scrambling around like heathen for a few hours. You know, you cannot imagine the problems that can be solved on the rugby pitch. Instead of brooding and arguing and plotting, you just run into somebody and release all of your frustrations at once.'

'Does Reverend Hampden play?'

'Ah. That particular prayer has not yet been answered,' he said, eyes dancing. 'But here is the man himself.'

Hampden, waddling down the driveway like a boozy walrus, had one mittened hand flapping at his side for balance; he guided Hannah down the walk with the other hand. The hand on Hannah's back wore no mitten, and his expression as she talked was somewhere between Extreme Interest and Suspicious Leer; the frequency with which his eyes flitted below her neckline and back while she wasn't looking moved him closer to Leer. When they drew close, he clapped a hand on my shoulder. 'Well, you know, Paul, I've asked our friend Hannah here all sorts of questions about you, and she couldn't tell me one darned thing.'

I wasn't sure what I was supposed to say, so I looked at Hannah and waited for her to jump in. She didn't.

'Well, I suppose you seem like a good enough fellow. What do you think, Luke? You gave him a good grilling, didn't you?' he asked, ostentatiously winking at Hannah.

'Oh, yes. He seems honorable enough to me.'

'Well, that settles it, then. Paul, great meeting you. You drive careful. Always lovely, Hannah,' he said, kissing her on the cheek and giving her an entirely unnecessary, and somewhat creepy, hug. 'I'll see you soon, I hope?'

'I hope so, too.'

'Great. Paul, you're welcome to drop by, too, see what we're all about over here.'

Several thousand responses skittered like tadpoles around my brain. Being unable to say something nice, I settled for a silent handshake. Reverend Makgabo told me to meet them on the Talcott playing field the next morning if I wanted to play. Hannah told me, with one finger against the small of my back pushing me toward the car, that it was time for dinner.

The trout sat by the side of a rill just south of the Massachusetts border, along a broad swath of meadow ringed with thickets of pine trees and hills that loomed against the blue night like the idea of hills.

'That's the Appalachian Trail right through those trees there,' said the bearded owner as he showed us to our table. 'Not too many know that; people think Appalachian, they think of Tennessee. But you finish your meal and go along that trail at the back of the parking lot, turn left at the first grove, Tennessee's where you'd wind up, you keep walking. When you're ready to order, come on up to the counter. Menu's on the blackboard above the bar over there. I was you, I'd stay away from the salmon,' he told us with a wink.

Hannah ordered their homemade ale and shepherd's pie. I asked for a cheeseburger with fries and a

Budweiser. The owner and Hannah both looked at me and winced, as though I had just asked for a sautéed baby. 'Are you sure you want Budweiser?' asked Hannah, implying that she was sure that I didn't. 'They make their own beer here.'

'Really?'

The owner nodded and grinned, his eyes closed beatifically: with that kind of self-satisfaction, I expected perfection in a pint glass. 'Then I'll have . . . Just bring me one of whatever you're bringing her.' He huffed a bit, gave a tight and extra-tolerant grimace, and walked away. I shrugged. 'I'm a philistine, I know. If they had cans, I would have ordered a can.'

She gave a look of mock pique. 'I just hope nobody sees me with a rube like you,' she joked, brushing her hand across mine.

I asked her what she thought of Father Hampden. 'Oh, he's a sweet old guy. He loves what he does, and he's just the perfect picture of a New England priest, isn't he? What did you think of him?'

I raised my eyebrows noncommitally. 'I liked Reverend Makgabo.'

'He's pretty quiet. I don't know him all that well. But Father Hampden, he just seems so authentic, you know? He seems like he belongs right where he is.'

I knew not 'seems,' but Hampden did, and better than he knew 'is,' too. Hardly worth arguing over.

'Can I ask you a question?' she asked.

I nodded.

'What kind of name is Tomm? I mean, when you first called, I thought of Billy Bob, or Becky Sue, or something like that.' I laughed and nodded: I had heard this before, and everyone asked about the name. 'I don't mean to pry,' she said, tilting her head to the side and pulling her hair back from her face. That was unfair, I thought; I'd tell state secrets to see that gesture again.

'My grandfather, my father's father, he came to Brooklyn from Poland. Only he was supposed to go to Liverpool, because that's where his brother went, and that's where he thought his boat was going. He couldn't read or write, and I guess he just figured he'd hop on the first boat with an English-speaking crew. So on the way west, he decides he has to anglicize his name. Anyway, he turns to one of the shipmates –'

'The first mate?'

'The boatswain? The keelhauler? Who knows; I've been on one boat in my life, and that's the Staten Island Ferry. So he asks this guy, "What's the most English name you can think of?" The guy says, "Tom." So that became his last name. How the extra *m* got thrown in, I don't know, but that, believe it or not, is the story of my last name. What about you? Rowe? You a *Mayflower* baby?'

She laughed, accidentally spitting a little beer back in her pint glass. 'Right. My father likes to think so. My mother, though, she's your basic generic midwestern girl. Scandinavian, Scots-Irish. Probably a bit of something else, too. It's the kind of ethnic background that doesn't really count as ethnic background.'

'Close family?'

'I'm very close to my mother. She lives on her own just outside Chicago. Schaumburg, if it means anything to you.' I shook my head. 'But that's about it. My father I see every so often, as infrequently as possible. He ran away with someone else when I was about six, then ditched her a while later. There've been lots of someone elses. Anyway, he lives down in Florida now, in a silly little bungalow right on a golf course where he can drink 7-and-7s and stay vain. He hates the cold, so he never comes up here. An added advantage to living in Lincoln.'

Our food had arrived while she was talking, and she dug into her shepherd's pie like she hadn't eaten in days. I guess I must have been watching her a tad too intently, because she looked up self-consciously and started wiping her chin and checking for food on her shirt.

'You're fine, don't worry. It's just that I like girls who eat.'

'Oh, thanks. That's me, I guess. A good little eater.'

'I didn't mean . . . I'm sorry, I just . . .'

She laughed and waved me off. 'I know. So what about you? You're a Brooklyn mongrel. What else?'

'Actually, my dad lives back in Indianapolis, where he grew up. My parents split when I was twelve. Mom still lives in Brooklyn. In fact, she lives in the

187

house where she grew up, this big three-story place. She always talks about renting the first couple of floors, but I think she wants to give the place to my brother and his wife.'

'Wow. A three-generation house in the United States. In New York, no less.'

'Yeah, well, I guess we don't get around all that much.'

'No traveling?'

'No, I guess no one in the family really likes to travel. My folks took us to London once when I was a boy, and my mom goes to Holland and Ireland every so often to visit family. My dad says he gets the bends anywhere east of Cleveland or west of Omaha.'

'Okay, here's the big question.' She did a little drumroll on the table with her fingers. 'How old are you?'

'What's your guess?'

'I don't know. Twenty-seven? Twenty-eight?'

I slumped backward against the red Naugahyde bench. 'That hurts. That really hurts. I just turned twenty-three.'

She put a hand over her mouth and her eyes widened, glittering as they picked up the candles on the tables around us. 'My God. A baby. I can't believe it. I guess I've dated people younger than me, but this is unprecedented. Cradle robbing.'

I blushed. Did she just imply that we were dating? 'Why? Can I ask . . .'

'Me? Over the hill. Done for. Past even the Christmas-cake jokes. You know, no good on the twenty-sixth? I'm thirty-one.'

I didn't say anything, which in retrospect was worse than saying something snide. I remembered my mother's twenty-eighth birthday party pretty clearly. Thirty-one was an adult's age. 'I've never dated someone this much . . . Well, I guess I was in college and just didn't . . .' The hole got deeper as my face reddened.

'Oh, quit blushing. Just get me a walker on the way out of the bar and slip a little Postum in my beer, and I'll be fine. Don't worry.'

I don't usually talk so smoothly with other people, especially women – especially women to whom I'm attracted. But our conversation just floated along, and the easier it got, the more I felt was at stake. The world grew wider and more benign at that table.

I confessed that I didn't really know what I wanted to do; she said neither did she. Before moving to Lincoln, she had lived in Boston, where she taught English, sang in a couple of choirs, and lived 'your basic lightly debauched life of a reasonably attractive single woman in a huge college town.' She moved here when she heard about the job at Talcott and was feeling like she needed an escape from the city, but said that she was 'more content than happy' with her life. She wondered whether this was a problem or something to which she should adjust. I shrugged and said I didn't know.

'Of course you don't; you're barely old enough to buy me a beer. Speaking of which.' She waved an empty glass in her left hand. 'Another of the same. And the promise holds: come back to this table with a Budweiser – or anything Bud-looking or anything in a can – and I'm leaving.'

We talked for another two hours and as many beers before she asked me what time it was. I got up to look at the clock behind the bar and saw beneath it, perched on a stool and not talking to anyone, a familiar-looking man. He had a kindly, seafaring face, blue eyes, and a white beard; he wore professorial clothes that seemed to lack shape and color (baggy, brownish beige). I couldn't place him, but I was sure I had seen him before.

When I sat down, I pointed him out to Hannah; I figured he came from Lincoln and thought she might know him. When she turned around, he was staring right at our table; Hannah turned back quickly and before she could completely mask the look of shock and fear on her face. 'I don't know who he is. I don't think I've seen him before. I think we should go,' she said quickly, with an obviously false smile stretched thin across her mouth. 'Plus, I'm tired,' she added, laying a hand across mine.

'What's wrong? Who is that guy?'

'I just told you, I don't know. Please, can we just go now? Please?'

'You still have half your beer left. Are you sure you don't . . .'

As I spoke, she was getting money out of her purse, preparing to pay the bill. At that, I relented. 'Okay, don't do that. Let's get out of here. But if you're worried, maybe you should talk to the police, or maybe . . .'

She forced a look of fatigued, beery calm across her face, but her expression seemed to hover just above her features like an imperfectly attached mask. 'That man just reminds me a little of my father, the way he looks in old pictures.' If this were true, then her father must have been pushing sixty when she was born, which was strange, if not completely unheard of. But I couldn't see this Old Mariner type in a golf-course bungalow in Florida.

Despite her casual smile and the affected jaunty walk toward the door, her hands shook as she fastened her cape.

XINJIANG'S IVORY
(EARTH)

❧❧❧

Earth: a barbarian poet noted, with unusual aptness, that from it we spring, and to it we shall return. It is the first and most important of the elements, as the Ancients have noted, principal in quality and dignity, noted mostly for its coldness and dryness but in fact a repository and breeding ground for the other three as well. Tsun Li Bai believed that the true Scientist should eat a tablespoon of his native earth each day, carrying it with him if he must travel. Of his unhappy fate we need speak no further. . . .

— YUN FEIYAN, *The Dragon's Wheel*

[The following is taken from the statement of Jakob Harve, an Estonian poet who was deemed an Enemy of the People and consigned to the Yamal Labor Camp in August 1974. It was written on his escape from Yamal seventeen months later. Initial page or pages missing.]

. . . because I understood they had all been collectivized and remade into dutiful *Homo sovieticus*es. I asked him whether this was not, in fact, the case.

'Mostly, yes,' he said, in suspiciously good Russian (this alone should have put me on my guard: the more fool I). 'But a few bands of our people still roam freely, as we always have and always will.' He looked down at my feet: I wore my thin, poorly made, prison-issue boots, and the soles were beginning to peel away from the boot itself. In fact, my feet had been totally numb for several hours – the tips of my toes were beginning to blacken – but I was so intent on putting some distance between myself and the hell from which I had escaped that I had barely noticed.

He laughed heartily and with his knife tore two strips of fur from the bottom of his own coat, telling me to wrap them around my boots. He then took off his massive, shapeless fur coat and wrapped it tight around my shoulders. I told him that I had never met a Yakut before; he said that the only Russians he and his people ever meet are escaping prisoners. He pulled two strips of dried meat – I didn't ask what animal it came from – from deep inside his clothes and handed them to me. My mouth was so dry and the meat so tough and frozen that I could do little more than roll a piece on my tongue like hard candy. The Yakut clapped me on the shoulder and pointed toward a yurt on the horizon. He asked if I was strong enough to walk; I of course said yes. But as we staggered off toward his camp, my lack of food and frostbitten feet got the better of me: I stumbled and pitched forward, hoping that the snow would buffer my fall. Instead, this far north, I received an icy blow to the jaw.

I awoke to my face being swabbed by a warm, wet rag with a curiously sweet, rather rank smell. I opened my eyes and saw that it was, in fact, a reindeer's tongue licking the fever sweat from my forehead and cheeks. In my shock I sat up too suddenly and upset the table next to my pallet, knocking tea, bread, and meat strips to the ground and sending my four-legged friend backward in shock. I heard laughter in a range of tones and styles: fluty girlish giggles, phlegmy old-man hacks, robust fat-man's guffaws, woodblock chuckles of indeterminate sex and age, and a number of nondescript laughs rounding out the party. I sat up slowly and dizzily and realized I was in a crowded, close, hot tent; it stank of sweat, flatulence, tobacco, alcohol, and tallow. Nonetheless, for the first time in 947 days, I awoke somewhere other than my cell, and for that I thanked God aloud for the first time in almost three years.

Seated on a bearskin on the ground nearest me was my savior, hatless and smoking a long, crudely made wooden pipe.

'Bulun?' he asked.

I nodded.

'How long?'

'Almost three years.'

He grunted and raised his eyebrows. A pudgy, flat-faced woman whom I took to be his wife looked up from the fur-lined boots she was repairing and clicked her tongue sympathetically at me. 'Not bad,' said the man. 'Last one through here had been in fifteen years. He died before we could reach my tent, but he was mostly corpse a long time before that.' He collected what I had spilled and handed it to me. 'Bread. My wife made it.' He nodded to the round woman, who smiled sadly at me. 'And reindeer meat. Healthy.'

'Also tea,' called a rough-voiced woman from across the tent. She sat next to a similarly aged man; both of them looked so old, so weathered, and so inscrutable that they seemed to be carved from wood. 'Drink tea,' she said, emphasizing the word 'tea' as though I were a foreigner (which, I suppose, I was). 'Warm in winter. Good for bones. Good, too, for thinking,' she said, tapping her head for emphasis.

'Tea, Mother. Bring the guest some tea,' said my savior. 'Eat up, now; it'll keep you warm. You smoke?'

I shook my head.

'First prisoner I ever met who didn't smoke.'

'I could buy more with cigarettes if I never smoked them.'

'Clever. You Russian?'

'Estonian.'

He said something to the two older people, who nodded inscrutably and in eerie unison. 'My parents,' he explained. 'And those three little ones are mine, too,' he said, gesturing to three young girls who eyed me warily from the far corner of the tent. 'Fourth one coming.' He winked. 'Snoring fatso over there is my wife's good-for-nothing brother. But family's family. You going home to someone?'

'A wife. I have a wife.' In prison I had learned to suppress all thoughts of her; now, warmed by the possibility of return, in my mind she thawed, first slowly and then uncontrollably. As I remembered her hands, her voice, her smell, I began shaking and bawling right there in front of a strange family. I couldn't bear thinking of her anymore. 'Please, who are you? And why did you help me?' I asked when I composed myself.

'I'm called Nei. We're Sakha, you know, Yakuts. The last free Yakuts in this region. Why did I help you? Because it's my duty, that's why.'

Shocking and unfortunate the speed with which one's prison crust melts when first exposed to human warmth. Even more unfortunate when that warmth is a simulation, a flashlight rather than a fire. 'It has been years, my friend, since I heard anyone talk about duty in that way. Duty as anything other than stepping on those below you and bowing to those above.' I reached out toward him, and I do believe I would have embraced him had not the tent flap opened and a familiar set of boots, followed by an even more familiar face, entered.

'Nice speech, poet.' He smirked. 'But Nei was talking about his socialist duty to me, not some retrograde, childish notion that would obligate him to assist enemies of the state.' Although I hoped never to see Commandant Zhensky's face again, I knew I would never forget it, and yet, despite all of my efforts – all the secrecy, bribing, digging, hoping, and waiting, the exposure and the risk of death or recapture that I thought I had avoided – here he was again, the same [SECTION CROSSED OUT] his resourcefulness.

'You've done better than most, you know. Getting past both sets of guards, living long enough to reach Nei. I really am impressed. Tell me, where did you do your military service?' He sat down closest to the fire, in an empty seat. Strange that it should have been empty, unless, of course, it was reserved for him (as I believe it was).

'Murmansk.'

'That explains it. You think you're used to the cold. Don't you?'

I said nothing.

'I'll tell you something: nobody ever gets used to this cold. Had you not run into Nei where you did, you would have been dead in hours. You think Bulun is a prison? Bulun is an oasis, a paradise of warmth and conviviality compared to the rest of this godforsaken region. This wasteland is the prison. Do you know how long I've lived out here? Eighteen years. And do you know why? Because they pay me. Well. I have a huge house on the banks of the Lena, where I can fish; I have foreign travel privileges, access to hospitals for me, my parents, and my children; I have cars and drivers and I live better than ninety percent of Party officials who technically outrank me. But I have to live in this misery. Nine months of bone-splitting cold and three months of mosquitoes.

'Comrade Poet, how many times had you been outdoors since you first arrived as my guest? No, no: don't tell me. I know already: you've been outside as often as we let you out. How do your hands smell?'

They smelled, of course, like fish, and I expect they always will. I sniffed, and I tried to stay expressionless but I must have wrinkled my nose, because Zhensky laughed.

'I thought so. We never want any of you ever to rid yourselves of that smell entirely. And we're increasing production, you know. They're sending more and more of you out here: more kike writers, more faggot actors, more long-haired singers. And we have room and work for all of you.'

Nei and his wife stared sadly at the ground. Zhensky looked over at them, and instantly their eyes widened, heads bowed, and insincere little smiles landed like insects between their noses and chins. He told Nei to pour me some tea and bring my plate of food to me. Zhensky sniffed the meat, exhaled his disgust, and handed it to me. 'I suppose eventually you might get used to that. I never have. Raw reindeer meat, frozen and sliced thin. Savage. Now, I prefer the osetra caviar that arrives each month, along with a case each of vodka and Crimean champagne. Only the best. But here: eat. Try to stay warm. Then I'd like to show you something, if I may.'

My appetite had vanished, but I didn't want Zhensky to think he had upset me, so I ate. When every last piece of meat and bread had gone, I handed the plate directly to Nei's wife, nodding in thanks. She beamed back at me, then glanced at Zhensky and scurried, head down, back to Nei's side.

'Come outside for a moment,' said Zhensky. 'I want you to see something.' I tried to push myself up from the bed but was frozen. A combination of the temperature and Zhensky's bloody reputation made my lower body useless. 'Poet,' he said, leaning his pockmarked face, the color of raw chicken fat, into mine, 'are you frightened of me?'

I didn't say anything but forced myself to stand up, and I wrapped Nei's coat around me. We lifted the flap and went out into a night so clear and cold it was like standing inside a pane of glass. The sky held more stars than I ever had imagined existed; it looked full. I could hear a quiet tinkling and crackling that sounded far away. Zhensky pointed behind us, and I barely made out a soft glow in the distance. 'Bulun. Not really all that far. Four kilometers, perhaps.

But do you see this camp? The shape of the camp?'

I hadn't even realized that we were in a camp. Then I noticed hide tents like ours at regular intervals, extending in a line in either direction into the distance. 'It's a line,' I said.

'No. Step over here and look again.'

We stepped to the other side of the tent. 'A circle. The tents . . .'

'A ring. Bulun and my house are at the center. Now do you understand? The Yakuts get to roam. They get their herds and their hides and their language. They're not in Magnitogorsk; they're not mining coal in Vorkuta or Voronezh; their children aren't sent to state boarding schools. All we ask in return is a bit of vigilance and some intelligence.'

A tear welled up in my eye, fell down my cheek, and landed on the ground, already frozen, with a plink. Zhensky leaned over and picked it up. Its trail stung my cheek, but the tear pearled in Zhensky's glove like a gift. 'The whispering of the stars,' he said.

'The what?'

'A poet like you should appreciate this. They call it "the whispering of the stars." Listen,' he said, raising a finger for silence. I could still hear the tinkling and craned my neck to see what it was. Zhensky laughed. 'No, here. Look.' He formed his mouth into a wide O and exhaled slowly. As he did, I saw the cloud of breath fall in droplets to the ground. That was the sound I heard: our breath falling. 'It's a Yakut expression. It means a period of weather so cold that your breath falls frozen to the ground before it can dissipate. The Yakuts say that you should never tell secrets outside during the whispering of the stars, because the words themselves freeze, and in the spring thaw anyone who walks past that spot will be able to hear them. In springtime the air fills with old gossip, unheeded commands, the voices of children who have become adolescents, and snatches of long-finished conversation. Your voice, Comrade Poet, our conversation, will remain here far longer than you.'

At that point I thought he meant to kill me. Instead he clapped me on the shoulder, walked me back to the tent, and stuck his head through the flap. 'Nei. You fat, lazy Yakut. Bring me that box, would you?'

'What box, Commandant?' Nei's face, so broad, plain, and full of concern when he found me wandering across the snow, had become a pointed mask of obsequiousness and terror.

'The ivory one, the carved ivory box that holds your snuff. The one that I told you I liked the last time I visited. The one you were rude enough not to offer to me.'

'But, Commandant, that box belonged –'

A loud bang and a shower of sparks made both me and Nei jump; I even fell backward, and when I looked up, I saw Zhensky holding a gun, from which smoke poured in billows. He aimed the gun at, and seemed to have just shot, a huge larch tree, which smoked prolifically. With a groan and an air of resignation, half of the trunk collapsed to the earth, and as it did, the rest of the tree – roots, branches, and all – toppled over in the other direction. Zhensky laughed and turned to me: 'They just explode, you know, in this weather. If you try to chop them down for wood during the winter, sparks fly from the trunk and the ax splinters in your hand. I had no idea I'd do that well, though. Shallow roots.' He laughed again and holstered the gun, turning to Nei. 'I believe you were telling me why I can't have that box I wanted.' Nei scurried back into his tent – when he went in, I could see his wife and children huddled in the far corner, crying – and came out carrying a small ivory box, which he handed to Zhensky.

'The Yakuts, you know, traded with merchants in Novgorod before they fell to the Golden Horde. Novgorodian merchants, in turn, received goods from all over the world. Including, I presume, this lovely box. And since nobody with any contact with the rest of the world ever comes out to this god-forsaken frozen land of shit hanging off the edge of the world, little prizes like this tend to stay in families for a very long time. Look here, look at this detailing. No Yakut could carve this, don't you agree?

'Well, whether you do or not, you should be honored, Comrade Poet; this box will preserve your words for me once you have gone. I'll tell you the truth now,' he said, reaching into his jacket pocket for a flask and a sheaf of papers. He took a deep draft from the flask and handed it to me. I expected vodka but instead swallowed liquid fire. 'Yakut *samogon*. Don't know what's in it, but it keeps you warm.' He drank again and put the flask back in his pocket. 'I have here' – he brandished the papers theatrically – 'the set of poems for which you were convicted. Do you know, by the way, the charges against you?'

I told him I never did.

'Bourgeois formalism. Using your university position to pervert the future leaders of the Soviet Union.' I began to protest, and he waved me away. 'Oh, please. Don't. All in the past. No, the truth is, I rather like these poems. They talk about nature and love; they follow nice little patterns, you know, the way the words match up –'

'Sestinas.'

'Excuse me?'

'They're called sestinas. Some of them. I also wrote villanelles. Both Italian forms that rely on wordplay and so translate quite well into Russian. You see, if you take the first line and transpose –'

'Please, no lectures now. It's too cold. My point is, these aren't dangerous poems. Some prisoners – drug dealers, deserters, Jews – I would have shot on the spot, but you're different. You might even have a future in this country. Of course, I can't let you escape; I'd lose my job. But if I sign your release papers and change the date of your release retroactively, who's going to question me, eh?' He winked, which I found far more frightening than I did his gunshot.

'You were always obedient enough, yet you showed far more ingenuity and spine than I would have expected from a poet, especially an Estonian poet, in escaping. I will ask only two favors of you, and then I'll leave you to spend the night here, in peace. The first thing you're going to do is write down how you escaped. Did you bribe guards? I want to know who. Did your fellow prisoners help? I want to know which ones. Is there a weak spot in Bulun's architecture? I want to know where. I don't want to hear any quibbling, I don't want to hear any professions of honor, any "I'm not turning this fellow in" – nothing like that. A full, honest, and detailed account, and you'll get to keep the fruits of your labor. Fair enough? Good.

'Now, your second task. Let's see . . . Ah, this way.' He beckoned me over to the fallen tree. It lay in the center of a slurry of ice, snow, wood chips, and black Siberian dirt.

He took a pinch of pinkish snuff from the box, poured the rest out, and guided me to the center of the patch of dirt. 'Breathe.' My breath fell in tiny hailstones onto the already frozen earth. 'Perfect. Now, what poem do you wish to read?'

'Pardon me?'

'Which poem? What's your favorite one? Here, here, maybe you don't remember. Maybe you just remember omul now. Take a look.' He sat down on the tree trunk at my feet and lit a cigarette.

'This one,' I said. It was called 'The Fruitseller's Lament.' I composed it during my first married summer in Kurgja, while making love to my wife and listening to a currant lady chanting in the square downstairs.

He signaled for me to begin. As I read the poem, he got down on his hands and knees and with a buck knife scraped up the earth onto which my breath fell and placed it in the box. When I finished, he sealed the box and bowed. 'There we are. Now, whenever I wish to remember the illustrious poet in my charge, all I have to do is open this box in warm weather.

'As for you, here is some paper, and here are two pens. Don't lose these. Start writing – everything, mind you, up to and including this conversation – and I'll be back in two days to check on your progress. Once I'm completely satisfied (as I'm sure I will be), I shall process your release papers and send you home.

'You look surprised. You shouldn't. We're not all monsters, you know. No, Nei and I, we've just figured out how to work the system to our advantage. He gets what he wants, I get what I want, and the only people who get hurt are criminals, reprobates, and enemies of the state who would have been caught anyway. Even the worst escapee gets to taste a few hours of freedom first, eh? A few hours munching reindeer jerky in the company of these pie-faced women who stink of reindeer fat. Better than nothing. Better than fish guts and snoring criminals. A worthwhile bargain, don't you think? Sleep well, Comrade Poet.'

Item 6: A rectangular ivory box, veined with silver and jade along the sides. On the top a jade inscription written in Arabic reads 'In the name of God, the Compassionate, the Merciful.' Inside, the word 'earth' has been inscribed, in Chinese, on the box's lid. The box is 12 centimeters long, 3 centimeters tall, and 4 centimeters wide.

Earth, of course, is one of the four Aristotelian elements (the others are fire, air, and water) and possesses the qualities of coldness and dryness (fire is hot and dry, air is hot and moist, water is cold and moist). Because each shares one quality with another, any one element can be transformed into another by heating or cooling, drying or adding water: this idea is the foundation on which alchemy rests.

Idris ben Khalid al-Jubir calls earth 'the most foundational of the four elements, the most ubiquitous and, in truth, the least useful. Earth, like water and air, simply is, but, unlike the other two elements, it cannot be altered in shape. It is the book of all matter: it is as it is, and what is, is simply the raw material for what will be, or what should be. The material world – the earthly earth – is silent, ignoble, and imperfect: just as a voice requires a mouth and breath to give it shape, so the tangible world requires a guiding hand to perfect it.'

Date of manufacture: The veining, though sophisticated in nature, is rather crude in appearance, and the signs of age around the box's corners date it back to the ninth or tenth century.

Manufacturer: Unknown.

Place of origin: The materials – ivory, silver, jade – are all common to China, but the Arabic inscription and the technique of veining one stone with another indicate an Islamic influence. The confluence of style and material suggests that the box came from Xinjiang, which enjoyed a flourishing Chinese-Islamic art when the Arabs first arrived at the Uighur court. Islam became a court fashion, though as Arab armies began arriving in greater numbers, it quickly became more than just a fashion.

Last known owner: Pavel Vadimovich Zhensky, chief engineer of the Bulun Fish Cannery and commandant of the Bulun Center for Labor and Higher

Education, both of which closed when the Soviet Union collapsed. Zhensky sold the box and its contents, along with a letter and the (since lost) last will and testament of Estonian poet Jakob Harve to an undisclosed buyer for an undisclosed sum.

At the time of the sale, August 1992, Zhensky's role in the liquidation of thousands of dissident writers at Bulun had just been made public. Two months previously he had been exposed as the architect of the CHP (the Northern People's Patrol, in which the KGB forced groups of native Siberians to act as informal camp guards in exchange for the appearance of liberty), and as a result was run out of his palatial home on the Lena River. The scandal that forced him to sell his possessions involved accusations that he suborned guards to facilitate the escapes of well-known dissident writers and then lay in wait for them in the Yakut camp that surrounded the prison. Once caught, the writers would be promised their freedom in exchange for a detailed description of who had helped them escape; he used these testimonies to blackmail virtually every guard who served under him. Without exception he either shot the escapees himself or paid their Yakut hosts to kill them in their sleep. A frustrated guard first leveled these accusations against Zhensky; they were subsequently corroborated by every living guard who had served under him.

Zhensky kept a range of memorabilia from the writers he killed or had killed, all of which he sold very quickly once his troubles became public. His wife, Lyudmila Yakovlevna Zhenskaya, speculated that the money went to bribe his way out of legal trouble and out of Russia: shortly before his trial was due to begin, he simply vanished and has not been heard from since. Lyudmila Yakovlevna noted that her husband was a prolific poet and essayist himself; he read and could recite by heart many of the works for which his inmates were sentenced to jail. His work, however, was rejected by virtually every literary publication of note in the former Soviet Union.

Estimated value: Given the box's age, its workmanship, and the silver and jade veins, it could probably command a price in the low six figures. It is something of a museum piece, which would increase demand at the same time it draws away more free-spending but secretive buyers, who have no desire to parse small bids in the company of tweedy near–public servants. Sold in the right way, with the appropriate selective advertising and emphasis on the proper details (the inscription, rather than the fine vein work and precious metal and minerals), the price could rise as high as $500,000.

The power thereof is perfect.

❦

The night ended, for better or worse, kissless in my car. Hannah, her patchy veneer of calm fraying at points over her unease, said that we would see each other tomorrow, though not where, when, or how. I tried a couple of times on the drive home to ask about the bearded man at the bar, but she stuck to her claim that he resembled her father, and once her voice began to rise and tighten with irritation, I backed off. This was obviously untrue, but she was even more obviously the most attractive woman who had ever been in my car. As I said before, I didn't want to press what seemed at the time – wrongly, as it turned out – a minor point.

As she left the car, she thanked me for dinner and a lovely evening and ran her smooth hand down the side of my face and neck, stopping just inside my shirt collar. I leaned across and reached for her, but unfortunately I had forgotten to put the car in park, and it started to inch forward. Suave, I know, ending an evening with a car accident. I pulled the emergency brake, and both of us just missed smacking our heads on the windshield. Fearing for her safety (I told myself), she shut the door, waved, and strode up the driveway to her house. Another wave from the top of the walk, and I drove off.

By the next morning, the weather had cleared and everything looked scrubbed and sparkling, the edges of buildings and tops of trees a bit too sharp to be real, the sky too glassy blue not to be painted. Intricate little frost fronds snaked across one of my apartment's windows from opposite corners, greeted each other, and merged into a white crystal bruise: a Saturday-morning gift. It was easily the most beautiful thing in my apartment, and it would melt by noon. Meanwhile, I pulled a blue button-down shirt – my only semi-ironed shirt – from where it hung, scrunched into the wall of my closet, put on a tie and a pair of slacks, and left my minimalist squalor to meet Professor Jadid for lunch.

On my way to Wickenden, though, I wanted to stop by the Talcott playing field. I had liked Reverend Makgabo immensely, though I could hardly say why: we hadn't really done more than exchange pleasantries. But his quiet self-possession seemed an antidote to Hampden's excessively hearty posturing. More to the point, I wondered whether he knew anything else about Hannah. I suppose I mumbled something to myself about checking any potential source, some sort of journalistic rationalization, but, really, I was just interested in her. As captivating and attractive as she was, there also seemed something closed and unreadable about her, and not just because of her reaction to the man at the bar. I did not have high hopes for a priest's gossiping, but I figured it was worth at least a greeting.

When I got to the playing field, Reverend Makgabo, dressed in a green-and-white-striped rugby shirt and shorts, stood in the center of about twenty seated teenage boys, holding and gesticulating with a rugby ball. '. . . and you must meet academic standards. This means that if you wish to play with us, no failing grades, no skipping classes, no fighting, no suspensions. They say that what you call soccer is a gentleman's game played by hooligans, and rugby is a hooligan's game played by gentlemen. I shall expect no less. Now, first, you must get your body prepared. Run around this field four times and then return here.' As the boys took off, some sprinting too soon, some loping, he looked up, saw me, and waved me over.

'This is an unusual clothing decision for rugby indeed,' he said, moving a hand up and down as though I were modeling my clothes. 'I haven't seen it since my primary school. You know, we used to tackle by grabbing ties.' He tossed me the rugby ball in an underhanded sort of spin move.

'I can't play this morning, unfortunately. I just stopped by to say hello and see whether maybe I

could write an article about the Lincoln rugby team.'
I tossed the ball back.

Makgabo laughed. 'No, no. The Lincoln Rugby
Club, I think. That sounds very nice, very professional. Yes, of course, I think an article would be a
good idea.'

'Okay. I don't have my notebook with me now,
but . . .'

'Ah, that's fine. I have no time to talk now anyway.
But we play here every Saturday, if you really are
curious. We try to begin around eleven. Then we
try to have the boys at the train station by three-
thirty.'

'Where are your players from?'

'Mainly New Haven. I know them from my
volunteer work there. Many of them, this is the first
time they have traveled outside of the city. And I am
guessing, for many residents of *this* fine small city,
this would be the first time they have seen so many
black boys in one place.' He laughed, and I giggled,
too, with that mixture of unease, guilt, and a desire
to please and ingratiate that follows almost any
cross-racial racial joking.

'So Reverend Hampden never shows up?'

'Ah, no. I do wish he would, but no,' he said,
chuckling to himself.

'How come? Your wish, I mean, not his absence.'

'My first coach told me that frustrations are best
excised and differences best settled on the pitch. They
cannot fester, they cannot breed resentment: You

tackle someone, you help him up again. He tackles you, he helps you up again.'

'The humanizing power of violence, is that the angle I should take?'

'Oh, no. Oh, no. The humanizing power of sport, perhaps. Anyway, this is perhaps too small and, shall we say, unimportant a crowd for Reverend Hampden.'

'You jealous?'

'No, no. I am quite happy working as I see fit. This field is also a ministry of sorts, you know.'

'I'll be sure to put that in the article.'

'Yes, I do hope that you would. Are you going to meet your friend?'

'Which one?'

'Which one?' he said, giggling. 'You know well which one.'

'Hannah?' He nodded. 'No, I'm going to meet an old friend in Wickenden for lunch.'

'Ah. I thought perhaps someone was getting married. Schoolboy dress so early on a Saturday. You must call or come by the church anytime if you really do wish to write an article about us. I hope you do.'

When I walked through the heavy mahogany front doors, then the glass-fronted, double swinging saloon doors of the Blue Point, Professor Jadid was sitting at a table by the window, smoking and chatting warmly with a middle-aged couple standing over his table. Jadid sat still, attentive and feline, while the smoke from his cigarette glittered with dust as it poured upward through the sunbeams. Both the man and the woman were speaking without gesticulating. They looked like a couple whose tastes had merged to the point where they dressed, stood, and held their heads alike, naturally and unaffectedly. Jadid saw me, grinned, half stood, and waved me over to the table. 'You're precisely on time, Mr Tomm. I'm glad to see you. I'd like you to meet Mr and Mrs O'Sullivan, the owners and dear old friends of mine.'

The man, I saw as I approached the table, was softer and more genial in appearance than his wife, who had a look of vague and permanent disapproval around the corners of her mouth. He introduced himself as Jerry. 'So, you're another graduate of the Jadid Academy of Fine Living, are you?' I didn't get the joke and looked from him to his wife, who didn't seem to find it funny. 'This man here's one of our best customers,' said Jerry, clapping Professor Jadid on the shoulder incongruously. 'Also probably the best cook in Wickenden.' He stood grinning, waiting a beat too long for the rest of us to appreciate the joke. The professor just smiled, closed his eyes, and bobbed his head slightly from side to side in a gesture of agreeable sufferance. 'Can we bring you gentlemen a drink along with the menu?'

The professor looked up at me. I asked for one of whatever they had on draft. Jadid ordered a glass of Fumé Blanc. I had no idea whether that was beer, wine, or liquor.

'I didn't know you cooked,' I said, slipping onto the banquette across from Professor Jadid.

'Indeed. A necessary and civilizing art. Culinary proficiency is not among my wife's many, many virtues. And in my family the men have always been cooks by proclivity and teachers and rabbis by profession. I suppose one out of two isn't bad for an immigrant.' Jerry brought an amber-colored beer for me ('Harpoon's Christmas') and white wine ('Sakonnet's finest') for the professor.

'Rabbis?' I watched him tuck his napkin into his starched collar and did the same.

'Yes, well, in most countries, at least, my name leads most people in another direction. I am now almost totally nonpracticing. I remain Jewish for persecution purposes alone, as my elder son jokes. A reverse casualty of the Second World War, I suppose.'

'What do you mean?'

He sighed. 'You know, I find nothing remarkable about my own speech, but for some reason the first question virtually every former student of mine ever asks, once we're speaking as friends rather than as professor and student, is where my accent comes from.'

I laughed, and he nodded slowly, eyes closed, grinning like a sleepy cat.

'Yes. Well, what would you guess? Bear in mind, you cannot offend me by guessing incorrectly, nor, unless I read you too simply, do I believe you will guess accurately. But first, while you're guessing, may I order us lunch? Is there anything you don't eat? No? Good.' He raised his hand, and Jerry's wife walked over, notebook in hand and smile half-heartedly plastered in place. Professor Jadid ordered a half dozen Wellfleets and a half dozen Malpeques, then a waterzooi for himself, a bowl of cioppino for me, and a half bottle of the Fumé.

'Maura runs the wine cellar and oversees the financial aspects of the restaurant,' he whispered as she walked away. 'I know she seems dour, but she's just a bit shy, and better suited to numbers than people. A wonderful palate, though. So let's hear your guess.'

'Well, I'd guess German, but you don't look very German. I would also guess that you would be a direct casualty, not a reverse one, whatever that means, if you were German, Jewish, and the age you are.'

'Good. Sound reasoning, and correct.'

'I also might guess Swiss or Austrian,' I continued, 'but the same reasoning probably holds as with German. Hungarian, maybe?' He was a little darker than me, with greenish eyes and gray hair: in Hollywood he could have played a dozen different ethnicities. 'Spanish? Turkish? Sure, I'll guess half Hungarian, half Turkish, but with something else thrown in.'

'As intelligent a guess as I would have expected from you, Mr Tomm. But –'

'Professor, could I ask you to call me Paul?'

'Of course. Paul. Born and raised in Tabriz, as a matter of fact.'

My geography got a little shaky east of Cape Cod and south of Baltimore. 'I don't mean to flaunt my ignorance, but where is Tabriz?'

'In Iran, actually, though we usually call ourselves Persian, if you don't mind. When Persian Jews were forcibly converted, they were called Jadid al-Islam, or new Muslims. For reasons lost to me, one of my forebears adopted that moniker as our family name. Persia, rather than Iran, connotes the tolerance and sophistication that once marked that part of the world, and I hope will again.' He raised his glass and drank to his own statement; I hurriedly tried to do the same but wound up slopping beer onto the table.

'So what do you mean by reverse casualty, then?'

'We were more or less run out of the country after 1948. It wasn't uncommon, you know, in those countries. One of history's crueler ironies. Israel was meant to give the Jews a safe haven in the world, a noble aspiration, especially in light of what had transpired so recently. As a result, though, all over the Middle East, Jews were made refugees from the cities – sometimes even from the houses – where they had lived for centuries. The house where I grew up had been built by my great-great-great-grand-father, almost two hundred years earlier. When we left, we left in a hurry. I don't even know who's there now.'

'So did you go to Israel?'

'No, no. My father briefly considered it, you know, but after centuries of living in Persia and among Christians, Muslims, Zoroastrians – all sorts, really – I don't know that he would have survived in an entirely Jewish atmosphere. Anyway, a friend of his, a Dutchman, in fact, whom he had known before the war and who survived the camps, contacted him in 1950 and invited him to become rabbi to what remained of the Sephardic community in Leiden. So we ended up there instead, which, I suppose, is why I sound partly German, though I don't mean to make your Dutch blood boil at the comparison. Add to that a doughty woman from Belfast, Mrs McClenahan, who raised me and my brothers after our mother died, and there you have my pattern of speech, which, I have been told, is almost totally unique.'

Just then Maura appeared at our table with two steaming bowls in hand and a dozen oysters on a glass plate, along with little pots of what she explained were cocktail sauce, a porter mignonette, and soy sauce mixed with ginger and lime juice. Ordinarily I run quickly away from raw seafood, and in all the years I had lived in the Northeast, I had never tasted an oyster. But I didn't want Professor Jadid to think I was some sort of rube. As it was, I just picked it up, swallowed, and as it traveled down my gullet like a refrigerated and reversed sneeze, I wondered why anyone would choose to eat these things and whether I could keep it from bouncing back up once it hit my stomach. She set the white stew in front of the professor and the red in front of me and asked, 'You know why he ordered these two dishes, don't you?' I shook my head. 'They're both his.'

I looked at the professor questioningly. Maura laughed. 'Anton comes in and messes around in our kitchen some Mondays, when the restaurant's dark. Both of these are his recipes. I think he's done . . . what? Four, five dishes that are on the permanent menu?'

'Five,' he said, grinning like a spelling-bee winner. 'Cioppino, waterzooi, shark tagine . . . what else, what else? Grilled fish with chermoula, and the Jadid martini. Gin with a dash of grappa and a lime peel on the rocks.'

'Sure, but, Anton, has anybody other than you ever ordered the Jadid martini?' she asked.

'The great and manifold deficiencies in other people's taste, my dear, are hardly my responsibility. All I can do is present a superior invention to the public. I can't force it on them.' She walked away laughing, and the smile erased about ten years from her face.

'So, tell me about your story now,' the professor said, dabbing soup from the corners of his mouth. The man probably could have found a way to spelunk elegantly. 'Tell me what happens in this "real world" we professors keep hearing so much about. I'm quite curious to know what you've discovered about Jaan.'

'Well, unfortunately, not too much. I still don't know how he died, and the coroner performing the autopsy was hit by a car two days ago.'

'My God. What happened? Is he all right?'

'No. It killed him. Hit-and-run. Driver didn't even stop.'

'How awful.'

'I know. He hadn't quite finished yet, but he did say that there was something odd about the body. The only person who seemed to know Jaan at all is Hannah, who –'

'Who is Hannah?'

'Sorry. She's a music teacher, a neighbor of his.'

'Whom you also know well enough to refer to by her first name in conversation.'

'Yeah, well . . . I do, I guess. She's unusual.'

'Unusual enough to make you stammer and blush. Go on.'

'Your nephew confirmed what you told me, that Jaan was arrested twice, both times for firing a gun.'

'That reminds me, this story piqued Joseph's interest. He ran into a bit of trouble this fall, and he's been kept firmly at his desk for the past several weeks. Your little problem has finally given him a bit of much-needed stimulation.'

'What sort of trouble?'

Professor Jadid sighed and crinkled his eyes. 'Joseph has always been something of a roughneck, I suppose. He gets it from his father, my older brother, Daniel, who was as enamored of Leiden's boxing rings and meaner quarters as I was of its libraries. Anyway, Joseph is quick-minded, diligent, and at heart really very decent, but he's stubborn as a cart horse and a bit too quick to resort to violence. In October a car hit his while he was waiting in it, in a parking lot. He began arguing with the driver; it escalated into shoving, and Joseph, sadly, struck the other driver, breaking his nose and knocking out two of his teeth. The driver happened to be a friend of the mayor's. So, much to his displeasure, Joseph has been, as he puts it, "riding a desk" for the past five weeks. I believe he has a case of cabin fever. In any event, he asked me to ask you whether you might be able to stop by and see him on Monday.'

'What, you mean at the police station here? Sure.'

'Wonderful. I'll tell him this evening. As I said earlier, Joseph can be rather difficult. But if he helped you once and apparently is about to do so again, then he must have liked you.'

'Can I ask you a question? Something that stuck in my mind from my conversation with Joe?'

'Of course.'

'Why did he call you Uncle Abe?'

'Ah. My given name is Avram. I changed it to Anton when I enrolled in university in Leiden. Consequently, my parents, grandparents, aunts, and uncles called me Avi; my university friends and professional colleagues here in Wickenden call me Anton; and my wife, younger relations, and close friends know me as Abe. Rather ludicrous, if you ask me, but, in my own defense, I'll simply say that changing my name seemed rather a modern idea at the time.'

'Impressive. Nobody has ever called me anything but Paul. But can I ask another question?'

'I believe you just did, but I assume you mean another one on top of that. By all means.'

'You told me that Professor Pühapäev wasn't fired because he had tenure. But how did that work? I mean, professors get suspended for stupid comments, for even hints of sexual harassment. But you've got a guy shooting guns out the window of your department, he barely taught anything, he didn't really advise anybody. I know you told me it was kept out of the newspapers, but the cops knew about it. Surely you could have dealt with him quietly, right?'

The professor wiped his mouth with the napkin and poured the last of the wine into our glasses. 'Tell me, do journalists actually use the phrase "off the record," or is that just in films?'

'No, we say that.'

'Excellent. Then this conversation is, as you would say, off the record.'

I nodded.

'The first time Jaan fired his weapon was in January 1995. He struck a cat, as I told you, and nearly frightened the department's night watchman to death. The chair of the department at the time was Professor Crowley. Now, Hamilton had been quite a vocal supporter of Jaan's during his early days here, when other members of the department had doubts about Jaan's fitness as a professor in a university of this caliber. He supported Jaan's application for tenure, which was ultimately successful.

'When Jaan first shot through the window, Hamilton worked assiduously to keep the information out of the papers, and to keep knowledge of the incident as quiet as possible. I don't know how he extracted promises from the police not to divulge the information to the press, but I would not be in the least surprised if money changed hands. It is Wickenden, after all. I believe that only four professors, myself included, knew what Jaan had done. This was the tail end of Hamilton's fame, but he still was a luminary here. He attracted plenty of students and attention, and he made it known that if we took action against Jaan – against *his* protégé, as he saw it – he would leave. I don't know what Hamilton's reputation is among students, but I presume that the force of his ego is well known. Consequently, no action was taken: Jaan promised not to carry a handgun to the university anymore, and we promised to say no more about it.

'Three years later, though, at the end of summer, just before the students were due to return, Jaan did the same thing again: nighttime, shadow, mistaken reaction, and so forth. This time, as it happens, the gunshot struck the hood of Professor Crowley's Mercedes. When he was in it. He was unharmed but quite terrified, and he insisted that Jaan be fired, jailed, fined – everything but drawn and quartered. I was chair of the department then. For better or worse, I did precisely what Hamilton had done the first time, reasoning that if we were to discipline him in any way now, then information about his infraction and our – for lack of a more delicate word – conspiracy would necessarily come to light. I wished to avoid a scandal. So the same promises were extracted, the same apologies made, the same reporters frozen out, the same newspaper editors – Wickenden grads almost to a man – cajoled and pressured, with the same result.

'The only strange thing was, when I told Jaan that he would go to jail, publicity be damned, if I heard even a rumor that he was carrying a handgun again, I received a letter the following day from Vernum Sickle.'

'That name sounds familiar.'

'Yes, it's almost unforgettable, isn't it? Dickensian, you might say, if you were the sort of person who said such asinine things. In which case we could hardly be having lunch together. Anyway, Sickle is perhaps the finest, and certainly the most expensive, criminal defense attorney in New England. He mostly represents organized-crime families, as I understand it, with the occasional high-profile politician thrown in for variety. Mr Sickle warned me to cease harassment of his client, Professor Jaan Pühapäev, or he would sue me, the department, and the university for slander, and if I took any action based on rumor, as

I had threatened to do . . . well, then something awful would happen, and so on and so forth. He also cautioned that although we were a private university, we nonetheless received federal grants and municipal support and therefore were bound by the Fourth Amendment, which meant that we had no right to search Jaan's office or person. I don't know that this reasoning was correct, but it was certainly intimidating. A great deal of legalistic saber rattling. But it worked: Jaan stayed on, and he never again fired his weapon, though I would bet my last sou that he carried one nonetheless.

'Sickle's involvement intrigued me, as it showed that Jaan was not nearly as unworldly as he appeared. Naturally, Jaan could have easily picked Sickle's name from one of the innumerable articles in which he manages to get mentioned, but the letter arrived so soon after the incident that I presume they must have already known each other. As I said, all off the record.'

'Well, Professor, you know, I really would like to use this information. It's not just an obit anymore. The story intrigued me as much as it did your nephew. Something isn't right with all this. As far as I'm concerned, I don't have to say it comes from you; I can attribute it to "a colleague" or "a source in the university." But the story does need actual quotes.'

Professor Jadid gazed out the window. We were right at the edge of downtown, and in the late-afternoon winter light, the buildings looked like a jumble of cinnamon-toast Legos, mellow and sweet. The river caught the light and looked warm and golden, though in fact it was probably freezing and corrosive to the touch. 'Let me consider that request. It would be a shame were my department to be maligned. You certainly are engaging in a commendable amount of investigation, considering the size of your readership.'

'Size of readership has nothing to do with it,' I said, perhaps a bit more sharply and defensively than I should have. 'Besides, there's an editor in Boston who's interested. Could lead to a job in Boston.'

'That's wonderful news. A prestigious paper in a major city at your age? Outstanding. Full congratulations are in order, as are two glasses of brandy,' he said, signaling Maura at the bar. 'It may not be my place to mention this, but you always struck me as the type of person who is both ambitious and frightened of your ambition. Is that accurate?'

'I don't know, really. Frightened? Probably not. I like doing well.'

'Indeed. I would hardly dispute that. I would just remind you that if ambition unleashed can be ruthless, ambition chained to as firm a sense of decorum and propriety as you clearly possess is essential. Do good, Paul, but that does not mean that you shouldn't also do well. Perhaps you require a few lessons on this subject from Ms Park.'

'Mia. How is she?'

'One of the smartest students I have ever had

the pleasure to teach. And one of the most argumentative. I must say, intending no offense, that I have no small amount of difficulty seeing the two of you as a pair.'

I laughed. 'You're not the only one. Much better as friends than we were as a couple, though I've hardly seen her in almost a year.'

'It happens. I won't pry too much by asking you about this music teacher, but if you're fond enough to blush over her, it must be something indeed. Good luck.'

'Thank you.'

'Now, we ought to have one last toast before braving the winter afternoon. Perhaps we ought to toast gloomy, possibly criminal professors with horrible aim but wonderful effects on the careers of young reporters. No, a bit long, I suppose. What about a toast to reporters and professors alike: To discovery.'

And to that we drank.

As I drove back along the purplish, dusk-softened streets, a thousand questions ran through my head: How and why did Pühapäev know Sickle? Was Professor Jadid's story about Crowley's cover-up true? Could I ever confirm it, if it was? What had Joe Jadid found, and why was he taking any sort of interest in some podunk reporter's inquiry?

One question, though, rose above all of them: Was Hannah busy tonight?

THE CRYING QUEEN

⌇⌇

Followinge the kinge's de-gradation comes his deathe, whereupon the Queen dothe bathe with most chaste and reverend tears the broken and disused bodye of her Lorde, and – Lo! – by those teares Chryste do it witness a rebirthe, which dothe free the kinge from all earthly suffering, and the filthe and quicknesse of this life, and he will be transformed into that which has no equal.

— JOHN FOXWELL, *On Rare and Wonderful Things*

The rickety silver bus chuffed slowly up Pragas *iela*, leaving a trail of brown slush and black smoke in its wake. The horn was whining and ineffectual, producing the sound of a goose trapped somewhere deep in the exhaust system. The driver sounded it constantly in a Morse code–like barrage of long and short blasts; the effect was more comic than imposing.

Before leaving the Latvija Hotel – a state-run,

concrete-drab monstrosity that held an inordinate appeal for cockroaches and rodents but almost none for humans – the driver had 'fixed' the bus's windshield wipers, which had frozen during the night, trapped beneath the gray highway slurry that accumulated in the windshield grooves. Using his shoe as a hammer and the jagged neck of a broken beer bottle as a chisel, he had chipped away the muck and pried them free, perhaps too enthusiastically: they now moved back and forth a good six inches in front of the window, repeatedly slapping into each other, ironically applauding his efforts as he blindly and instinctively pulled into the bus station's parking lot.

As his passengers disembarked, each one thanked him for the ride. No Soviet passenger would ever have done that. But these riders were British, and they disembarked in a funereal procession of beige raincoats, gray caps, taupe and vomit-green scarves, patchy galoshes, and spindly umbrellas. The tour guide and the bus driver agreed that this was the easiest job they had ever done: no drunken factory workers from Krasnoyarsk; no hectoring babushkas from Petrograd; no condescending 'Comrades' visiting the provinces from Moscow. These tourists were polite, obedient, snaggle-toothed fellow travelers from Islington and Jericho spending their winter holiday (none of them called it 'Christmas') in the socialist paradise of Latvia.

When the bus stopped, the guide used his sweaty

hand to plaster a few strands of hair over his spotty pate. He cleared his throat noisily and spit something foul onto the floor of the bus as he disembarked. 'If you will please to follow me,' he called, raising his red umbrella above the crowd, 'we now go to wondrous Central Market of Riga, where to find all manner of production from across workers' state of Soviet Union. Please to come this way, please.'

As the guide turned around, one of the Britons caught him by the arm and whispered something into his ear. Alone among his companions, he possessed both a hairbrush and proficiency in Russian, and he looked to be about twenty years younger than the youngest of his countrymen. A ripple of concern briefly disturbed the guide's bored expression, and he instinctively looked over both shoulders to see if anyone had heard what the young man had asked. No one had. 'Here,' said the Briton, placing a reassuring hand on the guide's upper arm, 'I promise to return this evening – ten at the latest – to the hotel. After that, please, send the police looking for me; tell them I sneaked out of my room; tell them whatever you like. But I would like just a little time to explore the city on my own. I promise to make it worth your while,' he said, holding out his hand with a twenty-pound note folded thinly between his third and fourth fingers. 'I'll have another one of these for you tonight.'

The tour guide shook his hand, pocketed the bill, and nodded quickly. 'If I were KGB, I would take this money, follow you, and arrest you. If you are KGB . . . well, I don't want to think about that. Slip away in the market. Do nothing illegal, do you hear me?' He jabbed a finger into the young man's side: his petty official's bullying manner returned when he spoke his own language. 'If you embarrass me in any way, I promise that your stay in the workers' paradise will be more work and less paradise than you can imagine. I will visit your room tonight at ten-thirty, where I'll expect to find you waiting for me with another little gift.' The two men shook hands again. The Englishman fell back in line and started chatting with a retired schoolteacher from St John's Wood.

As the group turned the corner, they saw five silver airplane hangars in front of them, from which spilled a busy and uncountable mass of people, goods, colors, and smells. 'Esteemed visitors, welcome please to Central Market of Riga,' said the guide, accenting his words with little punches of his red umbrella. 'Here to find what souvenirs and gifts you need from Soviet Union, remembering to give gifts to inspector of customs at the hotel for checking. Meeting back here please at one-thirty for driving to hotel and lunch.'

The Englishman waited for the retired schoolteacher to toddle off in the direction of some carved Georgian wine horns, shook off the Tatar with a well-placed elbow, and pulled a sheet of paper from his pocket. Following the paper's directions, he walked past a knot of suspicious-looking Uzbek pumpkin sellers, nearly ran into a clutch of Kyrgyz men in tall black-and-white *telpeks* chattering and sipping from bowls of tea, briefly paused before an array of Dagestani daggers (all fake, all dull), and noticed a small wooden door wedged between two stalls on the back wall. He paused to taste some acacia honey – not only did the old seller's eyes light up, but his beard seemed to rise from his chest when the Englishman smiled – walked a short ways past the honey stall, doubled back behind it, and slipped through the door.

In near darkness, around a round wooden table, sat two men. One was dark-skinned and rough-looking, with vaguely Asiatic features, a menacing expression, and a broad mustache that drooped downward at the corners of his mouth. He glowered as the door opened, and he reached his right hand under the table, never taking his eyes from the Englishman. Next to him sat a slender little birdlike man, with sandy hair, unmemorable features, and a bemused welcoming smile. He could have passed for a care-worn thirty or a well-preserved sixty.

'You Voskresenyov, then?' the Englishman asked.

The avian man nodded. 'You look like your father,' he said in slightly accented English.

'Not anymore I don't.'

'Mr Hewley, that's in rather poor taste, and completely unbecoming a young man as fortunate as yourself.'

Hewley laughed. 'What, you mean fortunate like I got debts to choke a pig? Fortunate like my flat's about to be seized? Fortunate like I can't get a draw at –'

Voskresenyov held up a hand and closed his eyes placatingly. 'Mr Hewley, I refer to your future position, not your present one. If I were unaware that your father's unfortunate and sudden death had left you, as you might say, in the lurch, I would not have gone to the trouble of inviting you here today. Sit, please.' He gestured to an empty chair, which the dark-skinned man kicked toward Hewley unceremoniously.

'Who's Charlie Chan there, then?'

'Fortunately for you, Timur does not understand English. He is Kazakh, not Chinese, and he takes great and rather violent offense at being mistaken for anything other than Kazakh. Timur is a friend. He oversees all arrangements for my physical security.'

'He's the muscle, then, is he?' Hewley stood up and walked over to Timur, making little feints and head bobs while carefully staying out of the man's reach. 'What's he, trained killer? Karate and nunchakus and all that?'

'No, Mr Hewley, I believe those are Japanese. Do sit down, won't you? Thank you. You brought what you were instructed to bring?'

'Hang on a minute. Let's see yours first. I reckon Mao Tse fucking Hirohito Kazakh Hard Man can just about rip my arms out whenever he likes anyway.'

Voskresenyov shrugged. 'No one is here to rob you, Mr Hewley, and certainly not to hurt you. After all, what would Sergei Kirilovich say if you opened the door tonight at ten-thirty with a twenty-pound note stuck to your bloody stump?'

'How did you –'

Voskresenyov waved the question away and pulled a briefcase onto the table. He opened it and held it toward Hewley. 'One hundred thousand pounds. Count it if you like. And more important than the money are these letters' – he pulled out several envelopes from his jacket and placed them on top of the money – 'guaranteed to placate any inquisitive customs inspectors in either of our countries. You'll want to keep those safe, even after you return to England. And more important than that, you have my word, as a friend of your father's, that should the letters fail, I will see that you return safely to London. With all your money and all your limbs. Now, if you would . . .' Voskresenyov's eyes lit up, and his very features seemed to sharpen as he leaned across the table toward Hewley.

Hewley reached into the inside pocket of his coat and withdrew a lacquer box, about the size of a pack of cigarettes. He pulled on a pair of white cloth gloves, opened the box, and carefully withdrew a deck of playing cards. Voskresenyov clapped his hands together. 'Ah. This is the first time I have seen these cards. The first time, I believe, that they have traveled out of England. And, judging from their extraordinary condition, one of the few times they have been touched since the late eighteenth century. Could I ask you, please, to place the four queens faceup on the table?' Hewley laid a maroon chamois on the table. He leafed through the cards, laying each queen as he found it on the cloth on the table. 'Thank you. That is all I wished to see. Please, if you would be more comfortable, put the cards back in the box and set the box between us on the table. I promise you, again, no harm will come to it or you.'

'So how should we do this, then? One-two-three go? I give you the cards, you pass me the satchel?'

'Certainly, if you wish. As I said, I do not intend to rob you, and, given Timur's presence and the unfamiliarity of your surroundings, you are unable to rob me, so however you wish to exchange the goods.'

Hewley drummed his fingers on the table and looked straight at the other two men. 'I could have done, though. Robbed you. Anywhere else.'

Voskresenyov laughed. 'I know. Your reputation did precede you. You descended from the best.'

'I got it,' Hewley said, escalating from finger drumming to slapping his palms on the table in a quick rhythm. 'How about we play a hand of poker, eh? These queens can't stay virgins forever.'

'I have no wish to handle these cards any more than necessary. The queens will stay undefiled. However, as you are technically my guest, I cannot refuse such a slight wish as a hand of poker. For what stakes?'

Hewley started to pull out his wallet, then stopped suddenly and looked at Voskresenyov: a cartoonish, but not inaccurate, representation of a sudden thought. 'Why not play for what we got here? One hand, winner takes all.'

'You certainly are a reckless young man,' laughed Voskresenyov. 'I offer you, in fair exchange, a sum sufficient to settle most, if not all, of your debts, and still you want more. What is that deck of cards worth to you anyway?'

'It's not me that's buying, my old son.' Hewley winked. 'If you'll pay a hundred grand in a back room, all secret, I reckon I could fetch a bit more by holding a proper auction. Have Sotheby's over to check out the cards, make it public, all that.'

'I thought we had a deal, Mr Hewley, and if you wish to go into the same line of work as your father, your word must be beyond reproach. His was.'

'Yeah, and look where it got him. You know, we couldn't even have a viewing for him? Pulled him up from the bottom of the Severn gray as an old fish, all bloated and peeling like one, too. Not for me, that sort of death.' Hewley shuddered, then straightened up and smacked the table. 'And I'm feeling in good spirits today. Lucky, you know what I mean? One hand of poker, and the winner walks off with a hundred grand and this deck of cards, worth – I don't know – we could say, maybe . . . twice that?'

Voskresenyov shrugged. 'If you like. Only I must beg you, if you should win, forgo the auction and name your price in this room. I really have taken a fancy to those queens.'

'You don't mind me asking, how's a Russian like you come up with this kind of bread? I thought all of you were supposed to be equal-like, you know?'

'Yes, equal. We are. But some are more equal than others. Without causing offense, I wish to observe that another reason your father lived as long and succeeded as well as he did was his distinct lack of curiosity. Never comes to any good.' He turned to the Kazakh and asked in Russian, 'Does Tezvadze still have a stall here?' The Kazakh nodded. 'He still sells the same wares as always?' Another nod. 'Fine. Go buy a deck.' He handed Timur a few bills, and as the Kazakh was leaving, he grabbed his arm. 'And bring back a dealer, too. The usual arrangement.'

As Timur left, Voskresenyov explained, 'Tezvadze sells Georgian playing cards. He claims they're hand-painted, but if that is so, they have been painted by a man with the steadiest hands I've ever seen. He sells them to Balts, Russians, and tourists too scared to wander down below the Caucasus. The suits are a bit different than what you are used to, but it should serve. As for the dealer ... well, let's see who Timur finds. Will you have a drink while we wait?' Voskresenyov brought a ceramic bottle up from under the table.

'What's that, then?'

'Balsam. Rigas Melnais Balzams. A local specialty.

Some never acquire a taste for it, but I have to say that since I started drinking it, I have never been troubled by illness. Particularly effective in dispelling the sorts of complaints common in an English climate.' He took a deep swig from the bottle and passed it across the table.

Hewley sniffed from the bottle and recoiled. 'Ugh. What is this muck?'

'Nobody knows, really. Some wormwood, hyssop, orange peel, oak bark, blossoms of some sort. It's a secret.'

Hewley took a deep draft, swallowed, retched, fell backward in his chair, righted himself, and ran his fingers through his hair. Voskresenyov laughed, and the door opened. Timur squeezed through the doorframe, followed by a slender girl of about twelve or thirteen in a dirty brown frock, blindfolded. He threw a deck of cards onto the table and said, in Russian, 'Found her wandering by the Bashkir tea women.'

The girl was trembling silently, and a tear ran from beneath her blindfold onto Timur's hand, which was laid across her collarbone, guiding her forward.

'Here, girl, come over here.' The girl straightened, sniffled loudly, and walked toward Voskresenyov with as much direction and self-assurance as if she had no blindfold on. 'You know how to deal cards?' She nodded. 'I'll give you a choice. In thirty minutes you can have more money than your father makes in five years, or in thirty minutes you can meet your first of thousands of husbands. Which would you prefer?'

The girl suddenly scratched Voskresenyov's face and yowled. 'Russian pig! Kazakh cunt! I know your voices –' Voskresenyov backhanded her hard enough to knock her to the ground. She inhaled sharply but did not bawl. Timur grabbed both of her wrists in one hand and yanked her standing.

'All we want you to do is to deal a simple hand of cards,' said Voskresenyov softly. He stroked her hair, and she recoiled as if burned. 'Deal fairly. Straight. If you do that, we will pay you handsomely and send you on your way. Understood? But if you act out, or struggle, or scream, or lay a hand on any of us, your life will suddenly become quite short and painful. Now, do you love your parents?' The girl didn't move. 'Well, fine. The money will be yours. Give it to them; hide it from them. Whatever you wish. Now, if you agree, my associate will release you. If he releases you and you do anything other than what we agreed, we will not have a second conversation like this. Clear?' The girl nodded.

Timur released her, and Voskresenyov handed her a deck of cards. 'Shuffle and deal these cards, please. No, wait!' Voskresenyov took the deck back, laid four cards on the table, and turned to Hewley. 'The suits, as I said, differ. Swords, stars, cups, and cudgels, in that order. Now, are you ready? One hand. What game?'

'I'm a hold-'em man, myself,' said Hewley, his

confidence much shaken and his voice therefore much louder since the incident with the girl. 'Texas hold-'em.'

'Agreed. Nothing wild.' He turned to the girl. 'Deal, please. Two cards facedown to each of us – that is, just put them down on the table, one at a time, the same way they are in your hand. Good. Now put one over to the side, your right, and put three faceup – turned over, that is – right in front of you. Now one more to the side and one more faceup. Now the same again. Good. Now step back from the table. Mr Hewley, does that deal seem fair to you?'

Hewley nodded, swallowed hard.

'Good. Now, girl, here is more money than you have ever seen before in your life. Timur will show you out and remove the blindfold, and you will forget any of this ever happened. Make up a believable story about your nose, and please accept my apologies. Now go, go now, and don't you dare glance back at this door.'

Voskresenyov looked at the cards arrayed on the table – a ten of swords, an eight of cups, a knave of stars, an ace of stars, and a ten of cups – and peeked at his two hole cards. Hewley did the same. 'This game loses something without any betting,' Voskresenyov muttered. 'Mr Hewley,' he said clearly and loudly, 'are you ready to turn?'

'I am.'

Item 7: A playing card, approximately 2.4 centimeters longer and 1.2 centimeters narrower than the contemporary standard English or American playing card. One side – the back – is dark vermilion with gold trim. Inside the trim, written in interlocking fanciful letters, beginning at the top left corner and continuing clockwise around the card, it reads 'Sutcliffe Sanderson & Trout, Expert Craftsmen in All Manner of Etchery, with Particular Skill in the Crafting of Cartes des Jeux and in Small Ornate Writing, by Appointment of His Majesty Duke Mulebollocks of Fiddle-Dee-Dee, Printed with Permission of Nobody but Ourselves, London or Someplace Other.'

On the other side is a queen of spades, possessing the blocky geometric form and generic courtliness common to English playing cards of the late eighteenth and early nineteenth centuries. To judge from the detail around her and the fineness of the lines that define her, she comes from a copper etching done in the style of a woodblock print. The card's background is a mosaic of interlocking diamonds that Yazdeh Samizdanji and his followers in Tabriz used on their nonrepresentational cards (the design was inspired by a rare but famed series of lithographs from the court of Sicily's King Roger II). The queen holds a green alembic in one hand and a small coffin inscribed 'The King is dead, long live the King' in Latin in the other. A single tear sits in the middle of her left cheek, with a faint streak connecting it to her eye. To the few who know of this card's existence, it is commonly referred to as 'The Crying Queen of Hoxton.'

The king is the original material to be transformed; the process begins when it first begins to shed water. The queen's tear represents both the purifying attributes of water (and, transitively, alchemy) and the sadness of the king at passing from one life, one form, into another.

Date of manufacture: Late eighteenth or early nineteenth century.

Manufacturer: No company named Sutcliffe Sanderson & Trout was ever registered in any guild in London, or in England for that matter. Jan Pieterszoon van Soudcleft, a Flemish count fond of whist, bridge, Spanish wine, arcane scientific subjects, and exceptionally young girls, lived just east of London from 1792 to 1820, when he died of exposure after going for a New Year's stroll around his heath, completely naked except for his wig. When his only son sold off his father's estate and anglicized his name to Sutcliffe, the items auctioned included a letterpress and engravers' tools, both of which had been used infrequently, if at all. Count van Soudcleft also possessed a vast collection of Islamic woodblock art, all of which his son cursed and burned rather than sell. Playing-card historians have speculated that this deck – the only one registered to Sutcliffe Sanderson & Trout and the only example of a hybrid Islamic-English woodblock-engraved design – was inspired by the burned collection of prints.

The identities of Sanderson and Trout remain complete mysteries.

Place of origin: The cards seem to be English, judging from the language on the back of the cards, their shape and size, and the generic courtly representations of the face cards (French, Spanish, German, and Dutch court cards were all based on historical personages; only the English used generic figures).

Last known owner: Hugh Hewley, British antiquarian, antique dealer, and compulsive pickpocket. After he drowned during a fly-fishing accident in Wales, all of his possessions – debts as well as antiques – passed to his Cambridge-educated son

Antony, who worked as a freelance Russian inter-preter in London but whose principal income came from the poker table. Immediately following Hugh's death, Antony traveled to Latvia for reasons that remain unclear. When he returned, he handily paid off all of his father's outstanding debts and sold the store and everything in it to the Southall Icemen, a mid-seventies London gang run by Azim Mehmood and Stony Rosen. The cards were found nowhere in the store, which is odd, as Hugh attested that he always kept them locked in a safe in the back of his store and repeatedly refused their sale at any price, to any customer. The story was given out that the cards were on his person when he drowned, and they disintegrated at the bottom of the Severn.

Antony died, supposedly of a heroin overdose, two weeks after selling the business to the Icemen. He left no descendants.

Estimated value: Singular decks of cards can easily command upward of $100,000: consider that the buyers tend to be gamblers, often have large amounts of cash that it behooves them never to deposit or declare, and they are paying, in effect, for at least forty separate individual paintings.

In 1889 Prince Albert decided to shave and regrow his beard during the annual summer holiday at Balmoral; he had the royal portrait artist paint his picture every day for fifty-two days and then had a deck of cards printed to commemorate the process.

In 1972 agents acting for Frankie 'Chicken Man' Testa bought the deck in a private auction for $120,000; the deck became known as 'Al's Chops,' after the prince's facial hair as well as the Philadelphia restaurant where the Chicken Man held court.

In 1993 Wei Xiang, a graduate student in robotics at the University of California at Berkeley, used a mechanical arm attached to an airbrush to create fifty-two microchip-size playing cards, each featuring a different figure from the history of computing sciences. One of his professors offered to buy the deck from him for $15,000, but Wei, who had a particularly cluttered apartment, lost the cards shortly after bringing them home.

One can only speculate on what the cards would fetch should their sudden reemergence be announced.

*If it be cast onto the Earth, it will
separate the element of Earth from that of
Fire, the subtle from the gross.*

❧❧

I spent the drive home from the Blue Point trying
to figure out whether I should be driving home.
After saying good-bye to the professor, I had tried to
dispel the midday brandy fog by taking a short walk
through the new park built alongside the river – the
brick sidewalks and curved footbridges were some
bureaucrat's idea of 'European' – and following that
with a four-dollar cup of coffee at an orange-walled
café that replaced Mama Fatima's. Apparently Mama
Fatima herself had died a little over a year ago; her
husband had returned to Loule, and her sons had
sold her restaurant. It had gone from a dockworkers'
lunch counter to a focaccia, sprouts, and mochaccino
place catering to the high-rent bohemians who were
moving into the warehouses. The actual bohemians,
of course, had long since abandoned the area once it

had soaked up all of their cachet; they had moved out to Olneyton, while the programmers, lawyers, and doctors who wore their edginess with designer labels in plain sight soaked up the self-conscious trendiness. Still, the coffee was better than Mama Fatima's had been.

Fortunately, the ride home was incident-free, and I pulled into my space behind the No Parking sign and between the Dumpster and the banged-up white Celica at around six o'clock. The night was clear and dark, with that wonderful autumn smell of rotting leaves and smoke, and there was the normal amount of Saturday-night foot traffic downtown: absolutely none. The Colonial, a tavern across the street, with neon beer signs in the window and a neon musket and tricorne hat above the door, seemed fairly busy, but that was the only sign of life.

As I climbed the last flight of stairs to my apartment, I saw a note attached to my door, and I rolled my eyes: Mrs Tawell, my landlady, had an irritating habit of taping remonstrances to my door anytime I committed an infraction against one of her many unwritten rules. She and her husband lived one floor below me; they owned the ten apartments in this building, as well as the other commercial properties on the same lot. They were conscientious, I suppose, but a little high-strung about renting to a young single man from the Big City. Last week Mrs Tawell left a typed note informing me that my habit of bouncing a tennis ball against the wall 'threatens to loosen the struts and may eventually lead to a complete collapse of the building.' I knew it was an irritating habit: back home a neighbor would just have pounded back. But I suppose that wouldn't have been Yankee. She and Mr Tawell had been known to spend a weekend afternoon checking the tenants' transparent recycling bags and pointing out the bottles of alcohol to each other.

When I reached the door, I saw that the note had been affixed with a rusty spike hammered weakly into the door. It was a standard postcard-size envelope; on the front was a thick staff, two-pronged at the top, with two snakes curling around it, the sort of symbol you see at the top of some doctors' prescription forms. It looked like a drawing rather than a print, stamp, or photocopy. Below the staff was taped a piece of newsprint: my name and byline from the *Carrier*.

I opened the envelope: no letter, but when I reached inside, I pulled out a human eyetooth. It looked freshly extracted: there was a bloody smear on the inside of the envelope, and the streaks of blood still on the tooth and root were red, not brown. A rotten-tooth reek wafted up from the envelope. I gagged, unlocked my door with shaky hands, and quickly went in. For the first time since moving to Lincoln, I dead-bolted my door.

My answering-machine light was blinking, and when I pressed Play, Hannah's voice came on: 'Hello, Paul Tomm. It's me. It's Hannah. I was just calling to see whether you were back from lunch with the professor. I wanted to invite you to dinner with a high-school teacher. Call me when you get in. Thanks.' I picked up the phone to return her call but figured it might be worth my safety to let someone know about this note. The Olafssons wouldn't do anything about it. Art would have been interested, but he probably would have either insisted on my moving in with him and Donna or called the cops himself. I didn't want to make that big a deal about it. For a minute I was tempted to call my mother, but she might have spontaneously combusted from sheer worry. Even though he had no jurisdiction here, Joe Jadid seemed like the logical person to call: he had taken an interest in the case already and had been straightforward and decent before he even knew me. I doubted he'd be at work on Saturday night, but it would ease my mind to call. If he wasn't there, I'd tell Art.

He picked up on the first ring. 'Homicide, Jadid.'

'Yeah, this is Paul Tomm —'

'Live, from the boonies: it's Paul Tomm. What are you doing calling me here on a Saturday night?'

'What are you doing in the office on a Saturday night?'

'You think bad guys take weekends off? All part of my rehabilitation deal: I work Saturday to Wednesday, either graveyards or four-to-twelves. You're coming here to see me on Monday, right? Got a couple of things I think you could use.'

'Yeah, I'll be there, but listen, something just

happened that I thought maybe you should know about. I don't know, though; it happened at my place, and you're out in –'

'What is it? What's going on?'

'I found a weird note on my door when I got home tonight.'

'What did it say?'

'Nothing. There was this picture on the front, one of those doctor's symbols, you know, the staff with two snakes?'

'Yeah. It's called a caduceus.'

'A what? How'd you know that?'

'Caduceus. One of the many benefits of growing up with Uncle Abe, the man who knows everything there is to know, long as it's impractical. Anyway, you found a caduceus tacked to your door? That it?'

'No. There was a tooth inside.'

'Come again?'

'A tooth. A human eyetooth, it looks like. I think there's fresh blood on the root. Nothing else. No letter, no writing, no nothing. Just a bloody tooth.'

'Broken or pulled?'

'Pulled, it looks like. Root still attached and everything.'

'You call the police?'

'That's what I'm doing. Isn't it?'

'No, I mean *your* police. Whatever sisterfuckers watch the rest of your sisterfuckers way out there.'

'No, I haven't. And if you'd met them, you wouldn't have either.'

Jadid took a deep breath. I heard him squeaking in his chair and drumming his pen on the table. 'Look, just do me a favor, okay? This is the kind of thing I could get in a lot of trouble for.' He lowered his voice, and it sounded like he was cupping his hand over the receiver. 'Courts take a pretty dim view of cops who think they're cops everywhere. But fuck it; they take a dim view of me anyway. Listen, put the tooth back in the envelope and bring it with you when you come in on Monday. We'll send it to the lab, try to figure out where and who it came from. You want me to send someone to keep an eye on you? Unofficial, of course. Won't even be a cop. But you'll be safe with him around.'

I thought about it. But then I remembered that Hannah had called, and, as skittish as I was, I didn't want to ruin my evening's plans. I didn't even know if I was in danger or if it was some sort of joke, maybe from a local dentist I had somehow offended in one of my articles. A local dentist who knew how to pick locks and knew where I lived. Selfishly or not, wisely or not, I declined and told Joseph I'd see him on Monday.

'Okay, tough guy. You staying at your house tonight?'

'Well, I'm not sure. I'm actually on my way out right now.'

'Oh, well, how about that,' he said in a mocking falsetto.

'Huh?'

'Nothing. You one of those Woody Allen–type ass chasers with brains?' he chuckled.

I didn't say anything.

'Come on, I'm only kidding. Don't be like that. I'm sure she's lovely. But look, you need to be a little careful, okay? You might be dealing with some tough customers. And you're a college kid and a friend of Abe's; I just want to impress this on you. You don't carry around any sort of weapon, right?'

'Is that a joke? I haven't even hit anybody since I was twelve.'

'Not a joke at all. Look, just be careful, okay? I still don't know. I mean, there may not be any reason to worry; it may be nothing; everything I found may just be circumstance and all that. But still: be aware of your surroundings, like we always tell people. Keep your eyes open, and don't go wandering around unless you have to. How's your lock?'

'Yale, double bolt, with a – what is it – Schlage door lock.'

'Okay, that's good. Yale's a good lock. Just because someone made it to your front door doesn't mean they can make it inside. You use that double bolt, you understand me? And you remember that if someone's sending you a message, and they want to – how should we say? – deliver another one up close and personal, they got experience here and you don't. Don't do anything stupid.'

'Jesus Christ, Officer –'

'It's Detective, but look, just call me Joe.'

'Jesus Christ, Joe. I was a little nervous before I called you, but I'm fucking terrified now. What are you trying to do to me?'

Joe gave a short, slightly bitter laugh. 'Not trying to do anything. You probably got nothing to worry about. It's the ones that don't send notes that tend to cause problems. Just be safe, keep your eyes open, and you ought to be fine. Any other kind of trouble tonight, even a hint of a feeling of trouble, you call me at home, you got it? It's 555-7077. I'll bring the cavalry. Figure I'll see you Monday, though, right? Shift starts at four, but you come in early afternoon, I'll be there. Stay healthy.'

He hung up. I poured myself three fingers of Beam Black, dropped in two cubes of ice, and called Hannah.

'Hello?'

'Hi, Hannah, it's Paul.'

'I know,' she said, voice rising on the second word. The happiness and recognition in that tonal rise, combined with the whiskey, warmed me like a blanket over my heart. 'You're home late. I wasn't sure when you'd get back, unfortunately, so I just ate. There's some soup left, though, if you don't mind eating alone. I mean, alone with some company. Come over anyway?' It fell between a question and a soft command.

'Absolutely.'

*

I parked out of the sight line of Hannah's house and shut my door as quietly as possible: I didn't want to have another conversation with Mrs DeSouza, especially when I was arriving after dark. I knocked at her door and heard Hannah running (running!) to answer it.

'Aren't you prompt?' She had her hair pulled back and clipped, and as soon as I walked in, she leaned forward to kiss me. Even the most successful romantics doubtless see more kisses than they participate in, thanks to television and the movies, so that first kiss, seeing an actual person's face so close, is always a surprise. Hannah had a C-shaped scar, curled like a tiny subcutaneous sleeping shrimp, between her bottom eyelid and the top of her cheekbone. Her gray eyes had glitters of green and brown, and beautiful little crow's-feet were beginning to form at their corners.

'I wanted to get that out of the way,' she said, tilting her head down and looking out from under her forehead. I reached for her again, and she put a hand on my chest. 'Easy there. At least take off your coat first.' But when I did, she went into the kitchen. 'Are you hungry?' she called. 'I won't be insulted if you say no.'

'Actually, no.' It was true. I was coasting on the fumes of lunch, but nerves had killed what little appetite I should have had.

'Would you like a drink?'

'Sure. What do you have?'

'Only whiskey, I'm afraid.' She reappeared in the doorway between kitchen and living room holding a bottle of Jameson. 'I know: Irish whiskey, the drunk's favorite. Mine, too. Want some?'

I nodded, and she came back with two tumblers with ice and whiskey and the bottle tucked under her arm, and sat down next to me on the couch. She aimed a remote control at the stereo. A swell of basses filled the room like steam, followed by a woman's voice, unusually deep, that seeped into the spaces that the chorus made for her. '"Bless the Lord, O my Soul,"' Hannah said. 'Rachmaninoff's Vespers. I always skip the first track; this is the second. It's from a service called the All-Night Vigil that begins with vespers and lasts until matins. They sing, cense the church while they circle it. You have to stay standing up and chanting all night.'

'You've done it?'

'Three times. There was a Russian Orthodox church a few blocks from me in Boston. You stand there, and the music and the service just soak into you. I felt like I had been steeped in the presence of God. Do you know what I mean?'

'It sounds beautiful,' I evaded.

'It was. Afterward, when we came out and it was morning, it felt like we had made the light. It felt like the day had broken for us. Just . . . I can't describe it. You have to see it. Will you come to a service with me one day?'

'Sure. When and where?'

'I don't know. Later. Somewhere else.'

'I'll be there.'

Hannah laughed and poured us both more whiskey. 'So how's the article shaping up?'

'Strangely. I had lunch with my old professor today, the one who worked with Jaan. He said that Jaan had been arrested twice. Both times for shooting a gun.'

She swallowed her whiskey and nodded slowly before exclaiming, 'Wow! That's amazing. I mean, I knew he was a gun collector – he had a few old shotguns locked in a closet at his place, but I never knew he actually shot them. He used to call them his "lethal sculptures." I thought they were just for show.' Just like last night at the Trout, I noticed something wrong with her answer, the timing of it, the pause before the expression of surprise, and again I didn't say anything.

'It wasn't a shotgun, actually, it was a handgun.' Her look stayed level. She nodded at me again. 'You're not surprised?'

'Well, sure I am,' she said, a little defensively. 'Why would you think I wouldn't be?'

'No, no, I'm not. I mean, I don't. I shouldn't. I'm just . . .'

'Just acting like a reporter. Aren't you ever off duty?'

'Yes. Starting now.' She leaned against me, her head fitting perfectly into the crook of my shoulder and chest.

'What else did your professor say?'

'Nothing, really.' I decided not to tell her about the police just yet. Something in her tone before made me think that she saw Pühapäev as her own project somehow, as a revealed instance of her generous nature, a Good Work, and I didn't want to tell her anything else about his legal troubles. 'I found something weird when I came home tonight, though.'

'What was it?'

'A note on my door.' She stiffened against me, just slightly, but enough to feel. 'On the note there was this drawing of a caduceus. See, I learned a new word today. A caduceus is –'

'I know what it is,' she said, beginning to get up but then sinking back against me and wrapping my arm around her chest. 'What did the note say?'

'Well, nothing. It had my name taped to the front, and inside there was a tooth. A human tooth.'

She sat up and stared at me. 'Are you joking?'

'No, totally serious. Looked like it had just been ripped out, too.'

Her hand went to her mouth. 'Have you told anyone about it?'

'You mean, aside from you?'

'Yes, smart-ass,' she said, playfully pinching my ear. 'Like the police, or your editor, or anyone like that.'

'I haven't told Art yet, but I guess I should. The cops here, well, you've probably seen them. What are they going to do?' I wanted to leave Joe out of it. I couldn't say why, though in retrospect it was the right instinct. 'What do you think I should do?'

'Honestly? I think you should just drop it. I mean, write the obituary like you were supposed to do at the beginning. Don't you know enough to write it? And the rest, you know, some people are just mysterious, just like some things always have to be mysterious. I knew Jaan better than anyone else in town, right? And better than anyone he worked with, too, probably. And I never knew about his arrests, or his childhood, or anything like that. If you're getting strange notes –'

'Getting strange notes makes me want to keep going. I don't like the idea of being scared away.'

'My tough man,' she joked, poking me in the stomach. 'Why not write the obituary, leave it alone for a little while, and see if you get anything else stuck to your door? If you do, then you know it was connected and you can start digging around again.' It was a decent idea, and coming from her it sounded almost persuasive. But it would have been giving up all the same.

'An editor from Boston is interested in the story,' I said. 'I can't give it up.'

'Ah. I hadn't pegged you as a careerist.'

'I'm not,' I shot back, a little stung. 'I'm just saying, I'm working on a story and I don't want to just drop it because someone somewhere doesn't want me working on it. Anyway, how do I know it didn't come from some dentist somewhere who I bothered with one of my old articles?'

'You don't, you don't. Fair enough. But be careful, okay? I want to see a lot of you. I just don't see any reason to risk anything for the *Lincoln Carrier*. Or for some other job in Boston that you'll probably get anyway. I mean, you're twenty-three, smart, talented. Other things will come along.'

It's easy to see through this conversation in retrospect, on paper, laid out like this. But I was charmed because I wanted to be charmed. 'Maybe,' I conceded. 'Maybe you're right.' That phrase was my mother's favorite for the few years preceding my parents' divorce. I used it all the time myself; what it actually means is 'I disagree but have no desire to argue about it now.'

In the middle of my third glass of whiskey – we had killed the bottle – I noticed that the room had turned freezing. I stood up and walked over to the radiator: bone cold, and a draft slithered beneath the windows. During the pause between songs, I heard the old house creaking and settling, heard the wind groaning against the house's sides. I got even colder. I tucked my hands inside the sleeves of my sweater and closed them into fists around the fabric.

'You look like a little boy when you do that.' I looked down at my sleeves and unclenched my hands, extending them out of the sleeves. 'No, no, I didn't mean . . . I know it's cold. The temperature drops all of a sudden when Mrs DeSouza turns off the heat. Fortunately, I have a solution.' From her closet she produced a huge, obviously hand-knit woolen afghan: brightly colored squares in blue borders made it look warm, homey, like the board of some sort of children's game. 'My grandmother made it,' she said, unfolding it and shaking it loose. 'Come here.'

We held each other tight on the couch, under the blanket. She smelled like whiskey, rose perfume, and herself. I kissed the side of her neck closest to me, and she grabbed both my hands. 'You're shaking,' she said.

'I'm cold.'

'Is that the only reason?'

Of course it wasn't.

I woke up at 3:36, confused and with a thick whiskey headache before I remembered where I was. Hannah was asleep next to me, her hair nimbused across her pillow. I bolted three glasses of water standing next to the bathroom tap and tiptoed through the cold back into bed. When I got there, Hannah wrapped her arm around my chest, tucked her knees into the backs of mine, and kissed my ear. We fit.

Sunday was momentous and unremarkable. Everyone is entitled to one – maybe two – such days in a lifetime: a day spent not in the middle of love but at the beginning of it, maybe, a day that passes like the morning after a snowstorm or a broken fever, when everything seems almost too sharp to bear. Our actual activities that day were prosaic: we rose late; I made toast and fried eggs; we went back to bed; we drove to the New York border and took a long walk along a river; we stopped at a large and empty roadside tavern with the memorable slogan 'Flyin' Darts and Chicken Parts,' where we ate wings and played darts until ten-thirty, when we drove home again. She did this adorable shoulder dip just before she threw a dart, like she was trying to shimmy arms-first out of a tank top. She stopped putting her hand over her mouth when she laughed; I stopped looking down when I told a joke. By the time we got home, we were treading a little less carefully with each other, though she clouded over as we headed back into Lincoln and, pleading desouzaphobia, insisted that I park along the adjoining street and we go the long way around the house, avoiding the sight line of Orchard Street and Mrs DeSouza's front windows, to get into her apartment. I thought nothing of it. I was in no condition for critical thought.

I thought we didn't sleep, but apparently we had: her radio alarm clicked on and pulled me awake. Hannah groaned. 'Drinking on a Sunday night. Why'd you make me do it? Go redeem yourself and bring me three Advils from the bathroom cabinet and a tall glass of orange juice from the kitchen.' She gave me a playful kick in the back of the legs while I rubbed my eyes.

When I came back to the bedroom, she was in her robe and running a shower. 'I need to be at school in about an hour. What's your schedule like today?'

'I have a meeting at around two, but nothing until then. Why?'

'Just curious.' She walked over and stood against me, smiling while I untied her sash. 'We don't have that much time, you know.'

'You around tonight?'

'Indeed I am. Who's asking?'

'I'll bring dinner. Something special.'

'I can hardly wait. What time?'

'Seven? Seven-thirty?'

'Either. Whenever. I'm already excited.' She pushed my hand away and tied up her robe. 'Right now, though, you're going to leave so I can become a clean teacher again. Okay? I'll see you tonight.'

I pulled on my coat and kissed her for a long time at the door. She ran a hand down my face, and I could feel the trail it left after she stopped. She gave one last smile, dip of the head, and finger-roll wave and locked the door behind me.

I felt great, so great that I tossed my car keys high into the air, clapped twice like I used to do at baseball practice, positioned myself under them, and completely missed. Bending down to pick them up, I noticed a small drawing in white chalk against the slate at the bottom of her doorframe: a staff, with two snakes wrapped around it.

THE SHENG (AIR)

'You hear how the wind approaches?'
'It approaches quickly, violently, and I know not
   where from.'
'Nor do I. Draw close the shutters: I would keep
   warm.'

— ARDAL GOGARTY,
Have I Lived Too Long, Too Long?

Abulfaz Akhundov – whose ability to flatten and
lengthen his short vowels, round out his *r*'s, and
keep his *v*'s and *w*'s separate in mind, use, and mouth
had earned him the temporary name of Chester
'Chet' Muncie – tied his Kmart blue-and-red rep tie
first in a four-in-hand and then in a Windsor before
finally settling, as he knew he must, on a clumsily tied
half-Windsor deliberately shoved three centimeters
down and to the left from his top collar button. Since

arriving, he had seen no man wearing any other type of knot.

Abulfaz's butterfingered half-Windsor was the knot of someone who nominally accepts but never enjoys wearing a tie, who believes that excessive attention paid to attire signifies dandyism or effeminacy, and who thinks that by paying evidently minimal attention to his knot, he shows his tacit contempt for it. In fact, Abulfaz noted as he winced at his reflection while thinking of his natty father, all it showed was that he was a slob; the notion that a man would do something poorly or incompletely because he objected to it was most common among adolescents, American office workers, and Russian military personnel. He grabbed the knot between his thumb and forefinger and squeezed while pushing in opposite directions with his fingers, until the knot became oblong and slipped even farther from his collar: a man at the end of a long, fluorescent-lit day. He applied some ballpoint ink to the base of his right hand's middle finger and gave himself two small paper cuts on his left first and ring fingers. Smoothing his sandy (dyed) mustache and adjusting the gold aviator-style frames of his glasses, he put on his rumpled suit jacket, turned off the motel-room light, and stepped into the hazy, gauzy summer afternoon.

He was staying in an anonymous, sterile motel with the wonderfully efficient name U.S. 30, near a strip mall complete with a grocery store (which naturally he never patronized). Where he came from, hotels were named for war heroes, political leaders, and mythic literary-historical figures that supposedly embodied a national trait. Hotels in the Soviet provinces tended to exalt Potemkin ideals with unintended irony: Baku's Friendship of All Peoples Hotel, for instance, had the surliest service in Azerbaijan; Yerevan's Industrialization of the Masses Leading to Revolutionary Peace Workers' Guesthouse had broken toilets, no telephones, and regular stabbings in the bar. That a proprietor would name his establishment simply and for no apparent reason with a number struck Abulfaz as absurd, delightful, and reassuring all at once.

The U.S. 30 was on Highway 30, in LaGrange Park. He selected this motel in this city virtually at random, though it had three important attributes in its favor. First, very few people stayed there: the parking lot had been empty when he arrived, and except for a chubby, amoebic-looking family who slubbered in and out of a van with Ohio license plates, nobody but he had stayed for more than two nights. Second, unlike hotels at home, where you had to show your papers and issue appropriately formal requests to three or four fat, gold-toothed old women in various stages of decay and ill temper simply to receive your door key, here Abulfaz could park directly outside his room and enter without talking to anyone, when and how he pleased. Third, his job was in Skokie, a good forty-five-minute drive from LaGrange Park. The commute was inconvenient enough so that he never regularly saw the same people in one place as in the other. Commuters from both LaGrange Park and Skokie went to Chicago; they didn't go to one another's cities, and Abulfaz (who in the past two decades had been called Fyodor, Istvan, Cinar, Chester, Paul, Sudat, Jean-Pierre, José, João, Wim, Klaus, Yahya, Bradley, Niall, Hamid, Shmuel, and, briefly and only by telephone, Katya) could live and work comfortably, obscurely, and, therefore, by his own temporary measure, happily for the twenty-eight days required to complete his task.

DAY ONE: He pulled into the restaurant parking lot at 12:12, the early middle of the midwestern lunch hour. The restaurant was an unremarkable, typically Chinese-American place: a pink-and-green neon sign advertising the restaurant's name (Pine and Bamboo) in the front window, a small red-and-gold awning above the front door, chintzy gold lions in either midroar or midyawn on either side of the foyer linking the outside door with the restaurant. Local office workers and klatches of suburban mothers came for predictable exoticism, and while Abulfaz's mouth watered at the sight of a stew containing eel and lotus roots being eaten by a chef, alone at the end of the long bar, he ordered a cup of egg-drop soup and chicken lo mein at his solitary table.

DAYS TWO THROUGH FOUR: Precise copies of the first day, except for the third day, when an accident on Dempster Street delayed his arrival until 12:18. He ordered the same food, gave the same cautious, expressionless nod when greeting the shabby and crepuscular host, and read the *Sun-Times* at the same table, sitting in the same chair, each day.

DAYS FIVE AND SIX: Saturday and Sunday. He did not eat at the restaurant but noticed on Sunday, while parked across the street, that He-li Yaofan appeared grayer, thinner, and more stooped than he had appeared in the black-and-white photograph that Abulfaz had been given. The restaurant's business card, which he kept in his glove compartment, listed the owner as Harry Yaofan. Abulfaz smiled and thought of Chester.

DAYS SEVEN THROUGH ELEVEN: He began to slide his arrival time a bit, so that by Thursday he was arriving between 12:45 and 1:00. Starting on Monday, he solicited his waitress's advice on what to order: the first day, she merely shrugged; the second, she smiled shyly, eyes still on her notepad, and said she didn't know; the third, she steered him away from the egg-drop soup ('Not fresh. Make from powder'); the fourth, she asked him what he liked to eat and simply nodded when he said, 'Well, anything good, I guess'; the fifth, she substituted squid and razor clams for the chicken in his lo mein.

DAYS TWELVE AND THIRTEEN: On Saturday night Abulfaz ran a short, lucrative, and exceptionally messy errand in Waukeshaw, Wisconsin; on Sunday he followed the crowds to Clark and Addison to watch the Cubs lose to the Phillies, despite two home runs from Jody Davis and a valiant eight-inning performance from Scott Sanderson.

DAY FOURTEEN: When he walked in at 1:07, the host nodded, smiled, and asked, 'How was your weekend, sir?'

Chet answered, 'Yup, real good, thanks for asking. Went to see a Cubs game and had some folks visiting from back home in Mankato.'

The host smiled again and bobbed his head but said nothing in response. He held an arm out like a magician introducing his assistant as Chet's waitress approached.

DAY FIFTEEN: 'You like our food, sir?' the host asked Chet.

'Sure do, yep. Like it a lot.'

'Yes. Come here a lot, yes? Chinese food very healthy!'

'What my wife tells me anyway. Tell me something, though: I'm trying to be a bit, you know, a bit more adventurous. Sort of shake things up a bit, lunchwise. What do you people think I oughta be eating? 'Cause I always seem to get the same thing here.'

'You eat spicy food, sir?'

'Sure.'

'I have special lunch for you, sir. Just one moment. Maybe a little more expensive than regular lunch special, okay? Little bit more only, okay?'

'Well, if it's just a little bit, sure, no problem.'

DAY SIXTEEN: 'Hey, buddy, can I ask you a question?'

The host replied, 'Of course, sir. Yes, please.'

'You guys do sort of catering deals? My firm – I'm in packing boxes and sealing tape, by the way, run a little firm over in Dearborn with an office here in Skokie. Anyway, we got to host some out-of-towners, big shots in from Omaha thinking about placing a major order, and what I want to know is, food here's good, so I was wondering if you could make a special lunch for maybe eighteen, twenty people.'

'Yes, sir, of course we can do. When for?'

'Ah, week after next, I think. It's not totally set yet.'

'Okay, so you get set let me know, or you want to talk about food maybe now?'

'I can just tell you later, I guess. Just wanted to make sure you do this sort of thing.'

'Yes, we do.'

'Should I talk to you about it or to the owner?'

'Either.'

'Say, great. So what's the owner's name? And what's yours, by the way?'

'I'm Wang. The owner, everyone calls him Harry.'

'Well, it sure is good to meet you, Wang. I'm Chet.'

'Okay, Mr Chet. Today I make for you a Shanghai soup with pork and preserved mustard greens. Not on the menu; only for Chinese people, but you will like very much, I know.'

DAY SEVENTEEN: He stayed away today, wanting to see whether his absence would be noticed. Naturally, he left his room appropriately dressed (white striped shirt, blue-and-green-striped tie, powder blue Sansabelt slacks, Dexter saddle wingtips) and at the proper time. He filled his time in the usual manner, too: driving, watching, getting the feel of the brief, cliché-based conversations so essential to American communication. Last week he worked on the phrases 'Just goes to show you' and 'Funny you should say that'; this week's tasks were 'If it works, it works' and 'Can't do a thing about it.' Two phrases of resignation, one of satisfaction with the present that implied a certain chariness of improvement, and one used to pivot a conversation away from one's interlocutor to oneself. Abulfaz vowed to stay away from the latter.

DAY EIGHTEEN: 'We miss you yesterday, Mr Chet,' said Wang.

'Yeah, gee, had to work all through the lunch hour there at my desk. Didn't get a chance even to get up.'

'You have delivery menu? You can call, and we bring food to you.'

'Yeah? That'd be great.'

'No, great for us! Great for us, to have customer who come back so much. You eat today something special?'

'Sure will. Whatever you bring me, you know that. By the way, just keep noticing, I like the music you play on the system here while I eat.'

'Oh, yes. Very good music. Chinese music. Different songs, different instruments.'

DAY NINETEEN: From across the street, Abulfaz saw Harry Yaofan and a woman he assumed was his wife – a plump woman with the pocked complexion and spherical shape of a lychee – enter the restaurant at 6:08. When they sat down at a table, some seven minutes later, they were the only customers there, and they ate, as far as Abulfaz could see through the window, in total silence. Wang brought them a succession of dishes without being asked and placed them in the center of the table with a dancer's arcing grace. Harry and his wife ate small bites of each dish and drank tea from lidded porcelain cups.

Twenty-eight minutes after they arrived, two men entered the restaurant, spoke to Wang at the front desk, sat down on chairs by the entryway, drained a beer each, received a plastic bag of food, and left eleven minutes after they arrived. No other customers entered. At 7:15, Wang hung a Closed sign in the window. Harry and his wife left thirty-two minutes later, and Wang, having cleared their plates, followed behind them, locking the door. One hour and fifty-seven minutes later, Abulfaz saw the kitchen light turn off, and two minutes after that, a red Datsun with rust patches and a sagging exhaust system drove off from behind the restaurant.

DAY TWENTY: Abulfaz had made a point of filling up his gas tank one gallon at a time at eleven different service stations between LaGrange Park and Skokie. Each time he bantered – or Chester bantered – with the attending gas jockey who checked his engine and oil; he wanted to give his accent plenty of practice, plenty of time to stretch out, be sure the *r*'s extended fully and roundly and his long vowels stayed flat and generically midwestern. He noticed no mistakes, and neither, apparently, did any of the men he spoke with, but seven of them were foreign and the other four so young, callow, and uninterested that they probably would not have noticed had his skin been green and antennae protruded from his forehead. As on any potentially final day of an assignment, he defecated frequently – at each service station, in fact – until he finally asked a Pakistani cashier, while patting his gut and grimacing, for 'something to kind of rein these horses in.'

At 5:59 he pulled into the parking lot next to Pine and Bamboo, opened a can of Old Style beer, and swished it around in his mouth before spitting it into a Big Gulp cup. He rubbed some beer into his neck and dribbled a spot onto his St Paul Saints T-shirt. When he was satisfied, he smelled like a man who had spent the afternoon drinking, and just after he saw Yaofan and his wife enter the restaurant, he pulled next to Yaofan's car, pinched his cheeks and nose until they were bright red, rubbed his eyes until he looked a bit bleary, and went in to have dinner and a conversation.

Wang looked at him uncertainly when he walked through the door; then his face broke and lit with recognition. 'Mr Chet. Here on Sunday! Dress very casual today – not recognize you for a minute.'

Chet grinned a little too widely and laughed a little too loudly, then emitted a sustained tuba-pitched belch, which made Wang giggle and Yaofan's wife jump in her seat. 'Yeah, was just grabbin' a few with some buddies right around here. Figured I'd stop in and see if you guys were open. Gettin' kinda hungry there, ya know.'

Wang glanced back over his shoulder at Yaofan, who nodded almost imperceptibly while looking squarely at Chet. Wang picked up a menu and gave Chet a relieved smile and an energetic arm wave, showing him to his usual corner table, which left just one empty table between him and the Yaofans, the only other people in the dining room. He adjusted his glasses – which were, in fact, entirely unnecessary – perused the menu, shut it, and looked up as bovinely as possible.

'Yes, sir,' said Wang, materializing helpfully at his elbow. 'What you eat tonight?'

'What are those other fellas having?' he asked loudly.

Yaofan looked over his shoulder at Chet and replied in an even, slithery voice, 'Stewed pig's intestines with dried shrimp and fermented black beans. I doubt you would like it.' His voice was as polished, dark, and hard as a gun barrel, with the musical English clip of an educated Hong Kong Chinese.

Wang, whose clueless unctuosity perfectly fit his role of troublesome but endearing sidekick, broke in, 'No, no, Mr Chet has Chinese stomach. Guolin face and Chinese stomach.' He laughed until Yaofan glared at him, whereupon he went instantly silent, as though he had been punched. Yaofan glanced back at Chet, shrugged, and began speaking to his wife in Chinese. Chet gestured at Yaofan's plate and gave Wang a thumbs-up, which Wang returned, grinning.

'Yep, I come here just about every day,' Chet said, looking at the back of Yaofan's head. 'It's near work for me, which is good, and the food's good, too. Pretty waitresses, too.' He had hoped to elicit a reaction with the last aside, but still nothing. 'They your daughters or something?'

At that, Yaofan swiveled around in his chair toward Chet, his face as placid and expressionless as a wooden carving. 'They are not.'

'Ah, well, just thought you kinda looked alike. The other thing I like about this place is the music. You know, I don't know much about music – well, I guess I know some, 'cause I played accordion and harmonica in the marching band back home in Walleye Creek, and I still play a little for my nieces' birthdays and such – but like I said, I don't really know much about music compared with anyone who knows anything, but I sure do like the stuff they play here. Do you have any of it for sale or anything?'

'I am afraid we don't. You'll have to excuse me now; my dinner seems to be cooling.'

'Yeah, sure, no problem, I don't mean to keep you. But it's just this thing I read the other day; my buddy, the guy who I first started taking accordion lessons with, he still plays a bunch, you know – he's got this Creole-zydeco thing going on in St Paul, and they're getting pretty big, at least for the Twin Cities – but anyways, he's the kind of guy who does a lot of reading, so he sends me this article, and it says that the accordion and the harmonica both actually come from a Chinese instrument called a sheng. I think that's it: a sheng, which he also called a mouth organ. Which is funny, 'cause that's what my gammy – Gammy's what I always called my grandmother, and she's from Denmark – what she used to call the harmonica is a mouth organ. Just kind of funny. Anyway, you know anything about that? Maybe that's right or not, something I can tell my buddy to maybe win a bar bet or two?'

Yaofan exhaled heavily but still refused to turn around. Wang entered with Chet's dinner – the same thing, in fact, that Yaofan was eating – and when he did, he saw Chet sitting in his chair smirking and not saying anything and Yaofan sitting similarly silent and bolt upright with his back to the talkative American, and he remembered keeping his sisters in one corner of their hut in Lengshuitan when his parents were fighting, remembered the contaminated air and the silences stiff and cold as batter, and he nearly dropped Chet's dinner in his lap, such was his hurry to leave. Yaofan turned around when he heard the plate clatter on the table.

'Anything about what?'

'About whether accordions come from shengs,' Chet answered, keeping any hint of a tremor or rise from his voice, remaining as calm as he could.

'Ah. No. Unfortunately, no, I don't.'

'Gee, that's too bad. Because what I was thinking was, my buddy's forty-fifth birthday is coming up, so I was thinking I'd like to buy him a sheng. I don't have a wife or kids, and he's my oldest pal, so I really could afford a pretty penny.'

Yaofan looked coolly at Chet and then smiled and lowered his eyes. He was about to turn his attention back to his neglected dinner and more neglected wife when Chet asked, 'So you don't know?'

'Don't know what?'

'Don't know where I could look for a sheng. Like I said, I really don't think money will be a problem.'

'Mr . . .'

'Muncie's my last name. People just call me Chet, though.'

'Chet. Yes, Chet, I unfortunately have no idea where you could procure a Chinese instrument. There are slightly more than one billion Chinese people on this planet, and probably several tens of thousands in this city alone. We do not all know each other.'

'Nah, it's just that I was sure you would know where to find one, you know? Come to think of it, I was pretty sure you had one here in your restaurant.'

Yaofan dropped his fork, and as his wife bent down to pick it up, he snapped at her in a voice no louder than silk swishing over glass. She rose, glared at Chet while clicking her tongue, and walked unsteadily into the kitchen. Yaofan wiped the corners of his mouth and took a chair opposite Chet. 'What I in fact have or do not have in my possession is, to you, entirely hypothetical. I do not suffer truth seekers; I have told you that I neither possess nor know anything about any instruments of any kind, Chinese or otherwise. If you have finished with your dinner – which you have – it really would be best for you if you left.'

Chet took his glasses off and leaned forward. Without them he looked hawkish – perhaps his expression grew sharper; he became more Abulfaz than he had been five seconds ago – and the mustache that had looked sloppy on a chubby, middle-aged American in a sports T-shirt now looked wild, almost feral, on this strange man who suddenly occupied Chet's body. 'We are in a position, Mr Yaofan, to offer you anything you would like in exchange for the sheng in your possession. We know it is here because we already searched your house; we know we can deal with you as we are doing because of the exemplary and ingenious manner in which you disposed of the Ghost Snakes in Macao and now control their operations from several thousand miles away. We are also prepared to rape and flay your wife, set fire to the houses of your brothers and sisters, and ensure that your nieces and nephews never again walk or speak unaided. We are not unnecessarily violent people and always prefer generosity to torture, but the choice between the two is in your hands entirely.'

Yaofan's face had turned pallid, and he was sweating. 'You say "we," but I see only you.'

Abulfaz withdrew three noodles from his bowl and twisted them into a shape on a plate: one straight line crossed repeatedly by two sinuous lines. Yaofan mopped his brow. 'Ah. I always thought you were a myth. Ghost stories, you know, monster tales.'

Abulfaz shook his head, smiling but saying nothing. 'What, in the world or out of it, would you most like, Mr Yaofan?'

'You know, my nephew –'

'Which one? The ophthalmologist in Phoenix, the stockbroker in Winnipeg, the restaurateur in Bourg-en-Bresse, the student in Hong Kong, or any of the five farmhands back home?'

'Ah. You have visited the restaurant in France? Also called Pine and Bamboo. David worked here, you know.'

'We do.'

'Ah.' Yaofan fidgeted in his seat and sopped the trickles of sweat running down his quivering temples. 'I am an old man, Chet, and there is little that I want.'

'We can give anything to anyone, as you no doubt know.'

'I did not finish. There is little that I want. My wife has an outlandish desire. I would never even speak of it to anyone other than you.'

Abulfaz raised his eyebrows and tilted his head upward.

'She is old, you know, old as I am. We have been married for forty-three years, since we were both seventeen. We left Lengshuitan together and have traveled to many places since then. But there are two things we never did. We have never spent a night apart.' Yaofan paused and cast his eyes to the red-carpeted floor. 'The other . . . the reason we left Lengshuitan . . . it is considered quite shameful, really . . .'

'We know,' said Abulfaz.

'Ah.' Yaofan looked up, relieved. 'Ah. Is this within your power, then?'

'It is.'

'What guarantees would I have?'

'Our promise. Nothing else.'

'Ah. Then by all means, please follow me into the kitchen, where we can speak more comfortably.'

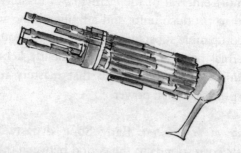

Item 8: A sheng, also called a 'Chinese mouth organ.' Generally, a sheng has between 13 and 17 pipes of different lengths mounted together onto a gourd- or drum-shaped base (although Fong Yu-T'sai, an eccentric nobleman from Guangzhou, constructed a plan for a sheng made of 75,346 tree-size pipes mounted around his home city). Each pipe has a free reed, and sound is produced by blowing through a single mouthpiece while covering circular holes cut into each pipe (in the case of Fong's city-size instrument, the wind itself would have produced the sound, and less fortunate villagers would have filled the holes).

This particular sheng had 16 bamboo pipes around a hollow gourd plated with gold; a thin gold band surrounded the pipes 13.5 centimeters up from the gourd. The sheng itself was 36 centimeters from its lowest point to its highest and had a diameter of 12 centimeters at its base.

Again we find an affinity between alchemy and music, and not surprisingly it involves air, the lightest and most ethereal of the elements. A mastery of air is said to produce unity and affinity among warring or incompatible substances, just as music soothes the proverbial breast. Alchemists frequently kept wind instruments to remind them that mastery requires more precision than power.

Date of manufacture: Early Song dynasty, which roughly corresponds to the period between the tenth and twelfth centuries A.D. inclusive.

Manufacturer: The name of Ping Yu-tsun is carved in an elegant, miniature calligraphy across the base of the gourd. Whether this means that Ping crafted the instrument or that it was crafted as a dedication to him is unknown. Ping was physician and court historian to Lord Menchou, known for his eccentric – not to say barbaric – habit of receiving foreign guests, which, during the Early Song dynasty, was unheard of. A Song-dynasty scroll unearthed during the building of a dam in 1978 refers to Ping as 'venerable, twice venerable, and again most venerable, . . . who has granted our lord the gift of long life.' The same scroll depicts a figure thought to be Ping himself transforming, in five stages, from a man into a dragon.

Place of origin: Menchou's court was between present-day Xian and Lanzhou. The wood and style of the sheng, however, is not specific to any particular region of China.

Last known owner: Yaofan He-li (Harry Yaofan), onetime enforcer for the Jackrabbit Sharks of Macao, currently a restaurateur and doting father to an infant son in Skokie, Illinois. Yaofan relinquished control of the sheng to a man whom his cousin, Yaofan Wang, knew only as 'Mr Chet.' Roughly nine months after Chet's last visit, Harry announced to his staff that he and Mrs Yaofan were parents to a baby boy; since they were both in their early sixties at the time, and since their youngest daughter was thirty-two, this claim was met with incredulity and suspicion from all who heard it. The staff reported that Mrs Yaofan ate her regular Sunday dinner with Harry for several months after 'Mr Chet' stopped patronizing the restaurant, and she never appeared pregnant, but, given her age, it seems unlikely that anyone would have even considered such a possibility. No records exist of an adoption, however, nor did any relatives contacted claim to have surrendered a child to the Yaofans. No Asian babies in the Chicagoland area were reported kidnapped at the time the Yaofans made their parenthood public. Mrs Yaofan referred to the birth as 'a miracle,' while Harry always called it either 'a gift' or 'a result.'

Estimated value: One baby boy.

With great sagacitie it doth ascend
gently from Earth to Heaven.

❦

When I saw the caduceus at the bottom of Hannah's doorframe, I felt the same little silver tickle of adrenaline at the back of my throat that I had felt at the door to my apartment last night. Only now the adrenaline wasn't backed by excitement but by fear for Hannah. I banged on her door. Nothing. I opened the mail slot and listened: a running shower with full-throated singing above it, loud enough to drown out the sound of my knocking. I heard the rustle of leaves on grass behind me but paid no attention to it until a dry hand grabbed my shirt collar and sharp fingernails scraped the back of my neck.

'Well, I guess it's my new tenant,' said Mrs DeSouza once I had turned around and stood up. She was wearing slippers, her housecoat, and a smirky, eyebrow-arched expression that mixed scorn, satisfaction, and glee. 'I heard Hannah's door shut this morning earlier than usual. She usually doesn't leave until eight-fifteen. I wondered whether someone might have been sneaking out. And look at what we have here: not only a suitor but a Peeping Tom, too.'

'I'm sure Mrs Rowe must be relieved that somebody's keeping such a close eye on her daughter.'

'Well, I just thought I'd remind you of our little talk the other night. You see, it's my belief that —'

'Mrs DeSouza, give it a rest. Hannah's over thirty, and she's not your daughter.'

At first her face reddened and tightened, like she had just been slapped; then it deflated, and tears welled up in her eyes.

I pawed the ground with the tip of my shoe, muttered a quick and almost heartfelt apology, and hurried toward my car. When I looked back over my shoulder, Mrs DeSouza was still standing there, shoulders sagging and shaking, one hand to her face. Not even eight in the morning, and I had already made an old lady cry.

Before heading to Wickenden, I stopped by my apartment to shower, change, and put the tooth in my pocket. No messages on my answering machine, no letters in my mailbox, nothing nailed to my door. Gone for two days, and nobody had tried to reach me, which wasn't unusual. But for the first time since moving here, I didn't feel as though I had been absent from my life. I felt that my life had moved and the details just hadn't caught up yet.

Parking spaces in downtown Wickenden are rare, and I was early anyway, so I left the car on Shelden Street, in front of a light blue clapboard house flying a huge Portuguese flag above the garage. At street level a purple door stood wide open, revealing a long, narrow room with a checkered linoleum floor, a bar with a few stools, a pool table, couches, and a television showing dog racing. A blue Bud Light clock hung above the bar. Next to it was a plastic letterboard – the type that shows the specials in diners – that read sannich, no hams fra tue. I used to live two blocks from here but had never noticed this little dive, and I liked the look of it. I poked my head in.

'Membership car',' said a fat man behind the bar. He wore a yellow-and-green-checked flannel shirt, untucked over sagging blue jeans, and was serving shots and beers to a pair of skinny, sleepy-looking guys at the bar.

'Sorry?'

'Membership car'. This a private club. Members only.' The last time I had heard that, a gold-toothed Albanian had threatened to kill me. And when did dingy bars in New England backwaters become so exclusive?

'I never noticed this place before. I used to live a few blocks over, and –'

'This ain't a student bar. Not for you here. This the Portuguese Men's Club. You Portuguese man?'

'I'm not.'

'Well, there you go. Some other bar for you. This my place here.'

I nodded curtly, and he did the same. Then one of the skinny guys walked over and shut the door.

I crossed downtown on foot in about thirty minutes and reached the police station at around two. Two pudgy beat cops were dragging a man in cuffs up the stairs when I arrived. The guy kept listing to his right and mumbling, while the policemen carried on a normal conversation about their wives: they looked like a percent sign slowly rising up the stairs.

I asked the desk sergeant where I could find Joe Jadid.

'Ain't on till four. You need to leave a message with me?'

'He told me to meet him here a little early. Any chance he's in yet?'

He huffed mightily, stood up, and leaned over the desk toward me. I stepped back and caught a faint stink of whiskey coming off him. He pointed to a glass-fronted door at the end of the hallway. 'See that door there? Interview Room One. Jadid likes to sit in there and read the papers when nobody else is using it. He ain't there, you go up one flight and ask for Detective Gomes. He'll help you.'

'Thanks.' He nodded and sat back down, puffing

out again as he did it, his belly jiggling and settling pouchily back onto his thighs.

I knocked tentatively on the door of the interview room. A deep voice told me to come in, and I did. Sitting at one end of a long metal table was a beefy, olive-skinned man with short, curly black hair and crow-black eyes. He wore a baggy gray suit that looked like he'd slept in it, and he was reading the international-news pages from that day's *New York Times*.

'Joseph Jadid?'

'That's right.'

'I'm Paul Tomm.'

He put the paper down, stood up, and walked over to me. He was almost a foot taller than me, and probably seventy pounds heavier, too. He had the all-over pudge of a football player gone to seed but still powerful, like if you locked him in a phone booth with an angry bear, he'd come out wearing a fur coat. The same ironic half smile as on his uncle's sat on his lips, and they had the same weak-tea skin tone, but where Professor Jadid was fastidious and feline, Joe spilled out of his clothes, and his features had a street fighter's fleshy roughness. He folded up the day's newspaper into quarters, which fit neatly in the palm of one hammy hand, and with the other he clapped me on the shoulder. I nearly fell over.

'I'm Joe. Good to finally see you. Good you made it in early, too: I'm starved. You eat lunch already, or you want to go grab something?'

'No, I haven't eaten yet.'

'Okay. The cop canteen here'll kill you quick, and it's still a little early for the Silver Shack to roll up. There's a decent grinder place around the corner, though. How's that sound?'

'Fine.'

'Okay. Meatball grinders. You tell me you're one of those college vegetarians, I'm throwing out everything I've done so far for you and kicking your ass back up the hill.'

'No, I eat pretty much everything.'

'Yeah? Don't look like it. I eat everything, especially recently, sitting on the desk like this, not going out, not on the street, no exercise.' He grabbed two big handfuls of his gut and jiggled it up and down. 'I must have added a sawbuck or two. You got lucky, though, 'cause these days I got nothing but time and a whole lot of useless energy.' I could tell. Some part of him was always in extraneous motion; as we crossed Patchett Street and started heading up Bishop, he clenched and unclenched his fists, ran his hands over his head, gesticulated as he talked. 'Want to know what else about sitting? The piles, I'll tell you, they make a grown man weep. Gotta walk around, pace, you know – sit down too long, it's like my ass is on a fucking griddle.'

'Yeesh.'

'So Uncle Abe likes you. That's good. He's my favorite uncle.'

'He said the same about you. Nephew, though, not uncle.'

'Yeah, we've always been pretty close. Big, tight family, mostly. The three brothers here in Wickenden – Abe; my father, Daniel; and Uncle Sammy. Two sisters, Amira and Claudia, over in Boston. Lot of cousins, too, especially now that my bunch is starting to have kids. Can't keep everyone's name straight. Tight family in general, but for some reason Uncle Abe and I always got on real well.'

'You have any kids?'

'Me? Naah. Not married. This is a bad job for steady things, you know, unless you're with someone else in the game or a high-school sweetheart or something. Lotta cops, they get married, they leave the force. Private security sometimes, or starting a business. My old partner quit to run a bar with his brothers-in-law in Olneyton. I tell him the only way I quit is feetfirst, you know?'

'You like it? Your work.'

'Love it. Some things I don't like about it, but mostly I can't think of anything else I'd rather do.' After puffing up the hill for a few minutes we came to a dingy little carry-out with a menu offering artery cloggers in about five different languages. 'You want my advice here, stick to the basics,' Joe said as he held the door open for me. 'Meatball sub. Deli sandwiches. You notice they call this dish here "Meat Lo Mein" without telling you what kind of meat? That's not an accident.'

I took his advice. The sandwich was perfect: not greasy at all, in fact, with fresh Italian bread, spicy tomato sauce that actually tasted like tomatoes rather than hot ketchup, and melted mozzarella that tasted like cheese and not library paste. With lemonade and sweet pickles on the side, it was the ideal Wickenden lunch. We ate it at the stand-up counter with a panoramic view of a parking lot.

'So what about that note?' he asked, spraying tomato flecks across my sweater.

'Right here,' I said, producing the envelope containing the tooth from my pocket and handing it to him. 'What do you do with this?'

'We'll give it to the lab, have them run some DNA tests, see if it matches. It's a long shot, but . . .' He opened the envelope, sniffed, and recoiled. 'Jesus. Put a man off his lunch. At least we know this came from someone who didn't own a toothbrush.' He stuffed the envelope into the pocket of his blue shirt. 'Anything happen since I talked to you?'

'Well, maybe.'

Joe widened his eyes and raised his eyebrows – his single eyebrow, actually, that made a little dip above his crooked boxer's nose – for me to continue.

'So I'm seeing this girl . . .'

'So I gathered. Why you need to be eating that beef there. Some shellfish and greens for dinner, you'll be going like a steam train. Sorry. Don't mean to embarrass you. Anyway, go ahead . . .'

'Right. You know that symbol on the front of the envelope?'

'The caduceus.'

'Exactly. Caduceus. I saw one on her doorframe this morning.'

'What do you mean? A note like this?'

'No, a little chalk drawing. Not on the door itself, but just next to it, you know, on the little indentation where the door meets the frame.'

'Hmmm. Who is this girl?'

'Her name's Hannah Rowe. She seems to be the only person in Lincoln who knew Jaan. Teaches music at the local boarding school.'

'What do you think of her?'

The million-dollar question. What did I think of her? 'I like her. That's why I'm worried.'

'About what?'

I shrugged and crumpled up my waxed paper. 'I don't know, really. That she's being threatened, maybe. The same symbol on the front of my envelope on the same weekend. It makes me nervous.'

Joe sniffed thoughtfully and ran a grinder-greasy hand over his already greasy hair. 'That's one way to see it, I guess. But how well do you know this girl?'

'I don't know. Not too well. We've only been out a few times, but I like her, you know? I get a good feeling from her.'

He looked at me sympathetically, eyebrow arched and mouth screwed tight. 'Exactly. So you're not even considering the possibility that maybe she sent you this note? Or knows someone who did? Or the caduceus on her door means something other than the caduceus on your envelope? You don't think she's the one who left this note for you?'

'Her? Hannah? What's she doing, pulling teeth in her spare time? Of course not. Anyway, where's she going to get a tooth like that? She had all her teeth when I saw her, and she's no dentist.'

'Yeah, I know. Still . . . I'm going to hold on to this. Meanwhile, just do me a favor and you be careful what you tell this girl. It's the Jewish mother in me, you know?' He nudged me in the ribs, trying to lighten the mood. I smiled despite myself: what else can you do when a lineman-size bruiser calls himself a Jewish mother? 'I know you like her, but as I said last night, I think you might be dealing with some bad, bad guys here. Gomes and I, we'll show you what we got, but any way you look at it, I don't think this was just an absentminded, sweet old guy. There's something else going on here, and if you've only been out a couple of times, I'd say you don't really know her all that well. I mean, I guess she's probably good-looking, right?'

'Right.'

'And sweet and smart, and she likes sensitive young guys like yourself, right?'

I nodded but didn't say anything. My ears were hot again.

He finished his lemonade, crumpled the wax cup, and shot it free-throw style into the tall trash can in the corner. 'Just watch yourself, is all. Hate to see anything happen to a friend of Abe's on my watch.'

*

Jadid tossed an underhand sandwich spiral to a dapper-looking man – slim-cut dark suit, as knife-creased as Joe's was slovenly, shaved head, round steel-rimmed glasses, mahogany skin – who was seated at the desk next to his. 'And what have you brought me here?' he asked, peering over the lenses of his glasses. I wasn't sure if he was asking Joe about the sandwich or me.

'Turkey on a roll, mustard, no mayo. One of those low-fat things like you always ask for. I told them to put extra tofu and granola on top. Side of wheat-berry and grass juice.'

The man smiled and reached for a bottle of water on the desk. 'Make fun if you want to, Fat Person, but when we're fifty years old, I'll be visiting you in the hospital on my way home from summer league.'

Joe dragged a chair over from an empty desk. 'Don't mind him,' he said, motioning me to sit down. 'He just hasn't had his spirulina today.'

The sharp-dressed man grinned and raised a middle finger. 'I'm Sal Gomes,' he said, pronouncing the last name with one syllable. He walked over to me and extended his hand. 'Joey usually rides with me when he's not on time-out for playing Mike Tyson with some friend of the mayor's. I've been helping him with your dead Estonian.'

'Paul Tomm. I appreciate the help.'

'Nothing to it. Anything to get a hopped-up Jadid off my back.'

'Paulie here is a graduate of your favorite university,' said Joe, looking over at me.

Gomes laughed shyly and waved him away.

'You don't like Wickenden?' I asked.

'I got nothing against Wickenden people as long as they behave just like anyone else.' He looked down at me. 'Where'd you live when you were a student here?'

'St Clair Point. Gano Street.'

'Oh, see, now we might have problems. You throw a lot of parties?'

'Not a one.'

'Okay. You take out the trash?'

'Yeah, sure. Twice a week.'

'And did you use those strange metallic objects some students refer to as trash cans, or did you simply eject said trash onto the street?'

'Cans.'

'Not bad again. Kid shows promise. Who'd you rent from?'

'Steve Terzidian.'

'Oh, I know Steve,' said Gomes, smiling wryly. 'Yeah, I've run across him a few times, buying up old people's houses in the neighborhood, turning them into rentals, some for students, some for other – shall we say less salubrious – purposes. Tell me, you never got anything stolen from your house, did you?'

'No, we never did.'

'And your neighbors, other folks you know down there, any of them have any problems with theft?'

295

'Yeah, actually, my girlfriend's place was broken into a couple of times. She lost a TV and a stereo. This other guy I know had his car stolen right in front of their house.'

'Either of them rent from Steve?'

'I don't know. I don't think so.'

'I wouldn't think so either. Funny how Steve always has such good luck in the theft department. What'd he charge you? Just wondering.'

'Three of us paid three hundred dollars each per month.'

He exhaled, sharp and bullish, through his nose. 'Okay. You probably weren't one of the bad ones, right?'

I didn't know what he was talking about, but it seemed smart to agree. 'Right.'

'Right, that's right. Listen, I have nothing against you, and probably nothing against your friends. But I'm St Clair Point born and raised. Student rentos don't respect the neighborhood and drive up the prices, is all. Don't take it personally.'

'I don't offend easily. Besides, I loved the neighborhood. Loved living there.'

'Hard not to love it, man, isn't it? Those pink-and-purple houses, the water right there, you got the park, ball courts, and football fields. All kinds of people now. Just bought myself my first house, almost down by the water, on the same street as my parents and uncles.'

'The Gomes Homes, he calls it. Not to be

confused with the Gomez Homezz, over in Coastal Falls,' said Joe.

'No, Gomes Homes *you* call it, Fat Man. Anyway, I truly am sorry if I made you feel uncomfortable, Paul. It's not what I meant to do.'

'Like I said, no offense taken at all.'

'Good. So,' said Gomes, dabbing his mouth daintily with a napkin, 'maybe we should talk about the dead professor.'

'We both of us did some legwork for you,' said Joe, pulling a manila folder out of his desk. 'Like I said, I got nothing but time these days, and Uncle Abe's recommendation goes a long way with me. Means a lot, too. Don't let the manners fool you: he doesn't really like that many people. But you didn't hear that from me. And Gomes here . . . well, he retrogressed – isn't that what that fake psychic we busted off of Tavey Street called it? – he retrogressed into a former life for you.'

'Painful, too,' said Gomes. 'All those repressed memories and shit. In my "former life," I was a distinguished officer of the United States federal government, in the employ of the Federal Bureau of Investigation. Made a few calls to some former colleagues about your boy. I'll tell you about that after Joey does his thing.'

Joe opened his folder, then opened a can of grape soda, draining it in two swallows, crushing the can in his paw, and hook-shooting it into a wastebasket about fifteen feet away. He cracked open a second can and downed half of it. 'So my question,' he said, belching loudly, 'after looking at this guy's arrest records, is why the university would let him keep teaching.'

'Your uncle told me about that.'

'Yeah, I talked to him, too. Probably the same story he told you.' He pulled a reporter's spiral, the same kind I used (I felt tough by proxy), from the top drawer of his desk and flipped through the pages. 'Let's see, first time this Crowley guy kept him on, second time it was Abe's decision?'

'That's right.'

'That's not right. Or not entirely right. What Abe told us is why the history department kept him. What I wanted to know was why the university kept him.'

'But he said nobody except a few history professors even knew about it.'

'I know that's what he said, and I know that's what he thinks, but in this case he's wrong.'

Gomes piped up from his chair. 'See, it's not so much that this is a small town as that it's a cone-shaped town, with the pointy part up top, and what we're talking about here – a crime involving a professor at Wickenden's most powerful institution – happens at the very top of the cone. No way, in my experience, something like this happens without somebody from the university finding out. Maybe the night watchman tells his wife, who tells her sister the teacher, who mentions it to another teacher, who's married to a reporter, who tells an editor, who tells an old friend, who tells a neighbor, and so on, like a game of telephone.'

'By the time it trickles up, though, the man might have become Son of Sam Two,' said Joe.

'Yeah, and news like this would have a way of distorting, especially coming from a group of people who probably hate guns and don't have much exposure to violent crime in the first place, you know?' Gomes had moved his chair closer to the desk where we were sitting. Something about spending time with the two of them made me feel good: safe but excited. They seemed intellectually intimate – finishing each other's sentences, refining each other's thoughts, each making the other better – and that, in my experience, is rare. Gomes continued: 'A man carries a weapon, and the Wickenden crowd turns him into some sort of Neanderthal.'

'Right,' agreed Joe. 'So the first thing I did was, I phoned Uncle Abe and asked if he could call in a favor, check the department's payroll records in the university offices. See what it was costing them to keep Pühapäev. You know what he made per year?' Joe leaned across the table, black eyes boring into me, hands clasped like a magician's enclosing a dove. 'A dollar.' He opened his hands.

'One dollar?'

'Yep. One dollar. That's not so unusual as you might think, though. You got a professor who maybe comes from money, or who's married to a doctor or a lawyer, and just teaches for the hell of it, doesn't need the salary. But the university needs to pay them for tax purposes. So they take a symbolic dollar and float the rest back.

'In Pühapäev's case, though, that wasn't all. He was also donating, on top of his salary, between five thousand and ten thousand per year, every year, to the university.'

'How'd you find that out?'

Joe held up a copy of Wickenden's yearly financial report. On the cover was the usual picture: a multi-ethnic group of students (none of whom anyone has ever seen before) sitting under a tree on the green, laughing up a storm, surrounded by books and good humor, steeped and rolled in luck. 'Name's here. Under "Patron," meaning he gave between five and ten thousand. We have these going back years, and he's in it, same level, every year since '92.'

'But what does this prove?'

'Listen to this kid,' said Gomes. 'He's got the courtroom manner and everything. Should have been a lawyer. You still could, young man, you know?'

'You been talking to my father?'

Gomes laughed and shook his head. 'It doesn't prove anything yet. But like Joey said, we have to assume that at least a rumor of his arrest got back to someone in the university's administration. And we have to assume that if it did, the administration would have overruled the department the first time out, because what university wants a professor with an itchy trigger finger? Crowley probably had juice, but no way he had that much. One guy? No chance. Pretty mediocre writer, too, you want my opinion. Anyway, what this does is, it provides enough for a working hypothesis on why the university would have kept your man Pühapäev. He was giving them . . . what? Including his salary, fifty, sixty, maybe even seventy grand each year? Lot of money. All they had to do was keep it quiet, and Crowley and Joey's uncle did a good job of that. So there we go. I got the good stuff, though, as usual.'

'Aw, fuck you, Gomesy.' Joe looked at me. 'This guy wanders around the desert for a couple of years chasing smoke thieves, he thinks he's Eliot Ness. Comes back here to join the real cops and never lets us forget his glory days.'

'Don't even talk about the desert, man. Gives me the shudders just thinking about it. I'll tell you this, young man, you ever do get the urge to enter law enforcement, let me counsel you to stay away from the FBI unless you got a whole lot of patience or a whole lot of luck. See, I wound up on assignment in Bisbee and Douglas.'

'Where and where?'

'Exactly and exactly. Chasing cigarette smugglers from Mexico between Bisbee, Arizona, and Douglas, New Mexico. I can't stand hot weather, and there the sun just leans on you, you know, so you drink six liters of water a day and never take a leak. Get a hangover as soon as you finish a beer. What kind of life is that? But I still got some friends in the Bureau, and they hooked me up.'

'With what?'

'Well, it turns out that your friend was a material witness in a jewel-theft case back in 1995.' Gomes moved the mouse on his computer, and the screen jumped to life. 'The feds still think he was the fence, but they never got enough to prosecute. You writing this down?'

'Always.'

'Good. Where are we . . . okay. In January of 1995, the Wickenden Museum of Fine Arts hosted a traveling exhibition of Iranian jewels. Very fancy material, some from the shah's collection, other stuff somehow trickled out of the country.'

'Hey, I saw that,' said Joe. 'Uncle Abe helped bring it here.'

'What do you mean?' I asked.

'All the fancy Wickenden Persians – meaning my uncles and cousins, mostly – chipped in a little money and matched the museum's funding. Besides, most of the stuff is in exiles' private collections anyway, so Persian expats all over the place had to do some sweet-talking, some convincing. Abe also wrote the proposal a few years back to bring the exhibit here. Beautiful stuff it was, too.'

'Certainly was, but it almost didn't open,' said Gomes. 'See, the exhibit came here from Manchester – the one in England, not New Hampshire. The jewels landed at Logan, and one of the workmen they hired to move the stuff from Logan to Wickenden tried to rip off some rubies.'

'What happened? How'd they catch him?' I asked.

'How'd they catch him? I would very much like to know that myself. Doesn't say here. Wait, no, it does. Here: "Acting on information provided by a confidential informant in Boston, agents apprehended Josef Khlopikov, an employee of a well-known courier firm that had responsibility for safely transporting the contents of the exhibit from the private air terminal at Logan to the Wickenden Fine Arts Museum. Agents followed Khlopikov from his Dorchester apartment to the terminal, where he was observed opening crate number twenty-seven, removing package number ninety-one, and secreting it in the pocket of his overalls. Immediately thereafter, agents Williams, Szalai, and Tadaki apprehended the suspect and took him to the federal detention facility in Springfield, Mass."

'Now, this is where it gets interesting. It appears Khlopikov tried to cop a plea. Any guesses what he said?' Gomes looked at me, and I shrugged. He looked at Jadid, who made a circular little 'get on with it' motion with his hand.

'Patience is a virtue, you know. Mr Khlopikov said he was carrying out the theft on the orders of one Jaan Pühapäev, professor of history and East European studies at Wickenden University. Mr Khlopikov said the professor promised him one million dollars in bearer bonds. Mr Khlopikov said that the professor told him that these rubies possessed some sort of magical power, but that only he knew how to use them. Convenient. Sounds like bullshit, naturally, to us right-thinking educated gentlemen, but notes here say Khlopikov was terrified. Said he only gave it up when they threatened to deport not just him but both his parents, his sister, and his nieces too.

'Anyway, Williams and Szalai visited Professor Pühapäev at his place of residence in Lincoln, Connecticut, where, naturally, the absentminded professor professed total ignorance of any traveling exhibition of Iranian jewels, any Josef Khlopikov, and any plot to steal any rubies. Washington told him to be prepared to come down to the Bureau in Boston for questioning. Three days later the Bureau office gets a letter from a lawyer claiming that Pühapäev is the innocent victim of a setup, that the Russian mafia organized the theft and picked Pühapäev as a patsy. My client is an immigrant, the letter says, a professor, unworldly, without family or close friends, consequently making him an easy mark for these sophisticated criminals –'

'This attorney,' I interrupted. 'Was he named Vernum Sickle?'

'Yeah, Sickie Sickle all right,' Gomes answered. 'You want my opinion, if Sickle's defending someone, it means two things: he's guilty and he's rich. Anyway, Sickle also threatened large and expensive suits for slander if any of this information ever leaked to the press. I suppose I'll expect a subpoena any day now. Agents searched Pühapäev's phone records, his home, his office — Sickle let them do it on a weekend night — but the only thing connecting him to Khlopikov was Khlopikov's say-so. No case, no prosecution. The end.'

'I want to talk to that thief,' said Joe.

'You do? Never pegged you for a séance man.'

'Dead?'

'Boy got his throat cut in a prison fight two days after sentencing. Assailant or assailants unknown.'

Joe sighed and scratched his head. 'So what we got here is a guy who with no apparent means of financial support, no known friends or relatives except this music teacher Paulie's keeping an eye on, and ties to Russian jewel thieves, probably mafia-related.'

'Why mafia-related?' I asked.

'I'll bet dollars to doughnuts that the snitch is low-level Russian mob. They got a presence in Boston.'

'Let me ask you something else,' I said. 'The theft happened in January 1995. That was also when Pühapäev was arrested for the first time for shooting his gun out the window. Do you think that's a co-incidence?'

'No such thing as coincidence in a criminal investigation, son,' said Gomes. 'Not unless you're a defense attorney.'

'This professor ever leave his house except to go to work?' asked Joe.

'Only to go to this bar out in Clougham,' I said.

'Clougham between here and Hartford?'

'That's right. The bar's called the Lone Wolf.'

'Lone Wolf, huh. You been there?'

'I have. Scrubby little neighborhood place. Totally unremarkable. The owner didn't really take a liking to me.'

'What do you mean?'

I told him about Albanian Eddie and his warm farewell.

'Albanian Eddie, huh? Sally, this worth a trip?'

'To Connecticut? You must be joking, desk rider. We don't have jurisdiction out there, and you're in enough trouble to last you a good long while,' Gomes said.

'We're investigating the possible murder of a professor at Wickenden University. We're not going to be arresting anyone. I just want to take a look, you know, get off my screaming ass. No one'll miss me if I'm not here bang on time when my shift starts.'

'You're not supposed to be investigating anything, man. And if you do, I'm sure not supposed to be helping you do it.'

'So you're coming?'

'Only to keep the Fat Person out of trouble, Fat Person.'

RAINBOW DUST AND
PEACOCK'S TAIL

⌣⌣

The peacock's tail, the rainbow: men smarter than I held faith that these symbolize the coming rebirth, and the inherent inconstancy of the new, which having replaced what is dead does not yet know what it is. Yet must I observe that rainbows are more often prismatic, brief, and visually incomplete than they are ·the arcing bands we see represented; and peacocks are exceptionally ill-tempered birds.

— BOUDEWIJN TEN HUYTEN,
The Arch of St Innocent's, or Flamel's Folly

November 18, 1986
Aubrey College
Oxford

To *[NAME DELETED], Commander: Soviet Navy, Baltic Fleet Haapsalu, Estonia*

I trust you will forgive the long silence between my receipt of your instructions and this, my proud announcement that I have, at last and only in part, succeeded. What you requested was not easy. It required patience, determination, and large amounts of research and travel. As you know, I grow exceptionally nervous and physically unwell whenever I travel southeast of London or northwest of Wales; I therefore feared, perhaps beyond reasonable measure, my recent journey to Gyumri and the surrounding region. Nonetheless, the chance to see the native soil from which my children originally sprang was ample incentive to overcome those fears (though I don't know what would have become of me had I not stuck to my daily regimen of Benzedrine, beerenburg, Seconal, and an ever-ready pipe filled with my own smokable shrubs). General Petrossian was a courteous and knowledgeable host; I understand I have you, at least partially, to thank for that.

Without causing offense, I feel compelled to tell you that much of my difficulty resulted from the bumbling ineloquence and needless position jockeying of your associate (and mine, I suppose, however reluctantly) Voskresenyov. In fact, his hunger to complete his task and move our Center west compelled me to write to you before finishing my task: I must register my objections at the earliest possible moment, and I want it on record that entrusting it to him, and allowing him to move it where he proposes to move it, is a mistake the likes of which we have not seen for centuries.

Now, you know that I would never question your judgment, nor do I have the slightest interest in assuming your duties: I find it a challenge to organize anything beyond the bounds of my own greenhouse, to say nothing of an organization such as ours. I must therefore accept that you had good reason to place Voskresenyov in charge of reassembling the Library, but I confess that in me he inspired scant confidence, particularly with regard to the particular item – or items – on which I have been working. I thought we had agreed, based on textual research, memory, and induction, that the Rainbow was purely metaphorical – a metaphor of a metaphor for a dissimulation – and I proceeded to breed for you ten living metaphors on that basis. Voskresenyov seems to view my work as some sort of placative, temporary, stopgap measure; he believes that a real Rainbow or Peacock's Tail of some sort can and will be found. He believes it to be some sort of jewel, he told me, most likely worn as a pendant or brooch. Where? When? How? Who has it? What trustworthy sources have written of it? On these questions he is, naturally, mute. Nonetheless, he insists that you seek my work only because it dies and can therefore be replaced with little agony one fine winter morning when he strides through the proverbial door with his prize. Fortunately, I trust I know you better than that. If I can presume to advise you: keep a close eye on this man. He has about him an air of incompleteness, and when he sits, he sits too far forward in his chair.

Were I a man who hungered for worldly fame, the contents of this package would ensure it. You hold ten unique beauties (red, orange, yellow, green, blue, indigo, violet, black, white, and translucent) crossbred and fertilized using techniques of my own invention. Some are fragile, and I will have to send replacements yearly; others should outlast us – or at least Voskresenyov, let us hope – after a single successful planting. All flowers descend in lineage from a tulip garden that the Petrossian patriarchs have tended for nearly fifteen hundred years. The same garden, I might add, from which the Petrossians – then Persian contract soldiers – sent tribute to the court of King Roger II. An average man will see these in bloom as beautiful flowers: you will see an unbroken line made of petals, alive and radiant before you.

I look forward to receiving payment in the amount, manner, and time we have previously discussed. Should you ever have occasion to skate across the North and Baltic seas, turning southward at the English Channel and following the fog that rolls off the Thames through the Meadows, up the cobblestone streets leading to the Bear, across the High Street and up Calx Street to the Porter's Lodge, you will find the warmest of welcomes, and in my greenhouse I will show you things of which even you cannot dream.

– DD

Item 9a: A glassine bag containing ten dried tulip petals, each of a different color.

Item 9b: The Peacock's Tail, a brooch that Valvukas, an early Lietuvan warlord, had made for his wife, and she gave to her lover, whom she never named but referred to in her diary as 'the dark man of riddles and directions.' Ten pieces of Baltic amber ranging in length from 3 to 6 centimeters, each of a different color (blood, cooling lava, late-August afternoon, Karelia, dead man's lips, January noon, wine, everything, nothing, God), each containing a single fly wing, set in a teardrop shape on a silver backing.

Alchemy supplants and hastens nature; gardening and husbandry merely follow it, so it should come as no surprise to learn that relatively few alchemists have kept bestiaries or ornamental gardens. Many were herbalists, just as many raised animals for food, but generally passion never leavened their curiosity about flora and fauna. Nonetheless, a peacock's feather (which in lore bears more color than it does on an actual peacock) or a multicolored bouquet of flowers both have always been welcome gifts. They refer, in metaphor, to the time during the process after the original substance is broken down and cleansed of its former self and before it begins to assume its new form. It then takes on a variety of colors and forms, depending on its nature and the skill and showmanship of the alchemist.

Date of manufacture (9a): The tulips bloomed in May 1983.

Date of manufacture (9b): Valvukas married on the summer solstice of 1152. He drowned his wife in a bog during the spring thaw of 1155.

Manufacturer (9a): Darius Dimbledon, university professor of botany and senior tutor at Aubrey College, Oxford.

Manufacturer (9b): Al-Idrisi, shipwrecked geographer of Baghdad and Palermo, and tutor to Valvukas.

Place of origin (9a): Oxford, England.
Place of origin (9b): The Estonian seacoast.

Last known owner (9a): Professor Dimbledon mailed the flowers along with the above letter to a Soviet naval commander with a reputation for eccentricity and erudition. From there they went to Ivan Voskresenyov, whose search for the Peacock's Tail continued, despite Dimbledon's derision.

Last known owner (9b): When Dimbledon died (suddenly and messily), the brooch was found in his nightstand. It was one of two jewels that he should not have kept; neither, fortunately, was found by the police.

Estimated value (9a): Negligible. About 7 cents for the bag, less for its contents.

Estimated value (9b): Those few who know it exists – not as few as Dimbledon pretended in his letter, but not terribly many – would easily pay $250,000. Amber of such clarity and variance of color, made into a single piece by such a renowned craftsman, can fetch a dizzyingly steep price.

*Again it doth descend to Earth,
and uniteth in itself the force from things
superior and things inferior.*

———

Jadid and Gomes bickered like an old married couple as they put on their coats and walked down the department steps. Gomes teased Joe about his clothes, calling his style 'neohomeless'; Joe snatched the car keys out of Gomes's hand and told me that he drove like he was always worried about giving himself a speeding ticket. Joe repeated his warning for me to be careful; Gomes told him I could take care of myself and then warned me himself. I thanked them again for helping me, and Gomes shrugged. 'You see the good stuff on TV. Interesting cases are pretty rare in life: when they come, we like to run with them.'

I headed over to Allen Avenue to pick up some dinner for me and Hannah. I figured I would surprise her, dazzle her with my culinary expertise, which typically extends no further than boiling water and pouring sauce over pasta. One night in college, drunk and hungry, I had invented a Toast Sandwich – one toasted piece of bread between two untoasted pieces of bread, with butter and ketchup. Fortunately, Allen Avenue caters to ambitious bumblers like me.

There exists no consensus on when or whether the Allen Avenue area of Carroll Hill tipped from being an authentic Italian-American enclave in Wickenden to being merely a collection of Italian food stores, wine stores, and wise-guy restaurants catering principally to tourists and crosstown shoppers. Ask a resident – one of the dwindling number of second- or third-generation Carroll Hillers – and you're as likely to get a lament as you will a defense; ask any other Wickenden resident and he'll probably tell you that it was really something when he was a kid, but now only red-sauce suckers and zoot-suit wannabes hang out there.

Of those two I consider myself more of a red-sauce sucker, which is how I found myself in Ciavetti's Pork Store buying some fresh arrabbiata sauce, sweet sausage, ravioli filled with fresh salted mozzarella, two handfuls of sweet basil, and two bottles of Montepulciano.

'You buying for a girl?' asked the old lady with the eye gleam and the faded-beauty half smile behind the counter.

'Yes, I am,' I said proudly.

'Yes. You see, I always can tell. You gotta little

bounce when you walk, and your eyes got the light. Cook this for her, easy-easy, and she gonna love you forever.'

'Paul?' a familiar voice called down from a window above my car. 'What are you doing here?'

I looked up and saw Mia leaning out of an oriel window that protruded from the roof of the powder blue house. She had her hair pulled back with a rubber band and a pencil through it, like she always did when she was working. She was wearing a Wickenden sweatshirt and glasses, which she never wore out of the house. 'Hey there,' I replied. 'Since when did you live down here?'

'Since my old place was bought. The new landlord painted the front of the house and doubled the rent, so we left. Hang on a sec, I'll come right down.'

'No, I don't have much –' But she had already shut the window. I tried to look cool and disaffected by leaning against my car nonchalantly, but in the mirror I saw that I only succeeded in looking sleepy, or like I needed glasses.

She opened her front door and walked outside in one quick, fluid motion, the same way I remember her doing everything. She looked down at her sweat-suit and shrugged. 'Work clothes. I've been writing for the last five hours. Funny that the first time I look out my window, I see Paul Tomm getting into his car in front of my place. It's either a coincidence or you're stalking me.' She spoke with the hyperaccurate pronunciation and perfect modulation of a child of immigrants, and she looked at me with the same appraising, half-flirtatious half-contentious expression I remembered from before.

'Don't flatter yourself,' I said, reaching out to hug her and laughing. 'You look great.'

'Paul, I've been reading German newspapers since six in the morning. I'm wearing oversize sweats and glasses, and I'm seven pounds heavier than when you last saw me. I've barely been outside in weeks. I look like shit. You're looking okay, though. What's going on?'

'Just in town working on a story, if you can believe that.'

'I can. What is it?'

'Professor Pühapäev. He died.'

'That's right; he lived out where you work. There's a rumor floating around that he was murdered, you know.'

'Really? How'd that one start?'

'How does any rumor start? I heard it from a guy in my Lübeck seminar, who heard it from someone else, who heard it from someone else, blah, blah, blah.' She took the pencil out of her hair and shook her head, maybe flirtatiously, maybe just because her scalp needed some air.

'It might not be inaccurate.'

'Really?' She sat down on the steps of her house and pulled at my sleeve until I sat down next to her.

'Stop standing there, you're making me nervous. So he really was killed?'

'Well, we're not sure,' I said, immediately self-recriminating for using that pompous 'we.' 'I was just talking to the police here about him. You know who the main cop helping me is? Guess.'

'Paulie, I don't know.'

'Go on, guess. Guess, guess, guess.' I poked her arm with each command. It really was sort of nice seeing her again.

'I don't know. Inspector Lestrade?'

'No.'

'Auguste Dupin?'

'Wrong again. That name sounds familiar. I'm almost sure I should know who Auguste Dupin is.'

'You should, but now will you please just tell me?'

'You always make me feel like I pay too little attention, you know? It's kind of charming in a masochistic way.'

She shook her head and looked pointedly away, her face so serious she was smiling by implication. 'Fine, I don't even care.'

'Joe Jadid. The big guy's nephew.'

She laughed with a hand over her mouth. 'I can't believe it. Or wait, yes, I can. He's a fascist anyway. It makes total sense.'

'He is not a fascist.'

'Yes, he is, and so are you. Fascist.' She stuck her tongue out at me.

I shrugged and turned my palms up. Arguments with Mia, even if they started at a level this childish, had a way of accelerating quickly and unpredictably. One minute we'd be arguing about whether to have dinner before or after the movie, the next she'd be blaming me for the rising prison population. Better to capitulate overtly and resist silently. 'So how's the thesis coming?' I asked.

'Great. Slowly but great. My entire life for the next five months is in that room up there. I'm not even going home for winter vacation.'

'What happens after that?'

'After winter vacation?'

'No, after the thesis is over. The dreaded question: What happens After?'

'After that we'll see. I've applied for the fancy England scholarships, and if I get those, I'll be over there. Otherwise law school.'

'And from there to world dominance?'

'And from there to world dominance. I'm going to need a minister of propaganda, you know. Interested?'

'Could be.'

'What else are you doing?'

'I might be working in Boston after this story. At the *Reader*.'

'Wow. Well done. I'm impressed, but not surprised. This kind of job seems about right for someone like you.'

'What does that mean, someone like me?'

'I don't know . . . Someone curious, but without a strong personality. Politically moderate. Personally moderate. Moderately moderate. Sometimes I felt you were like a sponge, you know, just sitting there listening to me talk or vent, without giving anything back. I guess that quality would make you a good reporter. A rotten boyfriend, but a good reporter.' I thought we had finished with these kinds of conversations. Oh, well. She smiled sidelong at me to see whether I was offended. I wasn't.

'Gee, thanks. So you seeing anyone else? Someone nonspongelike.'

'Yeah, my computer.' She stared at me. I braced; she relented. 'I really don't have the time now, with the thesis and everything. Besides, who knows where I'll be in six months? What about you?'

'Yeah, sort of.'

'Yeah, sort of and . . . ? Who is she?'

'She teaches music. Her name's Hannah.'

Mia nodded and gave a tight smile. I hoped she'd want to hear about Hannah less than I wanted to talk about her. 'Is that something for her in the bag?' She reached over and peered in. 'Smells good.'

'From Allen Avenue. I'm cooking.'

'You can't cook. I know you can't cook.' She pulled out the tub of pasta and looked quizzically at me. 'Have you learned to cook?'

'Yeah, maybe. Listen, I have to take off. It's a couple hours' drive back, and I don't want to sit in Wickenden rush hour.'

'Oh, yeah, that's a rough two blocks, isn't it? Listen to you, a New York boy, complaining about rush-hour traffic here. So it was nice to see you,' she said, dropping the pasta in the bag, standing up, and brushing paint chips and twigs from the seat of her sweats. 'Are you going to be back here again?'

'I don't know, really. Why?'

'If you are, you should stop by.'

'Okay.' The promise was maybe 70 percent hollow, but well intentioned, if that counts for anything. It probably doesn't.

'I'll be at my desk right next to that window for the next five months. Come throw pebbles or something.' She leaned over and kissed me on the cheek. 'Great to see you, Paul. Sorry about the "rotten boyfriend" comment.'

'Nothing to be sorry about. But I'm trying to get better.'

'I know. You always did. It's a charming quality of yours. Don't let it go to your head.'

'Nice to see you, too, Mee. Good luck with the Germans.' She gave a mock–Hitler salute, giggled, and went inside. It was an ideal conversation with an ex: flirtatious enough to produce residual little flutters, but noncommittal enough to avoid trouble; long enough to end with an ellipsis, but not so long that either of us got any ideas; glib, but with a warm and serious turn at the end, but not so serious that either of us brought out the knives. I was feeling ticklish; she tickled, and I went home almost missing her.

When I returned to my car, I saw that someone had taped a cloth Portuguese flag to my antenna. On the red half, I wrote 'Thank you' and slipped it through the mail slot of the Portuguese Men's Club.

This time I parked directly in front of Hannah's house, figuring that Mrs DeSouza would want to see me less than I wanted to see her. I let a wave of guilt wash over me, decided that what's past repair should be past grief, and continued feeling guilty as only a Jewish-Catholic-Calvinist can. I was owed an apology as much as I owed one, I said to myself as I semislunk around to Hannah's entrance.

Through Hannah's front window, I saw her seated at the piano bench but facing the couch, her hands in her lap and her head slightly inclined forward, as if she were listening to someone with a quiet voice. Her generally placid, content expression had risen and sharpened into an almost beatific eagerness – her gray eyes crinkled at the edges and visibly aglow and her mouth slightly open, caught in early laughter – as though she wanted her interlocutor to see how much, how deeply she enjoyed and believed what she or he was saying. There isn't enough dinner for three, I thought uncharitably as I knocked at her door.

She opened it warily and greeted me with a strained smile. I leaned forward to kiss her, and she blocked me, her hand flat on my chest as she turned her head to the side and gave a quiet, tight-lipped double hum of refusal. When I stood back, confused, she opened the door and invited me in. Sitting on her couch, a mug of tea in his lap and a kindly, open expression on his bearded, craggy face, was the man from the Trout.

'Paul, this is Jaan's brother, Tonu.' He rose slowly and creakily, exhaling with effort, to greet me, but he gripped my hand firmly, exerting a surprising amount of strength through a hand that was all callus and knobby bone. He looked like a combination of a lion and a bird, with watchful, bright blue eyes set on either side of an aquiline nose and above a poorly trimmed beard that seemed of a single piece with his shaggy white hair.

'You are Paul?' he asked in a booming and strongly accented voice. An odor of age and pipe rose and reached me just before he did. 'My name is Tonu Pühapäev. Your friend and I, we have been holding a sort of remembrance – a small wake, you might say – for my poor younger brother.'

'Nice to meet you. I didn't know Jaan had any family.'

'Oh, yes. Oh, yes. Not many family, of course. Just me now. One old man and another.' He chuckled absently, patted the pockets of his baggy corduroy trousers, and withdrew a stubby brown pipe, a packet of Shipman's tobacco, and a box of wooden matches. 'You also were knowing my brother?' His mustache and the beard near his mouth were yellowed, and he had to run the match over the flint three times before he finally struck a flame. When he lit the bowl of his pipe, he sat back down as carefully and hesitantly as he had stood. Next to him on the couch was a burled mahogany walking stick with a round silver head and a broad black rubber tip.

'No, I never did, unfortunately. I'm sorry for that.'

'Paul is the reporter I was telling you about,' Hannah said. 'The one working on an obituary for Jaan for our local newspaper.' I wondered about the ethics of deceit by omission: she knew – didn't she? – that it wasn't an obit anymore. Maybe I would have corrected her (or maybe not) had Tonu not started speaking again so quickly.

'Ach, yes, I remember now. The memory, you know . . . not so good. This is very wonderful custom, and I am so glad to you for doing this. When does the newspaper print your obituary?'

'Not for a long time, I hope.' The joke went over like a fart in church: I guess poking fun at ancient Estonians for ambiguous pronoun usage isn't actually that funny. Hannah grimaced with displeasure, and Tonu just looked up at me, confused and expectant. 'I'm sorry. That was a joke. I actually don't have a running date for the article yet.' I guess he was here, so why not? 'If you don't mind, perhaps I could ask you a couple of questions about your brother?'

'Yes, of course, but, you know, I've lost so much up here' – he tapped the side of his head and smiled apologetically – 'and Jaanja had lived in America for so long time, so maybe some things I don't know too good. But go, please, ask as you like.'

'Thanks.' I sat down in my usual chair, next to the table that I had knocked over the first time I came in, took out my notebook, and smiled nonthreateningly. 'Can you tell me when Jaan was born?'

'Well, we had not these calendars, so like today, on the farm where we were born. My mother would say that I am six years older than Jaanja, and I think that he was born in the wintertime, but for the question when? This nobody can know.'

'But when Estonia was part of the Soviet Union, wouldn't everybody have had official documents of some sort? And for that matter, he would have come here with a passport, right?'

'Oh, sure, sure, that garbage, ya, of course, but we just make up what sounded right, you know, for the papers. I have an old passport of Jaanja's at home. Maybe I have two. You know a Russian saying: "Without a little piece of paper, what are you? With a little piece of paper, you're a man."' He cackled, shifted in his seat, and drew on his pipe until his blue eyes glowed orange, as though lit from within.

'So what was your date of birth?'

'Mine? Ha! This is a clever reporter. I chose November seventh, 1917.'

'Why then?'

'Ha again! Maybe not so clever. It was a very patriotic Soviet day, and it helped to show yourself a patriotic Soviet man. Of course, no Estonian really *was* a patriotic Soviet, but as I said, you only had to show, not to be.

'So you know the Great October Socialist Revolution? It actually happened in November! Ha! Lenin's New Style calendar – he introduced this, you know, just after the Revolution: thirty days every month, twelve months in the year, with five extra days as national holidays, outside the calendar: very rational, very antireligious, antibourgeois, anticounterrevolutionary, and ridiculous, because it managed only to confuse everybody. When Lenin makes this new calendar for our new socialist workers' paradise, the October Revolution became on November seventh.'

'But don't people still refer to Red October?'

'Yes, yes!' He leaned forward excitedly and knocked tobacco ash onto his blue sweater. 'Of course. Completely Soviet. They replaced the seven-day week with a five-day week – weekends were for capitalist idlers, of course – and made every day a day of rest for one-fifth of the population. They gave slips of colored paper to every citizen – again, you see, this Russian love for bits of paper – so a husband and wife, maybe, had different days off, if he was a pipe fitter and she was a teacher. All to encourage constant production and to make it so impossible for people to celebrate the old holidays, which were, of course, religious holidays. But of course it made chaos! Nobody knew when to work; everybody felt everybody else was getting holidays when only they had to work; nobody could see families for spending time; so they tried to make a six-day week, but still it would not work, so they go back to as normal during the war. They said to improve morale, as a gift from the Great Leader to his subjects. Foolishness. Trifling.' His rant wound down and cooled, and he puffed contentedly on his pipe, sending up regular little smoke puffs like a dying factory.

'So there you see my birthday. So you can write for Jaan 1923, yes?'

'Unfortunately, I don't think I can. I really should either know an official date or just say that his birthday is unknown.'

'Yes, so, as you like,' he said, shrugging and bobbing his head from side to side. 'What else you want to know?'

'Where was he born?'

'Ah, this I can say for sure, that he was born on our family's farm, near to Estonian city of Paide. You know to spell this?'

'I'll figure it out.' I had no idea where that was, but figured I might as well feign journalistic integrity. 'Are you his only living relative?'

'Yes. Only me. No one else.' He laughed and scratched his head. 'He never was married, and I never was married. Only us.'

Hannah hadn't sat down yet; she stood in the same expectant position – watching our conversation as though she hoped it would end soon, laughing when Tonu laughed and refilling his mug of tea when he finished – as when I'd first walked in. For the first time since I met her, she seemed uncomfortable; a certain tightness around her temples and jaw muscles and an expression of fixed low-level alacrity made her look worried and on edge. 'If you don't mind,' I said to Tonu, 'how did your brother support himself?'

'Paul, that's a rude question. He was a professor, wasn't he?' Hannah said sharply.

'No, no,' said Tonu, 'he is reporter, he must ask rude questions.' He looked at me and raised his eyebrows mockingly, as though emphasizing that he had gotten the better of me in that exchange, and laid his cane across his lap, rolling the silver head across his thigh. 'Our family farm was collective farm, but really it was in so small town that all the workers were cousins, old friends, grandchildren, and great-grandchildren of people who had worked on this same farm for centuries. So when Russia left, the family again owns the farm. And I am the oldest son, so really it becomes my farm. And it became most successful: the largest dairy farm in the Baltic states. I live quite simply and do just my work, my walks, and my books. Jaanja loved always to wander, and he wanted always to teach in America, so when it became possible, I simply gave him what he needed.'

'He was lucky to have such a devoted brother. So you paid his living expenses and also let him donate to Wickenden University every year?'

At that question Tonu drew in a breath. 'Yes. For me, no problem. For Jaanja, he wants to give something as a gift for such a wonderful university.'

'It *is* wonderful. I graduated from there.'

'Ah, yes! You see, it is a university that makes its students into such fine newspaper writers. So you see why he wanted to give this money there.'

I hesitated before asking the next question. Hannah's expression had gone from unease to suspicion, and when I looked up at her, she subtly widened her eyes and nodded at me, clearly telling me to finish my interrogation. Interview. Whatever I was doing. I only had one more. 'In addition to paying his living expenses, did you ever pay for a lawyer for your brother as well?'

For just a moment, his amiable-old-codger veneer slid, and he glared at me with curiosity and loathing. As soon as he did that, I remembered where I first saw him: the Lone Wolf. He was the old guy sitting by himself at the end of the bar, the only one who didn't talk at all. Now he knew I knew that his brother was something different, something more than he appeared, and with the kindled hawkishness of that look, I knew he knew I knew. He clouded and widened his eyes, opened his mouth slightly into its vacant grin, and scratched his thigh absently while looking at me. 'Lawyer? What Jaanja did with his money I never knew. But why do you ask?'

'Well, according to someone in Wickenden's history department, he had a bit of trouble with the law.'

'Paul!' Hannah spoke so sharply I jumped. 'Tonu has come all the way from Estonia to collect his brother's body, not to hear about some problems he might have had. Does this really matter now?'

'It's my job to be curious about this sort of thing. And yes, it might matter very much, because –'

'I cannot see how,' said Tonu, standing up slowly and leaning on his cane. 'I have told you, I think, what you need to know, yes? Now it is time for an old man to go back to the comforts of his little room.'

Hannah helped him on with his coat and hat. 'Do you have enough food? What will you eat?'

'There is a small tavern, I think, just down the road from my guesthouse. I will eat American hamburgers and listen to Elvis Presley on one of your jukeboxes and then sleep in my big American bed.'

'I didn't know the Lone Wolf had a kitchen,' I chanced.

He paused briefly while putting his coat on and exhaled with impatience. 'No, this place where you first saw me does not,' he said, staring fixedly at me. 'I was there, since you do not ask but wish to, because Jaanja had written about it in his letters home. I wished to get some sense of my brother's American life, so I went there for an afternoon glass of brandy. But still I cannot see why this will be a part of my brother's obituary, and I ask that if you really are planning to write such a thing, you do so quickly. I ask also that you respect the sanctity of the dead and not speak ill of him.'

He kissed Hannah on both cheeks and bade her good night with a courteous bow. To me he slung a glowering harrumph as he teetered out the door and around the side of the house. I braced myself, expecting a torrent from Hannah for insulting her guest, for my impious curiosity, and for any number of other things that I might have done or omitted doing that I did not yet know about.

Instead she shut the door behind him and closed her eyes, leaning her head on the doorframe. I thought she was crying. I saw her wall of reserve and poise slip and crumble, and as she lifted her head, I saw her try to rebuild it. By the time she turned to look at me, she was smiling, but the smile was thin and brittle. 'Oh, Paul. What a mess.'

'What do you mean?'

'Just that . . . I don't know, Paul. You read *Hamlet*, right?'

'Sure.'

'I was Ophelia in a production in college. I lived with that play for a year. Do you remember it well?'

'No, unfortunately. Why?'

'The Player King's speech?' She took my hand, interlocked her fingers with mine, then dropped it. I nodded uncertainly. She looked grave, older, tired, and troubled: her eyes flickered instead of glowing, her face was pale, and her features had a fevered sharpness that made me think she was sick. 'Do you remember how it ends?'

'I don't.'

'"Our wills and fates do so contrary run, / That our devices still are overthrown: / Our thoughts are ours, their ends none of our own."'

'I don't . . . What's the matter, Hannah? Do you want to sit down? I have some wine and food if you're hungry. What's wrong?'

'How do we know when we've done well and when we've just intended well?' She clenched her fists and her jaw, dropped her head into her hands. When she looked up again, she was her old self, and she suggested that we go back to my place so I could cook her dinner.

'Sure,' I agreed. 'But are you sure you're feeling all right?'

'I'm fine. Really. I think I'm just hungry. And talking to Tonu made me realize that Jaan really is gone, and that I miss him.'

'Is that all? Hannah, I'm worried about you. This morning I found –'

She leaned forward and kissed me, running a hand down my cheek and around my neck. 'You have nothing to worry about,' she said, holding my face in her hands and looking straight into my eyes. 'Remember that: you don't ever have to worry about me.' She nodded my head for me, then let go and locked an arm in mine. 'Should we go? I've never seen your place, and I'm hungry. I didn't know you could cook.'

'I'm not sure I can. The ingredients are mine, their ends none of my own.'

THE KAGHAN'S CAGES
(FIRE)

❧

The Inner Fire is divine love. I discovered this after
burning my hand on a manifestation of the outer fire
while attempting to light my pipe while hanging
upside down from a roof beam.
— C. MORTMAIN, *Not Alone the Dragon*

'From the Arabic word *ashk*, which means "love."
This is the city of love.' The guide grinned and
bowed his head slightly as he turned it toward his
employer, who looked downward at the stone balcony rather than outward across it. A grenade-sized
black scorpion shadow-danced at the men's feet.
The guide teased it with his cane, eliciting five rapid
but ineffectual strikes, before he sent it flying with
an expert wrist shot. 'Hockey player. In school. The
officers' rink.'

The guide swept his cane across their field of vision, constantly darting his head to see whether his employer was pleased. A servile and insincere smile bounced from his mouth, and he was worrying a thread that hung from his robe's sleeve, balling it, twisting it, rolling it, pulling it, making the thread longer and the sleeve shorter. The Kopet Dag Mountains loomed in the distance like mounds of crumpled purple foil. The city itself seemed perpetually covered with a layer of dust; it never fully came into focus, and the minutiae shifted with each breeze. The streets and houses ran along a precise grid; in true Soviet fashion, all traces of imagination or inventiveness on the part of the city planners had been eliminated. 'New city, sir. All new. An earthquake destroyed the true Ashgabat nearly forty years ago.'

'So I read. But I don't remember hearing anything about it.'

'No. In those years we did not . . . you would never . . .'

'Earthquakes didn't happen in socialist countries,' said the employer with a low-wattage knowing smile.

'Of course not. The Iron Eagle was guiding us toward a glorious future, and we were building the ideal state of relations on earth. Working in harmony with nature. Mastering it. How, then, could nature turn against us, you see? You remember?'

'I do.'

'And if I can ask, where were you then?'

'Not yet born, actually. But I teach in the Department of Marxist-Leninist Dialectical and Historical Concepts in Rostov-na-Donu and have read a great deal about those years. Difficult times, particularly in these republics.'

The guide, more out of habit than necessity, glanced over each shoulder before turning uneasily back to his employer. He clicked his tongue quietly, nervously through the space where his top three front teeth should have been. People still never spoke of such things openly. The new frankness rumored to exist in official circles in Moscow and Leningrad had not yet blown southward to this desolate capital of a perpetually forgotten region.

'Shall I address you then as "Professor," or simply as "Comrade," or perhaps in some other fashion?'

'As you wish. Professor Ostrov is perfectly acceptable.' In fact, it was far from perfect: this was the first time he had worked as a Russian, and while he spoke the language fluently, his Caucasian accent defied his best efforts and fluttered occasionally into his speech. He hoped that it would be mistaken for a southern accent – hence his claim to come from Rostov-na-Donu.

Naturally, he backed up that claim – and all others Professor Ostrov made – with the requisite signed, sealed, decorated, embossed, and stamped papers. In eliminating religion, the Soviet Union had changed its icons from the hollow-eyed, mournful, incense-cured figures on its church walls for little sheets of paper and rubber stamps. When he registered at the Hotel Turist, he presented to the *dezhurnaya* a stamped letter from the Technical Institute of Rostov-na-Donu that identified him as a historical researcher come to Ashgabat to view the works of the heroic Turkmen people on display at Tolkuchka Bazaar. She looked at him with the bored superiority of the provincial official exercising petty and circumscribed power. Shuffling down the hall like a turtle looking for its shell, she showed him his room, told him when he would receive hot water, and reminded him to leave his key with her whenever he left the hotel.

Ashgabat's People's Leadership Technical Institute wished to extend a courtesy to a distinguished visiting scholar from Russia, so they provided Ostrov with a guide. He rejected the first four until they sent him the man whom he had come to see, Murat, who at this moment was cracking pistachios with his molars and spitting the shells off the balcony. That Murat did not know that his employer had come to Ashgabat to see him made the job that much easier. Ostrov saw him aiming for pedestrians.

To become Ostrov, Abulfaz had shaved his beard as well as the top of his head, and wore an ill-fitting blue blazer with a Lenin pin on the lapel, a cheap white shirt, and a stained and fraying red tie. He raised his eyebrows but turned the corners of his mouth down, making him appear watchful but perpetually disapproving: a professorial expression. When he turned his gaze toward Murat, the guide pocketed his pistachios and slunk back from the balcony's edge.

'Shall we go?' asked Abulfaz.

'Of course, Comrade Professor. Where do you wish to go?'

'Well, as you know, I have come to observe and record traditional Turkmen crafts, particularly carpets, so . . .'

'Indeed. So we shall go to Tolkuchka? We shall have to arrange for transport, then.'

'Of course. I shall expect you in front of my hotel with a car in one hour. I suppose I shall have to pay for private transportation. Preferably by car, and preferably in a car not likely to break down today.'

'Yes, sir. One hour.'

Sixty minutes and thirty-two seconds later, Abulfaz/ Ostrov and Murat wedged themselves into the backseat of a purple Lada. Murat's cousin, a huge man with a beard so thick and sprawling that it seemed to sit spherically on the lower half of his face, extending equally in every direction, drove the car in a manner consistent with his belief that fate was the exclusive determinant of human destiny. Willpower, industrial glue pilfered from a Soviet air base, and the occasional rubber cord kept vehicular entropy at bay. Abulfaz, who had driven in worse places with worse drivers, was not scared, but Ostrov would be, so he tensed his muscles and produced visible drops on his bald head and half moons beneath his arms. Murat and his cousin chatted animatedly in a patois of Turkmen and Russian; the latter man frequently turned fully around in his seat and gesticulated at his cousin with both hands while he steadied the steering wheel between his knees.

As they rounded a bend – driving, of course, as fast as the car would go – they nearly smacked into the back of a filthy gray truck whose flatbed was filled with sheets of color, rich colors of every hue in patterns such as you see on the insides of eyelids when you turn squinched-shut eyes toward the noon sun. The cousin sounded the horn and swore. Carpets, hundreds of them, gathered from the pages of fairy tales and forgotten songs and loaded onto a rickety old vehicle in this dusty and forgotten corner of a crumbling country. Abulfaz rubbed his eyes; Murat laughed.

'Beautiful, Comrade Professor, yes? Turkmen carpets, the finest in the world. This is what you are here to see?'

'Beautiful,' Abulfaz agreed.

In the desert afternoon, the market shimmered into view, but once they were inside, Tolkuchka quickly shed its desert-bazaar pretensions and became a Soviet market: car parts, single hand-rolled cigarettes, and shapeless beige clothing. Repetition and a surfeit of useless goods fostered an illusion of plenty.

Murat instantly became a guide, protector, hawker, and translator for Abulfaz, who needed nothing but for Murat to feel comfortable, expert, and therefore off his guard. So Abulfaz permitted himself to be led by the elbow, offered live chickens, gold teeth yanked from corpses, embroidered square caps, hairbrushes, younger daughters, illegal shortwave radios, bricks of hashish, bolts of greasy fabric and bolts of brilliant fabric, and sad-eyed pack animals, all the while maintaining a fixed look of intellectual and ethnic superiority.

'How do people buy things here?' he asked Murat.

'Many ways, Comrade Professor. Sometimes foreign cash, especially with tourists. Mostly bartering, trading. You are asking because . . . ?'

'Because I would have thought that most goods of quality are dispatched to Moscow. Like that pile of carpets or those sheets of maroon silk.'

'Yes. Many are sent, but people save, people save for themselves, and everyone saves maybe a couple of extras to sell or trade here. And you must remember that people come here from everywhere, everywhere, everywhere. From all over. And it looks huge today, but there are thousands of others who will come tomorrow when the thousands who are here have sold what they have to sell.'

'From everywhere?'

'Well, yes. Certainly no, not literally everywhere, but all over this area, all over Central Asia.'

'What about Russians from Central Asia?'

'Ah. Ah, yes.' Murat giggled and rubbed the fingers of one hand nervously over the fingers of the other. 'No Russians. Except you. You are the Russian here today,' Murat replied with a forced laugh.

'Ah.' Abulfaz looked around, careful to keep his mask of unease from revealing his curiosity. 'And what would happen if you were to wander away from me? To leave me here in the middle of the market, dressed as I am, looking as I do.'

'Not worth thinking about. I won't leave you.'

'I know you won't. But just for argument's sake.'

'Ah. Well, look behind you. Slowly.'

Abulfaz turned around. Behind him a barrel-chested man with a thick mustache and a missing eyebrow was hitting another man with a car's muffler. A woman in a head scarf the color of sand in moonlight stood impassively before rows of burlap spice sacks being slowly baked by the high afternoon sun. Abulfaz thought of his grandmother's stained fingers when the scent of roasting cloves wafted his way; the breeze changed, and he smelled sumac and thyme – *za'atar* – and thought of his half-Arab baker uncle and the hot, herby bread he would tear with his fingers. Storytellers and spice sellers, he reflected, had an unnatural power over the memory and should be avoided.

Just then he felt a warm drop of liquid spatter against his hand. He heard a hideous shriek and saw blood rainbowing from the throat of a freshly slaughtered lamb. With a few slits and tugs, the butcher pulled the skin off like a glove. Murat poked Abulfaz

in the back and nodded his head almost imperceptibly toward a group of three men – all tall, slender,
and almost regal, with long noses, green eyes, and
leathery skin – standing silently between the butcher
and the spice seller, their eyes fixed on Abulfaz.

'You see? Your friends. Your new friends,' Murat
giggled. 'We are in the Soviet Union, so all brothers
in socialism, of course, but you, Comrade Professor
– you are the older brother. You are the parents'
favorite.'

'So?'

'So here, maybe we younger brothers like a
little space for ourselves. We cannot keep out the
Russians, not really, but we make it so that if they
do want to come here, they must come escorted by
one of us, or they would have to bring a battalion
of soldiers, and even then maybe it would end badly
for them.'

'Those men are armed?'

'Armed? This is the land of the Turkmen!
Everyone is armed. See here,' Murat said, parting his
robe and revealing a Walther strapped to his side.
'But you, do not worry. We will go where you want
to go, and you will be fine.' As Murat tied his robe
back in place, Abulfaz walked over to the three
men and began talking. Murat stared openmouthed,
but then he saw handshakes all around, followed by
suspicious smiles and nods. Abulfaz moved his body
in front of theirs; Murat saw him reach inside his
jacket, shake hands with the three of them carefully

but emphatically, and touch his hand to his heart and bow slightly. When he turned around, Murat fleetingly saw him as another person – the way he held his head a bit higher, perhaps, or a much harder expression than disdain momentarily rested on his blank face – but Ostrov again was Ostrov when he rejoined Murat.

'What have you done?' the guide asked splenetically. Abulfaz could not tell if Murat was angry or terrified. 'You were provoking them? I told you, Comrade Professor, for your own safety, look at them slowly. Do not draw their attention. What have you done?'

'Ahmot, Ilham, and Mundir are now my protectors.'

'My cousin and I are your protectors,' Murat spit, 'and you have insulted us, insulted our honor.'

'I intended to do no such thing, but I do need insurance. In case you decide to leave me to chance.'

'Why? Did I not show you my gun? Do you not see my cousin standing ten paces from us, watching watching watching, for you? Why them, too?'

'Murat, I want you to take me to your cousin.'

'What? He is right there, you can –'

'No, your other cousin. I want you to take me to the Legend Seller.'

After passing the fourth spice seller – all women, all with the same blank, bemused expression, all with their neutral-colored head scarves wrapped two and a half times around their middle-aged heads – Abulfaz began to think that the market was a labyrinth of mirrors. There was one lamb and one butcher, one glass-eyed hawk seller, and Murat was guiding him in concentric circles away from the market's center of activity. Fortunately, his three protectors followed behind them; he need only throw his glasses to the ground and they would cut Murat's throat and lead him away, to safety for him and riches for them. Abulfaz's entire career was witness to what wonders could be accomplished with rudimentary knowledge of the local language, a modicum of charm, and an inexhaustible supply of Benjamin Franklin portraits in black and green.

Murat sucked his teeth, turned his head, and spit. He let go of Abulfaz's arm to wipe his mouth with his sleeve, and as soon as they fell out of step, Ahmot shoved him forward, roughly, and gestured for him to take Abulfaz's arm again.

'What language do you speak to them?' Murat asked his charge.

'Tajik. I know relatively little, but apparently it was enough.'

'Do you understand when my cousin and I speak to each other in Turkmen?'

'Not as much as I should. Perhaps after we see your cousin, you could give me some training.'

'Perhaps for the right price. If you can turn these men into your guards, perhaps you also can accomplish more wondrous things than simply learning another language. How many is it that you speak?'

'More than you would believe.'

'I am not surprised. Most men here know two languages – Turkmen and their clan version of Turkmen. The educated, like me, also know Russian. We see the Uzbeks coming here speaking four or five. Everyone in this country knows more than the Turkmen. Everyone gets more, everyone earns more, everyone always always always forever.'

'Shall I tell you a joke about languages?' Abulfaz asked.

'A joke. Yes, okay.'

'What do you call a Russian who speaks four languages?'

'I don't know.'

'A Zionist. What about a Russian who speaks three languages?'

'I don't know.'

'A spy. And two? . . . No? A nationalist. And only one? . . . An internationalist.'

'This is not very funny to me.' Murat pouted.

'I would have thought someone from the internationalized provinces of Mother Russia would appreciate the humor.'

'Are you trying to get me into trouble for speaking badly of the Soviet Union? Because I will tell you directly that I love the motherland, and I truly believe that we are forging the path to a beautiful future, united under socialism's red banner.'

'Yes, naturally. And I believe that every winter

Grandfather Frost and Snow Maiden emerge from the forest distributing gifts to all the good little girls and boys.'

Murat ran his tongue over his dry lips and stared at the man he was guiding. He was smaller than Murat, and rounder, too, with a face so lacking in character and detail, in defect or allure, that it seemed incompletely formed. He mocked Soviet principles (fearlessly, no less) but carried Soviet accreditation that entitled him to examine a market in which he apparently had not much interest. He came from a provincial town in southern Russia but befriended three Tajiks who, at the slightest provocation, would have killed him. And he knew about something that had remained not only within Murat's clan but almost entirely within his family for centuries.

In front of an otherwise barren stall, Murat kissed an old woman who wore around her neck sixteen cages, each containing a large, long-horned, feisty black beetle. 'For luck,' Murat explained. 'These *khorens*, you release it on the threshold of your house. If it walks outside, your house is blessed for seven harvests and seven winters. If it walks inside, you follow it as it collects the spirits lurking inside, and after it has walked one time all through the house, you set it in the fire. My aunt is the only one in our clan allowed to catch them from the desert.' The woman gave a curt half nod to a mean-faced, narrow-eyed boy attempting to pluck a live caged chicken; he took the necklace from her, and she showed the men into a small makeshift yurt that stood behind her stall.

She invited the men to sit down on a carpet with a pattern of interlocking vermilion, moss green, and burnished gold triangles. She sat across from them, withdrew a circular fringed carpet from a trunk behind her, and spread in on the ground in front of her. She looked at the men blankly, expectantly, warily.

'Do you know who I am?' asked Abulfaz in Russian.

'I knew a foreigner would visit today,' she answered. Her voice had the soothing rasp and timbre of a wooden flute. It sounded infrequently used and therefore younger than any other part of her. 'More than that is not my affair, but it has been many generations since one of my line traded with a foreigner. I did not know that any of you knew that we existed, but I assumed that you knew of my ignorance, and I in turn suspected your assumption of my lack of knowledge. This is a chain, you see, and, like most chains of information, it is both endless and inane. But it is also auspicious, in that it formed the subject of our first conversation, and it impels me to offer you this chain.'

From her trunk she withdrew a thick black belt that appeared to be in constant turbulent motion: three snakes, each attached mouth-to-tail to one another with crude, double-sided fishhooks. 'The

Circlet of Munatir, Seljuk Snake King, and my many-times-great-grandfather. To help you present many faces to your enemy. But perhaps a foreigner such as yourself has no need of this device.'

'I haven't,' said Abulfaz, recoiling from the proffered snakes.

She put the three snakes, still writhing, back into her trunk and turned to face Abulfaz, her hands folded genteelly in her lap, a gesture at once judicial and disconcertingly girlish. 'Why have you come?' Her voice fell somewhere between teasing and genuine inquiry.

'The Kaghan's Cages.'

At that she giggled and clapped her hand over her mouth; years fell from her like dead leaves in a breeze. 'This is indeed an honor. Even most of our people have forgotten about these. I should ask you how you know about them, but I fear you might tell me. In any event, I am only a poor market woman. What will you give me for them?'

'Do you have them?'

She sighed and reached behind her. Her entire arm up to her shoulder had disappeared into her trunk, and she rummaged around with her eyes averted, as though she were blind. She raised her eyebrows and withdrew a clay pot. The pot was as wide as a man's palm and twice as tall; its thick lid had a crude knob in the center. It looked as if it had been made by a child and left to dry in the sun, without any glaze or finish or ornamentation of any kind. Abulfaz wondered how many people had seen this pot by the side of the road and passed it by; he wondered how many times the clan had been robbed and had retained the Cage because it looked so homely. He wondered how different the world would have been if any of those robbers had known its value.

'Show me,' said Abulfaz to the woman. She held the pot up before her, as though inspecting it, and then toward Abulfaz, so he could do the same. He nodded. She lifted the lid, struck a match, and dropped it into the pot. The pot's clay walls warmed and glowed like a lantern. The light bounced off Abulfaz's glasses and landed on the woman's cheeks, making her look as though she were crying glowing tears. He reached out a hand, and the woman pulled the light away.

'This is why you came?' she asked. Abulfaz nodded. She smiled knowingly, lifted the lid of the pot, and blew out the light. 'The light of a tiny sun. A single spark will last until deliberately extinguished. You can carry this anywhere, through any weather.'

'How does it work?' asked Abulfaz, his eyes afire with something close to lust.

'There the stories end. I do not know. I doubt anyone does. My ancestor, maybe, she was the last Kaghan's vizier and doctor, but nobody else. What does it matter?'

Abulfaz nodded gallantly. 'Where is the sister?'

'The sister?'

'Cousin, did I not ask for the Kaghan's Cages, not the Kaghan's Cage? There are two. I wish to buy them both.'

'Ah.' She folded her hands in front of her again and looked down while speaking. 'Here I must confess that you are the second foreigner to visit a Legend Seller, not the first. In fact, you are the second foreigner to visit me in one moon's time. Another came – Murat showed him here, too, along with his cousin. Those three lions in men's bodies were not guarding him, though. And he barely spoke Russian. And he knew about the Cages but thought it was a Cage. He only bought one, you see. The Moon Cage.'

'And you sold him one? You split the sisters?'

'Well, yes. I had a debt, you see, a very grave debt that was left to me by my great-grandmother's great-grandmother. He settled it in exchange for the Cage.'

For the first time in years, Abulfaz was surprised. 'Who was he? Where did it go?'

'He never said his name. He said he was an Englishman, and he grew plants. Some of his plants were very special and grew only in moonlight, and the English summer days, he said, are so very long.'

Item 10: A round clay pot, 10 centimeters in diameter, 20 centimeters tall. Neither glazed nor painted, composed of crude clay, with the maker's fingerprints still visible on the outside. One of two 'Kaghan's Cages,' this one emits a glowing yellow light and is called the Sun Cage. Its sister, composed of black clay, shines hard and silver and is called the Moon Cage.

Date of manufacture: Little, if anything, about the Cage's manufacture belies anything time-specific: the potter was either primitive or clumsy; he either did not know about glazes or chose not to use any; ornamentation was either foreign to him or inappropriate for this creation; he either had no knowledge of oven baking or chose to sun-bake it. The pot's ability to gather, emit, intensify, and preserve light, of course, is completely sui generis.

Manufacturer: Legend puts the Cages in the court of the Khazar Kaghans. The title 'Kaghan' comes from either the Hebrew word *cohen*, meaning 'priest,' or the Tatar *khan,* meaning 'ruler'; which etymology you accept depends on whether you believe that the Khazars accepted Judaism or Islam (or Christianity, historically the most probable if linguistically the least interesting alternative). The Khazar state vanished sometime around the tenth century – again, the precise manner of its evanescence and the pursuant stories of its inhabitants vary according to Abrahamic faith – but al-Idrisi placed its heart between the Volga and Don rivers, near the modern-day Russian city of Rostov-na-Donu.

Representatives of all three faiths mention the Cages in their writings on the Khazars. Solomon Benjamin ben Benjamin, an Andalusian rabbi, composer, theologian, and theorist of color, reported that 'the Kaghan you would call Yusuf and I Joseph demanded of me whether there might be found on earth a quality of light more lasting than that of either the sun or the moon, which extinguish themselves every night, and more faithful than that of fire, which can rage and die like an old man whose only daughter marries an infidel. I replied that the sun is everlasting and night is only earth's blindness, but he forestalled this argument and brought forth two earthen containers, one light and one dark, both cruder than any item befitting a caliph, and dipped into each a lit reed, whereupon the lighter container glowed first the color of the cheek of a young girl in love, then took on the shine seen in the eye of a man who has discovered the answer to a vexing problem, and then steadied into the shine of a child sun in training. The other glowed hard as a proud woman pursued by an ardent but poor scholar, silver like a lake at night, like the moon's daughter.'

A cleric known only as Sa'ad was dispatched from Tripoli with a retinue of 1,000 soldiers, as well as 250 women and 250 boys for the Kaghan. Sadly, the most wellborn and promising of his soldiers died at the Kaghan's court 'for, upon seeing these lamps which replicate the heavenly spheres, my beloved Ibrahim grew offended, remembering the Qur'anic prohibition against replication of divine creations, and attempted to smash the jars with the flat part of his sword. No sooner had he lunged forward, his hand moving toward his scabbard, when twenty arrows, fired by unseen archers hidden in the infinite folds of the Kaghan's chamber, cut him down where he stood. I explained to the Kaghan why Ibrahim died as he did, and the infidel king was mightily impressed with a faith that frees its adherents from a fear of death. His vizier maintained that those of our faith fulfill the human need to live in terror by replacing fear of death with fear of transgression, except that death arrives only once and man, being mortal and disgusting, transgresses with every breath.'

The Bishops Dulcinius and Sandromes also visited the Kaghan, sometime in the ninth century A.D., when the Khazars were embroiled in a great war with the Arab armies advancing from beneath the

Caucasus. Dulcinius – who was martyred at Tyre and became the patron saint of the wayward, the laconic, men who walk looking at the ground, and editors of manuscripts – reported enigmatically to the emperor Tiberius that 'the Kaghan can hold in his hand the light of the sun and the light of the moon, but he has not yet in his heart the light of Christ our Lord, and it is this light that I will bring to him, making him thrice blessed on this earth.'

The original maker is unknown.

Place of origin: The Khazar state was in the Caucasus and Volga regions. Its precise boundaries were unknown; it certainly encompassed parts of Russia, and may also have included parts of present-day Georgia, Armenia, Azerbaijan, Nagorno-Karabakh, and eastern Turkey.

Last known owner: Following the almost complete ingestion of the Khazars by Judaism, Christianity, Islam, or simply history, the location of the Cages passed from written record. People still spoke of them, but their size and power grew greater and vaguer in the retelling. At the Seljuk court, the Sun Cage became the name of a constellation and the Moon Cage the name for wispy clouds bracketing a harvest moon on three sides. Following the dispersal of the Seljuks, there were only disembodied echoes of the Cages, stories about stories about an original referent buried somewhere in the desert, swallowed in the endlessness of the steppe. Every clan of wheat farmers with ancestral memories of conquest, every clan of shepherds and nomads who had once ruled their neighbors remembered themselves as the original owner of the Cages and saw their disappearance as a metonym for their lost prominence. After the British and the Russians snapped Central Asia like a cursed wishbone, and especially after the Russians baked these warriors and seekers into *Homo Sovieticuses* in the putative historical fires (metaphorical fires always seem to work better when there are actual fires nearby to heat up the pokers), the Cages became the Loch Ness Monster of Central Asian historical scholarship, a spook story bandied around the Pitt-Rivers and the Eagle and Child.

Though lost to the wider world, the Cages in fact passed into the ownership of a single clan, whose name is unpronounceable in any language but whose lineage can be verifiably and directly traced back to Oghuz Khan, the conquering Turk who ruled an empire stretching from the Arabian Sea to the Irtysh River and who, according to legend, planned his battles with the aid of a lone gray wolf. The women of that clan remained doctors of sorts, 'cunning men,' as Robert Burton would almost have called them: psychiatrists and charlatans who possessed a trove of folksy mythical stories and grandiose-sounding remedies of little or no value beyond suggestion. The last of these Legend Sellers held Soviet papers identifying her as Yomtuz Muramasov:

she and her nephews Murat and Mahmut, along with three unidentified Tajik nationals, were found slaughtered in a yurt just beyond the boundaries of Tolkuchka bazaar in August 1985.

Estimated value: Inestimable. Yomtuz may have traded them for a nearly dead Lada; she may have demanded the Kremlin itself. Determining a price requires examining comparable goods; no such goods exist.

*Thus wilt thou possess the glory of the
brightness of the whole world, and all
obscurity will fly far from thee.*

I made a few abortive attempts at conversation on
the drive from Hannah's place to mine. Hannah
responded monosyllabically and stared out the
window. I tried to be blithe, but in fact I was queasily
curious, about both Hannah and whether we would
find another body part nailed to my door. I thought
about insisting that we stay at her place, but I didn't
know how to do that politely. I also considered
telling Hannah about the symbol on her doorframe,
but she seemed in no mood to talk. I figured if
something needed explaining, I would improvise,
and if something or someone threatened us ... well,
I guess I would try not to run. Those under-thirty
advice columnists, the latest crop of pop-culture
mushrooms in the 'lifestyle' sections of newspapers,
tell you how to meet your in-laws, how to reconcile

religious differences with a spouse, and how to confront your paranoid girlfriend who's been checking your e-mail. None of them, to my knowledge, has written about what to do when you find a human tooth and an occult symbol on your door and you don't know whether your girlfriend is on your side or the extractor's.

'Which one's yours?' Hannah asked as we parked behind my building.

I pointed up at the third floor, where a light glowed yellow from behind the (perpetually) drawn curtains. 'Electricity waster, I see,' said Hannah, smiling thinly. She looked more tired than angry.

'That's my kitchen. I guess I must have been careless this morning. You'll remember that I didn't get much sleep last night.' She smiled, this time more warmly, kissing the corner of my mouth while brushing her fingers down my face. We got out of the car, and she took the bag of groceries over my protestations.

Across the street two round-bellied guys with mustaches wearing Lincoln Municipal High School letter jackets tottered, bandy-legged and unsteady, out of the Colonial Tavern, arm in arm. Both were laughing too loudly to be sober. Suddenly one of them spun around as if he had been shot and vomited into the bed of a red pickup truck with a hunting rifle on a rack in the back window. 'Ah, shit, the guy's a shooter. Let's get the fuck outta here,' he slurred, and clambered into the passenger seat of the other's car.

'Home sweet home,' I said.

'Those guys look a little bit too old to wear letter jackets, don't you think?'

'Either that or they're in the thirty-fourth grade.' I held the outside door open for Hannah, and we went upstairs. A sliver of light sliced across the landing just below my apartment. The light was coming from my apartment door, which hung slightly open. My stomach tried to escape through my mouth, and I started to sweat.

'Shit.'

'What?'

'Let me go first,' I said in a quivering voice. I didn't even convince *myself* of my bravery, much less Hannah, who looked at me wide-eyed and mute. 'Sometimes I forget to turn off my lights, but I never forget to lock my door. Could you wait here?' She nodded and stood where she had a clear view of the door.

I pushed it quietly, leaving it open behind me and calling out as I entered, 'Hello? Hello?'

In response a deep voice began singing from my kitchen. The song was familiar, Latin and churchy-sounding. It didn't make me feel any more comfortable, though.

I picked up the only thing even vaguely weapon-like in my apartment: a miniature blue baseball bat, the type given away free at stadium promotions, bearing the signatures of the 1985 Mets. Hoping not to get any blood on Hubie Brooks, I eased toward the kitchen, clutching the bat in my sweaty, upraised hand.

There, standing on one of my rickety kitchen chairs and belting out the Latin, was Sal Gomes, the glare of the kitchen lightbulb turning his head into a disco ball. Joe Jadid sat in the chair next to him, shaking with silent laughter. Two open bottles of Heineken were on the table. 'How did you . . . ?' I sputtered.

Joe slapped Gomes on the calf, pointed to the bat in my hand, and let loose a cackle so loud and violent that it forced his head backward. He toppled over, breaking one of my two kitchen chairs with a gunshot crack and spilling beer down the front of his rumpled and mustard-stained shirt. Gomes stopped singing and helped his partner up. 'This was his idea, man,' said Gomes, struggling to lift Joe, who was still convulsed with laughter. 'We'll pay for the chair.'

'Jesus Christ, Paulie, you'd really scare the living shit out of a starving, nervous, nearsighted midget burglar with that thing. Pass it over here,' said Joe, lumbering onto his hands and knees like a man climbing a hill. The bat looked like a Magic Marker in his paws. 'This Mets team broke my heart. Mookie Wilson. Ron Darling. Ray fucking Knight.' He snapped out of his baseball reverie, tossed the bat to the floor, and looked back up at me. 'By the way, you remember what I told you about your lock at the station this afternoon?'

'Yeah.'

'I was wrong. Really, it's a piece of shit; I picked it in, like, ten seconds.'

'You should understand,' Gomes interrupted, wiping up the beer from the table with my ratty kitchen sponge, 'that the Fat Man here can pick locks with the best of them. I know you'd never guess with those baguette fingers he's got, but it's true.'

Joe shrugged and stared at his fingers. 'I didn't even have to break it. Oughta work just fine. But you need to invest in a better one, and you need to do it tomorrow.'

'How'd you guys get my address?'

'From your esteemed law-enforcement agents, Mutt and Jeff,' said Gomes, tossing my sponge back into the sink with a look of disdain.

'Bert and Allen.'

'Whatever. The one with the big walrus mustache is a real charmer. Smalltown police, they're some other kind of people out here. We had cops like that in St Clair Point when I was a kid. Not too fond of the darker nation, that one.'

'Not too fond of anyone. What did he do, just give you my address?'

'Well, we did a little cop improvisation.' He looked over at Joe, who was mopping the beer from his shirt with his tie, my other kitchen chair creaking ominously every time he shifted his weight. After a couple of seconds, Joe noticed that nobody was talking and looked up.

'Yeah, he gave us your address right away, no problems,' he said, breaking into a canary-eating grin. 'All we had to do was tell him about the complaint pending against you in Wickenden. He wanted to escort us here himself.'

'What? What complaint? What did I do?'

'Exposing yourself to a minor,' said Joe, breaking into loud cackles again.

'What?! What? Of course I never – You didn't. Tell me you're just joking and that you didn't give Olafsson any more against me than he already had.'

This time Gomes failed to stifle his laughter, and it burst forth, first out of his nose like a sneeze and then in a cascade of descending tones. 'Of course we didn't. Joey wanted to, though. We just told him that we wanted to talk to you in connection with an ongoing investigation in Wickenden. He was ready to saddle up the cavalry himself, though, break down the door and drag you away for questioning. Look, if it makes you feel better, we'll send him a letter saying that we talked to you and –'

Suddenly he straightened up; his laughter stopped and resolved into an alert, good-natured grin; he raised his eyebrows in interested greeting. Joe stood and wiped his beery hands on the seat of his trousers.

'Is everything okay?' Hannah asked from behind me. I turned around: her gray eyes were wide, her lips pressed tight and slightly turned up in a look of bemused curiosity. It really was a wonderful face, all swooping high-cheekboned space, quick-change expressions, and watery calm.

'I'm very sorry, Paul, we had no idea you had company,' said Gomes.

'Yeah, you got a lovely lady waiting on the stairs, and you come in here and break your kitchen furniture all over the place,' said Joe.

'Everything's fine,' I said to Hannah. 'These are two lock-picking friends of mine, Joe Jadid and Sal Gomes. This is Hannah Rowe.'

'It's a pleasure to meet you, Miss Rowe. You ought to know, by the way, that Fat Person over here wrecked the kitchen chair, not Paul,' said Gomes.

Hannah said hesitantly, 'Okayyy?' then turned to me and crisply asked, 'Paul, where do you want me to put the groceries? Should I run out and get some more food if there are going to be four of us?'

The question had its intended effect, and Gomes stood up, saying, 'Thank you, but we need to be getting out of here. Really, it was rude of us to break and enter like this.' He kissed Hannah's hand, and she responded instantly with a mock curtsy.

Joe settled for an awkward handshake that completely engulfed her avian hand in his.

'That was the "Libera me" from Fauré's Requiem, wasn't it?' she asked.

'Indeed it was,' said Gomes, turning around and bowing. 'One of the lasting benefits of a Catholic education.'

'I love the piece.'

'"Free me, God, from eternal death." So do I.'

Gomes gave us both an inclusive wave, and Joe knocked me on the shoulder and asked me to follow him outside to his car. I asked Hannah to lock up behind me. She agreed, but a suspicious look floated across her face.

'So you guys decided you didn't need to go back to Wickenden after sneaking around outside your jurisdiction? Instead you wanted to come and pick a reporter's lock, probably ruining whatever chance he had of a pleasant evening with a beautiful woman in the process?' I asked.

'She really is lovely,' said Gomes. 'You've done well. But isn't involvement with a source some sort of violation of journalistic ethics?'

'Yeah,' Joe picked up, 'the desk sergeant just gave me a sheet about something like that in our department the other day, too. No more sex with suspects' girlfriends. From now on only blow jobs.'

'Shit, listen to him,' said Gomes, chuckling along with me. 'I'm a family man, and you're probably too young to hear that kind of talk.'

Joe put a bearish arm around me and leaned over. 'Paulie, does she –'

'Hey, leave the kid alone,' said Gomes. I'm not sure if he noticed, in the dark, that I was blushing. Joe's expression wavered between shamefaced and devilishly pleased. I grinned in spite of myself. 'We went to see your dead man's bar, is why we're here. The Lone Wolf. We figured we'd stop by as long as we were out for a country drive.'

Joe said, 'Strange place, that one. Every town's got a morning-and-afternoon bar or two, but I've never seen one as all-over sad as that one. I mean, it's got the patchy linoleum, the Salvation Army couches, the little black-and-white, no-reception TV behind the bar. A real no-hoper kind of joint.'

We arrived at their car: an unmarked blue Crown Vic that, in fact, could not have been any more marked if someone had spray-painted FUZZ across the hood.

'Yeah, this Albanian Eddie guy's a real charmer,' Joe continued. 'One thing, though: I don't think he's Albanian.'

'He's not? How do you know?'

'Well, Uncle Abe, he speaks God knows how many languages. I think he speaks like ten, maybe twelve, fluently and then can hack around in another ten or so. Anyway, when we were kids, me and all the cousins, he taught us two sentences in every language in Europe. Well, not every single language, naturally, but what he said was, "Every language worth knowing, even Albanian." That was the kicker for him – "even Albanian."'

'What were the sentences?'

'"This is a beautiful country" and "He's buying."'

'And so . . .'

'And so these things stuck in my head, you know,

so to sort of loosen things up, the first thing I said to this Albanian Eddie was, "This is a beautiful country," in Albanian. He didn't know what the fuck I was talking about.'

'Maybe it was your pronunciation,' I said.

'Yeah, everything's always my fault, right?' asked Joe, belching heartily. 'I guess maybe I wasn't saying it right, but I tried it four or five times, until he finally told me to order a drink or get out. So we ordered shots and beers, and then I asked him if his name was Eddie. He looked surprised and asked how we knew. I said we were friends of Jaan Pühapäev, and he got really agitated, saying how Jaan always had too big a mouth, and he's dead and he's sorry, but why did everybody want to talk about Jaan now, and it didn't matter anyway, and all this bullshit.'

'So then what?'

'So then Gomes and I flash our shields, but quick-like, so he doesn't see they're from Wickenden, and he goes apeshit. Says he pays the cops every month. You believe that? Calls me a greedy American pig and tells me to get out of his place. Says he's going to call the chief. I tell him go right ahead, that's his right. Then he's pounding on the bar, telling us over and over to just get the fuck out. So we drain our beers, and he snatches the glasses away and puts them in the sink. While his back's to us, I drop one of the shot glasses in my pocket. It's there now – thank fuck I didn't fall on it,' he said, flicking his front blazer pocket with his middle finger and producing a clinking sound. 'So we're heading back to the station now, and Sally'll run the prints through as many people as he can, see if anything comes up. Probably a long shot, but you never know.'

'Where do you think he's from?' I asked. 'And why would he tell people he's Albanian? And who are you sending the prints to?'

'Inquisitive little fucker, ain't he?' said Joe to Gomes. 'Don't know where he's from. I couldn't place the accent, and I'm usually pretty good with accents. Why's he tell people he's Albanian? I don't know, but it seems like a good story if he didn't want people to know where he's really from. I mean, how many Albanian immigrants is he going to run into up here? Who the fuck knows what an Albanian sounds like? How many people can even find it on a map? Could you?'

'Probably not,' I said ruefully. 'Could you?'

'Fuck yeah, I could,' said Joe proudly.

'Big Joey here's a map freak,' said Gomes. 'I've never seen a man just sit down and read maps before: road maps, city maps, world maps – anything like that. Plus he's got this memory that just holds on to everything. I know he's kind of a slob, and he looks like he sleeps in his clothes, but his brain's wired up deep.'

'I like this suit,' said Joe.

Gomes looked down, smiled, and shook his head.

'Anyway, your last question,' said Joe. 'Who's running the prints? State and local, no problem. FBI,

Sally can probably do. Interpol, even. They make this big deal about their record system, how it links hundreds of countries and all that, but their records are usually shit. A lazy bureaucrat in Lisbon's no different from a lazy bureaucrat in Wickenden, right? Anyway, we'll see if anything hits. We'd be better off if we knew where he came from – we'd be better off if we knew his last name, for Christ sakes – but we'll start and go from here.'

'You know,' said Gomes, blowing into his hands to keep them warm, 'we might want to run Pühapäev's prints through the same people. He just gets weirder and weirder, the more we dig into this. We got his prints on file, can't hurt anything.'

'Yeah,' said Joe. 'We could maybe send his name and prints to Estonia. See whether they got anything on him. I don't guess we got an Estonian speaker on the force, though, right?'

'Don't think so,' said Gomes. 'But what about that young guy, though, always looks spooked at something, works organized crime? You know the one I mean?'

'Yeah, I think so. Real skinny, looks like he shops at the same places as you?'

'If by that you mean he cares about his clothes,' said Gomes, looking over the tops of his glasses at Joe, 'then yeah, we're thinking of the same guy. Where's he from?'

'Priyenko. He works Russian mob stuff. Always figured him for a Russian, too, but I don't know.

Yeah, he might be able to give us a hand with Estonia, I guess. Probably still speak some Russian there. Never really talked to the guy, though. Maybe you can warm him up. Compare ties and aftershaves or something.'

'Funny. And you, young man,' said Gomes to me, 'best get back upstairs and rescue that lovely young lady from herself. Like the big guy said, the lock should work fine, and Joe here was just about to pay you for the kitchen chair, right?'

Joe sighed, rolled his eyes, and pulled a fist-size billfold fat with scraps of paper and receipts from his back pocket. Lugubriously, he handed me a fifty and asked whether that would be enough. I said it would, and he nodded.

'By the way,' I said, 'I met a guy who said he was Pühapäev's brother today. Not that I really think he is.'

'Yeah?' asked Gomes. 'Where'd you meet him?'

'At Hannah's. She said he was there to pick up the body.'

'Doesn't mean he was his brother, though, right?'

'Doesn't mean he wasn't either. Even the bad guys got brothers,' said Joe, batting his eyelids in mock Disney sentimentality. 'Time for us to go home, though, Sally. Places out here, they give me the creeps. And don't forget to get a new lock tomorrow, Paulie. They even have locksmiths out here?'

'Nah, usually we just nail a tree across our doors

before going to sleep. Makes it tough if we have to use the outhouse at night, though.'

Hannah was standing in the doorway between living room and kitchen when I walked in, her arms crossed, the bag of groceries at her feet, an expression mixing irritation with confusion darkening her face.

'Who were those guys?' she asked as soon as I had shut the door. Joe was right: the lock worked perfectly; the only evidence it had been tampered with was a couple of scratches next to the keyhole. I bolted the door and pulled the chain across it.

'A couple of friends from Wickenden. They've been helping me with Jaan's story.'

She raised her arms and let them fall to her thighs with a slap. 'How many people are you going to tell about this? Aren't you supposed to be a writer? Are you actually planning to do any writing, or do you want to just drive around and get strangers to make my friend look bad?'

'Who said they were making him look bad?'

She exhaled impatiently and lowered her head so she was looking out from beneath her forehead, like a bull. She spoke slowly and deliberately: 'Who . . . were . . . those . . . two . . . men?'

I ran through a semicoherent two-second argument with myself about whether I should lie or come clean. I sided with lying but couldn't come up with a good one fast enough: what could I possibly have to do with two grown men who pick locks, sing in Latin, drive a Crown Vic, and wear blazers indoors with suspicious-looking bulges on the sides of their chests? Who else could they be? 'They're two detectives from the Wickenden Police Department,' I said, more than a little sheepishly.

Hannah blew up. 'Police! You've been talking to the police? For how long? Why? What are they doing? What did they tell you?' She strode toward me, abruptly stopped, and walked back to where she was standing, then came at me until she was close enough to kiss. I put a hand on her shoulder, and she slapped it away, looking searingly at me.

'I talked to them this afternoon. That's how I know about Jaan and the lawyer. They told me he'd been arrested a couple of times.'

'And?'

'And nothing. The big guy's my old professor's nephew. He's been suspended, and he's got the time to help.'

'Suspended for what?'

'For hitting someone he shouldn't have at a traffic stop.'

'Oh, that's good. That's just great, just the kind of cop you want on your side.'

'He's not like that, and he and I aren't on any side.' I stopped and waited for her to respond. She just stared at me. Any ability I had to read her expression was gone; I had no idea what she was thinking.

I felt as though I had done something wrong; anything that upset her was inherently wrong. If I could have told Joe and Sal to drop it, I would have. But then a question occurred to me: 'Don't you want to know what happened to Jaan? How he died?'

She sighed and ran a cupped hand across her forehead, then flattened it and ran it through her hair. 'Of course I do. Of course. He was *my* friend, not yours; he wasn't just a stepping-stone to a new job for *me*.'

'Nor me, and that's not fair. I'm sorry, but I don't understand what you're so upset about. We're trying to figure out what happened to Jaan. To *your friend*. What's wrong?'

'Paul . . . Look, I don't want to talk about this anymore, okay? I'm going home.' She put her coat on and unlocked the door.

'No, wait. Why?'

She just shook her head.

'I'll call you later,' I said halfheartedly. Whoever thought that up as an appropriate placative response?

'Do whatever you like,' she said softly, almost smiling at me. She shut the door quietly behind her, and I heard her footsteps receding downstairs and the outer door closing behind her.

What I would have liked to do was have a meal and a long night with Hannah. I thought about running after her, but as odd as it sounds at this point in the story, I do in fact have at least a modicum of pride. I had bought the makings of a gourmet feast, planned the dinner as I drove back from Wickenden, and savored the postdinner evening in a thousand delicious imagined permutations.

My actual night, of course, accorded with none of my imaginings: dipping uncooked ravioli into a plastic container of cold arrabiatta sauce and accompanying this lachrymose meal with Montepulciano straight from the bottle, I watched syndicated sitcoms that were never funny during their initial runs and certainly weren't now. Sometime during the seamless chain of smarmy yet resilient families, dysfunctional adult-adolescents sharing an apartment and discussing their failed relationships with other dysfunctional adult-adolescents, and whiny narcissistic Manhattanites who spoke in declamatory catchphrases, I fell asleep on my couch and awoke to a test pattern (the glory of small-market stations), as red wine seeped into my shirt and stained my chest pink.

THE WHITE MEDIKO

❧

White is the color of middles: of uncuckolded
husbands, not young men in love; of disappointed
writers, not adolescent poets; of half-*finished* castles,
not *half*-finished houses.

— GEORG NAGY, *Sorrati's Tragedy*

18 March 1987

My Friend,
Enclosed you will find one of the two coins you sent me and
Abulfaz to recover. I will accept your thanks but sadly can proffer
none in return: my travels with that loathsome cipher to that
abhorrent country have quite depleted your stock of good graces in
my books. This marks the third time in as many years I have had
to leave home on a vanity mission inspired by Voskresenyov's
project: Armenia and Turkmenistan were intolerable enough, but
I had always been rather proud of not setting foot on American
soil. That I had not only to abjure this claim but to have had to do

372

so with a man in whose company I have never spent an easy moment is almost too much to bear. I should be cross, were I not myself and you not you. No matter, though. My erstwhile companion insisted that this division of the treasure was your idea; I agreed to it for that reason alone. I can only assume that you have requested it for the same reason you arranged this whole bloody mess of a trip: The American Question. You know my views on that matter well; this trip merely confirmed them.

As for my account's veracity, I feel sure you have never known me to be dishonest, whereas deceit is just one of many unsavory practices from which my traveling partner earns his living.

We met, as arranged, at one of the innumerable dreary little bars that litter the Brussels airport. I was privately musing, as I always do when I have occasion to visit Belgium, why earth's most boring nation should devote itself to producing such a remarkable variety of beers. Do the Belgians think that this mitigates their dullness? It doesn't. Do they think it provides some valuable service to the planet? It doesn't. Whenever a nation's pride can be swallowed by the glassful — each in its own proper glass, no less — then that is a nation hardly worth the mention. And please don't start expounding on King Boudewijn, whom nobody remembers, or Tintin, who is, after all, a cartoon produced by a man too dim — his supporters substitute 'good-natured' or 'trusting' for 'dim,' as people so often do — to realize when he was being taken advantage of by the Nazis. The world would feel no loss had Belgium itself been swallowed by France, or Germany, or (dare I dream?) the North Sea.

No matter: there I was, peacefully enjoying my Leffe, when a man dressed like an East End sheeny who'd finally picked the right horse slithered into the chair across from me. It took me a few moments to register that this was, in fact, Abulfaz: he had whitened his hair, grown an asinine little moustache, and was wearing a laughable pair of gold glasses shaped like television boxes. No sooner had I greeted him than he informed me that, even in private, we were not to use each other's real names: I was to call him Riley and he would call me Parker. He was naturally unaware that I had gotten the better end of the stick there – who would voluntarily be an Irishman? – even if his accent sounded like it came from BBC World Service rather than Auld Erin (or even Kilburn High Road). Still, maintaining this cloak-and-dagger charade in front of a snaggle-toothed barmaid and a couple of fat Continentals seemed rather much of a muchness, but he insisted that we must 'remain in character at all times,' both for continuity's sake and because 'we never know who might be listening.' Yes, he actually said that, just like one of those tawdry spy films they show on Sunday afternoons. It seemed easier to relent than protest, so I relented.

On the interminable flight, Riley also insisted that I read the dossier – 'dossier' he called it, not 'materials' or 'papers' but 'dossier' – he had prepared on the Mediko coins, assuming that I was as uncultured, ignorant, and crass as he. I pointed out that one of the articles (a derivative little squawk that appeared in one of those area-specific journals that nobody reads, written by a turnip-shaped Greek graduate student whose builder father had bought her way into College) had, in fact, been written under my supervision, and I was cited four times in its bibliography. This time he relented.

Briefly, the coins' story is this: Medea, as he no doubt did not know before he began preparing for this assignment, is considered one of the matriarchs of certain arcane branches of botany, and numerous plants of medicinal, therapeutic, or recreational value

*whose origins lie in the Caucasus have been named for her.
According to legend – often the most reliable source in my field –
these two coins were responsible for the flourishing gardens at the
court of King David the Builder, who ruled Georgia at the end of
the first millennium. They were given as a gift to a certain Arab
geographer whom we all know, who performed an unnamed but
valuable service involving the king's homely daughter, a hollowed-out
tree stump filled with vermilion paint, a male donkey in the early
stages of arousal, and four handkerchiefs. When the geographer
announced his intention to carry the coins to Baghdad, David's only
condition was that the geographer return them to Katusi after three
hundred new moons. One can safely presume that David never
envisioned the glories that would follow in Baghdad and Sicily: no
one did. No one could have, and since then no imaginative feat in
gardening – with the possible exception of Capability Brown's
designs – has matched them. That the geographer kept his end of the
bargain through no conscious act of his own is one of the odder
coincidences (or proofs, if you are that way inclined) in botanical,
Arabic, numismatic, or Caucasian history.*

*After he ceased trying to edify me, Riley devoted the remainder
of the flight to prettifying himself: apparently, though academics fly
cattle class, they still spend hundreds – no, thousands – of pounds
on fancy suits. And his was a corker: three-piece, naturally, dark
green, a perfect silk four-in-hand with a sapphire stickpin and a red
handkerchief in his breast pocket. The effect was utterly absurd:
somewhere between Victorian dandy and Al Capone's second –
everything but the spats and a walking stick, really – yet he seemed
rather proud of himself.*

*As we descended, a pack of squealing schoolgirls and their spotty-
faced, simian escorts all crowded into one small half row of seats by*

the window. I never understood the cooing tenderheartedness that children seem to inspire in some people. Children – and I extend that term to anybody younger than forty – are bloody miserable little creatures: brutal, wilful, noisy, extruding pheromones and fluids in all directions. In any event, I imagine the brats were hoping to see the Statue of Liberty or perhaps superheroes jumping off buildings. Maybe they were trying to catch the glint of gold on the streets. What we saw instead were street after street of little matchbox houses, rickety and depressing things (even from this height) that would barely have brightened up Luton or Slough.

Finally we escaped from that silver whale coffin and slothed our way to customs, where they waved us through with barely a glance. Can you imagine? In Armenia and Turkmenistan, they really put me through my paces – where was I from? what was I doing? what papers did I have? – and as a result I was safe as houses the entire trip. Here I suppose they use good old 'Murrican intuition and just see whether you're a good guy or bad guy, whether you've got a white- or black-handled six-shooter at your side, and that's all. Just go straight on, yes, mind you don't eat less than your daily allotment of eight hamburgers per day, and that's that. Instead of scrutinising our documents – instead of doing their jobs, that is – the customs agents all genuflected before some fifth-rate Adonis, all teeth and manicured nails, with hair that looked like a bird's nest standing on its side. Riley told me he was an American television actor; he even knew the name of the particular program he appeared on, information that I of course forgot as soon as possible.

Once we had passed through customs, we claimed our paltry one bag each and bundled into a taxi to the 'guesthouse' Riley proudly claimed to have booked us into. Between mouthfuls of some reeking muck he ate out of a foil packet with his greasy hands, our driver

insisted on speaking to us for the entire journey. After fighting our
way through the line at the taxi stand and a veritable United
Nations of the unwashed and undesirable skulking behind the
wheels of these ghastly yellow beasts, all I wanted to do was shut my
eyes and get the ride over with. No such luck: the driver had to tell
Riley (and Riley had to keep asking) about his entire bloody family
– all his children and his village back in Wogistan or whatever hole
he crawled out of – until finally I gave Riley an elbow to the kidneys
and he ceased talking.

I had been looking forward to a nice snug room with a bed and
basin and maybe even a hot water bottle, where I could stretch out in
peace. Instead we arrived at this filthy little restaurant with the most
garish neon signage in the window – I don't even remember what it
said, nor do I know how anyone could possibly read words that flash
incessantly. The restaurant itself . . . well, there were peanut and
almond shells scattered across the floor, it stank of garlic, and it was
packed with fat, gold-toothed Yids jabbering at each other like they
always do. The men all had those silly little school beanies on; the
fat-lipped women wore huge jeweled pendants, of course: I shall leave
you to imagine the rest. Even though the proprietor could barely
speak English, he introduced himself to us as 'Sam,' casual as you
like. Riley, finally showing some backbone instead of bowing and
scraping in front of every foreigner who speaks to him, asked him
whether Sam was, in fact, his real name, and he admitted that it
wasn't: he had some typically unpronounceable name that he had
shed, as they always do. It doesn't matter, of course; you can always
tell a Person of the Book – it has to do with the shape of the
forehead, the slope of the nose, and the prominent ears – and in
New York, they're everywhere.

The rooms themselves were scarcely better than a prison: nothing but a bed that was rather too wide and rather too short and a desk in each room. Not even a basin, to say nothing of a sink or even a private toilet. Through the floor we could hear some vulgar screeching music, which our host would have turned off except for Riley's insistence that he 'not change any practices on our account.' When valiant old Sam finally took his leave of us, he simply gave us the keys and retreated back downstairs, not even reminding us about payment (which frankly shocked me, given the six points of the star that hung around his flabby, liver-spotted neck), much less mentioning when we had to return at night, or what time breakfast was served, or whom to ring if we needed hot water, or anything of the sort. He seemed pleased to allow us to fend for ourselves, as though we were already members of the household or intimates of the family (can you imagine?). Naturally, I wanted Riley to complain, or at least to ensure that we understood the rules of the house in which we were guests, but he simply smiled pompously, took a deep breath, and told me he was sure we would have no problems, as we had no plans to leave that evening. Well, that was hardly the point, was it? Standards must be maintained – except in Queens, it would appear.

We went to the shop early next morning, and a good thing, too, I thought at the time, as it meant we might leave America that evening. 'Sam,' Riley explained, was a cousin of the man who 'owned' the Medikos, and he had been in correspondence with the owner for several months before receiving assurances that the coins were what he thought they were, and settling on a price. It just goes to show: there's a storekeeper or trader in every pack of them, and there invariably has to be some negotiation over the price; they can never just come right out and give you a proper, honest, firm answer.

Still, I suppose Riley – who is at heart nothing more than a rug merchant with some fancy clothes and a bit of education – enjoyed this sort of haggling.

The shop itself was every bit as filthy as you might expect: horrifically dusty, the greenish carpet strewn with cigarette ash and God knows what else, and cabinet after cabinet of coins, nothing but money money money – sort of a Jew's paradise, I should expect. The owner introduced himself to us as 'Hank,' which was every bit as much of a contrivance as his cousin's 'Sam.' He and Riley naturally got on like the proverbial house on fire.

I really can't see how you can place so much trust in someone like Riley/Abulfaz/whatever other name suits his current purpose: he has no identity or personality; he is a human palimpsest sustained by his endless barrage of questions and a constant influx of useless information. Someone like him – someone always escaping from himself, playing dress-up in Mummy's coat closet with accents and passports – would of course take to this miserable, cacophonous, mongrel nation.

I have the shop owner's business card next to me as I write this letter: 'FOREST HILLS COIN SHOP, Hank Tonchailov, Numismatist and Collector Specializing in the USSR, Open Sunday–Friday Regular Hours and at Other Times by Appointment Only.' Of course he makes himself sound much grander than he actually is. In fact, Tonchailov is a grubby junk dealer who takes from his own people the last trinkets they have brought with them from their homelands: he's an Americaniser, in other words. I even started to ask him how he could possibly barter and sell his people's memories (and I use 'his people' quite loosely), but he mistook my tone and grew quite aggressive. Riley attempted to smooth things over between us; fortunately for the minuscule Tonchailov, he physically restrained me from teaching the obstreperous little Yid the lesson he needed.

Such an education would have been entirely superfluous, as we were to be Tonchailov's last customers. Riley bought the coins from him for $7,300, which he counted out meticulously as the shopkeeper's eyes grew larger with each hundred-dollar bill placed before him. The deal complete, Tonchailov extended his hand to Riley (I had been banished to a chair in the corner of the shop, where bad children wait for their daddies to finish their grown-up business), who shook it with one hand and with the other withdrew a sapper and delivered a fantastic crack to the back of his head. Tonchailov collapsed as though someone had simply withdrawn his spine. Riley went to the back of the shop, found the gas main, punctured it, and left a small homemade bomb set to go off in forty minutes. Then, in that disgustingly breezy manner of his, he wiped down everything we had touched and handed me a pair of driving gloves. We returned to his cousin's shop, collected our suitcases, paid for our lodging, and boarded the next flight to Brussels.

Item 11: The White Mediko. A large (5.3 centi-meters in diameter) and imperfectly circular, rough-edged coin. One side is plain copper; the other is

coated with white enamel, and on the enamel is painted the figure of a woman with one outstretched arm, as though calling for someone. In her other hand she holds a green bottle.

Alchemists value the coin not only for its portrait of Medea but for its whiteness, which color, coming after the crazed indecision of the rainbow, signals the calm and purposeful birth of the shape to come.

Date of manufacture: Unknown. Presumably post-Christian (see below), but Georgia adopted Christianity in the first century A.D.

Manufacturer: Most enamel work was also monastery work, and just as we do not know the faces and lives of those nameless Celts who spent their lives illuminating the pregnant *B*'s and made the *S*'s curves as alluring as those of the women they would never see, so the name of the monk(s) who painted Medea calling to her children is similarly lost. The legend itself, though best known through Euripides' tragedy, belongs at least as much to Georgian mythography as to Greek.

Medea herself was the daughter of Aeetes, king of Colchis, which today is the part of Georgia bordering the Black Sea. The Thessalian prince Jason, challenged by his uncle Pelias to find the Golden Fleece, sailed up the Phasis River to Aeetes' capital, most likely Kutaisi or Vani. Aeetes promised Jason the fleece if he could yoke two fire-breathing bulls to a plow and sow a dragon's teeth, from which an army of men would spring. Medea, a skilled maker of potions and charms (the modern word 'medicine' has its roots in her name, and Mediko is the Georgian nickname for Medea), gave Jason a charm that enabled him to survive the bulls, best the dragon, and win the fleece.

From here the stories diverge. In Euripides' version, of course, Jason brings Medea home and spurns her in favor of a career-advancing marriage to Creon's daughter Glauce. Medea subsequently descends into mania and infanticide. Euripides ends his tragedy with her riding off in a chariot drawn by the sun god, her grandfather. Georgian tradition, however, holds that Aegeus, king of Athens, eager to gain the favor of such a wise scholar and her renowned warrior-king father, spirited Medea and her children out of Thessaly and into Athens, and thence home. The potion she gave her children temporarily stopped their breathing; she then slaughtered a lamb over them and presented them – lifeless and bloody – to her husband in order to drive him mad. Once her ruse had worked, she revived the children, escaped, and lived a full century as a healer, mother, and counselor (but never bedfellow) to the Athenian king.

Place of origin: The emerald, saffron, and ultramarine geometric design around the coin's edges indicates a Persian influence, as does much medieval Georgian art. Medea's wine-dark skin, her attenuated face with remarkably detailed features and expression (worried, expectant, with raised eyebrows, hollow cheeks, and slightly parted lips), the folds of her robe, and the stylized position in which she holds her slender hand are all typical of Georgian cloisonné iconography. The subject matter is typically Colchian.

Last known owner: Lavrenty Mashenabili, descendant of priests, father of monsters, husband of a harridan (actually, husband of Batumi's Party chief), a fixer and stuffer of broken teeth who spent his days knuckle deep in other people's saliva and decay, master of the Soviet trick of always being third or fourth best: good enough to inspire confidence but not so excellent as to arouse suspicion. Lavrenty performed two brave deeds in his entire life. This low total shamed him; that it was two more than most people could claim did not comfort him.

Lavrenty's father escaped death in the 1924 insurrection by hiding beneath a mound of corpses into which an inspired or insane Red Army conscript from Voronezh emptied 564 revolver-fired bullets. Eighteen months later he was deported to Siberia and died on the way, leaving behind three sons and a pregnant wife.

Local Party officials watched David, the eldest son, carefully: he was a deportee's child. When his time came to serve in the army, they sent him to a remote outpost in the middle of the Kara-Kum Desert. One endless desert day, fueled by boredom and home-distilled vodka, he accepted a dare from his commanding officer and swallowed six live scorpions, whereupon he died a death so agonizing that his commanding officer's grandchildren still dream of it.

Zviad, the second son, drowned during submarine training in Vilnius.

Leon, the third son, rather than serve in the military that had killed his father and two brothers, escaped through Turkey and settled in the foothills of the Talis Mountains, where he converted to Islam, cut off contact with his family, opened a small café in the shade, and lives still: wealthy, anonymous, and haunted.

Lavrenty married a snaggle-toothed, ham-calved girl of average intelligence and became a respected if somewhat indolent and dreamy dentist in Batumi. In 1983, when everyone, including his wife, assumed he was too old to defect, he was chosen to represent the Soviet republic of Georgia at an international dentistry convention in Philadelphia, where he defected.

Four months before he left, his cousin Boris (the son of Lavrenty's father's betrayer, it was whispered) returned to Batumi from Leningrad. Not to stay, of course – he had become famous, fat, and greasy as an instructor of Marxist-Leninist seaborne maneuvers at the Soviet Naval Officers' Training Institute – but to inquire as to the whereabouts of 'those two funny little coins that Grandfather always swore he would bury in the church before he allowed the Russians to get their hands on them.' They were doing nobody any good buried, he reasoned, whereas they would be a source of Batumian pride if displayed at the Museum of the Socialist Brotherhood of Native Peoples in Moscow. He would ask nothing for himself, naturally, simply an additional school in his ancestral home, and if the authorities saw fit to name the school for its renowned son – well, he would not object. Lavrenty was older than Boris, and perhaps remembered Grandfather's stories better; did he, by any chance, remember where around the church Grandfather had buried the coins, or would Boris have to send Russian excavators to dismantle the church brick by brick and comb through the rubble?

Estimated value: Lavrenty dug up the coins with his bare hands in the middle of the night – the same way he and his grandfather had buried them – and sewed them into the lining of his suitcase. During his first trip to New York, he noticed an ad in the back of *Novoye Russkoye Slovo*. He sold the coins for enough to pay for a one-way ticket to California, establish a dental practice in Bakersfield, and change his name to Larry Mack.

*The thing is the fortitude of all strength,
for it overcometh every subtle thing and doth
penetrate every solid substance.*

❧

I was at the bottom of the ocean with electric eels stinging my ears, and I was screaming. I was stretched out on the desert floor and left to become reporter jerky next to a braying hyena in heat. A fat man was sitting on my head and blowing the highest note possible on a clarinet. Someone had stuffed my mouth with rotten horsemeat mixed with gum from the floor of a subway station, then sealed it shut; the train doors sounded the warning bells, loudly and repeatedly.

I had drunk almost two bottles of red wine, and the phone was ringing.

Lumbering woodenly from the couch – I was still wearing all my clothes, including my shoes – I grabbed the phone with my lobster claw of a hand. 'Ggrrmmffrmmf,' I said.

'Paul?'

'Yeah?'

'You still work for me?'

'Art. Jesus Christ.' I reeled a bit, tripped on the open container of pasta sauce, and collapsed like a leaky water balloon onto my couch, now spattered magenta and reeking of spilled wine.

'You sick? You are, Donna says to tell you that she'll bring over some soup for you.'

I rubbed my dry, papery face and shut my eyes. Even then the room pendulumed irregularly, side to side. I was still drunk; the hangover hadn't even begun yet. 'Not sick. I had sort of a rough night last night, is all.'

'Aha, I see,' Art said, sounding as if he did. 'Well, Eileen Coughlin just called. She wants to know how the story's coming, and I had to tell her that I just plain didn't know.' He paused, and though I knew I should have said something, I didn't know what to say. 'So how's the story coming?'

'Fine,' I said. I was in neither the mood nor the condition to recount the past few days for him. In my condition I was barely even aware that I had arms.

'Okay, fine. If it's fine, then it's fine. You should call Leenie yourself sometime before the end of the week, though. She really was interested in the piece, and in you. You shouldn't let this one pass, Paul, trust me.'

I didn't feel like hearing a pep talk. I didn't deserve one either. So I just said, 'Okay.'

'Fine. Okay. Okay. Fine. Like talking to my daughter when she was thirteen. Listen, get some rest and drink some water. Maybe swing by this afternoon, I'll have something else for you to do. Austell says he misses you.'

'Yeah, I'll bet he does,' I croaked. 'I'll see you in a few hours, then.'

'Listen: water, sleep, hot bath, shave. That order. Repeat if necessary. This is the kind of stuff they teach you in J-school, you know.'

'Is that right? I thought they just taught you what "TK" means.'

'Yeah, that, too. Another thing they teach you? Not a good idea for a reporter to date his source.'

'Art, I –'

'I'm just giving you a hard time. Small town, word gets around. Your personal life's none of my business, and I don't mean to butt in. I don't assume you'll be making a habit of it, but it's the kind of thing you don't want to get a reputation for.'

'So noted.'

'So it should be. Soldier on. See you in a few.'

After several glasses of water and several of ginger ale, a long doze-soak in my lime-scaled bathtub, and an exceptionally attentive shave with menthol shaving cream, I upgraded myself from nightmarish to merely awful. After another forty-five minutes, my mouth was no longer cottony, nor was my stomach filled with vinegar and depth charges: I was once again almost human, and I figured that almost-humanness is the perfect condition for sitting in an office.

My drive to the office took me past Talcott, and until I was in sight of the front gate, I pretended to myself that I wasn't going to turn in and see Hannah, just like I pretended that it was coincidence that I left around lunchtime, when I knew she'd be free. As an experienced self-deceiver, though, I knew when to quit: I turned in at Talcott's gate.

The school office was a beehive of nonactivity. Three attenuated secretaries of indeterminate middle age sat at three identical wooden desks equidistant from each other: the one on the left stared balefully at her empty desk; the one on the right talked quietly on her telephone; the one in the center looked up at me with a total absence of expression on her face. They looked as though they slept in mothballs and lived on weak lindenflower tea, Platonic forms of an ideal New England private-school secretary. I nodded amicably (I thought) at the one in the middle, and she tucked an invisible strand of hair behind a prunish but sparklingly clean ear without taking her eyes off me. I asked where I could find Hannah Rowe's office. She cleared her throat and picked an invisible puff of lint off her desk, depositing it neatly in her top drawer.

'Follow Mr Heatherington,' she said, pointing to a man standing at a bank of mailboxes. Upon hearing his name, he stood bolt upright and looked quizzically in our direction. He walked over to me and extended a hand in greeting. Shaking it was like holding a wet bag filled with twigs. I thanked the secretary, but she was already busy erasing something from an index card and didn't even acknowledge me. I followed Mr Heatherington's elbow patches down several hallways and up a flight of stairs. He pointed to a set of double doors at the end of the hallway. He never said a word, and if I had believed even slightly in ghosts, he would have confirmed my faith.

From the double doors, I heard laughter, a man's and Hannah's, and inside I saw Hannah and an irritatingly handsome, slab-faced guy, the type who wouldn't look out of place modeling cable-knit sweaters or running for public office. He looked at me with condescension (easily mistakable in this case for friendliness, except to the knowledgeable and paranoid), then lazily back to Hannah.

'Paul, what are you doing here?' she asked. Her voice had walls around it.

'I was passing by on my way to work and just wanted to talk to you for a second.'

She smiled, first at me and then knowingly at the white teeth sitting next to her. 'I'm sorry,' she said unapologetically. 'Paul, this is Chip Gregson, one of our science teachers. Chip, this is my friend Paul. Chip and I were in the middle of a planning discussion.' Chip raised his eyebrows and nodded but neither stood up nor extended a hand to me.

'I'm sorry. I really didn't mean to interrupt you and Chip over here, but if you've just got a second for me . . .'

'Fine,' she sighed. 'Chip, I'll come find you after eighth period. You'll be around?' she asked, smiling.

'Yeah, I will. If I'm not here, I'll be running some drills on first field with the JV defense. Come find me; we'll hang out.' I wondered how easily he could break his leg 'running some drills.' Chip drained his cup of tea and strode athletically toward me, slapping me on the back as he passed. 'Good to meet ya, buddy,' he said.

'Yeah, you, too.' He left, and I sat down next to Hannah. 'Chip has beautiful shoulders,' I said.

She didn't say anything, didn't even look at me. Maybe it was the wrong moment for sarcasm. I reached for her face, and she let me raise her chin until she was looking at me. 'I don't understand any of this,' I said quietly. 'Can you please let me in? Tell me what I've done wrong, or what's happening inside your head? Or even outside it?'

She didn't say anything.

'Are you still upset about Jaan?'

A look of sadness fluttered around her eyes, then settled across her face. She looked like she was either trying hard to cry or trying hard not to. 'Paul, can I ask you a question?'

'Of course.'

'Why do you care?'

'About what?'

'Any of this. About Jaan, about what might have happened to him. About me.'

'Well, the first one's easy: Jaan's an inherently interesting character. Look . . .' I said. I gathered my thoughts and stared at the Olympic pattern of teacup rings on her desk. 'He's a professor who barely taught. He had connections to jewel thieves. Can you think of a more cloistered and safe life than teaching Baltic history at Wickenden University and living here in Lincoln? And still, he not only carries a gun around but fires it twice, both times evading any sort of censure thanks to protection from the history department and the university – to which, incidentally, he donates his entire salary and then some. How does he live? How does he know someone like Vernum Sickle? What's he so frightened of? I want to know who he was.' I stopped. She was unimpressed. It's times like these that I wish I had a better screenwriter to give me my lines.

'Also,' I said more slowly, 'someone left a threat – a bloody human tooth – nailed to my door. That just pisses me off. I mean, I'm not brave; I've never had to be. But it makes me angry that someone threatens me instead of showing me enough respect to explain why I should not report the story, what the consequences would be if I did, then letting me make up my own mind.

'The second question's easy, too.'

'Don't say anything stupid,' she said, eyes shining.

'It really is an easy question.'

She pushed into me with her chest and shoulders and put her hands against my bare back, under my shirt, kissing me like she was looking for food, then pulled me onto the floor and straddled me. She rolled me over so we were looking at each other – me on my right side and she on her left – lying on the bare linoleum floor. It smelled of disinfectant and decades of chalk dust. 'I don't understand any of this,' I said quietly. 'What are you doing?'

'Don't ask me that. Please. Will you do something for me?'

'Sure.'

'Give Jaan a rest. Let Jaan rest. Just for a day or two.'

'What do you mean?'

She sat up. Dust had gathered in her long hair, and she shook it out. 'Just promise me,' she said, pressing against me again, 'that you'll let Jaan alone for a couple of days. Then do anything you want. Please.'

'Why?'

'Will you do it? Please, if not for his sake, then for me? Please?'

I sighed and got up, moving to a chair by her desk. 'For only a couple of days?'

'Two. Give Jaan a little peace. Then do whatever work you want to do. Ask whatever you like.' The lack of pronoun in that sentence should have struck me more than it did.

'Fine.'

'Really?'

'Really. I can take a couple of days off, I guess. I have other stories I should be working on anyway.'

She sat on my lap and cradled my head in her hands. 'I owe you an explanation, I know. But can you just trust me, for now, that this really is the best thing to do? For Jaan, for everyone who cared about him, and for me?'

'I wouldn't do this for anyone else,' I said.

'Thank you, Paul. Paul.' She let my name in her voice hover between us like a sturdy soap bubble until she moved off my lap and I stood up, and it broke.

'I actually need to go into the office now.'

'And I've got a class here in four minutes. Why is it that the only piece of classical music teenage boys like is "Bolero"?'

'What's "Bolero"?'

'You're worse than useless. Promise me you'll learn something about music,' she said, looking unusually serious.

'Will you teach me?'

'I'd like to. I want to.'

'What's going on, really?'

She kissed me twice and let her hand linger on the side of my face. 'My class is coming. Call me later?'

'Sure.'

'Dependable Paul. Thank you. For all of it.'

I really did mean to back off, God help me. It violated all my instincts, but I would have done it because I could taste Hannah at the back of my throat every time I saw her. If it meant busying myself with other stories (which I had to do anyway) and letting Jaan's drop for a couple of days (after all, it was a forgiving two-week cycle), then fine: I could live with it, and so could Art. Not that he'd know.

But as it happened, I walked into the *Carrier* office just in time to give a quick wave to Austell before grabbing my ringing phone.

'Yes, Paul Tomm, please.'

'Speaking.'

'Ah, excellent. I thought it might have been you. This is Anton Jadid.'

'Professor, good to hear from you. Thank you again for lunch last weekend.'

'My pleasure, entirely my pleasure. Actually, the reason for my call this afternoon is that I would very much like to invite you for another meal.'

'Of course. When?'

'This evening.'

'Tonight?'

'Yes. I really do apologize for the short notice, but I've found something that I think would be of great interest to you.'

'Connected to Professor Pühapäev?'

'Connected very intimately with Jaan, indeed. I would prefer not to discuss this just now over the telephone. But are you free to meet me at the department this evening? Shall we say five-thirty? Again, I apologize for the short notice and the early evening, but that really would be best.'

Was I free? I suppose my promise to Hannah was wrong, and I was under no illusions – or at least nothing more than superficial and self-imposed illusions, illusory illusions – about why I had made the promise. When I made it, I think I intended to keep it, but it wasn't a terribly strong intention. First, everything I had said to her about why I wanted to stay with the story held true. Second, Jadid and his nephew had gone to unnecessary lengths to help me; I could hardly tell them that I was just dropping the story cold. And third, I know it's not the done collegiate thing to seem careerist, but that's a whole lot easier when you have no career to worry about: I wanted that job in Boston. 'I am free,' I said. 'Should I bring anything?'

'No, no, of course not. Arrive curious and hungry, is all I ask. My wife, sadly, left for a conference in Cincinnati this morning; she would very much have liked to meet you. The cooking responsibilities, therefore, are mine. Come to the department at five-thirty. It will most likely be locked, but I shall listen for your knock, which will have to be loud. Until this evening, then?'

'Until this evening.'

I checked my watch: 3:15. If I wanted to make it to Wickenden on time, allowing for the evening rush, I should have left fifteen minutes ago. From behind his closed door, I heard the creak that Art's chair made whenever he stood up. His desk drawer shut, and footsteps advanced toward the door. No reason to explain to the boss why I was putting in a whole three minutes' office time on a weekday, right? Of course not. By the time I considered counter-arguments, I was already on the outskirts of Hartford, heading east at seventy miles per hour.

I pulled into the history department's parking lot as the last filaments of sunset faded into the Wickenden River behind me. There were no other cars in the lot, which disturbed me; I had expected to find at least Professor Jadid still here. Cupping my hand around my eyes to peer in the front window, I saw only the fluorescent hall lights on, but I figured they always were. No doors were open inside; the threadbare gray carpet, sagging wooden stairs, paint chipping off the wrought-iron banister, and the whistling of the evening wind against the siding made the department seem a dozing, snoring old man. I knocked at the door, first politely, then firmly, then insistently, then loudly, and finally with my fists in tandem with the toe of my shoe. Professor Jadid hurried downstairs wearing an open-neck blue oxford shirt and neatly pressed jeans; I had never seen him in anything other than tie and blazer before. His glasses bounced on a string around his neck as he came down the stairs. He looked like somebody's kindly young grandfather without his professorial armor.

'Paul, lovely to see you again so soon. I apologize if I've kept you waiting: have you been out here long?'

'Not too long, thanks.' Long enough to break a couple of toes, is all. 'Good to see you, too.'

'Excellent.' He stood aside and ushered me into the dark hallway. 'My office, you see, looks over the courtyard in back of the building. A lovely, quiet place, totally deserted once the department closes. I chose it precisely for that reason, but this evening, unfortunately, it made it rather difficult to hear you knocking. I'm glad I finally did. Come in, come in.' He put a paternal arm around me as he pulled me into the musty, silent building and locked the door behind us.

'I'll tell you why I called you,' he said, rubbing his hands together, whether out of eagerness or cold, I couldn't tell. 'No, actually, I believe it would be best if I showed you. I suppose we won't be violating any expectation of privacy now, right?'

'Whose privacy?'

'Ah, the right question. Whose indeed? Jaan's, of course. You see, he . . . I really never have been good at giving presents. Come this way, upstairs.

'Our department, like most in the humanities, has a severe shortage of space,' the professor said as we ascended the stairs. 'Professors Ryerson and Zinoman, both of whom we hired at the beginning of this year, have been sharing an office, and good sports though they both are, I would guess that neither finds the situation ideal. So I decided to begin clearing out Jaan's office today to give each his own office by next semester. But I found I was impeded,' he said, pulling me to a stop in front of Jaan's door. Next to it I noticed that Crowley had pasted both his book jacket and three favorable reviews to the outside of his office. 'Does anything strike you as unusual about this door?'

It had four sides, a metal doorknob, a lock, and a sloppy coat of white paint, just like every other door in the department. 'No, nothing.'

'Ah. So I thought, too. Look down, if you wouldn't mind.'

I did, and saw two steel keyholes, one on either bottom corner. The keyholes were large and lozenge-shaped; ordinary toothed keys would have been swallowed in them. Professor Jadid had the satisfied smile of a scientist who'd just completed an un-usually difficult and showy experiment. 'Interesting, no? I certainly did not authorize those locks, nor indeed do I know when Jaan installed them.'

'Do you have the keys?'

'Of course not. I believe he wanted nobody other than himself to be able to enter that office.'

'Why? And how should we get in?'

'Well, I'll take the second part first: I already have. I understand that Joseph gave you a display of his lock-picking abilities last night. An unwelcome one, perhaps?'

'He told you about that, did he? No, not too unwelcome, I suppose, at least in theory. I mean, I was glad to see him. But maybe afterward, well . . . Never mind.'

'Hmmm.' The professor peered over the tops of his glasses at me. 'Joseph felt that your companion reacted with far less equanimity than you did.'

'I didn't think they were in the same room together long enough to notice,' I said defensively.

'No doubt, no doubt. Joseph can be quite a sensitive observer of small details, particularly small personal details. An invaluable ability in his line of work. Perhaps in this instance he was mistaken,' the professor said charitably. 'In any case, Joseph managed to pick these locks, but it took him the better part of an hour, which, according to his Olympian standards, means the lock is essentially tamperproof. And see here,' he added, pushing open the door and leading me into the unusually cold and musty office.

Six long steel cylinders, each a good inch or two in diameter, transversed the back of Pühapäev's office door, three linked by a bar on the left and three on the right. They fit into two bars, one on either side of the doorframe. 'Each lock controls three of these sturdy rods,' said the professor, running his hand along one of them. 'Joseph said that this sort of lock is standard for bank vaults, though they usually put the rods inside a thick steel door to boot. I suppose that would have been too conspicuous for a simple history department. But this was the first such private system he had seen. Why do you suppose that is?'

'I don't know. Expense?'

'Surely, that would be a part of it. In fact, there are a limited number of companies in our part of the world that install these kinds of locks. Joseph said he would phone those in and around Wickenden today and see whether any has records of working at this address. He imagines that wealthy private collectors of art, for instance, probably have similar locks on their doors. The reason he gave, though, for not having seen any, is that these work well enough so that the police generally have no occasion to investigate crimes involving those objects which they protect. Of course, Joseph *is* Joseph – he occasionally exaggerates for effect – but his essential point is well taken: that anyone who can afford such a complex and impregnable lock not only means to protect but usually succeeds in protecting whatever lies behind it.'

'What lies behind it?'

'Ah, now *that,* I believe, is not merely a fascinating question but a central one, too, and one that may well reach far, far beyond the bounds of one professor's death. It may seem, well . . .' He turned around to face the office, and so did I. I wish I could say that there was a body suspended from the ceiling, or a secret door in the back, or huge sacks of coke and measuring scales, but it really looked like any other professor's office: bookcases with books and papers spilling out of them, a large unruly desk covered with more papers, a computer and an electric typewriter on an adjacent small table. The one striking thing about it was that there was only one chair, and it was behind the desk: Pühapäev seemed to have given up on office hours.

'What are you going to do with his things?' I asked.

'I suppose the department will keep them, unless someone comes forward. He has no dependents, isn't that right?'

'I met his brother, actually.'

Professor Jadid turned toward me, eyes glowing, looking less surprised than I would have thought. 'His brother? Really? Tell me, did they look alike?'

'Not really, as far as I remember. They were both old, white, and bearded, but that's about it.'

'Ah,' he said, smiling distractedly and tapping the toe of his shoe against the doorjamb. 'Still, that really proves nothing. Did you form an impression of this brother?'

'Not particularly. He didn't seem to like me asking questions, though.'

'No doubt, no doubt. No doubt he didn't. Well, well. Examine the bookshelves, if you would, and tell me whether you find anything unusual.'

The books were in so many languages that I had no way of knowing whether they were unusual or not. I saw a few in English: *Poly-Olbion,* by Michael Drayton; *Brief Lives,* John Aubrey; *The Patterne of All Wisdome,* Geoffrey LeMetier; *Collectea Chymica,* Sir George Ripley; *Arabs of the North Sea,* Herve Tiima; *Pale Fire,* Vladimir Nabokov. 'I'm not sure. Unfortunately, I can't really read anything except English and very basic Dutch.'

'And I can read eight languages well, and another six in addition to that with the aid of a dictionary. But I count no fewer than thirty languages among these books. Arabic. Chinese. Russian. Urdu. Several scripts that appear Arabic here but use different diacriticals. Romanian. Hungarian. Finnish. Do you know of anyone who can speak or read that many?'

'No.'

'Nor do I. Learning that many languages would take decades. Centuries, perhaps, to be able to read every book in this office. Still, it proves nothing. But of those which I can read, not a single one – except for that volume about Arabs in the North Sea, which, to the best of my knowledge, do not exist – not a single one has anything to do with Baltic history, his supposed field. And look at this,' he said, walking over to the tallest and broadest bookcase in the room. 'Do you know what's behind these books? . . . No? A window.'

'So?'

'Departmental politics revolve around windows. A sociologist could produce a wonderful paper about windows as status symbols in academic departments. Most offices have two windows; professors wait for years to move into a room with a view. And Jaan deliberately blocks his. Little matter, of course; this window looks into an alley, affording a spectacular view of La Tortilla's Dumpsters. I examined the window from the alley and saw that the curtain was drawn. A drawn curtain – and, you can see behind here, a very sturdy curtain that appears to have been glued to the wall around the window – and an immense bookcase protecting it. Again, unusually cautious, wouldn't you think? Perhaps he simply preferred a dark room, but that seems unlikely, as he left the other window, the one behind his desk, unobscured.'

'Is that the one he fired a gun from?'

'Indeed it is. But he seems to have made a few modifications since then. Please, if you would, take this book.' He pulled a heavy Hebrew tome, bound in red leather with gold lettering, off the shelf and handed it to me. 'Take this book and hurl it through that window behind his desk.'

I stood with the book in my hand, puzzled. The professor's face was lit with energy, his perpetual cat's grin broadening beneath his glowing eyes and taut cheeks. 'Here, give the book to me. I don't wish to pressure you, but you needn't have worried.' He walked over to the window and swung the book against it. He dented the book's spine, but the window was undamaged. He knocked against one pane with his knuckles, producing a heavy thudding sound, as though knocking on stone. 'Plexiglas. Bulletproof, I should expect. It looks to be four inches thick. I seriously doubt whether small-arms fire could penetrate this window. And see here,' he said, leaning down to the frame and running a finger along it. 'Sealed shut, not merely painted. This room is a fortress.'

A beeping tune emanated from the professor's jeans: 'Jeanie with the Light Brown Hair.' He reached into his pocket and pulled out a cell phone; it would not have surprised me more if he had pulled out a crack pipe. He looked at the identification panel and gave a satisfied nod. 'Joseph? Yes, fine, thank you, how are you? Good. Good. What? Really? Well, what do you . . . Okay. No, no, he's here. Here with me in Jaan's office. I think I've found . . . You, too? Good, good. I was going to lay mine out before Paul over dinner this evening. Would you like to join us? Of course I am. My house. Yes, we'll leave now. See you shortly, then. Okay. Good-bye.'

He slapped the phone shut and turned to me. 'My nephew: police detective, gourmand, walking memory, and stealer of thunder.'

'What do you mean?'

'I thought that I had discovered what Jaan was actually about, if not who he was. I was looking forward to presenting my theory to you this evening. Now Joseph believes he has made a similar discovery. Mine hinges on the contents of this strong-box here.' He pointed toward a small, cubical black safe beneath Jaan's desk. Its door hung open, and it was empty. 'Joseph was kind enough to open this for me. But look, this really is ingenious. Come here and look.'

I bent down beneath the desk and peered into the

safe. Professor Jadid pointed to two small cylindrical protrusions at the top back corners of the safe. 'Do you know what those are?' he asked.

'No idea.'

'Gas jets. Apparently this safe is rigged to incinerate its contents should someone try to force it open. Isn't that wonderful? Like a spy film.'

'So how did Joe get it open?'

'Well, first he pried off the bottom panel and then the two side panels. He withdrew both gas canisters. Then he did something extraordinary with a stethoscope and two long flexible pieces of metal, and the door popped open. You know, his mother always wanted him to become a doctor. And I must say, I find the image of Joseph in a white coat inveighing against the dangers of overconsumption with a grinder in one hand and a beer in the other rather charming. I have the contents of the safe here.' He triumphantly held up a black litigation box. 'You don't see anything else, do you?'

I peered inside. It looked empty. I was about to stand up and close the door when something glinted on the bottom of the safe. 'Wait. There's something here. Could I ask you to pass me a sheet of paper? Thanks. Here we go.' I brushed some small shards of what looked like broken glass onto the paper, but none of them cut me. More dust than shards, really, they sparkled green in the office light. I held the paper out to Jadid, whose own face glowed along with the green dust. 'What is that?' I asked.

'I believe that is what my nephew might call "a smoking gun." Come on,' he said, pulling me to my feet. 'Time for supper.'

AL-IDRISI'S KAMAL
(WATER)

༺❦❦༻

At no time can a man say, 'It is,' only 'I believe it
was,' and 'I hope it shall be.' Transformation is the
only constant. From earth we come and to earth we
shall return, but while above it we shall be shapeless,
unsettled, as water.

— TANDOU ARMAH CISSÉ,
So Far, So Far from Home

During the 1980 Olympics, the regattas were
held at Pirita, a dock on the Tallinn Bay in the northeastern corner of the city. Even eight years later, as he
looked at the parklands that abutted the city walls
across from the train station, Voskresenyov could still
see the results of the money that Moscow had sent to
beautify the city. Even the apparatchiks raised their
own snouts briefly from the trough and allowed some

of the slop to flow northwest for the sake of putting on a good face for the international guests. Of course, the guest it had most been meant to impress stayed home, but Voskresenyov remembered clearly how his fellow officers had beamed – Russian-style military beaming, that is, marked by eye contact, set jaws with a smile like a lazy trout almost but never quite breaking the surface, and drink-scarred voices croaking 'Correct!' – at hearing Radio Free Europe and the BBC World Service speak admiringly of 'the jewel of the Baltic.'

But the beautification project had an unintended consequence: Estonians became fiercely proud of their Estonian – not Soviet – capital. Voskresenyov could see it as he walked from the station through the Old City on his way to his meeting: after so many years, so many revolutions, and so little change, he had developed a sense of social instability.

Things begin to happen. FUCK THE whoever's-in-charge is graffitoed across a prominent bridge. A stone sails through the governor's window at night; the street below is empty. Before accepting a policeman's order or greasing an open palm, a citizen hesitates and stares at the uniform – for that is what he sees, just the uniform, not the man – for two seconds longer than usual. Forms are lost, not remitted. Fines go unpaid. The governor wakes in the middle of the night to the smell of smoke: his flag, still atop the flagpole outside his window, burns. Political prisoners become symbols instead of ciphers, heroes rather than outcasts. Fat, bald, gray men in suits hurry; young, thin ones in leather jackets loiter. Time bends: one side pushes it forward; the other tries first to stop it, then slow it, then hide from it, then just get out of its way.

In the skeptical glance a young man on Pühavaimu gave his medals, in the unrepaired key scratch down the side of a police car on Müürivahe, and in the strains and pattern of a guitar coming from a second-story window on Pärnu maantee, Voskresenyov could feel it beginning here.

The Old City itself looked like a postcard vision of Europe: cobblestone streets trickling past soft-colored gabled buildings, thick grass-topped walls, a castle at the crest of a hill. The Hanseatic influence made the city look Old High German, like Bruges or Danzig, civilized and maritime and, this late in the twentieth century, pleasantly irrelevant. It was impossible to love both Moscow and Tallinn: one either thrived on Moscow's grotesque energy or found it inhuman; one either warmed to Tallinn's Teutonic coziness or was bored by it. Voskresenyov had grown bored with it, though he did love it once and might again, after another revolution passed it off into someone else's hands. He walked beneath the Raeapteek arch and heard the Pühavaimu bells tolling 11:00 A.M., wondered what would be kept and what would be burned off in the coming years, grateful that this was one Estonian revolution whose progress he could follow from a distance.

He drove out to the sprawling suburbs where the city's gloss faded and turned Soviet before stopping altogether at the edge of Keila-Joa. As soon as he stepped out of his car, Voskresenyov could hear the waterfall at the town's center and he could see the wooden roof of the manor house behind the falls. Behind the manor house was a typical Estonian forest – dark pine interspersed with white birch – that ran from the town's edge to the sea's. He saw a young couple disappear into the woods, hand in hand. They were both blond and willowy, so alike in appearance and so striking in their good health that they would be instantly suspect in any major Russian city.

Next to their vanishing point began a row of small wooden houses, attractive and innocuous enough to somehow escape the eyes-with-wrecking-balls-attached of Soviet urban planners. Voskresenyov knocked on the door of the house farthest from him and noticed as he did that he could see the sea sparkling through a clearing behind the house.

The man who answered Voskresenyov's knock looked like a weathered tern. He towered over the commander by more than a head and stared down at him past a long, thin nose and a tattered white beard. One eye had gone milky and indistinct with age and drifted like a broken compass in its socket; the other was black as a crow's eye. Both sat at the center of a network of crags and wrinkles. He pushed the sleeves of his baggy sweater halfway up his forearms, as though preparing to throw a punch, and waited for his guest to speak.

'Comrade Tiima?' Voskresenyov asked. The old man nodded, and Voskresenyov showed his military identification. 'Comrade Tiima, I am here to investigate a complaint brought against you by your neighbors. Your papers.' Voskresenyov extended his hand and looked as blankly as possible at the old man, who withdrew a leather-covered internal passport from his pocket without taking his eye from Voskresenyov's. The commander made a show of scrutinizing it, though in fact he was thinking only of how long he had to look at each page to make Tiima think he was looking at each page. He snapped the passport shut and returned it after the old man shifted his weight for the fifth time.

'May I come in?' asked Voskresenyov.

'Depends.' Tiima's milky eye rolled up into his head as he fixed his good eye on Voskresenyov's mouth.

'On what?'

'Who you are. What the complaint is. What happens if I say you can't.'

'I'm Voskresenyov, commander in the Soviet army, chief of the Baltic Forces. If you prevent me from coming in, you will be guilty of inhibiting the process of justice.'

The man raised his eyebrows wearily. 'Army man's coming to my house now?'

'We can discuss that later. But just because I'm

not a policeman doesn't mean I can't arrest you.'

'So it sounds like you better come in, then.'

The cottage smelled of pipe smoke, wood smoke, coal smoke, and the sea air that the wind carried in through the back window. The air stung Voskresenyov's eyes, and the old man smiled when he removed his glasses to wipe the tears away. A small victory. 'Want to go back outside?'

'No, no. I just need a moment. May I sit?'

'Suit yourself. But aren't you going to tell me first?'

'Tell you what?'

'What the complaint is.'

'Your neighbors, Mr Tiima, believe you are holding religious services on these premises.'

'Never happened,' he spit. 'This isn't Moscow. I know my neighbors, and they know me. None of them said that, because I don't do it.'

'I have here a signed statement that says –'

'Statement says anything you want. Doesn't mean I did it. You can get anyone to say anything.'

Voskresenyov continued, voice raised slightly and lips curled into what he hoped was a contemptuous sneer. He kept his eyes on the paper in front of him; he didn't want the old man to see the hunger, the acquisitiveness in them. 'It states that you hold unlicensed meetings in the back of your cottage and that "iconic symbols and ecclesiastical paraphernalia" have been clearly visible through the back window. Apparently the woods behind your house are a popular hiking path.'

'Always have been. Those paths I cut myself fifty, maybe sixty years ago. They'll take you right down to the sea.'

'And did you obtain the proper permit for cutting those paths?'

The old man grimaced, shook his head with disbelief but no surprise, and said nothing.

'May I see the room behind this one now, please? I can easily verify whether this claim is valid or false.'

'It isn't a church,' said the old man, not moving.

Voskresenyov stood up and looked around the room. The house could have been more than two hundred years old; it could have been twenty. The woodwork was too skillful to be Soviet, and what few decorations there were – a vibrant hanging rug, a painting of the sun rising over the Baltic coast, a row of carved wooden ships on a rough ledge above a potbellied stove – looked simple and rustic, more in keeping with the nineteenth than the twentieth century. Voskresenyov's thighs and the tips of his fingers were tingling, as they always did whenever he was near something he wanted. If he was wrong, of course, he could simply apologize and disappear, but he was not wrong: even in the Soviet Union, the right combination of money and privilege conjured up accurate information. 'I will determine, Mr Tiima, in keeping with national principles and the welfare of the Soviet people, whether it is or is not a church. Just take me to the room.'

Item 12: A rope, rotten in spots and indistinct in color, 35 centimeters long, with eight small knots running along the length. One end of the rope ends in a knot; the other is tied to a playing-card-size copper-plated board gone green with age. This is an Arab seaman's navigational device, known as a kamal, used to maintain a particular latitude on a familiar journey.

Alchemy can add to the number of years a person lives, but it cannot extend a single life indefinitely: no matter the precautions taken, lives are populated, and people inevitably begin to wonder when a neighbor, an acquaintance, a frequently passing apparition, or even (occasionally) a friend fails to age. Alchemists revere Mercury rather than Nebuchadnezzar or Tithonus for a reason: alchemists escape. None ever became, or becomes, known for extraordinary longevity: when one's age or appearance becomes conspicuous, he simply disappears, casting off an old life as a snake sheds skins, and reappears as someone else, somewhere else. A compass, or in this case a kamal with a telling history, reminds its bearer that he must eventually make peace with his life and abandon it, though this admittedly means something quite different and altogether less painful and permanent than it does for most.

Date of manufacture: 7 Jumada 'l-'ula 538. In the Western calendar, this date fell during the period of Advent, A.D. 1150.

Manufacturer: This is engraved on the copper board's edge: 'In the name of God, the Merciful, the Compassionate. In your hand is the kamal of Yahya Rifaat Tawfit al-Hashemi, artisan of Umm Qasr. His hands wove the final strand and struck the final blow to this copper on 7 Jumada 'l-'ula 538. May it bring God's blessing on its user and guide him through calm seas and gentle breezes wheresoever it pleases God to send him.'

Place of origin: See above.

Last known owner: Herve Tiima, tinker, tailor, soldier, sailor, galley cook, hermit, priest, and purveyor of strange and unsubstantiated historical theories.

Tiima was the son of Paldiski's mayor, Jaan-Uus, who wrote but never published a 'hexadecalogue' of novels that told Estonia's history from the perspective of a series of waves trapped in between the Baltic Sea and Matsalu Bay, dreaming of oceans but batted for centuries between Hiiumaa and the western mainland coast near Rohukula. The only wave to escape this purgatory was the protagonist of the fourth novel, who carried a Danish ship from King Sweyn's court to western Estonia to Hiiumaa during a winter storm.

Tiima became obsessed with the metaphorical implications of the fourth novel in the series and eventually wrote a manuscript of his own about the passengers of that ship, which, he believed, was not fictional. His manuscript, *Arabs of the North Sea,* contended that the key to Estonian identity was an item of tremendous power and worth that al-Idrisi brought from the still center of the earth, Baghdad, to the frozen and benighted wastelands between the Baltic Sea and Lake Peipsi. In the dying days of the Soviet Union, when faith healers, fortune-tellers, tyromancers and pyromancers and gyromancers all became temporary norths for the wildly wavering needles of lost citizens' need to believe, Tiima's theory enjoyed a brief vogue in villages west of Tallinn. He even dared to hold a reading and discussion group in the back room of his cottage, whose walls he decorated with seamen's memorabilia inherited from his father: a mariner's astrolabe, a sextant, and a copper board attached to an old rope.

Local citizens held an illegal vigil in Keila-Joa's main square when Tiima was found murdered, shot once in the back of the head in the forest behind his house by a pistol of the same type that local policemen carried. The vigil stayed peaceful, but the citizens did not disperse when ordered to. News of the civil disobedience spread quickly throughout the country, and though no violence, rioting, or even further sympathetic demonstrations followed, every single citizen of Keila-Joa participated in the 'Baltic Way' chain three years later.

Estimated value: A nine-hundred-year-old rope attached to a greenish rectangle of copper might fetch $10 at a junk store. It might fetch nothing; it could easily be mistaken for garbage. It might fetch $30,000, as did a kamal supposedly used by Vasco da Gama's chief navigator.

Thus was this world created.

~~~

Ihadn't realized how filthy my car was until I opened the door for Professor Jadid: he furrowed his brow and paused, quick enough to remain polite but visible all the same, before climbing in. I grabbed a few handfuls of paper cups, sandwich wrappers, and newspapers as well as two broken umbrellas from beneath the passenger seat and threw them into the back. Then I swept crumbs of every color of the beige rainbow onto the ground. He climbed in gingerly. 'Out of curiosity,' he said as I pulled out of the parking lot, 'more than idle curiosity, in this case – I have been wondering whether you consider yourself religious.'

'What do you mean? A believer in what?'

'Oh, the "what" doesn't much matter. I suppose religion would be a natural place to start. But I mean, are you, as a matter of temperament, inclined more toward belief or skepticism? Not that the two are irreconcilable, of course.'

'Well, religion I guess I never had much of. Went to church every so often when I was a kid, but I was never confirmed or anything. I never really got a feeling for it, and both my parents are mixed, too, so they never really took to any one church or one community. Or any one family, but I guess that's another story.'

'And do you feel that you have missed anything as a result?'

'I guess I'm a little jealous of people who find something in it, you know, or even people who make the rituals part of their lives.'

'Indeed. I suppose that even if religion fails to provide ontological comfort, it can at least provide structure. Chronological structure, if not spiritual structure.'

I asked him what had led to this topic of conversation.

'Curious, just curious, just simple curiosity. I must say, I rarely make my way into a synagogue these days. My wife, as you may know, is an Orthodox Christian, born in California to Syrian parents. We raised our daughters in the church, which caused no small amount of commotion in my family. As I age, though, I increasingly feel drawn not toward the cosmogony or theological substance of Judaism but toward its rituals, as you said earlier. Toward a sense of participating in something ancient and unbroken. I feel, with no small amount of shame, that I have proven myself the defective link in a chain of believers, son to father to grandfather, stretching back centuries. Were I more detached, I might be able to appreciate the irony that prosperity accomplished what adversity never could. Finally left alone to assimilate, I suppose that is precisely what we did. And by we, of course, I mean I.

'Well, well. I don't mean to prattle. Please, keep heading straight up Grover Street and turn left onto Appleman. My house is just past Torrance.' Professor Jadid switched on my radio to a classical station, and we drove without speaking for about ten minutes.

'There, that's it there,' he said. 'Pull into the driveway or park along the street, whichever you prefer.'

I left the car on the street in front of his house: a small, immaculate, and typically Wickendenian place, with a clapboard front, porches on all three stories with staircases leading from one porch down (or up, I suppose) to the next, and a widow's walk. It didn't look too different from my old place, or Mia's current house. I'm not sure why I expected anything different, but I did: a castle, maybe, a mansion or a cloister. A farmhouse out in the country. Seeing Professor Jadid in a parka and boots, walking past a lawn mower and stopping to pick up a free community paper from his stoop, seemed incongruous: he was meant to dissolve into a late-nineteenth-century Viennese café at the end of every day.

*

Professor Jadid's kitchen was long and low, warmly lit, with plenty of dark wood surfaces: the sort of room to pass a childhood in. He deftly chopped two tomatoes and two small red onions into tiny cubes, then mashed them to a paste with the back of a wooden spoon, adding a few cloves of garlic, the leaves from three sprigs of marjoram he pulled from a pot on the windowsill, a glug of olive oil, and a splash of white wine. He cubed a hunk of lamb and added the pieces to the vegetable slurry, and dumped the whole mixture into a ceramic dish that he put in the oven. He poured us both glasses of white wine and insisted that we toast the bulky rectangular briefcase sitting in the corner.

'Why?' I asked.

'All shall be revealed,' he said, with a showman's raise of his eyebrows.

I exhaled impatiently. We sat at a round wooden table in front of two sliding glass doors that opened onto a back garden, but because of the night and the light above and behind us, all we could see in the doors was ourselves. A sudden knock at the glass doors, and the erasure of both of our reflections made me jump and spill my wine.

Professor Jadid grimaced sympathetically at me ('Joseph always parks around back'), then stood up to open the doors. His nephew, holding a six-pack of Newport Storm in one hand and a file in the other, squeezed through the doorway. He hugged his uncle, almost completely enveloping him, and they kissed three times, alternating cheeks. Joe was followed by a tall, whip-thin young man in a knife-pressed maroon suit, pin-striped shirt, and maroon tie with a garnet stickpin, carrying a leather jacket; he looked like a half-starved, worried musician from 1950s Greenwich Village.

'This is Lyosha Priyenko,' said Joe. Priyenko slipped through the door gingerly, as though afraid of being noticed, and extended a bony hand to both me and the professor. 'Lyosha Priyenko, this is my uncle Abe, and Paul, who started this whole thing. Lyosha works organized crime.'

'A pleasure, Mr Priyenko. Come in,' said the professor. 'What can I get you to drink?'

Priyenko put a hand up, palm out, and waved it back and forth in time with the shaking of his head. His prominent, ax-shaped cheekbones seemed to divide his face into a rectangle on top of a trapezoid, and his awkward manner made the two facial halves move slightly out of tandem with each other. 'Ah, nothing, sir, thank you: I'm still on duty.' He spoke with a trace of an accent – his vowels were long and rubbery, while his consonants collided with one another on their way from throat to tongue – and he stood with the squared posture and blank face of a military recruit.

'Of course, of course. Please.' The professor pulled out chairs for Joe and Priyenko, and we sat back down in ours. Joe opened a bottle of beer and declined his uncle's offer of a glass.

'So which of us would like to speak first?' asked the professor.

Joe wiped his mouth with his sleeve. 'Lyosha here needs to get back to his real job, so let's us two go first.' He scratched his broad stomach and sniffed, as though insulted or pensive. 'Abe, something smells great. When's dinner?'

Professor Jadid snapped his fingers and touched a finger to his temple. 'Thank you, Joseph, for reminding me.' He set plates and cutlery on the table and opened the oven to check on the lamb. 'Dinner in a short while; nothing until then. You know my rules.' He walked over to the counter and began chopping vegetables for a salad. 'I'm still listening,' he called out over his shoulder.

'Well,' began Joe, draining his beer and moving the empty to the floor, 'you remember yesterday when we went to that Lone Wolf place, how I told you we took a glass and would run the prints?'

'Yeah.'

'Well, Sally and Lyosha here ran them. By the way, Uncle Abe, Sal said he's sorry he couldn't stop by. One of his kids is in a play tonight.'

The professor nodded and raised his knife in acknowledgment.

'Anyway, Priyenko here, he has a brother – is it a brother or a cousin?'

'Two brothers, actually,' said Priyenko, sitting up straighter, as if a teacher had just called on him. 'One is working as an investigator with the Moscow town prosecutor's office, the other is an assistant to the minister of internal affairs.'

'Right. Now, from what he says here, that's like Russian royalty, right? These guys have serious juice?'

Priyenko shrugged and looked down at the table. 'Juice, yes, I think so. Good jobs, I guess, get you that. I'm giving many presents to my nieces and nephews next visit, so they helped us.'

'Okay, so anyway,' said Joe, perching excitedly and dangerously on the edge of his chair, 'I gave both that bartender Eddie's prints and a copy of Pühapäev's prints to him and to Sally. Now, Pühapäev you already knew had a local record and had been a federal material witness, right? Not really a record, but the feds in Wickenden knew who he was.' I nodded.

Professor Jadid carried a salad to the table with the same disapproving scowl that froze students' blood and reddened their faces.

'Yeah, I told Uncle Abe about it yesterday. Wasn't too happy to hear that Jaan tried to steal the jewels he helped bring over,' said Joe. 'Turns out that Eddie had feds, too. They list him as . . . let's see,' he said, unfolding a sheet of paper that Priyenko handed him. 'Edouard Ivanov, convicted February 4, 1992, Kings County, New York, receipt of stolen property, served sixty on ninety at Ossining, saw his parole officer regularly, good behavior, no complaints, blah blah blah. Subsequently never heard from again in Kings County Court, or any other federal court either.'

'What sort of stolen property?' I asked.

'Gold. Gold icons stolen from a Ukrainian Orthodox church outside of Bridgeport, Connecticut. State lines: there's the fed charge. Looks like the same kind of deal as Pühapäev: whatever dumbfuck thief these guys paid was arrested with the goods on his person and claimed Ivanov suborned the theft. It looks like Eddie had some court-appointed scarecrow in a suit instead of our hometown Johnnie Cochran defending him. Why the fuck are both these guys using such dumb fences?' Joe looked up at us as though he expected an answer, but all we heard was the sizzle and pop of lamb roasting in the oven.

'Money?' ventured Priyenko. 'Maybe they were stingy old Soviets.'

'Yeah, maybe,' Joe agreed halfheartedly. 'So you never ran across either of these guys before?' To me and his uncle he added parenthetically, 'He works the Russian mob in and around the city.'

'No, I have never heard of either of them. But, you know, neither of them lived in Wickenden, and I've only been here for maybe nine or ten months.' Priyenko pulled a pack of Parliaments out of his shirt pocket with long, feminine fingers and looked the question at Professor Jadid, who put an ashtray and a book of matches in front of him.

Joe nodded philosophically and scratched the underside of his chin. Every man has a part of his face that he is condemned to miss whenever he shaves. That was Joe's: an oblong patch of thick beard grew like moss in the fold between his second chin and his neck. 'Tell him the better part, though.' Nobody knew who he was talking to. His uncle served a plate of baked lamb to each of us. Joe elbowed Priyenko amicably and almost knocked him off his chair. 'Go on,' he said, a pink trickle of lamb juice running inside his collar. 'Tell him.'

'Oh, me. Sure. Well, it turns out that Ivanov and this man called Pühapäev have Russian records.' None of us said anything. Priyenko made a little fluttering gesture with his smoking hand. He wasn't eating. 'Yes, well, this is nothing surprising, you know. Anyone going into the army or in Komsomol or living in big cities really had to get fingerprinted. Surprising is that I managed to find this out in a single day,' he said, giggling. 'My brother, the one in the town prosecutor's office, told me that they just put newer records on computer, but the old ones are still in the same huge room underneath Novokuznetskaya, where they've always been. Fortunately, he's had affairs with four of the six records clerks, and three of them ended happily. The only man in Moscow who can find out what we need to know.' None of us was laughing, but he seemed to find this pretty funny.

'Get to the point, how about? And eat something, Slim.'

As soon as he was given permission, Priyenko also began eating enthusiastically. 'Thank you, this is wonderful. Turkish?'

'The recipe?' asked the professor. Priyenko nodded. 'It may have been Greek originally, but it's entirely my own now. Excellent guess, though. I suppose it could be Turkish. Next time I could add a bit of sumac, and perhaps –'

'Abe, sorry, but Priyenko's got to walk soon. Can we trade recipes next visit?'

Professor Jadid looked first upset, then shrugged affably. 'I am sorry. Most old men potter in a garden or on a golf course; I potter in the kitchen. Please continue, Lyosha.'

'Yes, okay, so anyway, according to my brother, these prints of Ivanov's belong in Russia to a man named Ibragim Ikhmayev, an Ingushetian sentenced to forty years' hard labor for running a contraband-goods ring in 1985.'

'How curious,' said the professor. 'In 1985? There was no process of criminal review when the Soviet Union fell?'

Priyenko twisted his mouth, raised his eyebrows, and shrugged. 'Criminals were not the highest priority at that time. In a situation like this, I suppose authorities would have said that stealing is stealing; there's no Communist stealing or free-market stealing. But I don't know . . .'

'Don't know about what?' I asked.

'Wait, and I will finish.' He pulled a notebook from his jacket pocket. 'Ikhmayev ran an elaborate theft and resale ring. To visiting Western tourists, he sold icons and Russian religious and historical artifacts. Most of them probably false, of course – Westerners can never tell,' he said with a rueful smile, looking down. 'No offense intended, by the way. For Russians he smuggled cars, Western clothes, pop music, and name-brand cigarettes in from Scandinavia and West Germany.'

'That seems pretty small-time,' said Joe, leaning back from the table and emitting a sustained and satisfied tubalike belch while opening his second beer.

'Yes, I haven't finished yet, though.' Priyenko paused to see that he was holding everyone's attention. He acknowledged that he was with an almost imperceptible nod of satisfaction. 'He also smuggled precious metals and jewels from Central Asia into Russia.'

'Always jewels with these guys,' I said.

'Indeed,' agreed the professor, smiling enigmatically.

Priyenko speared a hunk of lamb on his knife and worked it back and forth with his molars. 'What is interesting,' he said through his full mouth, 'is that this sort of thing should have gotten him shot. The sort of organized crime, *mafiya,* that Russia is famous for now didn't really exist under the Soviets. No, that's not true: it existed, but only as a system of government.' All of us laughed, and he looked up, eyes twinkling, but not smiling. 'This is not a joke. Or it's a joke and a not-joke. Every bunch of Russian mobsters I've ever seen model themselves, consciously or not, on the Communist Party of the Soviet Union. The only difference is, the mobsters do their stealing without prefacing it with long speeches and lofty ideals that nobody believes.

'No, so like I was saying, really it should have been that Ikhmayev was shot for this crime. But he wasn't. I would guess that he had some sort of connections. Army or intelligence, probably: how else could he organize something like this? But even this,' he said, finger raised like a conductor's baton in the instant before the music starts, 'isn't the strangest thing about Ikhmayev.'

'Jesus, kid, this isn't a play,' said Joe. 'Just spit it out.'

'Well, the point is, according to the Russian police records, Ikhmayev is still in Magadan.'

'Where's Magadan?' I asked.

'A few thousand miles north of Japan, a few thousand miles southwest of Alaska, and a few million miles from anywhere. It's a prison,' said Joe.

We looked at one another, confused, and Priyenko burst out laughing. 'I cannot believe an American police detective knows where Magadan is. Why do you?'

Joe gave a satisfied shrug and a big-lug grin.

'It's just funny that the records are such a mess,' Priyenko continued. 'I told my brother that this man Ikhmayev was over here, and he started swearing and cursing, you know, because if someone is listening to his conversation on the phone, they know that he knows there's a problem with the records. Maybe then they make him go out to Magadan and verify it.'

'How's somebody escape from a prison like that?' asked Joe.

'Oh, many ways, really. If he really did have the connections that it looks like he had, escaping would have been no problem; all it would take is a phony order sheet or a bribed guard or two. No, the interesting question is how he managed to get out across the frozen desert. I guess some Yakuts live out there, but everyone knew that they were recruited to turn people in. The Northern People's Patrol. How he got out of Yakutia, this is a more interesting problem than how he left the prison. But I suppose this is what a smuggling ring does: it gets things safely from one place to another.'

Professor Jadid cleared away our plates and refilled our glasses. Joe helped himself to his third beer, and the professor also had one. 'I'm saving you from yourself, Joseph,' he said, 'as so often happens with you and a table of food and drink within arm's reach.'

The professor also helped himself to one of Priyenko's cigarettes. 'And I believe you also have some information about Jaan, do you not?'

'Yes, of course,' Priyenko said. 'This might be nothing, but the detective wanted me to mention it anyway.'

'That's me, by the way,' Joe said. 'The detective. Why I could convince him to poke around like this for a case so far out of his jurisdiction. Thinks I'll owe him one.' Priyenko looked up as if he'd been bitten, startled and angry. 'And of course I will. I mean, I do. Owe him, you know?'

'I can vouch for Joseph,' said the professor reassuringly, 'even if he were not my nephew. We Jadids do not forget our debts, nor do we lightly make ourselves indebted.' Joe nodded and patted Priyenko on the shoulder.

'Yes, of course. I have no worries. I'll continue? Good,' said Priyenko. 'I faxed my brother Pühapäev's fingerprints, and he said that they were about a forty percent match with the fingerprints of Ivan Voskresenyov, a naval commander stationed first in Murmansk, then in Riga, and then at the Directorate for Naval Strategy and Security in Moscow.' He glanced at his notebook. 'Notes say he retired in 1991 and has not been heard from since. This means no visits to a naval hospital, no naval burial. Maybe he's still in Russia but lives a terribly quiet life.'

'And how conclusive is a forty percent match?' asked Professor Jadid.

'Wouldn't hold up with most judges; I'll tell you that for free,' said Joe.

Priyenko tilted his hand first left, then right, then left again. 'It is difficult to say. Voskresenyov's prints were taken – let's see – in 1957. They were scanned onto microfilm and loaded onto a primitive finger-printing database in 1989 and then transferred to a more sophisticated imaging system just this last year, but my brother said the picture quality is still quite poor. They mostly still rely on human comparison when they use fingerprints at all. One reason is that picture quality on their machines rarely provides an accurate reading. What are those machines called again?'

'Who gives a shit?' asked Joe.

'Joseph, please.'

'Sorry, Abe. Sorry. It's a bad habit.'

'Okay, anyway,' said Priyenko, 'it could be an exact match, it could be no match, but we'll never know. By the way, something curious: *Voskresenye* means Sunday in Russian. Sergeant Jadid said that Jaan Pühapäev means "John Sunday." Ivan, of course, is the Russian version of John. Just curious.'

'Is Voskresenyov a common Russian surname?' asked the professor.

'Well, not common, but you know there are many, many last names in Russian. Maybe fifteen or twenty first names, but very many last names.'

'Yeah, also, by the way,' said Joe, 'Sally says his friends say that there's no record of anyone named Jaan Pühapäev ever emigrating from Estonia. There's an American passport issued to that name, though, and it was issued in the Hartford passport office.'

Joe slapped Priyenko on the back. 'Okay, kid, good work today. Listen: you can't pay me any attention when I start giving you a hard time, okay?'

'I have a thick skin,' Priyenko said, standing up and putting his jacket on. It was a fingertip-length tobacco brown leather jacket, the kind every city-dwelling man wishes he looked cool wearing. Priyenko did.

'Good. Gold star for today.' Priyenko smiled and waved Joe's comment away. 'You think I'm kidding? Take off now. We'll work together again.'

Priyenko shook hands all around, thanked Professor Jadid for the meal, and left.

'So,' I said.

'So,' said Joe. The professor hadn't turned off the oven, and the heat began to build in the kitchen, along with the smell of all the previously cooked bits burning inside. Still, nobody got up.

'Extraordinary,' said the professor after a long pause. 'My colleague was not what he was.'

'How do you mean?' I asked.

'That he served in the Soviet navy does not surprise me. That his name is an alias should also be obvious to anyone who chooses to think about it. But he tried to steal a very particular set of rubies: rubies set into rings crafted secretly, by a Sassanid jeweler who also had a reputation as something of a "cunning man." These rubies supposedly confer upon the right bearer a long life and, if properly treated and invoked, protection from enemies seen and unseen. Whether you believe that or not, the legend certainly adds to their value. This surprised me. Add to that he spent his leisure hours drinking in the establishment of another Soviet émigré and, apparently, another jewel thief. Also this matter of his alias sounding so suspiciously like that of a high-ranking navy commander who happens to have disappeared. Add to that Priyenko's suspicion – which seems to me quite well founded – that Ikhmayev's cohorts had military links, and we begin to get an altogether stranger picture.'

'You think Pühapäev was some sort of jewel thief?' asked Joe.

'Not precisely, and probably not in the way that you understand that occupation.'

'What do you mean?'

The professor sighed and brought the litigation box over to the table. Without saying anything, he opened it and withdrew a ten-by-fourteen yellow envelope. 'I realize that the large box is rather farcical, but it produces the required dramatic effect. In any event, it was all I had at hand in my office today. I lugged a great many student essays from home to work and had intended to bring it home empty. No matter. Paul, you know, but Joseph, you do not, that I have here the contents of Jaan's safe.

'Item number one.' Professor Jadid pulled a long, folded piece of paper out of the envelope. It was the type of paper that fit in old-style computer printers: both sides bore perforated, detachable edges with regularly spaced holes on them. Who still used paper like that? 'A travel itinerary.' Of course: travel agents did. 'Jaan was due for a rather adventuresome and expensive winter vacation. He was to fly from Boston to Berlin. Three days later from Berlin to Moscow. Five days after that to Tehran. From Tehran he would go to Riyadh, then to Amman, then to Baghdad, then to Jerusalem by some other means, because the next leg would take him from Jerusalem to Bombay, then to Los Angeles for a brief stopover, and then back to Boston.'

'The grand tour,' Joe joked.

'Indeed. Quite an adventure for an aging professor, wouldn't you say?'

'What was he doing?' I asked.

The professor held up a finger for silence and dug into the litigation box again. 'Items two through six: passports. Estonian, Russian, Dutch, British, and Iranian. Joseph, can you tell me whether the United States permits dual citizenship with any of these countries except for the Netherlands and Great Britain?'

'Don't think so.'

'Correct. We don't. Presumably, then, these passports – which are completely blank, as you can see, without even a photograph or a name – could well have been intended to replace, rather than augment, his American identity, which, as we have discovered tonight, appears to have replaced his Estonian identity. And so on back, perhaps.'

'So on back?' I echoed. 'How old is this guy? I mean, how many people can you be in one lifetime?'

'Now *that* is a fascinating question. Joseph tells me that the medical examiner who performed the autopsy on Jaan reported an abnormal lack of wear on his organs.'

'Yeah, but what's that prove? And the coroner

died, remember; never finished the autopsy. He could have been just saying something off the top of his head, you know? Long day, take a peek, get to it tomorrow. Haven't called whoever replaced him; maybe he found something, but this . . . I don't see what it means.

'Perhaps nothing. But this particular claim – that his organs seemed in unusually fine fettle – seems more compatible with close observation than a lack of observation, does it not? If the coroner were lazy or performing a hasty or incompetent autopsy, surely he would have assigned Pühapäev's body the qualities he most expected to find rather than unlikely ones, would he not? Why would a seasoned coroner make dubious but easily disprovable claims?'

Good point, and I didn't have an answer. Neither did Joe.

'Item seven,' the professor continued, 'a sheet of paper with a handwritten list of fifteen arcane objects: an alembic, a castle, a golden ney, a silver ney, an Ethiopian triptych, Xinjiang's ivory, the Crying Queen of Hoxton, a sheng, rainbow dust, the Kaghan's Cages, the White and Red Medikos, al-Idrisi's kamal, Ardabil's Yellow and Rising Sun, and the Shadow of the Sun.'

'Rainbow dust?' sneered Joe, drawing out each syllable until it snapped from the weight of his contempt.

'What's a *mediko*?' I asked.

Professor Jadid smiled and looked at us indulgently. 'I'm not certain what rainbow dust is either, but I would guess it has more significance than your tone affords it. And you should recall, Joseph, Mediko Tshvalianidze, that lovely Georgian woman who sang with the choir at St Cyril's.'

'Never went to church, Uncle Abe, remember? I bat for the other side.'

'Of course, of course. The confusion of an old man. In any event, I would guess that these were antiquities of some sort that had recently come into Jaan's possession. Notice the check mark next to each item in many different colors and styles of pen, probably because he acquired them at many different times.'

'Jeez, Abie, you should have been a cop.'

'You flatter me, Joseph, please.' Again he reached into the leather box and pulled out six leather-bound checkbooks. 'Items eight through thirteen: bankbooks. Citibank, Barclays, ABN AMRO, as well as banks in Switzerland, the Cayman Islands, and Liechtenstein. Tucked inside each bankbook are deposit instructions. In the latter three books, you will notice that there are no checks. They probably require that you present yourself in person in order to make withdrawals, but I may be wrong about that. In any event, all three of those countries are known for banks friendly to those wishing to either conceal or launder large sums of money.

'Now we come to something interesting. Item

fourteen is, as you can see, another sheet of paper. I will read what Jaan has written on it. By the way, I know the handwriting to be Jaan's:

'True it is, without falsehood, certain and most true.
That which is above is like to that which is below, and that which is below is like to that which is above, to accomplish the miracles of one thing.
And as all things were by the contemplation of one, so all things arose from this one thing by a single act of adaption.
The father thereof is the Sun, the mother the Moon.
The Wind carried it in its womb, the Earth is the nurse thereof.
It is the father of all works of wonder throughout the whole world.
The power thereof is perfect.
If it be cast onto the Earth, it will separate the element of Earth from that of Fire, the subtle from the gross.
With great sagacitie it doth ascend gently from Earth to Heaven.
Again it doth descend to Earth, and uniteth in itself the force from things superior and things inferior.
Thus wilt thou possess the glory of the brightness of the whole world, and all obscurity will fly far from thee.
The thing is the fortitude of all strength, for it overcometh every subtle thing and doth penetrate every solid substance.
Thus was this world created.
Hence there will be marvellous adaptions achieved, of which the manner is this.
For this reason I am called Hermes Trismegistus, because I hold three parts of the wisdom of the whole world.
That which I had to say about the operation of Sol is complete.'

'What the fuck was that?' asked Joe, speaking for both of us.

'That was Holmyard's translation of the Emerald Tablet, which is sometimes also called the Emerald Table or the Tabula Smaragdina, and which is one of the foundational texts of medieval alchemy. Stapled to this sheet are translations into German, Farsi, Arabic, Hebrew, as well as sixteen lines each in Cyrillic and in two Sanskrit-derived scripts, none of which I can read, but all of which I assume are also translations of the Tablet. Items fifteen through twenty-one, incidentally, if you are still keeping count.' The professor sat with his hands flat on the table, looking from me to Joe and then back again. His eyes were alight, and he was smiling. From the litigation box, he pulled out a book bound in green leather, with Gothic German script on the spine and front.

'Both of you, I am sure, noticed the breadth of languages represented on Jaan's bookshelves. I doubt, though, that you perceived a corresponding narrowness of subject matter. Virtually all of the books dealt, in one way or another, with the practice and history of alchemy. Of those, a large number dealt either with the Emerald Tablet itself or with the traditions known as Hermetism, Hermeticism, or Gnosticism, from which the Tablet so clearly sprang.

'This book, for instance, is a curiosity of which I have often heard but never seen. Do you know why that is? No? Because this is one of only three copies ever printed. One supposedly exists somewhere in

Germany. One burned with Hitler in his bunker. That the third existed just one flight of stairs above my office . . . well, I never would have dreamed of such a thing.'

'What the hell is it?' asked Joe.

'I was coming to that. This is the personal diary of Volker von Breitzlung, one of Hitler's astrologists. No, no, don't laugh: Hitler relied more heavily on occult practices than any other Western leader, more even than Reagan.' He paused and grinned. 'Or her husband. In any case, scholars are divided on whether such a book exists, and were I not convinced by the age, press marks, and signs of wear, I might believe this to be a fake. It might even *be* a fake, but a fake of such workmanship and thought as to be valuable in itself.

'Here,' he said, opening to a place marked with a scrap of yellow paper. '"The Führer asked me about the Great Green Stone again, whether it could do what I said yesterday it could. I told him it certainly could, that a man who gained control of the Stone and knew how to wield it would without doubt face no obstacles over which he could not triumph. Again I told him that it had long been rumored to be in Estonia, and he affirmed that the Soviets had designs upon the three Baltics, but that even if he ceded political power to those hateful atheists, he still would maintain a vigilant and clandestine network of loyal German patriots and supporters to seek, seek, seek, until they found the Stone."

'And finally,' said the professor, closing the book and withdrawing a folded sheet of paper, 'we come to item twenty-two.' He unfolded it carefully, revealing the green dust that I had found on the bottom of Pühapäev's safe. 'I believe that Jaan, or whatever his name really was, had somehow found the Emerald Tablet. I believe he was trying to sell it, or at the very least peddle its influence.'

After a few moments of silence, Joe leaned across the table toward his uncle. 'Its influence? Abie, have you lost your fucking mind? What influence? You're talking about an astrologer's fairy tale, for Christ sake. Alchemy? What's he going to do, jet off to Baghdad or Saudi and turn some fucking sand into gold?'

'First of all, young man, I will not have that kind of bigot's talk in my house.'

Joe flopped back into his chair, chastened eyes poking out from under his slabby brow.

'Secondly, alchemy is far more than turning lead, or sand, as you so meanly phrased it, into gold. It is the science of transformation, of understanding the fundamental nature of the universe and all of its objects. Theoretically, an accomplished alchemist would be able to turn anything into any other thing. Physical metaphysics, you might call it. And finally, why do you disbelieve so strongly even in the possibility that this particular object might have certain powers beyond the ordinary?'

'Abe, what powers?'

'I don't know, to be honest. Not precisely. But take the state of Jaan's body. Something must have made it possible to halt, slow, or perhaps even reverse the ordinary process of aging on his organs. How else do you explain his condition?'

'An incompetent coroner, that's how.'

'Ugh. Cynic. A premature cynic. Joseph, I am not talking about the sort of thing that you could find at that crystal shop on Prescott Street. I am not talking about a fashionable New Age trend or something to nod sagely about over a cup of – what is that garbage that your cousin Mira likes so much?'

'Chai?'

'Right – chai. I will grant a certain vagueness, a lack of specificity in describing precisely what it can do, but there are remarkable similarities in literature about the Tablet. Similarities across cultures, across time periods, similarities between authors who could not possibly have read one another's work. Furthermore, references to a large tablet made of green stone appear in the alchemical literature of numerous countries, always referred to as something that separates and purifies, as something that leaves the dead matter behind and rejuvenates the living. How do you explain that?'

'Well, coincidence, first of all . . .'

'Nonsense. Literature does not permit coincidence.'

'Maybe not in one book, there can't be coincidence,' Joe argued. 'But sure, all sorts of myths are alike from all sorts of places. Anyway, given a choice between coincidence and some kind of circumstantial proof – and that's "proof" with big, huge, giant, flaming red neon quotation marks around it – I'll take coincidence.'

'Does it really matter?' I asked. They stopped bickering and looked at me. 'I mean, let's say Jaan had this jewel, or had found this jewel. You'll both agree that's possible, right? He tried to fence something before, and that bartender, Albanian Eddie, is really a smuggler of some sort. So it's possible he has this jewel. Whether it has unusual power or not, he's still trying to sell it, right? The process – finding a buyer, contacting associates in other countries, putting money into an untraceable offshore account – that's still the same. So I can see why, as a matter of academic interest – offense unintended, of course – whether the stone had powers or not might matter to you, Professor. But all this stuff – the travel, the sales, what Jaan did – it'd be the same whether the stone was just a big hunk of emerald or a big hunk of magic emerald, right? I mean, the only thing that would really matter is whether his buyers believed it.'

'Kid's got a point,' said Joe. 'By the way, how big do you think it is, Abe?'

'I don't know, exactly. According to the most common legend, Noah carried it with him on the ark, and Abraham's wife, Sarah, found it in the arms of a priest who lay dead in a cave. Here in the von Breitzlung book it's called a "Great Green Stone."

The English words "table" and "tablet" aren't terribly indicative; neither really indicates size, and both are used with roughly equal frequency, as far as I know, to refer to the same object. But if dust from the Tablet was indeed found on the bottom of Jaan's safe, and if the safe was indeed purchased with an eye toward holding the Tablet, it would almost certainly be the single largest emerald on record. Roughly the size of a sheet of legal paper, let's say? It would have to be, would it not, for a grown man, even a small grown man, to cradle it to his chest with his arms? Could you imagine the worth of an item like that? Millions? Tens, hundreds of millions? It would be incalculable. I mean that it *literally* would be incalculable.'

'Hey, what were those other things you read from your list?' asked Joe.

'What other things?'

'The Crying Queen, the alembic, the castle – that stuff.'

'Antiquities, I suppose. I can see no link between these rather disparate items. Can you?'

'Yeah. They're all antiquities.'

'Well, obviously, yes. I mean any real connection.'

'That's real enough. You call something an antique instead of an old piece of shit in the attic, you're implying it has value. Worth something. Maybe Jaan wasn't just a jewel thief; maybe he was a fence for a ring of specialized thieves. Makes him a natural, I'd think.'

'Interesting. He does seem rather interested in items that have an occult history.'

'There you go,' said Joe. 'Makes them even more valuable. Rich nuts who spend all day doing yoga and tai-chi, sleeping in oxygen tanks, looking for a way to live longer. That'd drive up the price of any of these things.'

'Hmmm,' grumbled the professor, removing his glasses and rubbing the bridge of his nose. 'I still posit that there are more things in heaven and earth, Joseph –'

'Yeah, I read that one, too. Let's agree to disagree on this one. What I want to do now is check out this guy's house.'

'No way the local cops would let us do that,' I said.

'Even if I don't bring Sally and you wait in the car?'

'No way.'

'So we don't ask. What about your friend the music teacher. She have a key?'

'Actually, I don't think that's such a good idea. I sort of agreed not to poke around this story for a couple of days.'

'She asked you to back off? Why?'

'She said she just didn't want to think about it. Said she wanted to let Jaan rest.'

'Bullshit.'

'Perhaps she's still rather raw,' Professor Jadid suggested. 'I don't find that implausible.'

'Fine, be raw, but why ask Paul to back off, too?'

'She was pretty angry that I had talked to the police,' I said.

'Yeah? Well, whatever. Let's worry about her later. I bet dollars to doughnuts I can get into the guy's house, though.'

Neither the professor nor I said anything.

'I'll take that as consent. It's only nine o'clock anyway; I don't want to go doing anything until much later. What I could use, though, is another drink.'

'Joseph, you've just finished as many beers with one meal as I consume in a month,' the professor wailed.

'Yeah, I know. Not here. I think we should stop by and see Eddie on our way out to Lincoln.'

THE YELLOW SUN

❧❧

There are no sunrises at sea. When from the crow's nest the observant watcher first spies yellow filaments trickling into the sky, whether he is ultimately delighted or warned, he is primarily relieved. Yellow sunrises signal land: he is almost once more on solid ground.

— SØREN ÅSTERGAARD, *Enquiries in Favor of Life*

15 December 1989
Aubrey College, Oxford

To the Chief Senior House Officer,
Psychiatric Wing, James Hinchcliffe Hospital:
    This letter accompanies Mr K. R. Prasad, the Junior Dean of Aubrey College, and Mr Benjamin Glantz, an Aubrey post-graduate student in no small amount of distress.
    As you will undoubtedly hear, the College has suffered a terrible loss today. Mr Glantz has inadvertently been most directly affected,

448

as it was he who discovered Dr Dimbledon's body. He was in such a state of nervous apoplexy this morning that I thought it best to remand him to your care for the time being. I know Mr Glantz to be a remarkably intelligent, capable young man (though he does possess a tense and rather excitable disposition), and I hope that after a few days' rest in serene environs, he will be quite himself again.

I have one particular request, and I hope that you will consider your long-standing relationship with this University and honour it closely. You will no doubt have heard rumours of what has happened here, and by tomorrow you may well choose to read all about it in our more speculative and less reputable papers. Please do not ask Mr Glantz about it, and please do not speak about it in his presence. He is a young man and a sensitive one, and has been most troubled by the small part he has played in these events. I ask that you restrain your curiosity as long as he is in your care. Naturally, I would prefer that you restrain it after that, too, but I know better than to moralise in the face of ink and fame, transient though both may be.

In any event, here he is. Treat him well. I remain

Most sincerely yours,

Sir Peter Allham

Rector, Aubrey College

15 December 1989

To the Staff and Fellows of Aubrey College:

By now you will most likely have heard that Dr Darius Dimbledon, our Senior Tutor and a distinguished Fellow of this

College for nearly fifty years, has died this afternoon. Dr Dimbledon first arrived at Aubrey in the early stages of the War, and since then has been a constant and familiar presence here. I need not tell you how sorely he shall be missed.

I am aware of the various and macabre rumours concerning the manner and circumstance of Dr Dimbledon's death, and I choose not to comment on them. I would ask you to do the same, particularly to the reporters stationed just beyond the College gates, as we shall no doubt attract a great deal of salacious and unwelcome attention from the media. It behooves us to remember that Dr Dimbledon lived in College for his entire tenure here: aside from us, he had no family, and at times like these we ought to treat collegiate matters as though they were family matters. The city and University police are carrying out a most thorough investigation, and should foul play be proved, I feel certain that whoever perpetrated this vile crime will be brought to swift and sure justice. I am sure that you will provide the investigators with your full and enthusiastic cooperation.

You will notice that a police guard has taken a post in the Porter's Lodge beside the usual porter. This is a routine measure to ensure the safety of all of our staff, Fellows, and guests (and, when they return, our students) and should not be interpreted as any cause for panic.

Tomorrow at 3 PM Dr Dimbledon will be buried in the University Graveyard. This evening at 7, please join me and Reverend Wethersby in the College Chapel for a Remembrance Service for Darius Dimbledon.

Most sincerely yours,
Sir Peter Allham
Rector, Aubrey College

The Times, *December 17, 1989*
[From 'M — D —'s Social Diary']

My old school chum 'Hammy' (Sir Peter to the likes of you) *Allham rung yesterday to invite me to use the Rector's Lodgings at Aubrey College if I were to put in an appearance at the Remembrance Service for Dr Darius Dimbledon, the last remaining Fellow from my halcyon days at Aubrey. Dimby was a fusty old sod even then, and anyway Mrs D and I were due to attend the* Rusalka *premiere at Covent Garden, so I made my regrets and he promised to ring next time he ventured out of the dreaming spires and into the big city. Hammy promised to take me up on the offer posthaste, as he said the past week has been most trying. And what does 'most trying' mean for a don, Hammy? Run through your supply of Fino and have to switch to Amontillado until the domestic bursar shells out for another case or six?*

17 December 1989

To Rector Allham:
   Herewith is a note for you to know that the police have completed their questioning of those who attended the conference and were staying in Aubrey College Lodging at the time of Dr Dimbledon's unfortunate death. It is regretful for me that I should have to tell you that one man who registered for the conference and picked up his key from me has seemed to have disappeared. His name is Mr Federico Soares, and I remember him to be a smallish, dark-haired chap of somewhat medium build and a complexion belonging to a Spaniard or one from thereabouts. I do not have his key back, and nobody

from the conference has seen him, or so I am told. I will leave further decisions in this matter for your capable hands, but now I felt it right for you to know, and may I also extend to you my personal deepest condolences, for I knew Dr Dimbledon also, but not as well as you did, I am sure.

Thank you,

Barry Finch

Head Porter, Aubrey College

17 December 1989

To Rector Sir Peter Allham:

This is a brief note to inform you that we are discharging Mr Benjamin Glantz tomorrow morning. We have prescribed a course of Diazepam and recommend that he continue with counseling and/or therapy for as long as he feels it necessary.

As you said in your note, Mr Glantz is an intelligent and accomplished young man, but his rather sheltered upbringing – no financial hardship, high premiums placed on academic achievement, parents whose concern for his well-being frequently assumed an overbearing and smothering character – left him quite unprepared for the shock he suffered. I trust you will forgive the generalisation here, but the American tendency to 'talk through' problems often results in an obsession of sorts: it is of course impossible for Mr Glantz to erase the horror he saw, but it has proven equally difficult for him to move past it. He now appears calm and rational enough, however, so that further detention here would likely do him more harm than good.

Thank you for commending him to our care. Naturally, I and

*my staff will continue to observe your request that we refrain from
discussing Mr Glantz with members of the press.*

*I wish you and the College the very best in putting this matter
to rest.*

Kind regards,
Dr Sanjeev Singh
Chief Consulting Psychiatrist
James Hinchcliffe Hospital

19 December 1989

To Sir Peter Allham, Rector of Aubrey College:

*Thank you for contacting the Home Secretary with your concerns
about one of the attendees at the European Management Conference
recently hosted by your College. The Secretary relayed your
conversation to me, and it has fallen to my department to look into
the matter of Federico Soares's disappearance.*

*First of all, I regret to inform you that we know nothing about
Mr Soares. The Luso-Iberian desk believes his name to be
indisputably of Portuguese origin. Whether the man himself is or
was of Portuguese or Brazilian citizenship or extraction, we do not
know. Judging from Mr Finch's description, we think it unlikely
that he hails from one of the lusophone African nations (Angola,
Mozambique, Guinea-Bissau, Cape Verde, or São Tomé and
Principe), though this is of course possible.*

*He registered for the conference as a representative of PDL
Industries, and his registration materials were sent to a Bremen
post-office box. No such company exists in Bremen – or indeed in
Germany – and the post office to which he sent the materials had*

standing instructions to forward received mail to another post-office box in Turkey. This alone does not indicate deceit, as the combination of a phantom business in Germany and a forwarding address in Turkey is not terribly uncommon.

That said, a German-Turkish businessman would presumably have a Turkish name, not a Portuguese one. And there are six German citizens and resident aliens named Federico Soares; four are under 16, one is 75, and the one of appropriate age is a product-development specialist for BMW and has not left Stuttgart in nine months.

In the six weeks preceding the conference, three men named Federico Soares entered Britain. Two departed within three weeks, and the one remaining FS has been hiking in the Pennines for ten days, on an organised tour and always in the company of trail guides and fellow hikers. In the three days since the conference, nobody named Federico Soares has left Britain. This means that either he is still in the country under a different name (in which case my department will find him) or he registered under an assumed name, in which case, sadly, we have very little hope of catching him.

Convincing foreign police departments to lend their support in a matter such as this, where someone is connected to a crime only circumstantially if at all, is particularly difficult.

But our investigation continues. We will be in touch with any new developments and trust that you will do the same.

Yours,

Reginald Danvers, Chief of Services
Immigration and Nationality Directorate
The Home Office

19 December 1989
The National Herald
Cyril Brackett, News Editor

Thames Valley Police have been stumped by the apparent murder of one of Oxford's longest-serving dons.

Four days ago Dr Darius Dimbledon, who had been a Fellow at Aubrey College for nearly fifty years, was found dead in his room.

He was discovered by a student who apparently entered Dr Dimbledon's rooms by mistake, thinking they were his own. The student, who lived in the room next to Dr Dimbledon's, was returning to college quite late and somewhat the worse for wear.

Aubrey College has not released his name, and College staff have persistently refused to answer any questions about him.

One member of staff, speaking on condition of anonymity, said that 'horrible things' had been done to Dr Dimbledon's body, but would not elaborate.

Officially, the police have refused to rule Dr Dimbledon's death a murder. When asked directly how he believed Dr Dimbledon had died, Chief Constable Henry Standage said, 'From injuries that may have been self-inflicted, that may have resulted from an accident, but that do not necessarily indicate foul play.'

Unofficially, though, police are proceeding as though a crime has been committed.

A Thames Valley Police source said suspicion had initially fallen on Benjamin Glantz, the student who discovered the body, but no link could be proven between student and don, and a source within the Thames Valley Police said that Mr Glantz was no longer a focus of their investigation.

The silence of the Thames Valley CID has given rise to all sorts of rumours. Nigel Blitherington, Middle East correspondent for the London Global Report, *opined from his villa in Beirut that 'the shadowy tentacles of the Mossad hang over the cruel, bloody, and expertly planned murder of Dr Dimbledon,' noting that 'both the first name Benjamin and the surname Glantz are frighteningly common in extremist-Zionist circles in the United States and Israel . . . Why has the Israeli embassy not confirmed that Glantz has never travelled to Israel? Which high-powered figures have forced the police to shift their enquiry so quickly? And who can possibly be surprised that the American media, always eager to soft-pedal Zionist deviousness, is on these questions characteristically silent?' So far no other newspapers have followed Mr Blitherington's speculations.*

One popular theory among Aubrey students was that the reclusive, unmarried don had been murdered by an angry lover.

The police have been frantically trying to look for controversy in Dr Dimbledon's work but have as yet found none.

At the time of Dr Dimbledon's death, Aubrey and Ripley colleges were jointly hosting a pan-European management conference. One of the conference's attendees has disappeared, and his whereabouts remain unknown, though police from across the country have been secretly mobilised in a manhunt.

Oxford City Council member Sharon Viers said it was 'a blessing that whatever happened, happened when students had mainly departed for the winter holiday, and of course we are all most relieved that this appears to be an isolated incident and not the work of a madman targeting the local community as well.'

19 December 1989

Dear Mr Bowman:

My name is Benjamin Glantz, and I am in my second year of a PPE at Aubrey College. I am writing to formally request suspension of my Rhodes Scholarship for the remainder of this academic year, as you advised me to do during our phone conversation earlier today.

As I assume you know, I have been centrally involved with the recent events at Aubrey. I discovered Dr Dimbledon's body and, as a result of that shock, spent two days in the psychiatric ward of James Hinchcliffe Hospital.

I am still very anxious in Aubrey College, especially because I live in the room next to Dr Dimbledon's. I think it would be best for my health if I took some time away from my studies here.

Should you have any doubts about my condition, or believe that I am malingering, please contact Dr Sanjeev Singh at the James Hinchcliffe Hospital or Rector Sir Peter Allham, who has been very kind to me these past few days. Should you have any doubts about my seriousness as a student, please contact Professor Trelawney, my course supervisor, who will vouch for the quality of my work. And should you require anything further from me to process or expedite this request, please do not hesitate to contact me. As you can imagine, I really want to be in the familiar surroundings of home as quickly as possible. Thank you in advance for your consideration, and I hope to hear good news soon.

Yours sincerely,
Benjamin Glantz

21 December 1989

    Dear Mr Glantz:

    Thank you for yours. Following our initial telephone conversation, I contacted the rest of the Rhodes Supervisory Committee.

    We see no reason to deny your request for a suspension of the Rhodes Scholarship, and we sympathise with your desire to return to your family with all due speed. We will expect you back in Oxford in October of next year. Please contact me no later than August 15, 1990, to confirm your intent.

    Please accept the condolences of the Rhodes Committee, as well as my personal best wishes to you.

    Yours,

    Mr William Bowman

    Chairman, Scholarship Supervisory Committee of the Rhodes Foundation Trust

22 December 1989

To Sir Peter Allham, Rector of Aubrey College:

    As you requested, I am providing you with a status report of our investigation one week after its commencement.

    I am afraid that this report finds us no further along than we were one week ago. We found no usable fingerprints in Dr Dimbledon's rooms; or rather, we lifted hundreds of prints, mostly his. It is important to bear in mind that scores of students, cleaners, and guests have no doubt passed through those rooms, and without a definite goal in mind or a set to match them against, progress is usually down to blind luck.

It is worth mentioning that the only places we found Mr Glantz's prints were on the doorknob and then on the carpet where he fell. This bears out our lack of suspicion towards the young man, and if we dealt with him more roughly than he was accustomed to being treated, I am sure he understands. If we knew more about this disappeared Soares chap, naturally we would be searching for him, but as he seems to have been a ghost, we have nothing to look for.

We also have no leads from our usual networks of informants and undercover officers in Oxford. I daresay the Oxford underworld is as baffled by Dr Dimbledon's death as we are, which is some comfort I suppose.

One ought to remember that most murder cases yield at least some scent, and that those without a lead within the first week often remain unsolved. Please do not construe this remark as an admission of failure, however, simply as a warning of what lies ahead. Our investigation continues.

Yours,
Henry Standage

23 December 1989

Dear Peter:

Well, I hope you're happy. This muddle at your College has cut into the Christmas holidays of a good number of your chums over here. They're ex-chums now, of course. Still, no rest for the weary, I suppose.

So Hammy rung up Bumster at the Home Office, Bumster rung Reg at Immigration, and Reg has been marching to and fro like the little martinet that he is. He's discovered absolutely nothing, which is par for Reg's rather limited course, but in this case — *painful though it is to say* — one cannot blame him, because there is simply nothing to discover. This fellow Dimbledon was done by a real professional.

Immigration's turned up nothing; we've turned up nothing; even Standage at Thames Valley (he's quite a good detective, by the way, as decent and professional as you'd hope to meet) turned up nothing. No sign of this Soares fellow — nothing in Oxford, nothing in London, nothing from any of 6's sneaks and spooks in Armenia, Turkmenistan, or New York (Dimbledon's only foreign travel in the last decade) — just total bloody silence. Phipps even sniffed around the Japanese mafia, what little there is in London (removal of a finger, apparently, is a traditional form of self-inflicted atonement among the yakuza) and found — *can you guess?* — nothing.

This Dimbledon's a real puzzler. Oxford don for fifty years, potters around in gardens for a living, suddenly on the receiving end of the most professional job Britain's seen in years. Something doesn't add up, and the rub is, we'll probably never know what it is. And I'm going to assiduously avoid caring for the next twelve days. I'd advise you to do the same. He's gone, Beanie, gone like they all go.

Do let us know if you see any promising third-years, won't you? Aubrey's been pretty thin on the ground in recent years here and in 6, you know.

Bah humbug & c.,
Crumms

May 23, 1997
The New York Times
Teresa Watkins & Benjamin Glantz

Teresa Althea Watkins, a daughter of Harold Watkins and Alice Watkins of Brooklyn, N.Y., was married yesterday to Benjamin Herschel Glantz, a son of Herman Glantz and Leora Glantz of Thousand Oaks, Calif. The Hon. Edward T. Harries, Associate Justice of the New York Supreme Court, performed the ceremony at the Brooklyn Museum of Art. Rabbi Adam Maisels, of Temple Beth Shalom in Los Angeles, and the Rev. Hosea I. M. Jefferson of the Temperance AME Zion Church of Fort Greene, Brooklyn, also took part in the service.

Ms Watkins, 27, is keeping her name. She is an assistant district attorney in Manhattan. She graduated from Johns Hopkins University and Yale Law School. Her father is chief curator for South Asian antiquities at the Brooklyn Museum of Art. He is also a founding member of and baritone in the Musica Antiqua Brooklyn, a vocal group dedicated to historically informed performance of Renaissance-era music. The bride's mother is the group's other founding member; she remains the first soprano. She is also a professor of visual arts at New York University.

Mr Glantz, 32, is a junior partner in the law firm of Sanders, Clark, Monk, Brown, & Garrett, working principally in government contracts. He holds a B.A. and a J.D. from the University of Chicago and an M.A. from Oxford University. His mother and father run Glantz's Delicatessen in Thousand Oaks, Calif.

Item 13: A platinum ring, with a bevel-cut 9.04-carat yellow sapphire set in its center. 'It is the morning sun and it is the end' is inscribed in Arabic around the outside of the ring. Around the inside are intertwined pointed leaves. It is believed to be one of a set of three rings made secretly in Ardabil by Osman, court jeweler to the deposed Farooz, last king of the Sassanid empire, in commemoration of his master's finished rule. This ring is commonly referred to as 'The Rising Sun of Ardabil.'

The other two rings are also sapphires; one is red and is called 'The Setting Sun of Ardabil,' and the other, 'The World's End Sun,' is black. Setting Sun and World's End Sun both reside in Manchester's City Art Gallery, though in the mid-1990s they and a number of other Persian antiquities toured four American cities.

Date of manufacture: The intricacy of the engraving and the combination of Islamic (the Arabic script) and pre-Islamic (representation of living things – leaves) dates the Rising Sun to the century immediately following the decline of the Sassanid dynasty (middle eighth century).

Manufacturer: In the Sassanid annals, he is known only as Osman the Jeweler, but whether this is because he had no other names (indicating humble origins) or because he was so renowned that he needed no other names remains a mystery.

Place of origin: Ardabil, a city largely constructed by the Sassanid king Farooz and previously an Achaemenid outpost city on the Persian empire's northern border. Today the city lies in northeastern Iran, close to the Azerbaijani border.

Last known owner: Darius Dimbledon, ageless wonder of Aubrey College. In 1988 Dr Dimbledon stole it from the luggage of his traveling companion while impersonating a museum curator in New York. The theft was not discovered until several months later, whereupon the previous owner, acting with the tacit consent of his employers, gained entry to Aubrey College housing under false pretenses and one evening visited Dr Dimbledon in his rooms.

He forced the professor to disrobe and sit in his favorite chair while wearing the stolen ring on his finger and proceeded to remove his fingers one by one with a small, sharp knife. He arranged the fingers in the pattern of a caduceus across Dr Dimbledon's desk (though he also needed several toes and one penis to complete the design), then departed with Dimbledon's ring, head, and a number of papers from his desk.

Estimated value: The sapphire is of unusual clarity and beautifully cut; it would easily fetch a price of $5,000 per carat. Consider also the fine workmanship on the gold ring, the value added by its age and pedigree, and its value would rise to the $100,000 mark.

Hence there will be marvellous
adaptions achieved, of which
the manner is this.

***

Driving from Wickenden to Clougham, Joe and I saw nobody. We passed no cars on the road, and there were none in the Lone Wolf's parking lot. Driving through Clougham was like driving through a painting of Clougham. Joe and I pulled up right next to the Lone Wolf's front door. The town's eerie, deserted feeling added to my uneasiness, and even Joe, who could probably have charmed and wheedled Pühapäev's eviscerated corpse into conversation, said almost nothing for the entire drive. I was thinking of Hannah, of course, and vacillating between anger, sadness, concern, and confusion, all underlaid with a bit of lust and a dash of regret. My usual emotional range, in other words.

All this for what could have been an obit at the back of a newspaper that a few hundred people would have run their eyes over before throwing away, a piece I could have written on the day of his death ('Distinguished Emigré Professor Dies,' a couple of grafs about his career, maybe a complimentary sentence from a colleague, and that sad and stark final sentence, 'He has no known living relatives'). But it had grown into something else, something that thrilled me even as it frightened me, made me feel that I had finally cracked through the pane of smudged glass, broken the surface of the sea. I finally felt like something other than an observer in my life. Whether it was cruising toward a resolution with Joe, working and thinking on something nobody else knew about when the rest of the world was asleep, or whether it had to do with Hannah, coming to feel so deeply but uncertainly for her in such a short time – or both bound up together – I couldn't say. I strained against my seat belt and drummed my fingers against the car door. I wanted to know how it would end.

The only light in the Lone Wolf came from a college basketball game on the television behind the bar. I immediately recognized the unrecognizably bland-looking guy watching the TV when we walked in. He sat behind a fortress of empty Rolling Rock bottles and wore that CHARLIE REED'S FEED & SEED cap.

'Help you?' he grumphed, turning his head beerily toward us like it was top-heavy and poorly attached.

'Yeah, you can,' said Joe, strolling in with his

466

hands in his pockets and looking around. 'We're friends of Eddie's. He here?'

'Haven't seen him all day.'

'You break in here? Or did he give you the Customer of the Month key?' Joe flicked the lights on to make sure they worked (they did), then turned them off again.

'Door was open when I came in. I didn't feel like going home, so I just grabbed a few from the cooler. Hey, I'm gonna leave him the money, that's what you're worried about.'

'It isn't, but do it anyway.' The guy exhaled loudly, shook his head, and turned his attention back to the game. 'Do it now,' said Joe, towering over the guy. Feed & Seed laid a ten-dollar bill on the table. 'You're a little light, but we'll let it go this time.' Joe waved his badge in front of the guy's face and snapped it shut quickly, so the guy didn't have time to read how far out of his jurisdiction Joe was. 'What's your name, sir?'

'Mike Venables.'

'Do us a favor, Mike: turn off the ball game and sit down over on that couch right there.' Any seventeen-year-old can testify to how quickly a policeman barking orders can cut through an alcoholic fog: Mike had probably not moved that fast in years. He took off his hat and sat on the couch with his hands in his lap. Joe walked to the back of the bar and opened the door.

'Mike, I see an upstairs here. You been up there?'

'No, sir, I never have.'

'You know what's up there?'

'I think that's where the Albanian lives.'

'Okay. You hear anything from upstairs since you been here? Noises, like people moving, water running, anything like that?'

'No, sir, Officer, I haven't. Just the game on the TV over there.'

'All right, Mike, I need you to sit tight right there on that couch. My partner and I want to see if Eddie's okay. You see anything, hear anything, you call us. But just stay there and don't do anything until we tell you, you got that?'

'Yes, sir, no problem. Don't do nothing at all.' Mike put his hat on his head and then snapped it off again. 'Sir?' He spoke in the quavering tones of someone beginning a confession. 'Sir, I got a little record, and I didn't mean to do nothing tonight, you know? I just came in, place was open, and Eddie knows me, you know? He knows I'm good for what I drink, and he knows where I live, so you know, if there's any way to, you know, just sort of let bygones be bygones and forget what happened, then, you know . . .'

'Jesus, Mike, will you just sit there and shut your fucking yap? No one's looking to arrest you tonight.' Mike nodded, exhaled, and leaned back into the couch. 'Okay there, partner, let's go see Eddie.'

I tried to do a cop walk across the bar but probably just looked like I had a bad sunburn on my legs.

'You think that guy knows you don't have jurisdiction here?' I whispered to Joe.

'Be quiet and be cool; of course he doesn't know. Sees a badge and does what I say. Come over here and stand behind me; anything happens, it should happen to me first.'

The back stairs were rickety and dusty; every step creaked and groaned under us. At the top of the stairs was a wooden door with peeling grayish paint and a lock that Joe picked in seconds.

Joe flicked the light switch, and by the sad glow of a bare bulb, we found ourselves in an immense, wood-floored room with high, pressed-tin ceilings and a fireplace across from the entrance. The room was about the size of the bar downstairs, large enough so that it was clear it comprised the entire apartment. It could have been grand, even elegant, but the floor had rotten patches, the ceiling was stained, and the paint on the walls bubbled and peeled away in flaps. There was no furniture at all; at the far side of the room, several pipes protruded sadly and ineffectually from a back wall where something (a stove? an oven? a range?) had apparently been ripped out. There was no smell of gas, though, and the apartment was much colder than the bar downstairs. Next to the absent stove was a door; Joe opened it onto a small white bathroom.

'Least something's clean,' he whispered.

'Why are we whispering?' I whispered.

He looked back at me with raised eyebrows and a

tight, forbearing smile, the same look his uncle gave students who made inappropriate jokes or offered feeble but well-intentioned answers to his questions. The bathroom was as empty as the rest of the apartment, as similarly devoid of specificity, as though it had been scrubbed not just clean but blank. I turned to face the open apartment through the door just as a car drove by playing a loud rock song.

Something in the way the wailing guitar's notes skidded and flowed downward reminded me of a passage from the cello music that Hannah had played when we first met, a passage that I hadn't even known I remembered, and suddenly she rose up through my memory so sharply and immediately that it physically hurt. The speed with which a couple of coincidental passing notes conjured Hannah stunned me, and I felt as though I was on the brink of understanding something important, when Joe tugged at my sleeve and settled me back within myself.

'Nothing here. Bring prints guys, maybe they'll find something, but looking around, the place looks clean. Take a look at the tub,' he said with a half nod toward it. I bent down and scrutinized it for as long as I thought I should, then stood up.

'I really didn't see anything,' I said blankly.

'Exactly. You ever see a tub without any hairs, or little puddles of water, or smears across the faucet handles? Only in a new house. Or one that's been so thoroughly cleaned it might as well be new.'

*

Downstairs we found Mike Venables fast asleep, snoring with his head back and his mouth wide open ('Catching flies,' Joe said). Joe put his finger to his lips as we walked past Mike and out the open door.

'Should we call the police?' I asked.

'What, like, I'm not police?'

'No, I just mean –'

'I know what you mean. What are we going to call in? A clean bathtub?'

'Missing person?'

Joe exhaled through his pursed-out lips and made a horsey sound. 'Sure, maybe. I guess so. We ought to do it anonymously, though, 'cause this kind of thing could mean my job. Other hand, though, how'd we call something like this in without letting anyone know who it is?'

'Pay phone?'

'Yeah, good idea. No rush, though, right?'

'What do you mean?'

'We're still going over to look at Pühapäev's place, right?'

'Yeah, maybe.'

'So let's go. What's the problem?' Joe hopped into the car, tapped 'shave and a haircut' on the dashboard, and when he got to 'two bits,' he belched twice, in perfect rhythm.

'Allen's still driving by the place every so often, and –'

'Driving by at . . . what is it, eleven-fifteen? Small-town cop? No way.'

'Says he has trouble sleeping.'

'Fuck 'em. We pull around back. Anything happens, we hide and drive.'

'You've hidden and driven before?'

'Shit, yes,' Joe said, putting the car in gear. 'I didn't waste *my* youth trying to get into Wickenden University.'

Like Clougham, Lincoln slept as soundly as a village in a children's book. We slowed down as we drove through the Station and up to the Common, and when I opened my window, all I could hear was our tires and all I could smell was the smoke of a late-evening fire.

'Smells like at least someone isn't asleep with the moon here,' Joe said. 'Place drives me crazy. Where's the banjos and the brother shacking up with his sister?'

'That kind of thing doesn't happen up north. This is a nice, clean town.'

'This were a nice, clean town, I wouldn't be in it, which would suit me fine.'

'I doubt it really would,' I teased.

Joe lit a cigarette, grinned, and tossed the match out the window. 'Where's the house, smart-ass?'

I directed him to a street just north of Pühapäev's (and Hannah's), and he pulled the car past the dark and dozing houses to a patch of woodland that separated the two streets, from which we could see the back of Pühapäev's house. We crouch-walked through the woods as quietly as possible – for Joe that meant light tromping – to the decrepit back door.

'You think a jewel thief maybe could hire a painter,' said Joe, picking scabs of brown paint from around the door's four-paneled window. He knocked once at the top, once at the bottom, and once at either side of the doorframe, then grabbed the door-knob and jerked it back and forth, his lips pressed together, white with the effort. 'Sturdier than I thought,' he said, withdrawing a pencil-size flashlight attached to his key ring and shining it through the door's window. 'Thought so. Come take a look at this.'

I walked over to where he stood pressed up against the doorframe and looked straight down through the window. Metal cylinders, just like in Pühapäev's office, spanned the inside of the door. Joe knocked on the glass; it sounded like he was knocking on concrete. 'Shit. Well, guess we got time. Take this,' he said, tossing me the light, which I dropped. 'And try not to drop it. Shine it on the knob here.'

'What are you doing?'

'What's it look like? Picking the lock,' he said. With one hand he worked a skeleton key in the lock, and with the other he unfolded a thin, flat strip of metal from his jacket pocket and began working it against the inside hinges. 'Why, you embarrassed? Afraid?'

'No, just that –'

'Relax. I'm the police. Anybody asks, I kidnapped you. You smell that?'

I sniffed and picked up a smell of acrid smoke. 'Just a fire.'

'You think? Doesn't smell like a cozy fireplace fire to me. I'd guess something burning that shouldn't be burning.'

'What should we do?'

'What you should do is hold your fucking hand steady and don't go wandering off. Here, I almost got it. This one's not as tough as the office one.' He leaned his considerable frame against the door, and it yielded. The lights flipped on: we were in a grimy kitchen.

'Motion detector,' he said, wobbling to his feet and wiping his hands on his trousers. 'Wonder why no alarm's sounding. Strange.' Two frying pans sat on top of the stove, both with a measurably thick layer of congealed white grease ('Bacon,' said Joe, sniffing them); three more sat stacked in the sink. Whatever was in them was beginning to rot. A roach peered over the side of the sink, took a couple of tentative steps forward, then rethought his plan and darted back into the sink. 'You know,' said Joe, 'someone ought to just throw some gasoline around and torch this place. Stinks. Greasy. You going to want to cook off any of this shit? I hate messy kitchens.'

A messy kitchen is a sign not merely of solitude but of the expectation of perpetual solitude. Either that or the expectation of indulgence, the expectation that whoever gets to see that you have such a filthy kitchen will be willing to accept it as either charming or irrelevant. I had a messy kitchen, I think I expected solitude, but I no longer felt very good about it.

'You waiting to make friends with the roaches or something? Come on through here,' Joe called from the next room.

The bedroom apparently had been caught in a storm of old man's clothes: variations on the themes of 'drab' and 'shapeless' were strewn several inches deep across the bed and floor. The dresser drawers had been pulled out and overturned; the mattress lay propped against the wall, and someone had taken a razor blade to the bed frame: strips of fabric hung from it in every direction, like hair from a drowned head. Joe moved some clothes around with his toe; I picked up an ash-stained brown sweater, and Joe immediately told me to put it down. 'Shouldn't do that. Jeez, I should have thought . . .' His sentence trailed off in an exasperated sigh.

'What? What's wrong? What did I do?'

Joe raised his hands and spread his fingers like he had just counted to ten: he wore thin latex gloves. 'You've been contaminating a crime scene. Should've given you these before.'

I dropped the sweater as though it were electrified. 'So what do we do?' Jokes about picking up the soap in the shower started whirring and raining inside my head.

Joe gave a twisted-lip grin and raised his eyebrows.

'Hope, I guess. Look, don't go worrying about any-thing now, all right? You did what you did – now let's just look around a little more and leave.' He reached into his jacket pocket and tossed me a similar pair of gloves, which I quickly put on.

I still wasn't moving. I couldn't go to jail.

'Hey!' barked Joe. 'You hear me? It's late, I want to go home, I shouldn't even be here. Quit standing there. You don't want to help, fine. Just sit there on that bench, out of the way.'

I walked over to the piano bench and sat down while Joe walked slowly around the living room, which looked exactly as it did when I first saw it. He lifted up a couple of plates and peered at their undersides; he ran his finger along bookshelves, occasionally flipping through a book and releasing a cloud of dust into the stagnant air; he riffled through some papers on the low table and pronounced them 'history stuff, stuff Abe would understand a lot better than I would.'

Finally he slumped heavily onto the couch. He puffed out his cheeks and exhaled, allowing fatigue to drag his facial features downward and make him look slightly melted. He sat absolutely still. It was the first time I had ever seen him not moving at all, not fidgeting or clearing his throat or smoking or eating. I wondered what he did for fun, what type of music and women he liked. Whether he preferred walking on the pavement or the grass, took vacations in cities or mountains or by the beach. Aside from

Art and the professor, he really was the first adult (not including relations) that I had spent time with, and I could tell you nothing about him that wasn't obvious. For better or worse (I choose worse), I could make that statement about almost everyone I knew, except one, and then only after the fact, after it became obvious that it would never matter to anyone but me how much she warmed, thawed, and moved me.

Joe put his head in his hands, rubbed his eyes, and seal-coughed twice. The noise startled me. I flinched and knocked a pencil from the keyboard cover to the floor. As I bent down to pick it up, I noticed, directly behind the pedals, beneath the broadest part of the piano's body, four clumps of mud. The two closest to the pedals were waffle-shaped and had clearly fallen from the soles of two boots; farther toward the wall were two smudges of mud, less distinct in shape but more deeply ground into the off-white, ash-flecked carpet.

'Joe?'

'Yeah,' he said, his head still in his hands, not moving at all.

'That anything? Under the bench there?'

He opened one eye skeptically, inhaled, and rose. 'What is it? What do you got?' He leaned over my shoulder, and I could feel the fatigue snap from him. 'Look at that. You know why the prints look like that?'

'Like what?'

'Gridded back here and ground in deeper up there?'

'No idea.'

'Someone squatted underneath the piano. Rested his weight on his toes,' he said, pointing with a pen to the two smudges, 'which is why it's ground in deeper. When you squat down wearing boots, the mud from the soles comes out when the soles get bent. Why you get the waffle shapes here.'

'Not bad,' I said, turning to face him.

He waved away the compliment. 'Look at this, though,' he said, still bent close to the floor. 'Gimme that flashlight you had. Here, see?' He shone a path from the piano to the door: it was littered with fresh mud treads, but except for the ones under the piano, they were light enough so that we wouldn't have seen them unless we were looking. 'Should've brought a camera. Shit,' he said, standing up and grimacing. 'Lug all this stuff in my pockets all the time and forget the one thing we really could have used. Oh, well.' He stretched with one arm, yawned, and shoved me out of the way, gently but firmly, with the other. 'Here, let me crawl under there, long as we're here.'

He wedged himself into the space between the floor, the pedals, the piano bench, and the piano's body so tightly that he seemed to have reshaped his body to fit the space. 'Hey, quit looking at my ass and get over here on the other side of me. What do you make of this?'

I crawled toward him from the other side of the

piano, trying to balance with closed fists so that I avoided getting fingerprints anywhere else. He shone his light on a patch of carpet that seemed to me no different from any other patch of carpet and glanced up at me. I shrugged and shook my head.

He sighed, looked at me as though I might evaporate from sheer dumbness, and traced a line with his finger in the carpet. 'Here. What's this?' A barely discernible line ran parallel to the keyboard, from my hands to Joe's. He dug a finger into the line and raised a flap of carpet, revealing the hardwood floor beneath. 'What do you think of that?' he asked. I sensed that there was a right answer. I sensed even more clearly that I didn't know it.

'I don't know. Maybe that's how he installed the carpet?'

'Oh, you think? Flap like this, this size, just right here. So tell me, what does it join? What does it do?' I just shrugged again. 'Here, let's try this.' Joe pounded on the carpeted floor behind him, then on the bare floor in front of him: the bare floor sounded hollow. 'See? Here, hold this, and shine it onto that patch of floor. Good. Now, see how the grain goes in this floor? All left to right, all short lines. Now look at that one long groove in the opposite direction. I'll bet –' He stopped speaking, stuffed his fingers into the groove, and pulled up a perfect square of wood. 'Still think he just installed the carpet like that?'

Joe held the square foot of floor above what looked like a corresponding square of pure emptiness beneath it. I think it was a combination of my fatigue, my uncomfortable crouch, and the sheer weirdness of my day, but as I peered into the emptiness underneath Pühapäev's floor, my peripheral vision went black, I leaned a little too far forward, and – for the first and so far only time in my life – I fainted. I came to when I cracked my forehead against something very cold and very hard, which argued strongly against Joe's having opened some sort of void beneath the floor. Joe grabbed me by the scruff of the neck and lifted my head up until it was right in front of his, and for a moment, before I regained my focus and told him I was fine, he looked terrified. I felt something tickle the side of my face, and when I brushed it away, the back of my hand was streaked with red. 'Yeah, nothing bleeds like a head injury, does it?' asked Joe, more loudly and jocularly than usual. 'Tell you what, you go sit down over there, and we'll get out of here in a minute. Just let me see what's what under here, and then we'll take off. You're sure you're okay?' I said I was. 'Okay, two minutes, then.'

'If it's all the same to you, I'd rather stay here.'

'Yeah, sure. Just stay out of the light. Here, sit on the other side so you got some room to stretch out.' I moved to his other side and had a better view of what was beneath the floor: a square foot of thick metal, with a lock set in the middle. 'Well, look at this,' said Joe, eyes twinkling as he took out the thin folding piece of metal from his jacket.

Ten minutes later he had taken off his jacket, loosened his tie, and untucked his shirt. He grunted as the crescent moons of sweat under his armpits turned into full moons and then into clouds, meeting halfway across his back. 'Motherfucker!' he swore, slamming his tool onto the floor next to the lock. 'Pickproof.' He stood up and stretched. 'Either pickproof or I'm losing my touch. I'll go with pickproof. It's a ring lock, looks like. Special key, maybe a combination or something after that. Short of blasting the door off, nobody's getting in there.'

'Safe place to keep jewels?'

'Safe place for anything. Especially jewels. Come on, let's go home. What time is it anyway?'

I rubbed my eyes and checked my watch. 'Three-fifty.' Suddenly I was exhausted.

'Let me just grab this,' said Joe, crawling once more under the piano bench for his picklock. 'Whoa. Fuck me. Hey, come here. And watch your head.'

He shone the light onto the sides of the recess, between floor level and safe level. There, dancing against the black walls like mica in sand, were flecks and flakes of green, lighter and dustier than glass, and less shiny, too. Joe scraped some of the flecks onto a sheet of paper, then folded the paper over and shoved it into his pocket. 'You know . . . Nah, never mind. Just one thing,' he said, standing up and walking over to the front door. 'Lock's intact. Need a key to open it, but the doorframe next to the lock looks smooth, doesn't look busted or anything. Can't see any forced entry. The windows, too, none of them broken, none of the locks broken or jimmied. I mean, you'd need a real forensic guy to work this thing over, but I'd bet you won't find any signs of a break-in.'

'Except ours, you mean?' I asked from the couch. Now I had my head in my hands, and I could feel my humor starting to sour.

'Yeah, except ours. Come on, let's get out of here and get you home. We got only a couple hours of darkness left anyway.'

So we left the way we came. We shut the door behind us, and Joe managed to force the lock back into place, but the back doorframe had obviously been cracked. My fingerprints were all over the house, and though Joe wore gloves, he had stomped and crawled through enough space so that his presence, too, would be obvious to anyone who cared to look. And all we found was more green dust. Joe said he'd tell Sal tomorrow afternoon and have the feds come out and look at the place, see if they could tie anything in Pühapäev's house to any known jewel thefts in the area. Still, it seemed pretty thin. Or perhaps I was just tired and inclined toward pessimism. Joe dropped me in front of my house; I think he wished me good night, but a few minutes of sitting in the car had already put me to sleep from the inside out.

I unlocked the door to my apartment, didn't even bother to turn on the lights or brush my teeth or take off my shoes. I was halfway across my apartment when the reading lamp in my living room flicked on and a familiar voice said, 'You work much later than I would have expected.'

THE RED MEDIKO

✎

Some men will see their blood on a battlefield and will engage in all manner of womanly behavior, such as fainting, or wailing, or purging, or shielding the eyes. Others will suddenly find courage where they had none: the samurai of Toyama, for instance, were known for writing their master's name in their own blood as they died. Men greet their ends as they have passed their lives; but for the coward as for the brave, blood betokens the end.

— YAMAZAKI HIDEO, *Famous Battles*

Item 14: The Red Mediko. A large (5.3 centimeters in diameter), roughly circular coin. One side is plain copper; the other is coated with red enamel, and on the enamel is painted the figure of a woman clutching two children to her side beneath one arm. In her other arm, she holds a green bottle, tipped slightly and extended toward the children.

Date of manufacture: See 'The White Mediko.'

Manufacturer: See 'The White Mediko.'

Place of origin: See 'The White Mediko.'

Last known owner: See 'The White Mediko.'

Estimated value: See 'The White Mediko.'

*For this reason I am called
Hermes Trismegistus, because I
hold three parts of the wisdom
of the whole world.*

❦

'You must be very tired. Are you tired?' Tonu sat in my reading chair smoking his pipe, the white of his beard like gold filaments in the twin glow of pipe and lamplight.

'How did you get in here?' I asked, still standing unsteadily in the doorway between my living room and the rest of my apartment.

'Oh, pssh,' he said, closing his eyes and waving a hand in front of his face as though declining a compliment. 'That lock' – he raised his cane and pointed toward my door – 'is worthless. You must look into getting it replaced.'

'Yeah, people keep telling me.'

'Not that you appear to possess much of value.' He looked up at me and waited for a response. I gave none. 'Do you?'

I shrugged. 'What are you doing in my apartment?'

'Would you like to sit down?' he asked, offering me my less-comfortable living-room chair.

'No. I'd like to go to sleep, and I'd like you to leave.'

'Yes. Yes, yes, yes,' he said peremptorily. 'And I would like to let you sleep, but first I owe you a remonstrance.' Again he motioned for me to sit. My legs were getting that simultaneously stiff and rubbery feeling that comes from exhaustion. I stayed standing. 'A remonstrance for not listening to the sound advice of your friend.' He spoke softly and crisply, as though he were breaking velvet saltines.

'All you had to do was listen. Listen to a pretty girl. How difficult can that be?' He held a questioning hand out, palm up, and shook his head with false pity. 'You might have led a long and happy life.'

'What do you . . . ?' I stammered, rubbing my eyes and feeling my bowels deliquesce as soon as he put my life in the past conditional. He stood up, and I took a tremulous and involuntary step backward. As I did, I stepped on my baseball, which somehow, no matter where I put it, always seemed to find its way to the most inconvenient place in my apartment. I fell backward like a cartoon character, landing butt first and feet up, knocking the wind out of myself. Tonu walked, chuckling pompously, over to the doorway between my kitchen and living room, where I was lying stunned on the floor.

'Nothing broken, I hope?'

I flapped my hands at the wrists and moved my feet up and down. Nothing broken aside from my pride. I shook my head and started to rise when Tonu shoved the tip of his cane into my shoulder.

'Slowly, if you don't mind,' he said, twisting the cane head. An ominous-looking little trigger popped out in the right place, and I noticed that the end of the cane was hollow: a barrel.

'What the hell is that?'

'Neat thing, this,' he said, lifting it off me for a moment to admire it. 'I got it when I was serving in the Ottoman Honor Guard.'

'The what?'

'Just stand up slowly, would you, and walk over to that chair across from mine, as I've already told you to do. We'll have one last brief chat, like civilized people.'

'Are you going to kill me?' I wish I could tell you I asked the question bravely.

'Let's not worry about the future just now. Have a seat there.'

I stood up, bringing the baseball with me so I would have something to fidget with, and sat down right where he told me to. Antiauthoritarian tendencies have a way of evaporating at the business end of a gun.

He walked over to the door and pointed the cane at me without his finger on the trigger, as though he were checking the barrel's alignment. Then he pulled on a pair of black leather gloves and put his dark topcoat on. He was getting ready to leave, and so, I presumed, was I.

'So,' he said, looking at me with a mixture of amusement and pity. 'Is there anything you wish to know? Any message you wish me to convey, perhaps, to your friend?'

My mouth felt like the inside of a sofa cushion, and I could hear the steady and alarmingly rapid rushing of blood in my ears. My hands were shaking, and a cold and narrow rivulet of sweat ran from one temple down the inside of my jawline and stopped at my collarbone. Any movie that shows someone delivering witty last lines is a lie. I doubt I could have talked if I wanted to.

Tonu shrugged. 'A silent exit, then.'

Then, more in anger than desperation, I wiped my clammy hand on my jeans, grabbed the baseball tight, and threw it as hard as I could at Tonu. I don't know what I expected, really. I suppose I just wanted to register a protest, however feeble: break a window, dent a wall, attract some attention. Instead what happened was, I somehow threw the most perfect strike of my nonexistent baseball career and delivered a fastball straight to his nose. His face jerked backward like it was on a pulley; both of his hands flew to cover his nose, which immediately began pouring blood; and the gun fell to the floor. In retrospect I should have grabbed the gun immediately, but instead I kicked it out of the way, and the adrenaline took over.

Understand that the last person I'd hit was my brother, Victor, when I was twelve and he was seventeen. I graduated from a liberal university, for God's sake; I prefer baseball to football; I dislike boxing; and when I get angry, I tend to go silent and sullen. All of which is by way of saying that before I fully knew what I was doing, I had my left hand around Tonu's neck, squeezing as hard as I could, while my right kept pounding and pounding on his face. I felt this strange tingling in my head, like I was swathed in electricity, and I saw everything that was happening from the end of a long and quiet tunnel. It was the most satisfying feeling of my life, and I'm sure I would have kept going until he was dead, if my landlady downstairs hadn't banged on my ceiling and screamed, 'Shut the fuck up! Do you have any idea what time it is?'

'Sorry,' I called back, my fist still poised at eye level to strike Tonu again. I had been kept awake by my neighbor's horrible music plenty of nights, but this somehow didn't seem the time to press that point.

When I stopped, I heard that we breathed in tandem. I panted – thrilled by myself, by this capacity to hurt that I never knew I had – and he gave a series of shallow, mucosal wheezes somewhere between hisses and puffs. When I turned my face back toward his, he instinctively shied away from me, and that felt great.

From the corner of my eye, I saw that my fist was a horrible mess, especially across the knuckles, where

I guess his teeth had cut me. I'm glad to say that he looked much worse. His beard was matted, blood-black, and dripping; his nose looked misshapen, almost piglike, and each time he breathed, more blood and mucus bubbled forth. I cocked a fist at him, and when he flinched, I spit on him.

I let go of his neck and picked up the gun. Through the door to my bathroom, I saw a face towel, and I remembered: I am the kind of man who gives a bleeding old stranger a face towel. I am the kind of man who does this even if it's his own towel. I am even the kind of man who runs that towel under cold water first, whatever the bleeding stranger has done, knowing he would have to throw the towel away afterward.

After a while – I don't know how long; it could have been thirty seconds, or it could have been thirty minutes – we were sitting opposite each other, the adrenaline having run out of us both, and Tonu said something I couldn't understand. I asked him to repeat it, and just for fun I pointed the gun at him. And it *was* fun.

'*Durak,*' he mumbled. His speech sounded muffled and squishy, but his eyes were still narrow, cunning, and alive. '*Durak.* In Russian it means "idiot" or "fool." But you also say it when you witness an act of pure and unadulterated good luck. Sinking a billiard shot with your eyes closed, for instance. Winning a lottery.' He grimaced as he touched the towel to his nose. 'What you did just now. Your aim. *Durak*.'

'How do you know? Maybe I do this all the time,' I said, checking to make sure I was pointing the right end of the gun at him.

He laughed feebly, more a series of croaks than anything else. 'Yes? This is why your hands are still shaking? This is why you look more afraid still than I do?'

I raised the gun and pointed it right at his head. 'You think I'm afraid?'

'To use that?' He paused, as though he was really thinking. 'No. To tell you the truth, no, I don't. Not at the moment. But I know you are no fighter. No killer either.'

'How do you know?'

'Because I am. A killer, that is. A very good one, too. Successful.' He spit a yellow-and-red gobbet into my towel. 'What you did was a direct result of my overconfidence.'

'You came here to kill me?'

'Well, yes. May I have another towel, please?'

'No. You came here to kill me?'

'Please,' he whined, almost ingratiatingly. 'This towel is soaked through. And a touch of brandy, if you have it.'

'No brandy. And use your coat if you want to clean up. You were coming to kill me?'

'Yes, and if you give me some brandy, I promise I will leave here without killing you. And I will never come back. I promise.'

'You'll leave here without killing me whether I give you brandy or not. I have the gun.'

'You do, and I will. You're right. Bravo. I can clearly see you are getting used to this business of violence. But if you didn't shoot me, I would probably come back, just out of pure spite for your manners. Who would refuse a bloody old man a drink?'

He was almost smiling now, and he held up his hands in mock defeat. 'My business depends on trust, just like yours,' he said. 'If you talk to a person for your newspaper, small and irrelevant though it is, and you promise not to use his name, will you? No. Your reputation. So with me. If I say a job is done, so it is. If I promise I will never come back, I will not. Besides, I have rethought the necessity of your immediate death. I now believe your eventual death will do just as well. For a generous glass of brandy, I shall explain why.'

With the gun I pointed to the bottom shelf of my bookcase, where I had half a bottle of Beam Black. 'No brandy. Just that. But help yourself. I'll get you another towel.'

He unscrewed the top clumsily and gulped straight from the bottle. I stood up and sidled into the bathroom, the gun still pointed directly at him, but he seemed more interested in polishing off my whiskey than in chasing me. I grabbed another towel from the cabinet and turned on the faucet. Instead of running it under the water, though, I dunked it in the toilet before giving it to Tonu. He rubbed it across the open wound that was his face. I hoped the towel gave him some sort of awful infection.

'Who are you really, and who sent you here to kill me?' I asked.

He took another swig from the whiskey bottle. 'The first question: My name certainly would not mean anything to you. I can promise you that it is not Tonu. I find things. I return things to where they belong. And I dispatch the people who have taken them. As for you . . . well, I usually prefer a neat ending, but as I said, I do think we can achieve that goal without resorting to any more violence. And as for who sent me, perhaps we ought to start at the beginning.' He lit his pipe and stared at me like a teacher about to chastise a student he finds amusing though he knows he shouldn't.

'You are far braver and more persistent than I – than anyone, really – expected you to be. I would guess you even surprised yourself.' He held the towel to his black and clotted lips.

'Maybe I did. But I'm not sure whether I should be insulted or pleased.'

He gave a little smoke puff of laughter. 'Neither, really. Simply an observation.'

'Based on what?'

'A young American man, privileged, educated. Soft, perhaps. Toiling so much for a newspaper with perhaps several hundred readers? First we thought you would simply grow tired of your investigations and reach the same conclusion anyone else would have: an old man had died alone. Then we thought receiving a rotten tooth nailed to your door would frighten you away. Finally we hoped –'

'So *you* did that. Who's "we," though? And whose tooth was it?'

Tonu paused with the bottle halfway to his mouth, then looked upward, as though waiting for an answer, then shrugged. 'The tooth belonged to a rather avaricious bartender of our acquaintance. As for "we," I have heard the phrase "doing God's work" several times since coming to America. Is it familiar to you?'

'Sure, I've heard it.'

'Well, this is who we are. We do God's work.'

'What does that mean?'

'What do you think it means?'

'I think I'm tired,' I said, raising the gun level with his head, 'and I'm not above shooting you.'

'You are very far beneath shooting me, you know,' said Tonu, laughing. 'But still, doing God's work, the way I have understood it, means doing work of which God would approve, yes?'

'Yeah, that's right.'

'Charity, ministry work. Sometimes used ironically, but mainly this is the meaning, is it not?'

'I just said yes.'

'Doing God's work means doing work for God, work on the side of God.'

'Yeah. And?'

'This is what we do. God's work. Except instead

495

of work *for* God, we do the work *of* God.' He took another gulp of my whiskey. I counted three swallows left in the bottle.

I laughed. 'Oh, right. That explains everything. Thanks.' He didn't crack even a small, sympathetic grin. 'Impossible,' I continued. 'Blasphemy. Besides, why should –'

'Blasphemous? Yes, absolutely. Impossible? Impossible, impossible ... You know, I have no idea anymore what that means,' he joked. 'No, not impossible.'

He picked up the baseball that I had thrown at him, now lying next to him on the ground. There was a blood smear between the seams, probably from where it hit his nose. I thought he was going to either pocket it or throw it at me.

'Just put that down,' I said.

'What? You are paranoid, are you not? I told you already you have nothing to fear from me. I simply wanted to examine –'

'Would you just put it down, please? Roll it over to me.' He waited a few seconds, then shrugged, smiled, and rolled the ball to me.

'Do you know what alchemy is?' he asked, shifting toward me in his seat.

I leaned toward him in mine. I might have jumped up in surprise if I hadn't been so tired. I would have given my eyeteeth – which were and still are, by the way, in pristine condition – for Anton Jadid to walk through my front door. I needed some help. 'No. I mean, I've heard of it before, I guess. Middle Ages stuff.' I considered telling him about what the Jadid boys had found but decided that I would rather hear him tell me.

'You know a bit more than that, I should think.'

'Not really.'

'No? Nothing? You and your police friend and his learned uncle snooping around Jaan's office found nothing that could enlighten you more than that?'

I didn't say anything. I hope I didn't show anything either, but I've always been a mediocre poker player.

'Really? Well, well. I can hardly force you to say what you don't wish to say. Not now anyway.

'Explaining what alchemy is, is as difficult – precisely as difficult, in fact – as explaining what the world is.' He began to stroke his beard thoughtfully, but his hands came away bloody, and he wiped them disgustedly on my couch. 'The concise explanation is that alchemy is the study, the science, and the process of transformation. Deliberate transformation. Of anything into anything.' He sat back in his seat, as though that had explained everything, and again went to the bottle. Two swallows.

'Like lead into gold?' I asked, making my expression as blank as possible.

He laughed condescendingly. 'Yes, well, just like, I suppose. Nobody expected that that particular feat would become quite the craze it did. But for centuries every ambitious and greedy fraud who knew how to read set up shop as "an alchemist." Young men wasted family fortunes, kings and princes threw away their reputations, playwrights and poets laughed at us. But when you –'

'I'm sorry, but "us"?'

'Yes, us. Us including me, and including your late townsman. Alchemists, as they call themselves but we never have – I am speaking now of the figures from popular history and the idiots that exist even now, in grubby little shops surrounded by crystals and cheap amulets with inscrutable symbols – alchemists have always believed that they could bumble their way forward, through trial and error, and eventually wind up at the goal. What that goal is changes with the age: nobody today, for instance, takes up the study of alchemy to get rich, though that was once the only reason to undertake such arduous study. "Enlightenment," or "cosmic understanding," or "harmony," or some such nonsense: those are today's worthy aims. But those will change, too.

'Whatever the course they follow, I suppose there is a theoretical possibility that one of these idiots could blindly and luckily make a few small steps forward, but that possibility is far more remote than, for instance, the proverbial monkey sitting down at a computer and managing, by chance, to type out *Hamlet*. And nobody has unlimited time or patience. People have their allotted threescore and ten. Besides, for sources they rely on other alchemists, or on horrible misinterpretations of Bacon or Paracelsus.

And they always have this great faith that they are one small adjustment away, that success awaits them the next morning if they simply believe harder and turn up the burner a bit.

'Now,' said Tonu, or whatever his name was, 'why don't you tell me the one thing that you found in both Jaan's home and his office?'

'We found lots of things in both places. Books. Papers. Carpets. Dust, lots of dust. Sophisticated locks –'

'Yes, locks. And also safes, did you not?'

'Yes, we found safes, but not –'

'And in both safes you would have found sparkling green dust, correct?'

I didn't say anything.

'And your educated professor friend, he knew where the dust came from.' The sentence rose at the end slightly; it fell somewhere between statement and question.

'What you found,' he continued, 'is dust from an instruction book to life. A manual that tells us how to be our own miniature gods. It explains –'

'What we found,' I interrupted, 'were traces of a huge and very valuable gemstone. What we also found is that Jaan had ties to jewel thieves that went beyond just circumstantial or probable.'

'Thievery is beside the point. What you found was more valuable than you can possibly imagine. Do you know, for instance, where the Emerald Tablet was discovered?'

'No.'

'Clutched to Abraham's chest as he lay in his cave, prone and dead. Sarah found it. No doubt you know what the Tablet says.'

'Professor Jadid read a translation, I think. I really don't remember it that well; it didn't make any sense to me.' I figured there was no point in playing dumb anymore.

'That does not surprise me; with a poor translation, that often happens. Also, what he read – what any of the scores of official translations and millions of inane interpretations of the Tablet claim to explain – is nothing but the preamble.'

'What language was it translated from?'

'The preamble? Aramaic. But the meat of the Tablet is written in a language long disappeared from human use. Human memory, even. Perhaps an unusually sharp expert in Semitic languages might, if he ever saw it, be able to piece together a few words, but the meaning would escape him.'

'And the meaning doesn't escape you?'

'Well, no. But then I was taught the language, and I have taught the language to others. A small number of us use it for communication, and we guard the language very carefully.'

'And was Jaan among that small number?'

'He was. He always had a facility with languages. But there is a more important reason that the main part of the Tablet has never been translated.' He paused here and looked at me. However strange this story, he told it well. He knew just how to hook his audience, where to drop opaque details, how to wheedle information from me that I didn't want to divulge.

'The reason is that it has never been seen,' he said, a smile writhing back and forth on his lips like a bloody eel. He took another gulp from the bottle. One left.

'When Sarah found the Tablet, Abraham was clutching it to his chest.' He wrapped his arms around the bottle, held it tightly to himself, and smiled through a matted beard. He looked like he belonged on the number 3 train at New Lots Avenue at 4:00 A.M. 'What do you think of this?'

'Of what?' I asked, tightening my hold on the gun.

He exhaled and rolled his eyes. 'What does this bottle say on the back?'

'I don't know.'

'Why not?'

'Well, because I don't memorize the promotional copy on the back of whiskey labels. And I can't see through the bottle.'

'Exactly. The reason you know what the preamble says is that someone must have accompanied Sarah and written down what appeared on this strange green object held in his dead friend's arms. But the Tablet had another side, too: the side that faced Abraham's chest. And it is this side that has never been seen.'

'So you're telling me that this precious, precious

stone, this gift from God or whoever to Abraham that Jadid said is so famous, we only know about half of it because nobody thought to look on the underside?'

'Indeed,' he said, laughing softly. 'Absurd, isn't it? Simple and obvious. Presumably, it was not that nobody *thought* to look underneath. People then were as curious as you today. Fewer journalists, perhaps, to feed the curiosity, but all the same . . . But after being discovered by Sarah, the Tablet passed from public view. She knew what it was. Or more likely, a rabbi knew what it was and knew that it had to be kept secret. It couldn't be destroyed, of course, and whoever it was, he couldn't protect it all by himself. Nobody can. So, presumably, he chose people around him he could trust, and they guarded the Tablet. Not only did they guard it with their lives, but with the Tablet's help, they prolonged their lives in order to guard it.

'And since then the Tablet has been a rumor. An inspiring rumor, to be sure, but then so was the Fountain of Youth. El Dorado. The lost city of Atlantis. The Chamber of Green Lions. That the Tablet actually existed never mattered if nobody ever saw it except those who wanted it to remain unseen.'

'What do you mean, they prolonged their lives?'

'Have you not been listening to me? Alchemy is the science of transformation. Rocks into diamonds, or money, or ducks, or other rocks. Whatever you like. An old body into a young one, for instance.

Or in my case a damaged face into a healthy one. I should be angrier if I thought my injuries beyond repair.

'But back to the point – the Tablet came and passed from vogue. Every few decades someone else claims to finally "understand" it. Only by now, especially in this country, the Tablet has become so obscure that even its supposed adherents and discoverers attract no attention. Every few years you'll have a book or a prurient television show about Atlantis, and children learn that the legend of El Dorado attracted Spanish explorers to the New World. But the Tablet, for some reason, became the whisper of a shadow of a rumor of a relic. And it would have stayed that way, had its current guardian not grown bored, and hungry for the things in this world.'

'Jaan?'

'Of course. I presume that one of the things you found in his office was a travel itinerary? A rather adventurous one?'

I nodded.

'You know, not everyone is as cynical as a callow newspaper reporter. The world, in fact, is filled with people who know what the Tablet is and are willing to pay immense sums of money for its influence.'

'Why would he need to sell it? If the Tablet can do what you say it can, couldn't Jaan just have made money out of grass clippings or pipe ash or something like that?'

He exhaled. Behind him the milky, silver, early-morning light had begun to show through the curtains. 'Jaan had changed. He grew messianic. Paranoid. It has happened before, occasionally, and no doubt it will happen again, despite our best efforts. There are bound to be some psychological effects, after all, from outliving everyone you know by centuries. He wanted to change the course of history. He grew tired of watching lesser men earn earthly glory while he, guardian and possessor of a treasure that could reduce anyone to dust, lived in obscurity. He lost sight of his mission, lost faith, lost . . .' His voice trailed off sadly, and he rubbed his eyes.

'May I ask a question?' I said, more timidly than I had intended. 'If it was found in Abraham's hands, how did you get it? How did it come to Estonia?'

'Accidentally, perhaps. Perhaps providentially. Perhaps there is no difference between the two other than the narrative we impose. In any case, one of the Tablet's early keepers – I say "early" for your benefit; it actually was many centuries after the Tablet went into hiding – was a librarian in Baghdad who became a geographer to the Sicilian court. He became infected with a similar sort of wanderlust, a similar craving for earthly glory, as did its most recent failed guardian.

'He wanted to map the world – this was in the twelfth century – and wound up shipwrecked in a frigid little backwater populated by half-starved pagans. He survived, of course – all of us survive as long as we want to – but eventually grew tired. He appointed new guardians to replace him, and he ended his life, leaving the Tablet as far from the world's center as it was possible to be. A resolutely safe place.'

'And there it stayed?'

'And there it stayed.'

'Why did you move it?'

'Why indeed,' Tonu said, stretching his arms and legs out before him. 'I suppose we allowed ourselves to become convinced that the changes in that part of the world meant that it was no longer safe there. And that the general indifference to history in this country made it ideal.' He slapped his thighs and polished off the whiskey. 'I was wrong, and one particularly dislikable botanist whom I ignored and subsequently dismembered was right, but everything's put right now. Obviously, given what I've just told you, we won't return to Estonia. But the world offers plenty of out-of-the-way regions of obscure countries where we can buy and burrow our way to safety.'

'How many is "we"?'

'Oh, not many,' he said, again going to work on his beard with the towel. He had cleaned most of the blood off his face, and except for a little trickle from his nose and a small blotch on his upper lip, his wounds had stopped bleeding. He pointed to the mug rings and empty beer cans and bottles of water on the coffee table. 'I see you share my late colleague's indifference to matters of cleanliness. We are not many at all.'

'One in every country?'

'Please,' he said, grinning.

'A nice round hundred? Two hundred?'

'Are you planning to write a little article about us?' he asked teasingly.

'Sure, why not. I've always wanted to try fiction.'

'I assure you this is not fiction,' he said, laughing, 'and anyway –'

'Is any of what you've just told me verifiable? It's pretty compelling, and you're a fine storyteller, but I'm sure you're a much better jewel thief. So was Jaan. Or whatever his real name was.'

'And anyway,' he continued, his voice rising with mirth more than anger, 'I don't think you have considered your own position. Yours or your friend's, Miss Rowe's.'

Hearing him mention Hannah sent me back into my chair like I'd been punched in the stomach. In retrospect I don't see how I couldn't have expected it.

'What does she have to do with it?' I asked this carefully, like I was afraid of tipping something over.

'Absolutely everything,' Tonu said, bringing his palm down on the table for emphasis. 'We would not have been able to do what we did without her. Not at all. I presume, dogged as you have been, you know of Jaan's scrapes with the law? The acquaintance he has – we have now – cultivated with Vernum Sickle?

Jaan lived in fear of us for the last few years of his life. Firing guns from windows, purchasing locks more suited to a bank vault than a professor's home. He's lucky he aroused no more suspicion than he did. We all are lucky for that. Do you think Jaan would have welcomed us had he known we were coming for him? We can defeat age and disease, but we are hardly bulletproof. Not impervious at all to physical violence, as you showed so well tonight.'

'So I still don't understand –'

'What this has to do with Hannah? She has a good heart, quite unaffected by the premature cynicism that infects so many of her contemporaries.' He wagged a finger at me mockingly. I had left myself no credible responses between stoicism and murder: I chose the former.

'We had been watching him for quite some time,' he continued, 'and noticed that the only visitor he ever received was this charming young neighbor of his. So I arranged several accidental meetings with her. This would have been, let me see, several months ago. She was quite active in the church's summer programs, giving children music lessons, swimming lessons. Quite selfless, Miss Rowe, and, between the two of us, rather proud of her selfless-ness. Only too happy to help.'

I exhaled disgustedly. 'So you just told her . . . what? You have to help us kill your friend?'

'No, no, of course not. Nothing so crude. Gradually I revealed to her who we were and who

Jaan was and what he planned to do. I explained to her – proved to her, in fact, detail by painful detail – just why and how goodness required her to assist us. To put her petty personal concerns, her feelings of friendship, to one side, if only for an evening.'

'And she believed you?' This fell somewhere between a fearful statement and a question. She believed in everything. She told me that herself.

'She agreed that we couldn't release the Tablet into the world, as Jaan wanted to do. At the same time, she was not ready – is still not yet ready – for some of the messier work we must do.

'Jaan gave her a key to his house, you see. She felt she was doing a good deed by cooking for him, taking in his washing, and he loved having a pretty girl attendant. He instructed her to hide the key, of course, and to notify him before using it. Which she did, naturally. Every time but one.'

After he said this, he sat silent for a time. 'For what it's worth,' he said quietly, 'all of us regret Jaan's death. Hannah more than anyone else. Her guilt, after all, forced this messy cleanup effort.'

'Murder, you mean. You regret having murdered Jaan. And what do you mean her guilt forced this cleanup?'

'Murder, death: semantics in this case. Whatever we did, it was necessary, and whatever Hannah did, it was also necessary. Now, the unnecessary thing she did was to try to salve her conscience by placing a telephone call to your policemen.'

'Hannah reported the death?'

'Who else? After doing so, of course, she realized what a compromising position she was in, and so she has been far more advisable, less truculent, since then. Anyway, at the very least, she had the sense of self-preservation to use an out-of-the-way public telephone at an obscure hour of night. But –'

'What do you mean, self-preservation?' I interrupted. 'You said all she did was step out of your way. She didn't actually do the killing, did she?'

'Of course not. But the conscientious Miss Rowe had her fingerprints recorded by the state of Connecticut last fall, during an initiative to ensure the easy identification of children should they, God forbid, be kidnapped. Everyone under thirteen at her school was fingerprinted. Hannah, wanting as ever to set a good example, went first, to show the children not to be frightened. She feared that the police would eventually question her, if they decided that Jaan had died under suspicious circumstances, and she feared – rightly, I might add – that under such questioning she would falter. Fortunately, we relied on the sloth of small-town policemen and our efficiency at making his death appear as natural as possible. Notwithstanding the coroner, whose death we naturally regret –'

'The Panda? That was you?'

He shrugged. 'Let us say that it suits me now to have you believe that it was us. Accidents do happen and, being accidents, sometimes they even benefit the unworthy.'

'And sometimes they aren't accidents.'

'Yes, of course. Sometimes. As I was saying, aside from this unfortunate coroner, only one person treated Jaan's death as suspicious. Only one person lacked the good sense to keep his nose out of what did not concern him. He became so curious, in fact, that he even broke into the dead man's house, in the company of a violent rogue policeman. And I would guess any interested party would find that person's fingerprints – your fingerprints – quite easily in the house, could they not?' My face stayed blank. 'And you, working ever so diligently – unusually diligently, one might say – on an obituary in an obscure newspaper? And you, having been seen with Miss Rowe, entering and exiting her apartment, spending an inordinate amount of time together for two people who, after all, only met so recently? Do you see? I am a foreign national traveling on a forged passport: the only way I will ever be found is if you decide to use that gun. Say Jaan had willed his estate to Miss Rowe – and say his estate was far grander than it appeared – you can imagine the sordidness of what might emerge.'

'Did he really leave everything to Hannah?'

He sighed exasperatedly. 'Did he, didn't he? Should you choose to publicize this story, that certainly is what he did. So you see, you really would have been better off had you just acceded to the request she made of you. To let the matter rest. You should have done it then, but you'll do it now,' he said confidently. 'The only difference is the burden it places on your shoulders, all these distressing events that don't concern you.'

'But the police already know,' I said pathetically. 'The man who brought me tonight –'

'Detective Jadid, you mean? Detective Jadid was photographed breaking into a man's home two hours outside of his jurisdiction,' Tonu said, pulling a tiny camera from his inside pocket. 'The film has already been sent to Mr Sickle, the late complainant's attorney. Detective Jadid was also photographed exiting a bar in Clougham, gun drawn; the bar's owner has also, shall we say, disappeared. By a strange coincidence, shortly before the bar owner's disappearance, he, too, had occasion to visit Mr Sickle for a bit of advice. These photographs will be on Commissioner Pereira's desk in a matter of hours, in fact, if not already.' He drew the curtain to let the morning air into the room. It was sunny and clear, and the light washed into the room like water into a wound.

'I know as well as you that Joseph Jadid is a good policeman and that he likes his work. I also know he has a fiery temper and an unfailing instinct for irritating his superiors. He will most likely retain his job. But he will never have anything to do with any of these matters again. This is the condition Mr Sickle has laid out for keeping this matter quiet, away from the press.'

He pulled a folded piece of paper from his jacket, and as he unfolded it, I noticed that the paper was of unusually good quality: thick and bonded, with a watermark visible in the morning light. Why that detail stays with me, I don't know. '"Detective Joseph Jadid is to avoid disturbing or in any way tarnishing the memory of Jaan Pühapäev, a valued member of Wickenden's academic community and an upstanding citizen of Lincoln, Connecticut." Mr Sickle's letter to Commissioner Pereira.'

'So what happens now?' I asked after a long, defeated pause.

'Now? Well, as I told you, I have no intention of killing you. Nor any desire, really, after our conversation. What happens now is entirely up to you. If you feel compelled to write about or further investigate this story, I can hardly stop you, though naturally it will most likely lead to the conviction of you, Joseph Jadid, and Hannah Rowe, at least for breaking and entering. But are you asking my advice?'

'Sure, why not?' I had thought him deluded, a little kooky, when he first started talking about emeralds and secret crystals and living forever. Even if his alchemy bullshit was just a screen, it was still first-rate bullshit. And I am nothing if not a producer and consumer of bullshit.

'Heed your friend's request, and just drop it. Just let it go. You are a young man; your capacity to forget, to heal, exceeds your expectations. Especially now, so lovelorn and deprived of sleep.' Tonu paused and gazed at me steadily, his eyes dropping to examine how I was holding the gun (lightly and away from him, until he looked and I snapped it back up).

'Besides, everyone loses once in a great while. Even me, as you can see. And in this case also you.' Again he paused, and again I didn't shoot him. 'If I can wonder aloud, you seem an intelligent and serious young man. I cannot understand why you remain in this town.'

'Well, there's Hannah. There was Hannah.'

'Ah. You will never see her again.'

'I'm sorry? How do you know? Just because –'

'You no doubt smelled smoke last night on your way into Lincoln?'

'Yeah.'

'Ms Rowe's apartment caught fire last night. Faulty electrical wiring. A tragedy.' I started up from my chair and trained the gun back on him. 'She's fine,' he said, raising his hands, palms out, motioning for calm. 'She's fine, as is her unusual landlady. In perfect health, but the stress of losing her friend and her home in such proximity have been rather more than she can bear. Her Christmas vacation has started early.'

'What do you mean? Where is she?'

'As I said, not your concern. It would be a shame, of course, if her name was tarnished in any way, now that she is unable to defend herself.' I walked over to him and put the cane's barrel against his temple. When he winced and licked his lips, I pressed harder.

'Do you really want to do that?'

I shoved the cane into his head until I heard him

whimper. Then, feeling my adrenaline rise again and knowing what I was about to do, I snatched it away and sat back down. 'Did you kill her?'

'No, of course we didn't kill her. Such a serious, committed, beautiful woman. A timeless type of beauty, don't you think? A timeless character? Eternal, you might even say.' He winked. 'No, I give you my word she is as healthy and robust as ever she has been, though the week's events have taken rather a grievous toll on her emotions. No matter. Anyway, as I said, you won't see her again.'

THE SUN AND ITS SHADOW

❧❧❧

As the wing the ground evades, / As the two surpas-
seth one, / As the day the night defines, / So the
Shadow and its Sun.

— JOHN DEVERE (SIXTEENTH EARL OF OXFORD),
The Tragic Tale of Posthumus Leonatus,
His Most Lamentable Death

In the popular imagination, Moscow's winters are
considered abominable: endless, sunless, cheerless,
colorless, a barren country beneath a sky that seeps
from black to tepid gray to black again, rolling over
in color like a patient in a hospital bed. In fact, while
the persistent and frigid drizzle in autumn and spring
turns the city into the inside of a tubercular lung,
winter brings Moscow to life like a slap to a sleeper.
For three or perhaps four hours a day on a good day,
from December to February, the city shines under
the most perfect light in the world. On the best of

days, a new snow will have fallen the previous night, covering the exhaust and snow and cigarette ash and sputum and spilled beer and torn papers in a sparkling jacket. The wide streets will be quieter than usual and the narrow old ones more bustling.

So it was on the morning of Voskresenyov's last visit to Moscow: at Soimonovsky Passage, near Metrostroyevskaya, he stepped out of the back of his chauffeured Zil, and a mother with her two towheaded and apple-cheeked children collided with him. He was reaching into the car for his attaché case, and her attention was on a girl about to toddle into the street.

After she walked into him, she gasped and a hand fluttered up toward her throat, and upon registering who he was – the car, the uniform, the medals, the real leather briefcase – her eyes widened and she jerked her head back involuntarily. But as soon as she had collected herself, she gave him a level, almost contemptuous glare, and instead of gathering her children in her arms to protect them, she simply held out her hands to them. The children grabbed on, and the three of them stared at their quarry, who considered smiling ingratiatingly but then decided that simply returning their gaze would be best. What happened to the awe? Why did the mother not wrap her arms protectively around her children, nod servilely, and hurry away? As Voskresenyov bent to pick up his briefcase, he couldn't help grinning; he stood up stone-faced, the mother gave a little puff-spit exhalation of dismissal, and the three walked on.

'You know, they're renaming this street,' said a familiar voice at Voskresenyov's elbow.

'Lubin. Thank you for meeting me. And in the old place, too.'

'Yes, well, *near* the old place, you might say.' Lubin touched Voskresenyov on the forearm and pointed forward to indicate that they should begin walking. They followed the small street northwest, away from the river, until it hit Metrostroyevskaya, where they turned right. Unlike many Russian men, Lubin was averse to physical contact or excessive displays of emotion. He and Voskresenyov habitually greeted each other with nothing more than a handshake and a brief nod.

'How do you mean, near? We are near. There it is. Shall we not go in?'

Dom Pertsova rose up red and gaudy, like a painted gingerbread house, in front of them. The fairy-tale panels on the outside and the spiraling snakes supporting one of the side balconies delighted Voskresenyov, and he couldn't help smiling as he saw it.

'Hard to believe that all of this was supposed to be torn down,' he said.

'This entire corner of the city: Metrostroyevskaya, Kropotkinskaya – all of these little winding streets between Kropotkinskaya Station and Park Kultury, razed to make a Palace of the Soviets. Tragic perhaps, but not really surprising. I'm just glad they didn't get to it,' Lubin said.

'*I* didn't get to it, you mean.'

Lubin shrugged equably and pointed to the white church with green domes in front of them. St Ilya Obydenny, where they and countless other clandestine government-to-government contacts had met through the Soviet years. Because citizens feared being denounced for entering churches, they became safe places for government officials to meet secretly; any ordinary citizen who reported anything would immediately be under suspicion because of his undue interest in a place of worship. As for officials' meeting each other, the very illicitness of the act made it safe for everyone. And this particular church had an out-of-the-way beauty, an incense-cured and ramshackle peace that made it one of the more popular assignation spots.

'See?' asked Lubin, gesturing toward the church.

'Ah.' A weak but steady stream of worshippers – men and women, old and young, poor and less poor – entered and exited the church, some crossing themselves fervidly, others awkwardly, as though the gesture was not yet familiar to them. 'In Estonia, too. Latvia. Lithuania and Ukraine even more.'

'Yes. I don't doubt it. So why don't we walk for a bit instead.'

'Of course.'

'Vsekhsvyatsky, since you didn't ask,' said Lubin after a few minutes of silent walking. 'And this street,

Metrostroyevskaya, will be Ostozhenka.' He grinned thinly. He had the opaque, ophidian manner of someone who has spent a lifetime manipulating and studying other people's reactions.

'Sorry?'

'This street. Ostozhenka it was, and Ostozhenka it will be again. The passage where we met will be Vsekhsvyatsky, not Soimonovsky. All still secret, of course, but the prerevolutionary names are coming back into use. Sverdlovsk went first, of course, because of that drunken buffoon. Leningrad's probably next. The street names, though, that's what really brings it home. Ah, well. You know, I never knew you had a brother.'

'Nor did I know you had a son.'

'Oh, yes,' said Lubin, smoothing his tie with paternal pride. 'Three, in fact. One a doctor – he's studying in Berlin at the moment – one a prosecutor here in Moscow, and then Sasha, the one after your own heart.'

'After my job, Lubin. I've never met the boy. And besides, how would the son of a KGB man know anything about a heart?'

'All right, all right. Steady on,' said Lubin, his voice tightening but not rising with irritation. 'I see no saints in present company.'

'Forgive me. I meant no offense.'

Lubin dipped his head in acceptance. 'I admire people who look after their family. Especially these days. You're sure about Sasha?'

'Absolutely. And you about Tonu?'

Lubin handed Voskresenyov a sheaf of poor-quality copies of official documents. 'Here he is. Tonu Pühapäev, an exemplary member of a Hiiumaa sheep farm, has recently been named chairman of the Paide Dairy Collective. You can see for yourself.'

Voskresenyov grabbed the papers and leafed through them hungrily. 'And this is the one going private?'

'Oh, yes. Private within a year. A consortium of Finns and Swedes are buying. They say it will be the largest dairy farm in the Baltics. Probably even supply some of Scandinavia, too. Given the low cost of Soviet labor, even ex-Soviet free-Estonian labor, it should also be the most profitable, too. We had to fight tooth and nail to install Tonu. Estonians smell money, they're worse than the Jews. And you?'

'As we agreed. Look there,' said Voskresenyov, pointing to the modest wooden house across the street. 'Turgenev's mother lived there, in that little house. It survived all the fires, all the destruction, all the blockheaded Soviet planning. And here it stands, plain and beautiful as ever, not even a plaque to adorn it.'

Lubin sighed impatiently and shifted his weight back and forth as he walked. Voskresenyov noticed. 'As I was saying. I am resigning my commission immediately after this conversation. I have the power to name my successor – not as commander of the Baltic forces, of course, which will cease to exist very soon – but as a general in the Russian army. And as I promised, Aleksandr Anatolyevich Lubin will become the army's youngest general. Naturally, I cannot guarantee his posting, but if it's Moscow he wants, I presume that Moscow he shall have.'

'And there's no way to tie the favor to me?' asked Lubin, somewhat anxiously. It was the first time Voskresenyov had seen Lubin act covetous, and the sight of this stone-faced and oily man suddenly widening his eyes, licking his lips, and clenching his teeth gave Voskresenyov a pleasant feeling of superiority. 'Sasha and I, we don't speak as much as we should. If he knew I was responsible for arranging this, he would spit on it, I'm sure. Hotheaded, like his mother.'

'No ties at all. Reciprocal anonymity, as always, right?'

'Of course. Although it's an odd thing, you know?'

'What?'

'Just something I found when I was working on Tonu and looking over your file.'

Voskresenyov stiffened. He thought he had taken care of that.

'There's no listing of a brother on your enlistment documents. No listing of a brother as next of kin anywhere. And certainly no explanation of why two brothers would have different last names. Different *uncommon* last names, both of which mean "Sunday" in different languages.'

Voskresenyov looked toward the sun so that he

could clench his eyes shut in self-remonstration. He had altered his files in the Central Army office, but the KGB would naturally have had the original documents as well. He should have thought of that before asking Lubin to meddle. 'Did you bring the file?' he asked, perhaps a bit too rapidly.

'Bring the file? What, here? Of course not, why would I do that? I'm not permitted to do that.'

'So it remains with all the other military files in the Lubyanka?'

'Naturally. Where else would it go?' They walked along through this unpretentious, meandering corner of the city in silence.

'What will you do?' asked Voskresenyov.

'Do? With what?'

Voskresenyov looked down at Lubin and put on an expression that he hoped bore some resemblance to wry yet earnest concern.

'Oh. Yes, I am quitting too,' Lubin said. 'Same as you. All accounts equal, I suppose.' His chuckle turned into a weak yet persistent cough that sounded like a scythe through dry wheat. 'They will let me keep a small dacha not far from Suzdal. My apartment will go to my oldest son, so he will have a place to live when he returns from Berlin. If he returns, I suppose, things being as they are. And my wife and I will live quietly in Suzdal. And that will be that.' Lubin nodded and made a chopping motion with his hand, as though by this very bank of trees at the intersection of Sechenovskiy and Ostozhenka he was dividing his past life from his present one, or perhaps his present from his future. 'And you?' he asked.

'Oh, you know . . . I have a couple of projects, I suppose. More free time. Army pension, no more uniform.' Voskresenyov fumbled for more telling but vague fragments.

'I've never really understood you. What are you doing? What are your plans? You know, I've heard rumors that you're springing some Ingush jewel thief from Magadan. Being kept very quiet. And can you tell me, you know, why is it that I look like a man who's spent forty years drinking and smoking living in a cold climate and you've barely aged a day?'

'Pickle brine,' said Voskresenyov, slapping his cheeks. 'My grandmother told me – pickle brine on the skin every morning.'

Lubin chuckled uncertainly. 'Pickles? Yes, well, I suppose if you say so, perhaps. I'm not sure, though . . . You know, you could buy the file,' he almost spit. 'Everything is for sale these days – if you wanted to keep that information to yourself, you could easily just arrange to buy the file.'

Voskresenyov kept his expression fixed, though he knew as soon as Lubin suggested it that this was what he would have to do. 'Make a purchase from the KGB?' he asked, feigning shock. 'Who does one contact to do such a thing?'

Lubin tore a flap from the box of Winston Lights in his pocket and wrote a name on the white cardboard inside, handing it to Voskresenyov. 'This is your man. Very discreet. Anyone with enough money and aspirations in the new Russia has been buying incriminating information from him. And because everyone goes through him, everyone knows it's him, so he's untouchable. Maybe it's the other way around, though: maybe even though everyone knows it's him, everyone uses him, and *that's* why he's untouchable. One or the other, anyway.'

'Yes, of course,' chuckled Voskresenyov, though he didn't really know why he should be chuckling. 'Could I not just give the money to you? Would you erase my record?'

'Me? Certainly not. I don't do that kind of thing, and besides, what would I need money for? But thank you for asking.'

For as long as the two men had known and done favors for each other, each had always tried to hold any advantage possible over the other. Not to use, of course, just to have. Constant infinitesimal re-adjustments of hierarchy allowed them to personalize their professional relations and professionalize their personal relations. Voskresenyov wondered what Lubin was planning to do with this information. He stared at the pouchy, slack face beneath brittle and graying hair, the trembling and liver-spotted hand, and concluded: absolutely nothing. Checkmate and tip the king over: Lubin was giving up. And nothing can be done with a man who wants nothing.

'No, no money for me,' Lubin continued in a near mutter, looking down as though speaking for himself. 'Just some quiet away from all of this. My wife and I, we are both country people, from around Tver. Forty years in this city, this shit. No money for me.'

As they walked, they came upon a little park at the intersection of five streets, with a copse of denuded birch trees whose branches splayed like skeletal hands of warning too high for anyone to see. At the center of the empty park was a fountain – really just a stagnant concrete pool of green-scummed water visible beneath a thin lattice of ice – surrounded by a bunch of bushes, and as they approached the fountain, they walked from crisp sunlight into the thicket's shadow. The bushes hid them from the street; Voskresenyov grabbed Lubin and kissed him fully on his open and surprised mouth. He felt Lubin shoving against him with his weak and spindly hands, and Voskresenyov reached into his pocket for his spring-loaded knife, flicked open the blade, sliced deeply into the nests of arteries on either side of Lubin's groin, and shoved him through the ice and into the fountain.

Voskresenyov threw the knife in afterward, checked his shoes, trousers, and topcoat for bloodstains (there was none), and continued on to the Lubyanka to buy the rest of his past.

Item 15: A pendant with a broad (3.6 centimeters across, 5.8 centimeters top to bottom) leather-backed charm attached to a thin looped strip of black leather 34 centimeters in length. On the charm were two stones: a topaz starburst – that is, a circlet of amber with eight thin spindles extending from it in the shape of a sun – and next to it an onyx oval.

Representations of shadowed or setting suns signify a nearly completed endeavor in danger of failure. They inspire hope and vigilance in equal measures.

Date of manufacture: Impossible to determine. The stones themselves are cracked and clouded with age; they appear several centuries old at least. The leather, though, is in reasonable condition, if a bit worn from regular use.

Manufacturer: Ivan Voskresenyov. He claimed that the design was based on a drawing of 'The Sun and Its Shadow' – an enigmatic alchemical hieroglyph –

found in the notebook of Arab-Sicilian geographer al-Idrisi.

But comic-book scholar Milos Smilos – author of the article 'Where's That Football, Charlie Brown? Illicit Sexual Desire in Daily Comic Strips' and the graphic fictional autobiography *Call Me Sir! Peppermint Patty, Warrior Dyke* – wrote in his unofficial embellished autobiography that leather pendants inlaid with yellow glass and polished obsidian became quite popular among artists and intellectuals in the Baltics during the interwar years. Their design came from an Estonian artist's interpretation of a jersey worn by Flash Gordon in the 1940 comic serial *Flash Gordon Conquers the Universe*.

Place of origin: As difficult to determine as the date. Estonia is one of the world's largest exporters of amber, and its tanning industry has always been quite active as well. Onyx, while not produced in the Baltics, is a common and popular gem.

Last known owner: Ivan Voskresenyov. Taken from his body following his murder by [NAME DELETED] and given to [NAME DELETED].

Estimated value: Smilos and his ilk would probably drive up the price of what ordinarily would, in perfect lighting and from an excited buyer, fetch $300 at best.

*That which I had to say about the
operation of Sol is complete.*

So,' said Tonu. He was standing at my open door,
topcoat on, one foot in the hallway and one
hand on the doorknob. 'I assume I have answered all
outstanding questions.' His voice and eyebrows rose
at the end of the sentence.

'Albanian Eddie?'

'Edouard, yes. I thought we had forgotten about
him.' He smirked. I felt at that moment as though
I were looking at a reptile made of glass, some sort
of poison-weaned creature that would cut you as
soon as you applied any pressure to it. How anyone
could trust him remains a mystery. 'Edouard had a
talent for smuggling. He learned it under the closed
and paranoid Soviets; we certainly thought he would
succeed in this trusting and open nation.'

'So what happened?'

Tonu advanced hesitantly back into my apartment

and had nearly shut the door behind him when he thought better of it and resumed the one-foot-in-and-one-out position. 'Same as Jaan. Greedy. Deceptive. Untrustworthy. But he was a temporary employee anyway. No sense of dedication. He did help acquire certain things we needed, but he really had no further utility.'

'What things?'

Tonu took a small step backward farther into the hall. I stepped toward him. 'No. No more questions. This is all you need to know.'

'No,' I sputtered. 'No, I have more questions now than I did three hours ago. I . . . You can't just . . . What you told me makes no sense.'

'Which part of it did you not understand?'

'Any of it. All of it. I just can't believe –'

'You don't need to. I know of no law that states a thing must be believed to be true. You really ought to be more grateful, you know. You've actually been entrusted with a piece of information that many people would kill for.'

'And you trust me to keep quiet about it?'

'Trust you?' Tonu laughed. 'Of course. Who would you tell? Who would believe you? I think we're quite safe on that score, and if not, we keep ourselves well camouflaged. Should you suddenly develop a chatty disposition, I might need to visit you again. Besides, now that Jaan has enticed Tablet seekers, you certainly would attract attention from the most unsavory and unscrupulous quarters should you decide to brag about your connection to him. And as I said, we would be long gone and unable to help you.'

'What if I decide to take my chances? It's a good story,' I bluffed, more testily than bravely.

Tonu gave me a disappointed smile, then shrugged and said, 'As I told you, I have no plans to take up residence in your apartment. I cannot control what you do. I can, however, remind you that you would be guilty of breaking and entering and, quite possibly, found guilty of murder. Should you wish intimate knowledge of Connecticut's prisons, Mr Sickle will ensure that you receive it. But if we thought you insensible or rash, neither you nor Joseph nor his uncle would still be alive. Be wise, Mr Tomm. This is the sum total of the advice I have. Be wise.' And with that he left, easing the door shut behind him, well mannered to the last. I heard him descending the stairs, and then from my window I saw him climb into an unmemorable car of unremarkable color. He started up the engine and, using the appropriate turn signals even though no other cars were on the road, headed south, away from Lincoln.

It was too late, or too early, to go to sleep that night. I don't mind admitting that I still don't sleep all that well. It's getting better, though: most things that grind can also mollify, and time is no exception.

Instead of sleeping, I showered, shaved, made and drank a pot of coffee – my pot held not quite two full cups: like everything else in my apartment, it was made for one and only one – and at seven-fifteen headed to work.

I felt like someone had hollowed me out and stuffed me full of cotton, like I was lugging around deadweight, and the deadweight was me. This feeling of trying to dance after the music has stopped, of realizing you've taken a dead-end turn in a maze, of having outstayed your welcome, strikes everyone, I imagine, everyone except the perpetually mobile and those with an unerring sense of timing. It hit me in my last year of high school, again in my last year of college, and now, like then, it was time to go. When it strikes, you can either heed it and move or wait for it to pass and spend the rest of your life sublimating the feeling of howling loss into low-level malaise. I chose option one.

'There he is,' said Art, not even looking up as I walked into the newsroom.

'What are you doing here so early?' I asked.

'Told you before, you get old, you don't sleep so well.'

I remember Art best as I saw him that morning: leaning back in his chair with his feet on the desk, a human hammock, flipping through the *Times* with a thermos of coffee open and steaming on his desk and a burning cigarette in the corner of his mouth.

With his right foot, he pushed an envelope across his desk toward me. 'Found it this morning under the door. Figured I'd wait to ask how the never-ending obit's going until after you read it.'

I nodded thanks, sat down, and opened the letter. Even before I saw the ballpoint spidergraph writing, I knew who it came from.

Dear Paul,

If you are reading this, then you have spoken to Tonu, and if you have spoken to him, then he has told you that I have left Lincoln. In fact, as I write this, a car is waiting outside with what few possessions I have allowed myself to carry with me into my new life. Funny what we choose to take and what we leave. All of my music, for instance, a collection that I built piece by piece over almost twenty years, I have left in Talcott's music room, but I would rather you take it than the school. I suppose I might miss some of what remains here, at least initially, but in fact I am leaving behind little that I care about, except for you, whom I had not planned to meet and was certainly not supposed to feel for as I did.

I never really thought of obituaries before. I never thought of them being written, and when I did what I did, meeting the writer of Jaan's obituary was not even remotely part of my thoughts. But I met him all the same. And the whole time I was willing myself to shove you further away and unable to keep from welcoming you into me. Maybe because I saw your obvious affection – and it was obvious, Paul, clear as water from the very start – as a sign that what I had done was really not so bad. You see, I believe in signs, though I suspect you do not. Our time together is in that sentence.

I take the broad view, as Tonu did, and I believe what he told me – told us – about Jaan, and the Tablet, and what Jaan wanted

532

to do. He told me that you did not, and I can just see you, Paul, arguing with him and shutting him out and refusing even the possibility that the world is broader and deeper, more numinous and mysterious, than it appears. For what it's worth, I cannot and do not hold this against you. I ask you not to hold my beliefs against me.

What happened to Jaan would have happened anyway. Even if you believe that Tonu and he were common thieves and not guardians of something extraordinary, you know this is true; you know that he was hiding something from them. A narrow moral view would probably say that this hardly matters, that we are finally accountable only and most of all for our own actions. But I have actually been given a chance to be responsible for something more than myself, and I ask that you at least try to understand, and perhaps eventually try to forgive me before you forget me.

I would beg only two favors from you. First, I was not just flattering you when I said that I liked your articles in the Carrier. I would consider it a tremendous gift if you could write down your recollections of the past week and send them to this address that I enclose here. I want to know how my actions looked to someone who lacks my belief in them. I know this is a burdensome gift, and it might strike you as vain, but I hope you will do it anyway.

Second, I want you to promise not to try to trace me. I do not plan to be here for very long, certainly not long enough for you to follow the trail that leads to me, and the closer you would get to me, the more worried I would become for your safety. We will agree to be glad that we knew each other, however briefly (too briefly!), but you must promise to go no further than that.

Tonu, as he told you, was not Tonu. Jaan was not Jaan. But I really was Hannah Elizabeth Rowe. While I write this, I still am,

and I will always remember you with great fondness, whoever I am
and wherever I go.

   Love,

   H.

Well, that last line was certainly a comfort, thanks very much: I helped kill an old man; I did it for reasons too elevated and noble for you to understand; I've disappeared with the murderer; but you write really well, and I want you to have my records, and I'll remember you fondly. What was I supposed to say, or do, with any of that? Out of either a misguided sense of chivalry or a well-guided sense of writerly egotism, I did write this account of our week, which I now disclaim all ownership of. I hope you don't mind reading about yourself in the third person; it was easier to talk and think of you that way. I also hope you read this and then burn it, to tell you the truth, but if you want to keep it, I can't stop you. Hell, I probably couldn't even find you.

The only thing left, I suppose, is to tell you what happened to some of the ancillary characters – some of the mere mortals – in this story, which is fundamentally yours. After I read your letter, I typed this up for Art. It appeared in the next issue of the *Carrier:*

Jaan Pühapäev, an Estonian-born professor of Baltic history at Wickenden University, died early last Wednesday morning at his home on Orchard Street. He had lived in Lincoln since he arrived in the United States in 1991. His age, the exact time of death, and the exact cause of his death remain unknown. He leaves no survivors.

Less than a minute after I put the text in the copy-edit file, I heard Art's chair creak.

'So this is it?' he asked, walking over to my desk and looking at me quizzically. 'Days of shuttling back and forth between here and Wickenden, a week of working police sources, and this is what you got?'

'Nothing really panned out,' I said.

'What do you mean, nothing panned out? What about the police records? What about, you know . . . what about . . .' He squinted and moved his hands in circles as though trying to conjure more information. 'You know this better than I do – what about the other stuff?'

'There was no other stuff, unfortunately. A lot of speculation and nothing firm. Nothing to go on.'

'So give it another week. You want to run this here now, fine, but don't give up on the story like this. Keep digging. For Leenie and your career, you know, if not for this paper.'

'Look, I really don't think anything else is going to pan out. And I want to move on to something else.'

'Anything you want to tell me?'

'Like what?'

'I don't know. You protecting a source?' I looked up at him. 'You know, my daughter used to look at me like that instead of telling me to mind my own business.' I smiled, but Art didn't. 'Couldn't force her to answer, though, because she didn't work for me.' He picked up my obit from the office printer and threw it away. 'So you want to tell me what's going on? Why you got nothing else?'

I sat there silently, looking down at my desk. 'I wish I could tell you, Art. I really do,' I said quietly. 'But I really can't, okay? You can print that obit, you can not print it. You can fire me, you can –'

'Jesus, Paul, I told you before: no one's looking to fire you. I'm just . . . You know, you been digging around with this for a while now, got real excited about it, even had an editor from Boston excited about it, and now it's like someone turned off the program. You don't want to tell me, fine, but my two cents? I think you're probably making a mistake.' He stopped and looked at me with his head to one side, like he was trying to guess my weight.

I shrugged and looked out the window at the lake across the street and at the dearth of activity. A weekender's town, because nothing happened here. I liked Lincoln, liked it a lot, and in a few years I might even come back to visit. But the town had ejected me. As Tonu said, sometimes you just take a loss on the chin and move on.

When I told Art I wanted to quit, he responded neither with total equanimity nor, unfortunately for my ego, with outright begging and bawling. At first he didn't say anything and went back into his office, while I tried to make myself busy at my desk without looking as though I was cleaning it out. Around noon, though, he took me over to the Colonial for lunch and what he called 'the options conversation.' He asked me where I was going, and since I hadn't really thought about it until he asked, I said I would just head home to Brooklyn until I figured out where I wanted to go. We strategized about whom to meet and where he should send his letters – he promised me 'a recommendation that'll get you into heaven.' He was one of the few people I knew who never steered me wrong, because he never tried to steer: he took things as they came, sized them up, and reacted to what was before him rather than what should have been before him. He didn't try to persuade me to stay, which I still appreciate. Instead, after we drained our beers, he asked me how soon I was leaving.

'As soon as I can load my car, I think.'

'Come by for dinner on Friday?' he asked, looking at me out of the corners of his eyes, as though afraid I would say no. 'Donna would love to say good-bye.'

'Sure. Sounds great.'

And it was – great, that is. They treated me like a son, and the send-off dinner felt like I was leaving home. Donna cried, Art and I drank too much, and Austell re-created Lincoln Common's only Revolutionary War battle using olive pits and corn kernels. The Rolens' daughter, Dana, was up from New York for the weekend, and I saw that she had inherited her father's long face, his gentle charm, and his uncanny and unlearned ability to see and bring out the best in other people. It's a rare and enviable quality.

Dana and I have been out a couple of times since I've been back in Brooklyn, holed up in my childhood room. From the window I can see the same vista of scrubby park grass, street, and the corner of Grand Army Plaza that I saw growing up. Prone on my bed with my head at just the right angle, I can see the top corner of the arch, just like my uncle Sean could when he had this room. My mother and I both regressed pretty much instantly to the roles we had when I was sixteen – she asks me where I'm going, and I grunt; I ask her when dinner's going to be ready, and she growls – both because it's easiest and because it somehow comforts us, because, like every time I go home, I always think it might be the last time I really 'go home.'

My sister-in-law, Anna, seems worried that I'll somehow contaminate my nephew into a do-nothing ex-journalist slacker just by playing with him in the wrong way. If that kid makes it to eighteen without breakdowns or serious chemical dependencies, he'll be absolutely insufferable.

And Art and I have been talking about where I should go next, though I feel no particular urgency about it. Maybe this is my last extended winter vacation. The break between semesters at Wickenden lasted more than six weeks – an unrectified holdover from the energy crisis in the late seventies, when they left the dorms empty and unheated during winter – and those vacations always seemed like hibernation, like I was lying low and storing up energy for the coming semester. Maybe this was because I didn't do enough. Anyway, I'm supposed to meet with editors in Hartford, Wickenden, Manchester, and Concord after the New Year. We'll see what happens.

A few days after leaving Lincoln, I called Joe Jadid to see what had happened to him. It turned out as Tonu said it would: he had photographed Joe breaking into Jaan's house, had sent the pictures to Sickle, and Sickle had sent the pictures to Joe, along with a note telling him to drop the investigation unless he wanted to lose his job. So he did (drop it, that is). Joe told Sal not to return calls from his federal buddies, and he served out the rest of his suspension all but chained to his desk, determined to keep out of trouble. Considering he could trace his troubles directly back to me, he was surprisingly friendly on the phone. I told him I was looking around for another job, and he said better me than him, and he also told me he hoped I didn't end up with a Wickenden paper because he'd never talk to me again.

He told his uncle about the pictures, and Anton immediately agreed not to say anything else to anyone else about Jaan and his curious hobbies. He had Jaan's modifications – the door locks, the Plexiglas windows, and the safe – removed very quietly one weekend, making the office ready for a new occupant by the start of spring semester. The books, of course, he gave to the department library, after picking out a few to take home. He promised to give them all back if a next of kin should materialize. We spoke once, briefly, by phone, and made all the usual promises to keep in touch. We – by which I mean I – might even keep them this time.

A couple of weeks ago, I couldn't leave Lincoln quickly enough. Now, though, after a few weeks of solitary work in my childhood bedroom, with NY1 and *Law & Order* providing pretty much my only human contact (well, except for Mom and Vic and Anna and Dana), at about 4:00 P.M. every day, I'm about ready to chew my arm off to go back again. The feeling passes, though. It's just a feeling, and I let it pass.

THE SUITCASE

꒰꒱

Blessed is He who has appeared to our
human race under so many metaphors.

— ST EPHREM THE SYRIAN

When he left Sicily, al-Idrisi's library had fifteen
items in it. I want to speak briefly in my own defense,
though, so I need a sixteenth item. Let's say it
was Omar Iblis's woven sack; and let's say that with
a very few carefully preserved exceptions, woven
material cannot last for a millennium; so let's say that
the sack represented the idea of departure, the necessity of flight; and so instead of a burlap sack, let's
make the sixteenth item the suitcase into which Tonu
and I put all fifteen of the items that Jaan had been
storing at his house. And let's add one item, too: an
airplane ticket. Tonu had just shown it to me when
Paul knocked on the door. One way, first class, along
with an envelope stuffed with enough money to get

me and my suitcase here without any unwanted interference from customs officials.

It is easier for me to say this in the passive voice: for whatever it's worth now, I feel that Paul was used rather badly by me. He was, and I very much hope he still is, a sweet boy. But he was still just a boy, in his early twenties, when most people's lives have not yet become interesting and their personalities are just beginning to deepen and fill out.

When we met, I had just helped one man kill another. I had helped a persuasive stranger kill a man who, in any worldly sense, had been in my care for the better part of a year. I was feeling guilty, and low, and ashamed, and frightened, and this young man literally appears from nowhere on my doorstep, wanting to talk to me, to pay attention to me. It was flattering. He found me far more attractive than I ever found myself, which was also flattering. And I needed the attention. I needed to feel like I was not damned or horrible. I wanted the spiritual assurance that my actions did not render me unfit for human company, but I also needed to be held and reassured. So that's what Paul was to me: my temporary crutch. I do wish I could apologize to him, but from the tone of his writing, I doubt he would listen. Anyway, he will certainly get over it. As the poet said: People have died, and worms have eaten them, but never for love.

For greed, on the other hand: that sin has plenty of corpses on its account. I told Paul that Jaan lived simply, and he did, in the way that the Paul Tomm of a week ago would have understood it. He wore shabby clothes, he drove a rust heap, he had a small house filled with books and dust and almost nothing else.

Aside from me, the only person he had any contact with was a bartender a few towns over, a bartender whose avarice not only matched but, Tonu told me, inspired Jaan's. Tonu told me that this Edouard used to be a smuggler in Russia when it was the Soviet Union and that he was brought to Connecticut to help Jaan get the library items into the country. Naturally, once he saw how much easier smuggling was in a little town in Connecticut than in Moscow, he expanded his enterprise, started free-lancing for wealthy clients, kept talking about how much money he had, how many more possibilities it gave him. This started Jaan thinking. And talking. And drinking with Edouard while he was thinking and talking. Rumors arose: the Emerald Tablet had been found, and its influence was for sale. Colleagues of Tonu's made inquiries under false identities, think-ing it was the beginning of another Tablet fad – another charlatan parting fools from their money – but, to their surprise, traced the whispers back to Jaan.

What Tonu said, then, about Jaan and his inten-tions was true, but he said it in the future conditional, and he was very efficient at doing what needed to be done, so there was no opportunity to prove it true.

Not to Paul anyway. But Jaan never groped Paul. He never thanked Paul for cooking him dinner by ogling him. He never asked Paul about pornographic films; Paul never had to endure an evening's conversation consisting entirely of clumsy double entendres and crass questions about money and prostitution. Naturally, none of this justifies killing him. And in retrospect perhaps I should have been less indulgent of Jaan. But from the first time I met him, when I knocked on his door to introduce myself and found this unworldly, tattered old man smoking a pipe on a sagging sofa in a house that smelled of dust and neglect, I felt sorry for him. The ruder and more familiar he became with me, the sorrier I felt for him. I suppose he reminded me of my own belligerent and smarmy father, exiled by his family for being unpleasant, living alone with a heart pumping ground glass through his veins whenever he thought of them. Of us. Whatever the reason, I considered Jaan's lewdness and prurience burdens I had to bear.

Tonu made me see that those traits in fact pointed toward and came from Jaan's propensity to do great evil. I learned so much from Tonu; he taught me so much about the world and about people. Practical and impractical, obvious and esoteric. And I could tell he liked me, too. Not in a sexual way – he seemed to have no appetites there at all – but he respected me for my faith and intelligence. So one day, after shopping for Jaan, I stayed to make him a pot of soup, and

I ate a bowl with him while he talked about bastards he had known, people who had undeservedly done better than he had, how nobody understood the world but him. I brought a bottle of brandy, and we drank it. He drank most of it. And when he grew drowsy, I poured the rest of the soup out in the backyard, washed the dishes, and left. All I had to do was leave the door unlocked, which I did.

But I suppose I had an overdeveloped sense of guilt, because I couldn't sleep that night. Nor the next night either. I tried forgetting it, I tried praying, but it kept eating at me. So that night I walked down to the pay phone outside Arliss's General Store, and I called the New Kendal police and told them that Jaan had died. And then I went back home, crawled into bed, and the world shut on me like an eye, and I slept.

I don't know what would have happened had I said nothing. Tonu thought that Jaan kept the Tablet in his office in Wickenden, so after he finished in Lincoln that night, that's where he went. But the Tablet was back in Lincoln. By the time he got back, it was nearly daybreak, and he wanted to wait until nighttime – until the early-morning hours – to sneak into Jaan's house again. Unfortunately, by then I had already reported his death, and Lincoln's policemen were already there. Joseph Jadid's suspicion that the police never drove by at night was wrong: he did, and irregularly, too. Sometimes the policeman stopped the car and shone a light through the windows. Tonu would have waited until he lost interest, but Paul started digging around, and more policemen got involved, and it became obvious – clear and ironic, Tonu said – that he did not have the leisure to wait. So we set a corner of my apartment on fire, called the local police, and when we saw them go into my house, we went into Jaan's and finished the job.

The one unexpected thing that happened to me in all of this was that Tonu could see that I was conflicted still, and in pain. He invited me to take Jaan's place as one of the Tablet's guardians. He told me that I understood the sanctity of every life on earth, but that I also understood that sometimes lives have to be taken. He told me that my grief was a sign of my goodness. He gave me the chance to belong to something greater than myself, the chance to dedicate my life to something more important than anything I could have dreamed of.

That is how I find myself here. And 'here' is a city you, reader, have probably never visited, but I still see no reason to name it. It could be anywhere, really. And here is where I will wait for Tonu. And here is where I, where Hannah Rowe, will disappear. She will have come here after a trying week. She will have come for peace and introspection: there are forested mountains laced with trails just outside the city. Perhaps she'll have a hiking accident on a winding path high above a river. Perhaps she'll leave a bar with a strange man and never return to her hotel. Perhaps she will simply vanish, as people sometimes do. I envy Huck Finn the pleasure of attending his own funeral, but a clean break really is best. I do wonder, at times, whether I did the right thing, and I have temporary feelings of doubt and recriminations. They pass, though. They are only feelings, and I let them pass.

Acknowledgments

First thanks in this as in any worthwhile endeavor of mine belongs to Zachary, Sally, Benjamin, and Rebecca Fasman, anchors and inspirations all.

While this book rests on the shoulders of too many books to mention, I must acknowledge *A Dictionary of Alchemical Imagery*, by Lyndy Abraham, as a particularly inspiring source.

Thanks to Peter Johnson, Sylvia Sellers-Garcia, and John Williams for reading and improving my early drafts, and also to Mildred Newmark, my eagle-eyed great-aunt, for catching several infelicities that otherwise would have escaped me.

Jim Rutman and Meredith Blum are the principal reasons this book is in your hands, rather than still in manuscript form at the back of my sock drawer. To explain even in part what their support has meant to me would be prohibitively long and mawkish, so: for Jim's candor and decency, for Meredith's editorial sensitivity, and for their enthusiasm, faith, diligence and wit, I am deeply grateful.

Thanks, too, to everyone at Penguin on both sides of the pond: Ann Godoff and Simon Prosser; Sophie Fels, Liza Darnton, and Juliette Mitchell; Bruce Giffords and Maureen Sugden. I could not have asked for better editorial support.

In Moscow, the *Moscow Times* gave me a home long before I deserved one; thanks and my deep respect are due to its entire talented staff, particulary to Lynn Berry, Sunny Bosco, and Joy Ziegeweid.

Also in Moscow, I had the incalculable good luck to meet Jeffrey Tayler, who illuminated so much about Russia that would otherwise have remained dark. His generosity, warmth, curiosity, bravery, and humor will remain a model to me for as long as I write and travel.

Finally, a note to my future self: If your son, two months after meeting a girl, tells you he's headed for a tiny island without electricity, running water, or a way off, with the girl and her brother, parents, cousins, aunts, and uncles, do not panic. It might turn out okay. Many thanks to George and Paula Krimsky for ensuring that it did, and for countless kindnesses large and small. But thanks to them most of all for raising an extraordinary daughter, without whom I would never have gone to Russia or written this book. *The Geographer's Library* is for Alissa. So am I.